H
Latin Lovers

Passionately dedicated to pleasure…

By
Request™

Hot Latin Lovers

THE ITALIAN'S REVENGE
by
Michelle Reid

ULTIMATE TEMPTATION
by
Sara Craven

THE LATIN AFFAIR
by
Sophie Weston

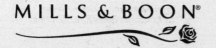
MILLS & BOON®

*MILLS & BOON and MILLS & BOON with the Rose Device
are registered trademarks of the publisher.*
Harlequin Mills & Boon Limited,
Eton House, 18-24 Paradise Road, Richmond, Surrey, TW9 1SR

HOT LATIN LOVERS © by Harlequin Enterprises II B.V., 2003

The Italian's Revenge, Ultimate Temptation and *The Latin Affair*
were first published in Great Britain by Harlequin Mills & Boon
Limited in separate, single volumes.

The Italian's Revenge © Michelle Reid 2000
Ultimate Temptation © Sara Craven 1997
The Latin Affair © Sophie Weston 1999

ISBN 0 263 83595 2

05-1003

*Printed and bound in Spain
by Litografia Rosés S.A., Barcelona*

Michelle Reid grew up on the southern edges of Manchester, the youngest in a family of five children. Now she lives in the beautiful county of Cheshire with her busy executive husband and two grown-up daughters. She loves reading, the ballet, and playing tennis when she gets the chance. She hates cooking, cleaning, and despises ironing! Sleep she can do without, and produces some of her best written work during the early hours of the morning.

THE ITALIAN'S REVENGE
by
Michelle Reid

CHAPTER ONE

STEPPING out of her son's bedroom, Catherine closed the door just as quietly as she could, then wilted wearily back against it. Santo had gone to sleep at last, but she could still hear the heart-wrenching little sniffles that were shaking his five-year-old frame.

It really could not go on, she decided heavily. The tears and tantrums had been getting worse each time they erupted. And the way she had been burying her head in the sand in the vague hopes that his problem would eventually sort itself out had only managed to exacerbate the situation.

It was time—more than time—that she did something about it, even if the prospect filled her with untold dread.

And if she was going to act, then it had to be now. Luisa was due to catch the early commuter flight out of Naples in the morning, and if she was to be stopped then it must be tonight, before it caused her mother-in-law too much inconvenience.

'Damn,' she breathed as she levered herself away from her son's bedroom door and made her way down the stairs. The mere prospect of putting through such a sensitive call was enough to set the tension singing inside her.

For what did she say? she asked herself as she stepped into the sitting room and quietly closed that door behind her.

The straightforward approach seemed the most logical answer, where she just picked up the phone and told Luisa bluntly that her grandson was refusing to go back to Naples with her tomorrow and why. But that kind of approach did

5

not take into consideration the fragile sensibilities of the recipient. Or the backlash of hostility that was going to rebound on her, most of which would be labelling her the troublemaker.

She sighed fretfully, caught a glimpse of herself in the mirror as she did it, then just stood staring at her own reflection.

Good grief, but she looked a mess, though in truth it didn't particularly surprise her. The battles with Santo had been getting worse by the day as this week had drawn to a close. Now her face was showing the results of too many emotion-draining tussles and too many restless nights while she lay awake worrying about them. Her eyes were bruised and her skin looked so pale that if it hadn't been for the natural flashes of copper firing up her golden hair then she would probably resemble some hollow-eyed little ghost.

Not so much of the little, she then mocked herself on an unexpected burst of rueful humour. For there was nothing *little* about her five-feet-eight-inch frame. Slender—yes, she conceded. Too slender for some people's tastes.

Vito's tastes.

The humour died as suddenly as it had erupted, banished by the one person who could turn laughter into bitterness without even having to try.

Vittorio Adriano Lucio Giordani—to give him his full and impressive title. Man of means. Man of might. Man at the root of her son's problems.

Once she had loved him; now she hated him. But then that was surely Vito. Man of dynamic contrasts. Stunning to look at. Arrogant to a fault. Exquisitely versed in the art of loving. Deadly to love.

She shuddered, her arms coming up to wrap around her as if in self-protection as she turned away from that face in the mirror rather than having to watch it alter from tired to bitter, which was what it usually did when she let herself think about Vito.

Because not only did she hate him but she hated even thinking about him. He was the skeleton in her past, linked to her present by an invisible thread that went directly from her heart, straight through the heart of their son and then into Vito's heart.

In fact Vito's only saving grace, in Catherine's view, was his open adoration of their five-year-old son. Now it seemed that even that fragile connection was under threat—though Vito didn't know it yet.

'I hate you! And I hate Papà! I don't want to love you any more!'

She winced painfully as the echo of that angrily emotive cry pierced her like a knife in the chest. Santo had meant those words; he had felt them deeply. Too deeply for a confused and vulnerable little boy to have to cope with.

Which brought her rather neatly back to where she had started when she walked into this room, she grimly concluded. Namely, doing something about Santo's distress and anger.

A point that sent her eyes drifting over to where the telephone sat on the small table by the sofa, looking perfectly innocent when in actual fact it was a time bomb set to explode the moment she so much as touched it.

Because she never rang Naples—never. Had not done so once since she had left there three years ago. Any communicating went on via lawyers or by letters sent to and from Santo's grandmother Luisa. So this phone call was so unique it was likely to cause major ructions in the Giordani household. And that was *before* she gave her reason for calling!

Therefore it was with reluctance that she went to sit down beside the telephone table. And with her bare toes curling tensely into the carpet, she gritted her teeth, took a couple of deep breaths, then reached out for the receiver.

By the time she had punched in the required set of digits she was sitting there with her eyes pressed tight shut, half praying that no one would be home.

Coward, she mocked herself.

And why not? she then countered. With their track record it paid to be cowardly around Vito. She just hoped that Luisa would answer. At least with Luisa she could relax some of the tension out of her body and *try* to sound normal before she attempted to break the news to her.

No chance. *'Si?'* a deeply smooth and seductively accented voice suddenly drawled into her ear.

Catherine jumped, her eyes flicking open as instant recognition turned her grey eyes green.

Vito.

Damn, it was Vito. A sudden hot flush went chasing through her. A thick lump formed across her throat. She tried to speak but found she couldn't. Instead her eyes drifted shut again and suddenly she was seeing him as clearly as if he was standing here directly in front of her. Seeing the blackness of his hair, the darkness of his skin and the long, lean, tightly muscled posture of his supremely arrogant stance.

He was wearing a dinner suit, she saw, because it was Sunday and coming up to dinnertime there in Naples, and the Giordani family always dressed formally for the evening meal on a Sunday. So the suit would be black and the shirt white, with an accompanying black bow tie.

And she could see the disturbing honeyed-gold colour of his eyes, with their long, thick, curling lashes, which could so polarise attention that it was impossible to think of anything else when you let yourself look into them. So she didn't. Instead she moved on to his mouth and let her mind's eye drift across its smooth, firm, sensual contours knowing exactly what to expect when another telling little shudder hit her system.

For this was the mouth of a born lover. A beautiful mouth, a seductive mouth, a disturbingly expressive mouth that could grin and mock and snarl and kiss like no other mouth, and lie like no other, and hate like no—

'Who is there, please?' his deep voice demanded in terse Italian.

Catherine jumped again, then tensely sat forward, her fingers tightly gripping the telephone receiver as she forced her locked up vocal cords to relax enough to allow her to speak.

'Hello, Vito,' she murmured huskily. 'It's me—Catherine…'

The bomb went off—in the form of a stunning silence. The kind that ate away at her insides and made nerves twitch all over her. Her mouth was dry, her heart having to force blood through valves that had simply stopped working. She felt light-headed but heavy-limbed, and wanted to start crying suddenly—which was so very pathetic that at least the feeling managed to jolt her into attempting to speak again.

But Vito beat her to it. 'What is wrong with my son?' he lashed out, grating English replacing terse Italian. The sheer violence in his tone was enough to warn Catherine that he had instantly jumped to all the wrong conclusions.

'It's all right,' she said quickly. 'Santo isn't ill.'

There was another short, tense, pulsing moment while Vito took time to absorb that assurance. 'Then why do you break your own court order and ring me here?' he demanded coldly.

Grimacing at his right to ask that question, Catherine still had to bite down on her lip to stop herself from replying with something nasty. The break-up of their marriage had not been pleasant, and the hostility between them still ran strong three years on.

Three years ago Vito had been so incensed when she'd left him, taking Santo with her, that he had made the kind of threatening noises which at the time had made her blood run cold with fear.

She had responded by making Santo a ward of court and serving an order on Vito prohibiting him any contact with her unless it was through a third party. Catherine didn't think Vito would ever forgive her for putting him through the indignity of having to swear before a judge that he would neither contact Catherine personally nor attempt to take Santo out of the country, before he was allowed access to his own son.

They had not exchanged a single word between them since.

It had taken him a whole year to win the legal right to have Santo visit him in Italy. Before that it had been up to him to come to London if he wanted to spend time with his son. And even to this day Santo was collected from and returned to Catherine by his grandmother, so that his parents would not come into contact with each other.

In fact the only area where they remained staunchly amicable was where their son's opinion of the other was concerned. Santo had the right to love them both equally, without feeling the pressure of having one parent's dislike of the other to corrupt his view—a point brought home to them both by a stern grandmother, who had found herself flung into the role of referee between them at a time when their mutual hostility had been running at its highest.

So Catherine had grown used to listening smilingly for hours and hours at a time while Santo extolled all his adored *papà's* many virtues, and she presumed that Vito had grown used to hearing the same in reverse.

But that didn't mean the animosity between them had

mellowed any through the ensuing years—only that they both hid it well for Santo's benefit.

'Actually, I was hoping to speak to Luisa,' she explained as coolly and briefly as she could. 'If you would get her for me, Vito, I would appreciate it.'

'And I repeat,' he responded, tight-lipped and incisive. 'What is so wrong that you dare to ring here?'

In other words, he wasn't going to play the game and allow Luisa to stand buffer between them, Catherine made wry note.

'I would prefer to explain to Luisa,' she insisted stubbornly.

She sensed more than heard his teeth snapping together. 'Then of course you may do so,' he smoothly replied. 'When she arrives to collect my son from you in the morning…'

'No, Vito—wait!' she cried out, her long, slender legs launching her to her feet as panic went rampaging through her when she realised he was actually going to put the phone down on her! And suddenly she was trembling all over as she stood there waiting to find out what he would do, while a taut silence began to buzz like static against her eardrum.

The line was not severed.

As Catherine's stress-muddied brain began to take that fact in, she also realised that Vito was not going to say another word until she said something worth him keeping the line open.

'I'm having problems with Santo,' she disclosed on a reluctant rush.

'What kind of problems?'

'The kind I prefer to discuss with Luisa,' she replied. 'Get her advice on w-what to do be-before she arrives here tomorrow…'

No wonder she was stammering, Catherine acknowledged grimly, because that last bit had been an outright lie. She was hoping to stop Luisa from coming here altogether. But the coward in her didn't dare to tell that to Vito. Past experience warned her that he would just go totally ballistic.

'You will hold the line, please,' his cold voice clipped, 'while I transfer this call to another telephone.'

Just like that, he was going to accede to her wishes and connect her with Luisa? Catherine could hardly believe her luck, and only just managed to disguise her sigh of relief as she murmured a polite, 'Thank you.'

Then the line went dead. Some of the tension began seeping out of her muscles and she sank weakly back down onto the sofa, her insides still playing havoc at the shock contact with their worst enemy. But other than that she congratulated herself. The first words they had spoken to each other in years had not been that dreadful.

They hadn't torn each other to shreds, at least.

Now she had to get her mind into gear and decide what she was going to tell Luisa. The truth seemed the most logical road to take. But the truth had always been such a sensitive issue between them all that she wasn't sure it was wise to use it now.

So, what do you say? she asked herself once again. Blame Santo's distress on something at school? Or on the dual life he is forced to lead where one parent lives in London and the other in Naples?

Then there were the two different lifestyles the little boy had to deal with. The first being where average normality was stamped into everything, from the neat suburban London street they lived in, with its rows of neat middle-class houses, to the neat, normal kind of families that resided in each. While several thousand miles away, in a different country and most certainly in a different world, was the other kind of life. One that was about as far away from normal and average as life could get for most people, never mind a confused little boy. For instead of suburban Naples, Vito lived out in the country. His home was a palace compared to this house, his standard of living steeped in the kind of luxury that would fill most ordinary people with awe.

When Santo visited Naples, his *papà* took time off from his busy job as head of the internationally renowned Giordani Investments to give his son his full attention. And if it wasn't his *papà*, his beloved grandmother was more than ready to pour the same amount of love and attention upon him.

Catherine had no other family. And she worked full time all the time, whether Santo was away or not. He had to accept that he was collected from school by a child-minder and taken home with her to wait until Catherine could collect him.

But all of that—or none of that—was what the child found upsetting. Santo was not really old enough yet to understand just what it was that was disturbing him so much. It had taken several skirmishes and a lot of patience for Catherine to begin to read between the lines of his angry outbursts.

Then, tonight, the final truth had come out, in the shape of a name. A name that had sent icy chills sweeping down her spine when she'd heard it falling from her own child's lips. And not just the name but the way Santo had said it— with pain and anguish.

She knew those emotions, had first-hand experience of what they could do to your belief in yourself, in your sense of self-worth. She also knew that if what Santo had told her was the truth then she didn't blame him for refusing to have anything to do with his Italian family. For hadn't she responded in the same way once herself?

'Right. Talk,' a grim voice commanded.

Catherine blinked, her mind taking a moment to realise what was going on. 'Where's Luisa?' she demanded, beginning to stiffen up all over again at the sound of Vito's voice.

'I do not recall saying I was going to bring my mother to the phone,' he responded coolly. 'Santo is *my* son, I will remind you. If you are having problems with *my* son, then you will discuss those problems with me.'

'He is *our* son,' Catherine corrected—while busily trying to reassess a situation that had promised to be complicated and touchy enough discussing it with Luisa. The very idea of having to say what she did have to say to Vito, of all people, was probably going to be impossible.

'So at last you acknowledge that.'

The barb hit right on its chosen mark and Catherine's lips snapped together in an effort to stop herself from responding to it.

It was no use. The words slipped out of their own volition. 'Try for sarcasm, Vito,' she drawled deridingly. 'It really helps the situation more than I can say.'

A sound caught her attention. Not a sigh, exactly, more a controlled release of air from his lungs, and then she heard the subtle creak of leather that was so familiar to her that she knew instantly which room he was now in.

His father's old study—now Vito's study, since Lucio Giordani had passed away eighteen months after Santo had been born.

And suddenly she was seeing that room as clearly as she had seen Vito himself only minutes before. Seeing its size and its shape and its old-fashioned elegance. The neutral-coloured walls, the richly polished floor, the carefully selected pieces of fine Renaissance furniture—including the desk Vito was sitting behind.

'Are you still there?'

'Yes,' she replied, having to blink her mind back into focus again.

'Then will you please tell me what problems Santino has before I lose my patience?'

This time she managed to control the urge to retaliate to his frankly provoking tone. 'He's been having problems at school.' She decided that was as good a place to start as any. 'It began weeks ago, just after his last visit with you over there.'

'Which in your eyes makes it my fault, I presume?'

'I didn't say that,' she denied, though she knew she was thinking it. 'I was merely attempting to fill you in with what has been happening.'

'Then I apologise,' he said.

Liar, she thought, heaving in a deep breath in an attempt to iron out any hint of accusation from her tone—though that wasn't easy, given the circumstances. 'He's been disruptive in class,' she made herself go on. 'Angry all the time, and insolent.' She didn't add that Santo had been the same with her because that wasn't important and would only confuse the issue. 'After one such skirmish his teacher threatened to bring his parents in to school to speak to them about his behaviour. He responded by informing the teacher that his father lived in Italy and wouldn't come, because he was rich and too important to bother with a nuisance like him.'

Catherine heard Vito's indrawn gasp in response, and knew he had understood the import of what she was trying to tell him here. 'Why would he say something like that, Vito?' she questioned curtly. 'Unless he has been led to believe it is true? He's too young to have come up with a mouthful like that all on his own, so someone has to have said it to him first for him to repeat it.'

'And you think it was me?' he exclaimed, making Catherine sigh in annoyance.

'I don't know who it was!' she snapped. 'Because he isn't telling!' But I can damn well guess, she tagged on silently. 'Now, to cut a long story short,' she concluded, 'he is refusing to go to Naples with Luisa tomorrow. He tells me that you don't really want him there, so why should he bother with you?'

'So you called here tonight to tell my mother not to come and collect him,' he assumed from all of that. 'Great way to deal with the problem, Catherine,' he gritted. 'After all, Santo is only saying exactly what you have been wishing he would say for years now, so you can get me right out of your life!'

'You are out of my life,' she responded. 'Our divorce becomes final at the end of this month.'

'A divorce *you* instigated,' he pointed out. 'Have you considered whether it is that little event that is causing Santo's problems?' he suggested. 'Or maybe there is more to it than that,' he then added tightly, 'and I need to look no further than the other end of this telephone line to discover the one who has been feeding my son lies about me!'

'Are you suggesting that *I* have been telling him that you think he's a nuisance?' she gasped, so affronted by the implication that she shot back to her feet. 'If so, think again, Vito,' she sliced at him furiously. 'Because it isn't me who is planning to remarry as soon as I'm free of you! And it isn't me who is about to undermine our son's position in my life by sticking him with the archetypal step-*mamma* from hell!'

Oh, she hadn't meant to say that! Catherine cursed her own unruly tongue as once again the silence came thundering down all around her.

Yet, even having said it, her body was pumping with the kind of adrenaline that started wars. She was even breathing heavily, her green eyes bright with a bitter antagonism, her mouth stretched back from even white teeth that desperately wanted to bite!

'Who the hell told you that?' Vito rasped, and Catherine had the insane idea that he too was on his feet, and breathing metaphorical fire all over the telephone.

And this—*this* she reminded herself forcefully, is why Vito and I are best having no contact whatsoever! We fire each other up like two volcanoes.

'Is it true?' she countered.

'That is none of your business,' he sliced.

Her flashing eyes narrowed into two threatening slits. 'Watch me make it my business, Vito,' she warned, very seriously. 'I'll put a block on our divorce if I find that it's true and you are planning to give Marietta any power over Santo.'

'You don't have that much authority over my actions any more,' he derided her threat.

'No?' she challenged. 'Then just watch this space,' she said, and grimly cut the connection.

It took ten minutes for the phone to start ringing. Ten long minutes in which Catherine seethed and paced, and wondered how the heck she had allowed the situation to get so out of control. Half of what she had said she hadn't meant to say at all!

On a heavy sigh she tried to calm down a bit before deciding what she should do next. Ring back and apologise? Start the whole darn thing again from the beginning and hope to God that she could keep a leash on her temper?

The chance of that happening was so remote that she even allowed herself to smile at it. Her marriage to Vito had never been anything but volatile. They were both hot-tempered, both stubborn, both passionately defensive of their own egos.

The first time they met it was at a party. Having gone

there with separate partners, they'd ended up leaving together. It had been a case of sheer necessity, she recalled, remembering the way they had only needed to take one look at each other to virtually combust in the ensuing sexual fall-out.

They had become lovers that same night. Within the month she was pregnant. Within the next they were married. Within three years they were sworn enemies. It had all been very wild, very hot and very traumatic from passionate start to bloody finish. Even the final break had come only days after they'd fallen on each other in a fevered attempt to recapture what they had known they were losing.

The sex had been great—the rest a disaster. They had begun rowing within minutes of separating their bodies. He'd stormed off—as usual—and the next day she'd gone into premature labour with their second child and lost their second son while Vito was seeking solace with his mistress.

She would never, ever forgive him for that. She would never forgive the humiliation of having to beg his mistress to send him home because she needed him. But he'd still arrived too late to be of any use to her. By then she had been rushed into hospital and had already lost the baby. To have Vito come to lean over her and murmur all the right phrases—while smelling of that woman's perfume—had been the final degradation.

She had left Italy with Santo just as soon as she was physically able, and Vito would never forgive her for taking his son away from him.

They both had axes to grind with each other. Both felt betrayed, ill-used and deserted. And if it hadn't been for Vito's mother Luisa stepping in to play arbiter, God alone knew where the bitterness would have taken them.

Thanks to Luisa they'd managed to survive three years of relative peace—so long as there was no personal contact between them. Now that peace had been well and truly shattered, and Catherine wished she knew how to stop full-scale war from breaking out.

But she didn't. Not with the same main antagonist still very much on the scene.

When the telephone began to ring again she went perfectly still, her heart stopping beating altogether as she turned to stare at the darned contraption. Her first instinct was to ignore it. For she didn't feel up to another round with Vito just yet. But a second later she was snatching up the receiver when she grew afraid the persistent ring would wake Santo.

'Catherine?' a very familiar voice questioned anxiously. 'My son has insisted that I call you. What in heaven's name is going on, please?'

Luisa. It was Luisa. Catherine wilted like a dying swan onto the sofa. 'Luisa,' she breathed in clear relief. 'I thought you were going to be Vito.'

'Vito has just stormed out of the house in a fury,' his mother informed her. 'After cursing and shouting and telling me that I had to ring you right away. Is something the matter with Santo, Catherine?' she asked worriedly.

'Yes and no,' Catherine replied. Then, on a deep breath, she explained calmly to Luisa, in the kind of words she should have used to Vito, what Santo's problem was—without complicating the issue this time by bringing Vito's present love-life into it.

'No wonder my son was looking so frightened,' Luisa murmured when Catherine had finished. 'I have not seen that dreadful expression on his face in a long time, and I hoped never to see it again.'

'Frightened?' Catherine prompted, frowning because she couldn't imagine the arrogant Vito being afraid of anything.

'Of losing his son again,' his mother enlightened. 'What is the matter Catherine? Did you think Vito would shrug off Santo's concerns as if they did not matter to him?'

'I—no,' she denied, surprised by the sudden injection of bitterness Vito's *mamma* was revealing.

'My son works very hard at forging a strong relationship with Santo in the short blocks of time allocated to him,' her mother-in-law went on. 'And to hear that this is suddenly being undermined must be very frightening for him.'

In three long years Luisa had never sounded anything but gently neutral, and Catherine found it rather disconcerting to realise that Luisa was, in fact, far from being neutral.

'Are you, like Vito, suggesting that it's me who is doing that undermining, Luisa?' she asked, seeing what she'd always thought of as her only ally moving right away from her.

'No.' The older woman instantly denied that. 'Of course not. I may worry for my son, but that does not mean I am blind to the fact that you both love Santo and would rather cut out your tongues than hurt him through each other.'

'Well, thanks for that,' Catherine replied, but her tone was terse, her manner cooling in direct response to Luisa's.

'I am not your enemy, Catherine.' Luisa knew what she was thinking.

'But if push came to shove—' Catherine smiled slightly '—you know which camp to stand in.'

Luisa didn't answer and Catherine didn't expect her to— which was an answer in itself.

'So,' Luisa said more briskly. 'What do you want to do about Santo? Do you want me to delay my journey to London until you have managed to talk him round a little?'

'Oh, no!' Catherine instantly vetoed that, surprising herself by discovering that somewhere during the two fraught telephone conversations she had completely changed her mind. 'You must come, Luisa! He will be so disappointed if you don't come for him! I just didn't want you to walk in on his new rebelliousness cold, so to speak,' she explained. 'And—and there is a big chance he may refuse to leave with you,' she warned, adding anxiously, 'You do understand that I won't make him go with you if he doesn't want to?'

'I am a mother,' Luisa said. 'Of course I understand. So I will come, as arranged, and we will hope that Santo has had a change of heart after sleeping on his decision.'

Some hope of that, Catherine thought as she replaced the receiver. For Luisa was labouring under the misconception that Santo's problems were caused by a sudden and unexplainable loss of confidence in his *papà*—when in actual fact the little boy's reasoning was all too explainable.

And she went by the name of Marietta, Catherine mocked bitterly. Marietta, the long-standing friend of the family. Marietta the highly trusted member of Giordani Investments' board of directors. Marietta the long-standing mistress—the bitch.

She was tall, she was dark, she was inherently Italian. She had grace, she had style, she had unwavering charm. She had beauty and brains and knew how to use both to her own advantage. And, to top it all off, she was shrewd and sly and careful to whom she revealed her true self.

That she had dared to reveal that true self to Santo had, in Catherine's view, been Marietta's first big mistake in her long campaign to get Vito. For she might have managed to make Catherine run away like a silly whimpering coward, but she would not send Santo the same way.

Not even over my dead body, Catherine vowed as she prepared for bed that night...

CHAPTER TWO

AFTER spending the night tossing and turning, at around five o'clock the next morning Catherine finally gave up trying to sleep, and was just dragging herself out of bed when the distinctive sound of a black cab rumbling to a halt outside in the street caught her attention. A couple of her neighbours often commuted by taxi early in the morning if they were having to catch an early train somewhere, so she didn't think twice about it as she padded off to use the bathroom.

Anyway, her mind was busy with other things, like the day ahead of her, which was promising to be as traumatic as the evening that had preceded it.

On her way past his room, she slid open her son's door to check if he was still sleeping. The sight of his dark head peeping out from a snuggle of brightly printed duvet was reassuring. At least Santo had managed to sleep through his worries.

Closing the door again, she went downstairs with the intention of making herself a large pot of coffee over which she hoped to revive herself before the next round of battles commenced—but a shadow suddenly distorting the early-morning daylight seeping in through the frosted glass panel in her front door made her pause.

Glancing up, she saw the dark bulk of a human body standing in her porch. Her frown deepened. Surely it was too early for the postman? she asked herself, yet still continued to stand there expecting her letterbox to open and a wad of post to come sliding through it. But when instead of bending the dark figure lifted a hand towards her door-bell, Catherine was suddenly leaping into action.

In her urgency to stop whoever it was from ringing the bell and waking up her son she was pulling the door open without really thinking clearly about what she was doing. So it was only after the door opened wide on the motion that she realised she had gone to bed last night without putting the safety chain on.

By then it didn't matter. It was already too late to re-member caution, and all the other safety rules that were a natural part of living these days, when she found herself staring at the very last person she'd expected to see stand-ing on her doorstep.

Her heart took a quivering dive to her stomach, the shock of seeing Vito in the actual flesh for the first time in three long years so debilitating that for the next whole minute she couldn't seem to function on any other level than sight.

A sight that absorbed in one dizzying glance every hard-edged, clean-cut detail, from the cold sting of his eyes to the grim slant of his mouth and even the way he had one side of his jacket shoved casually aside so he could thrust a hand into his trouser pocket—though she wasn't aware of her eyes dipping down that low over him.

He was wearing a black dinner suit and a white shirt that conjured up the picture she had built of him the night be-fore; only the bow tie was missing, and the top button of the shirt yanked impatiently open at his lean brown throat.

Had he come here directly from storming out of his house in Naples? she wondered. And decided he had to have done to get here to London this quickly. But if his haste in getting here was supposed to impress her by how seriously he was taking her concerns about Santo—then it didn't.

She didn't want him here. And, worse, she didn't want to watch those honeyed eyes of his drift over her on a very slow and very comprehensive scan of her person, as if she was still one of his possessions.

And the fact that she became acutely aware of her own sleep-mussed state didn't enamour her, either. He had no right to study the way her tangled mass of copper-gold hair was hanging limp about her shoulders, or the fact that she was standing here in thin white cotton that barely hid what it covered.

Then his gaze moved lower, jet-black lashes sinking over golden eyes that seemed to draw a caressing line across the surface of her skin as they moved over the pair of loose-fitting pyjama shorts which left much of her slender legs on show. And Catherine felt something very old and very basic spring to life inside her.

It was called sexual arousal. The man had always only had to look at her like this to make her make her so aware of herself that she could barely think straight.

'What are you doing here?' she lashed out in sheer retaliation.

Arrogance personified, she observed, as a black eyebrow arched and those incredible eyes somehow managed to disparage her down the length of his roman nose, despite the fact that she stood a deep step higher than him, which placed them almost at a level.

'I would have thought that was obvious,' Vito coolly replied. 'I am here to see my son.'

'It's only five o'clock,' she protested. 'Santo is still asleep.'

'I am well aware of the time, Catherine,' he replied rather heavily, and something passed across his face—a weariness she hadn't noticed was there until that moment.

Which was the point when she began to notice other things about him. He looked older than she would have expected, for instance. The signs of a carefully honed cyn icism were scoring grooves into his handsome face where once none had been. And the corners of his firm mouth were turned down slightly, as if he never let himself smile much any more.

Seeing that for some reason made her insides hurt. And the sensation infuriated her because she didn't want to feel anything but total indifference for this man's state of mind.

'How did you get here so quickly, anyway?' she asked with surly shortness.

'I flew myself in overnight,' he replied. 'Then came directly here from the airport.'

Which meant he must have been on the go all night, she concluded. Then another thought sent an icy chill slithering down her spine.

After flying half the night, had he then driven himself here in one of the supercharged death-traps he tended to favour? Glancing over his shoulder, she expected to see some long, low, sleek growling monster of a car crouching by the curbside, but there wasn't one.

Then she remembered hearing a taxi cab pulling up a few minutes earlier and realised with a new kind of shock that Vito must have used it to travel here from the airport.

Now that must have been a novelty for him, she mused, eyeing him curiously. Vito always liked to be in the driver's seat, whether that be behind the controls of his plane or the wheel of a car—or even in his sex-life!

'Which airport did you fly in to?' she asked, the thrifty housekeeper in her wanting to assess the cost of such a long cab journey.

'Does it matter?' He flashed her a look of irritation. 'And do we have to have this conversation here on the doorstep?' he then added tersely, his dark head turning to take in the neat residential street with its rows of neat windows—some of which had curtains twitching curiously because their voices must be carrying on the still morning air.

Vito wasn't a doorstep man, Catherine mused wryly. He was the greatly admired and very respected head of the world-renowned Giordani Investment Bank, cum expert troubleshooter for any ailing business brought under his wing. People valued his opinion and his advice—and welcomed him with open arms when he came to call.

But she was not one of those people, she reminded herself sternly. She owed Vito nothing, and respected him not at all. 'You're not welcome here,' she told him coldly.

'My son may beg to differ,' he returned, responding to her hostile tone with a slight tensing of his jaw.

Much as she would have liked to protest that claim, Catherine knew that she couldn't. 'Then why don't you come back—in a couple of hours', say, when he is sure to be awake?' she suggested, and was about to shut the door in his face when those golden eyes began to flash.

'Shut that door and you will regret it,' he warned very grimly.

To her annoyance, she hesitated, hating herself for being influenced by his tone. And the atmosphere between them thrummed with a mutual antagonism. Neither liked the other; neither attempted to hide it.

'I would have thought it was excruciatingly obvious that you and I need to talk *before* Santo is awake,' he added with rasping derision. 'Why the hell else do you think I have knocked myself out trying to get here this early?'

Once again, he had a point, and Catherine knew she was being petty, but it didn't stop her from standing there like a stone wall protecting her own threshold. Old habits died hard, and refusing to give an inch to Vito in case he took the whole mile from her had become second nature during their long and battle-zoned association.

'*You* called *me*, Catherine,' he then reminded her grimly. 'An unprecedented act in itself. You voiced your concern to me and I have responded. Now show a little grace,' he suggested, 'and at least acknowledge that my coming here is worthy of some consideration.'

As set-downs went, Catherine supposed that that one was as good as any Vito had ever doled out to her, as she felt herself come withering down from proudly hostile to childishly petty in one fell swoop.

She stepped back without uttering another word and, stiff-faced, eyes lowered, invited her husband of six long years to enter her home for the first time. He did it slowly—stepping over her threshold in a measured way which suggested that he too was aware of the significance of the occasion.

Then suddenly he was there right beside her, sharing the narrow space in her small hallway and filling it with the sheer power of his presence. And Catherine felt the tension build inside her as she stood there and absorbed—literally absorbed—his superior height, his superior breadth, his superior physical strength that had not been so evident while she'd kept him outside, standing nine inches lower and therefore nine inches less the man she should have remembered him to be.

She could smell the unique scent of his skin, feel the vibrations of his body as he paused a mere hair's breadth away from her to send her nerve-ends on a rampage of wild, scattering panic in recognition of how dangerous those vibrations were to them.

Six years ago it had taken one look for them to fall on each other in a fever of sexual craving. Now here they were, several years of bitter enmity on—and yet she could feel the same hunger beginning to wrap itself around her.

Oh, damn, she cursed silently, though whether she was cursing herself for being so weak of the flesh or Vito for being the sexual animal he undoubtedly was, she wasn't quite certain.

'This way,' she mumbled, snaking her way around him so that their bodies did not brush.

She led the way to her sitting room, shrouded still by the curtains drawn across the window. With a jerk she stepped sideways, to allow him to enter, then watched defensively as his eyes moved over his strange surroundings.

Plain blue carpet and curtains, two small linen sofas, a television set, a couple of low tables and a bookcase was all the small room would take comfortably, except for a special corner of the room dedicated to Santo, where his books, games and toys were stacked on and around a low play table.

It was all very neat, very—ordinary. Nothing like the several elegant and spacious reception rooms filled with priceless antiques in Vito's home. Or the huge playroom her son had all to himself, filled with everything a little boy could possibly dream of. A point Catherine was made suddenly acutely aware of when she glimpsed the brief twitch along Vito's jawline as he too made the comparison.

'I'll go and get dressed,' she said, dipping her head to hide her expression as she turned for the door again and— she admitted it—escape, before she was tempted to say something nasty about money not being everything.

But his hand capturing her wrist stopped her. 'I am no snob, Catherine,' he murmured sombrely. 'I know and appreciate how happy and comfortable Santo has been living here with you.'

'Please let go of my wrist,' she said, not interested in receiving his commendation on anything. She was too concerned about the streak of heat that was flowing up her arm from the point where his fingers circled her.

'I am no woman-beater either,' he tagged on very grimly.

'That's very odd,' she countered as he dropped her wrist. 'For I seem to remember that the last time we stood alone in a room you were threatening to do just that to me.'

'Words, Catherine,' he sighed, half turning away from her. 'I was angry, and those words were empty of any real threat to you, as you well know.'

'Do I?' Her smile was wry to say the least. 'We were strangers, Vito. We were strangers then and we are strangers now. I never, ever knew what you were thinking.'

'Except in bed,' he said, swinging back to look at her, the grimness replaced by a deeply mocking cynicism. 'You knew exactly what I was thinking there.'

Catherine tossed her head at him, matching him expression for cynical expression. 'Shame, then, that we couldn't spend twenty-four hours there instead of the odd six,' she said. 'And I really don't want to have this kind of conversation with you,' she added. 'It proves nothing and only clouds the issues of real importance where Santo is concerned.'

'Our relationship—or the lack of it—*is* the important issue for Santo, I would have thought.'

'No.' She denied that. 'The important issue for Santo is the prospect of his father marrying a woman his son is actively afraid of.'

Vito stiffened. 'Define "afraid",' he commanded.

Catherine stared at him. 'Afraid as in frightened—how else would you like me to put it?'

'Of Marietta?' His frown was strong with disbelief. 'He must have misunderstood something she said to him,' he murmured thoughtfully. 'You must know his Italian is not as well-formed as his English.'

Oh, right, Catherine thought. It couldn't *possibly* be Marietta's fault. Not in a Giordani's eyes!

'I'm going to get dressed,' she clipped, abandoning the useless argument by moving back into the hallway.

'Do you mind if I make myself a cup of coffee while you do that?'

Without a word, she diverted towards the kitchen—but,

aware that Vito was following her, Catherine sensed him pause to glance up the stairwell, as if he was hoping his son would suddenly appear.

He didn't—and he wouldn't, she predicted, as she continued on into the kitchen. Santo was by nature a creature of habit. His inner alarm clock was set for seven, so seven o'clock was the time he would awaken.

She was over by the sink filling the kettle with water by the time Vito came in the room. The hairs on the back of her neck began to prickle, picking up on his narrowed scrutiny of her, which once again made her acutely aware of the unsuitability of her present clothing.

Not that she was in any way underdressed, she quickly assured herself. The pair of shorts and a shirt-style top she was wearing were adequate enough—it was the lack of anything beneath them that was making her feel so conscious of those oh, too knowing eyes.

'I don't suppose you expect to hear from him until seven,' he murmured suddenly.

Catherine smiled a wry smile to herself as she transferred the kettle to its base and switched it on. So, his attention was firmly fixed on Santo—which put her well and truly in her place!

'You know his routine, then,' she answered lightly. 'And, knowing it, you must also know that if I try to wake him any earlier—'

'He will not be fit to live with,' Vito finished for her. 'Yes, I am aware of that.'

She glanced up at the kitchen clock, heard a sound of rustling cloth behind her and had an itchy feeling that Vito was also checking the time on his wristwatch.

Five thirty, she noted. That meant they had a whole hour and a half to endure each other's exclusive company. Could they stand it? she wondered, counting coffee scoops into the filter jug.

'Your hair is shorter than I remember.'

Her mind went blank, the next scoopful of coffee freezing on its way to the jug. After only just reassuring herself that he wasn't interested in anything about her personally, it came as a shock to discover that her instincts had indeed been working perfectly.

What else had he noticed? The way her shorts tended to cling to the cleft between her buttocks? Or, worse, that as she stood like this, in profile to him, he could see the shadowy outline of her right breast through the thin white cotton?

'I'm three years older,' she replied, though what that was supposed to mean even she didn't know, because she was too engrossed in a whole host of sensations that were beginning to attack her. All of them to do with sex, and sexual awareness, and this damn man, who had *always* been able to do this to her!

'You don't look it.'

And did he have to sound so grim about that?

'You do,' she countered in outright retaliation.

The rollercoaster of her own thoughts sent the coffee into the jug and saw the scoop abandoned onto the worktop with an angry flick of her slender wrist before she turned almost defiantly to face him, with a flat band of a false smile slapped on her face meant to show a clear disregard for his feelings.

But the smiled instantly died, melted away by the megawatt charge of his physical presence. He looked lean and mean, with his shirt hanging open at his brown throat and his jaw darkened by a five o'clock shadow. He had the arrogant nose of a Roman conqueror, the dark honeyed eyes of a charming sneak thief, and the wickedly sensual mouth of a gigolo. His body was built to fight lions in an arena, but men no longer did that to prove their prowess.

'And memories are made of this…' a silk-smooth voice softly taunted.

Her eyes closed and opened very slowly, bringing her fevered brain swirling back from where it had flown off to, to find him standing there taking malicious pleasure in watching her lose herself in memories of him.

It was like being caught with her hand in the sweetie jar. Sweat suddenly bathed her body, heat flushing her fine white skin—not the heat of arousal but the heat of a humiliation that completely demolished her. She didn't know what to do; she didn't know what to say.

'I'll get dressed…' was the wretched thing she actually came out with, and forced her shaking limbs to propel her towards the door and escape—again.

But Vito was not going to let her get off as lightly as that. Oh, no, not this man, with his lethal brand of wit, who also had so many axes to grind on her exposed rear that he was almost gleeful at being given this heaven-sent opportunity.

'Why bother?' he therefore drawled smoothly. 'It is already way too late to cover up what is happening to you, *mia cara.*'

'I am not your darling!' she snapped out in retaliation, knowing she was only rising to his deliberate baiting but unable to stop herself anyway.

'Maybe not,' he conceded. 'But I think you are wondering what it would be like to relive those moments when you were.'

If she didn't suffocate in her own shame then there really was no justice in the world, because it was what she deserved to do, Catherine derided herself bitterly.

'Not with you,' she denied, with an accompanying little shudder. 'Never with you again.'

'Was that a challenge? For if it was I might just take you up on it. You never know,' he mocked. 'It could be an—interesting exercise to see how many times we can ravish each other in the hour and a half we have free before our son comes down. It would certainly keep our minds off all our other problems…'

If the kitchen door handle had been a gun, she would probably have fired it at him. 'And if you need to sink yourself that low just to keep your mind occupied—then call in Marietta!' She used words to slay him with instead. 'She always was much better trained than me at servicing *all* your requirements.'

So what's really new here? she asked herself as a large hand came to land palm flat against the door to hold it shut, making her blink as it landed. 'You may still possess the body of a siren, Catherine,' Vito bit out, 'but you have developed the mouth of a slut! When are you going to listen to me, you blind bitter fool, and believe me when I tell you that Marietta is *not* and has *never* been my mistress!'

She should have left it there; Catherine knew she should. She should have remained perfectly still, pinned her 'mouth of a slut' shut and ignored his wretched lies until he gave up and let her out of here! But she couldn't. Vito had always been able to bring out the worst in her—and she the worst in him. They'd used to fight like sworn enemies and make love as if nothing could break them apart. It was like meeting like. His Latin fire versus her Celtish spirit. His oversized ego versus her fierce pride.

It had been a recipe for utter disaster. But for the first few blissful months of their relationship it had been a glorious blending of both passionate temperaments fused together by that wonderfully enthralling sensation she'd used to describe as—true love.

It hadn't seemed to matter then that the words were never actually spoken, for they had been there in each look, each touch, in the way neither had seemed able to be apart from the other for more than a few hours without making contact—if only with the intimate pitch of their voices via the telephone. Even when she'd fallen pregnant and the warring had begun, she had still believed that love was the engine which had driven them towards marriage.

Meeting Marietta on her wedding day, and learning that this was the woman Vito would have chosen to marry if she had not instead married his best friend Rocco, had placed the first fragile seeds of doubt in her mind about Vito's true feelings for her.

Yet neither by word nor gesture had Vito revealed any hint that there could be truth in the whispers, and she had very quickly managed to dismiss them when his attention towards her remained sound right through her first troubled pregnancy and into her second.

Then Rocco had been killed in a tragic boating accident, followed within weeks by Vito's father dying from a massive stroke. And before she'd realised quite what was happening, Vito and Marietta had hardly ever been seen apart.

'A shared grief', Vito used to call it. Marietta had called it—inevitable. 'What do you think Vito did when you trapped him into marriage—put on a blindfold and forgot it was me he was in love with? While Rocco was alive he may have been willing to accept second best in you. But with Rocco gone…?'

'I'll believe Marietta's not your mistress when hell freezes over.' Catherine came out of her bitter reverie to answer Vito's question. 'Now get away from me,' she commanded, trying to tug open the door.

But Vito's superior strength held it shut. 'When I am good and ready,' he replied. 'For you started this, so we may as well finish it right here and now, before my son arrives.'

'Finish what?' she cried, spinning to stare at him in angry bewilderment. 'I don't even know what it is we're fighting about!'

'This thing you have against Marietta,' he grimly enlightened her, 'is *your* obsession, Catherine. It always has been. So it therefore follows that it must be *you* who has been filling Santo's head full of this nonsense about Marietta and me.'

Catherine stared at him as if she didn't know him. How a man as intelligent and shrewd as Vito was could be so fatally flawed was a real mystery to her.

'You are the blind one, Vito,' she informed him. 'You are a blind, stubborn and conceited fool who could never see through the charm she lays on you that Marietta is as evil as they come!'

'And you are sick,' he responded, his dark face closing into a mask of distaste as he stepped right away from her. 'You have to be sick, Catherine, to think such things about a person who only wanted to befriend you.'

Befriend me—? 'I'm sorry if this offends you, Vito.' She laughed, almost choking on her own fury. 'But I don't make friends of my husband's lovers!'

Honeyed eyes began to flash dire warnings of murder. 'She has never been my lover!' he repeated furiously.

'And you are such a dreadful liar!' she sliced right back.

'I do not lie!'

'I know Marietta has been feeding her poison to Santo just as she once fed it to me,' she doggedly persisted.

'I will not continue to listen to this,' Vito said, reaching out as if to grab her arm so he could shift her away from the door and leave himself.

'Then will you listen to Santo?' she challenged.

The hand dropped away, his chin lifting stiffly. 'It is what I am here for, is it not?'

Why did his accent always thicken when he was under stress? she found herself wondering. Then blinked the silly question away because it had no bearing on what was happening here.

'But will you believe him?' she wanted to know. 'If *he* tells you that what *I* have been telling you is the truth?'

'And what if it is you who has fed him his version of the truth?' he countered.

Catherine sighed in disgust. 'Which I presume means that you have no intention of believing your own son's word—any more than you once believed mine!'

'I repeat,' he said. 'You are the one with the obsession. Not Santo and not me.'

And I am banging my head against a brick wall here, Catherine decided grimly. But what's new about that? she asked herself, with a deriding twist of her mouth that seemed to set his tense frame literally pulsing.

'Then I think you should leave,' she said, moving away from the door and crossing the room to get right away from him. 'Now, before Santo wakes up and finds you here. Because he will not thank you any more than I do for showing such little faith in his word.'

'I did not say that I disbelieve what Santo is thinking, only that I disbelieve his source.'

'Same thing.' Catherine shrugged that line of argument away. 'And all I can say is that I find it very sad that you can put your feelings for Marietta before your feelings for your son—which makes your journey here such a wasted gesture.'

Vito said nothing, his face locked into a tight, grim mask as he went over to the kettle and began pouring boiling water into the coffee jug. From her new place by kitchen sink Catherine watched him with an emptiness that said she saw no hope for happiness for him. The man was bewitched by the devil. He had to be if he was so prepared to risk the love of his son for the love of that woman.

But was he? Catherine then pondered thoughtfully. For he was *here*, wasn't he? Breaking a court order, willing to risk his visitation rights, because it was more important a present for him to be where his troubled son was. Be of help, if he could. Reassure, if he could…?

'Well, as a tit-for-tat kind of thing,' she murmured slowly, 'let's just test your love for Marietta against your love for your son, Vito.'

'It isn't a competition,' he denounced.

'I am making it one,' she declared. 'And I'm going to do it by giving you a straight choice. So listen to me, Vito, for I am deadly serious. Either you renounce all intention of ever marrying Marietta,' she said, 'or you marry her and forfeit all rights of access to Santino.'

Turning with his coffee cup in hand, he murmured levelly, 'Word of warning, *cara*, You will not come between my son and me again, no matter what tricks you try to pull.'

'Yet pull them I will,' she instantly promised. And the tension between them began to edge up to dangerous levels again, because she wasn't bluffing and Vito knew that she wasn't.

Her father had been an eminent lawyer before his premature demise. He'd had friends in the profession, powerful friends, who specialised in marital conflicts and had been more than willing to come to Catherine's aid three years ago when she had needed their expertise. They'd tied Vito up in legal knots before he'd even known what had hit him.

She would let them do it again if she felt she had to protect Santo from the evil that was threatening to take up permanent residence in his father's house. Vito must be as aware as she was that he had already given her the ammunition to fire at him by breaking a court order to come here like this today.

One phone call and she could make good her threat; he knew that.

'So, what is it to be?' She flashed him the challenge. 'Is Marietta out of your life—or is it going to be Santo?'

He dared to laugh—albeit ruefully. 'You sound very

tough, Catherine. Very sure of yourself,' he remarked. 'But you seem to have overlooked one small but very important thing in all your clever plotting.'

'What?' she prompted, frowning, because as far as she could tell she had all the aces stacked firmly in her hand.

'Our son's clear insecurity and what you mean to do to ease it,' he said, taking a sip of thick black coffee. 'The last time you went to war against me, Santo was too young to know what was going on. But not any longer. Now he is old enough and alert enough to be aware of everything that takes place between the two of us.'

Pausing to watch as the full weight of his words settled heavily on her, he then gently offered a direct counter-challenge. 'Are *you* willing to risk hurting *his* love for me with yet another one of your vindictive campaigns aimed to make me toe the line…?''

CHAPTER THREE

'NO COME-BACK?' Vito softly prompted when she just stood there, staring at him while the full import of what he was pointing out to her slowly drained all the colour out of her face. 'Am I to assume, then, that your lust for revenge on sins imagined done to you does not run to hurting your son also?'

No, she thought on a chilled little shudder that spoke absolute volumes, she wasn't prepared to risk hurting her son's love for his *papà*.

'Well, that makes a refreshing change,' drawled a man who sounded as if he was beginning to enjoy himself. 'It almost—almost—restores my faith in you as the loyal loving mother of my son *cara*—even if it does nothing for my faith in you as the loyal and loving wife.'

Her chin went up, green eyes suddenly awash with derision. 'If we are going to get onto the subject of loyalty, then you're moving onto very shaky ground, Vito,' she warned him darkly.

'Then of course we will not,' he instantly conceded. 'Let us see instead if we can come up with a more—sensible compromise between us, that will adequately meet both our own requirements *and* fulfil our son's needs in one neat move…'

Was there such a thing? Catherine's eyes showed a blankness that said she couldn't think of one. 'So, don't keep me in suspense,' she snapped. 'Tell me this compromise.'

He smiled an odd smile, not quite wry, not quite cynical. 'I am not sure that you are going to like this,' he murmured.

39

'So long as it will put Marietta out in the cold, I'll be agreeable to anything,' Catherine assured him recklessly.

He didn't answer immediately, but the way his eyes began to gleam in a kind of unholy way made her flesh turn cold on the absolute certainty that she was about to be led somewhere she had no wish to go.

'Look, either cut to the bottom line of what all this taunting is about or get out of here!' she snapped in sheer nervous agitation.

'The bottom line,' he drawled, dropping his eyes down her body, 'is resting approximately midway down your sensational thighs and has the delicious potential of dropping to your lovely bare feet with a bit of gentle encouragement.'

Glancing down to look where his eyes were looking, she almost suffocated in the sudden wave of heat that went sizzling through her when she realised he was referring to her shorts!

'Will you just stop being so bloody provocative?' she choked, not sure if she was angry with him for saying such an outrageous thing or angry with herself for responding to it!

'I wish I could.' He grimaced, taking a languid sip of his coffee. 'But seeing those exquisite legs so enticingly presented has been driving me crazy since I arrived here.'

It was sheer instinct that made Catherine take a step forward with the intention of responding with a slap to his insufferable face!

But his hand deftly stopped her. 'You still have a great body, Catherine,' he told her, his eyes pinning her eyes with a look that made her feel as if she was drowning. 'All long sensual lines and supple curves that stir up some very exciting memories. So exciting in fact,' he murmured, gently stroking his thumb over the delicate flesh covering her wrist where the pulse-point was fluttering wildly, 'that it occurred to me—long before you showed your attraction to me, should add—that with you back in my bed I would not need to look elsewhere to fill that particular place in my life.'

A stunning silence followed. One that locked the air inside her throat and closed down her brain in complete rejection of what he was actually suggesting here!

'How dare you?' she breathed in harsh denunciation. 'How dare you make such a filthy suggestion?'

'I need a woman in my bed.' He shrugged with no apology. 'And, since my son must be protected from the seedier side of that need, then that woman must therefore be my wife. My proper wife,' he then succinctly extended. 'One who will proudly grace my table, eagerly grace my bed, and love my son as deeply as I do.'

'And you think Marietta fills all of those requirements?' she scoffed in outright contempt for him.

His golden eyes darkened. 'We are not talking about Marietta now,' he clipped. 'We are talking about you, Catherine. You,' he repeated, putting down his cup so he could free his other hand to slide it around her waist. Her flesh tightened in rejection. He countered its response by pulling her that bit closer to the firmness of his body. 'Who, even dressed as you are, would still manage to grace any man's table with your beauty and your inherent sense of style. And as for the sex,' he murmured in that sinfully sensual tone that helped make him such a dynamic lover. 'Since I know your rich and varied appetite as well as I know my own, I see no problem in our resurrecting what used to be very satisfying interludes for both of us.'

Interludes? He called what she would have described as giving herself body and soul to him *satisfying interludes*? She almost choked on her own outrage, feeling belittled and defiled.

But—maybe that had been his intention! 'You're disgusting!' she snapped.

'I am a realist,' he said.

'A realist who is hungry for revenge,' Catherine extended deridingly, well aware of his real motive.

'The Italian in me demands it,' he freely admitted. 'Just think, though,' he added softly, 'how your very British yen for martyrdom could be given free rein. How you could reside in my home with your head held high and pretend that you are only there because of Santo. How you could even share my bed and enjoy every minute of what we do there while pretending to yourself that keeping me happy is the price you have to pay to keep your son happy.'

'And you?' she asked. 'What do you aim to get out of such a wicked scenario?'

'This…' he murmured, and with a tug she was against him, his mouth capturing hers with the kind of kiss that flung her back too far and too swiftly into the realms of darkness, where she kept everything to do with this man so carefully hidden.

Well, they were not hiding now, she noted painfully as the heat from his kiss ignited flaming torches that lit their escape. And suddenly she was incandescent with feeling. Hot feelings, crazed feelings, feelings that went dancing wildly through her on a rampage of sheer sensual greed.

Only Vito could do it. Only he had ever managed to fire her up this way. Her body knew his body, exalted in its hardness pressing against her. His tongue licked the flames; his hands staked their claim on her by skimming skilfully beneath the hem of her top, then more audaciously beneath the elasticated band of her shorts.

She must have whimpered at the shock sensation of his flesh sliding against her flesh, because his mouth left hers and his eyes burned black triumph down at her.

'And I get my pride back,' he gritted. 'A pride you took from me and wiped the floor with the day you forced me into court to beg for the right to love my own son!'

And without warning she was free.

Standing there swaying dizzily, it took several moments for her to realise just what he had done to her. Then the shock descended, the appalled horror of how easy she had made it for him, followed closely by an all-consuming shame.

And all in the name of pride, revenge and of course passion, she listed grimly.

Her chin came up, her green eyes turning as grey as an arctic ocean now as she opened her mouth to tell him what he could do with his rotten proposition, his lousy sex appeal—and himself! when a sound beyond the closed kitchen door suddenly caught their attention.

It had them both turning towards the door, and freezing as they listened to Santo coming down the stairs, bumping something which sounded rather heavy down behind him. And in perfect unison they both then glanced up at the kitchen clock to note that it was only six-thirty, before they looked back at the door again.

The time was significant. It meant that their son was so disturbed by his worries that they'd woken him early.

From the corner of her eye Catherine saw Vito swallow tensely and his hands clench into fists at his sides. His face was suddenly very pale, his eyes dark, and the way his lips parted slightly in an effort to help his frail breathing brought home to her just how worried he was about what his son's reaction was going to be towards him.

She then suggested to herself an alternative. Afraid? Was Vito's expression the one Luisa had described as his frightened look?

Her heart began to ache for him, despite her not wanting it to. Vito loved his son; she had never doubted that. In a thousand other doubts she had never once doubted his love for his son.

Yet still he didn't deserve the way her hand reached in-

stinctively out to touch his arm in a soothing gesture. And
beyond the residue of her anger with him over that kiss she
felt tungsten steel flex with tension as the kitchen door flew
open, swinging back on its hinges against the wall to reveal
their son standing there in the opening.

Dressed in jeans and a sweatshirt, a baseball cap placed
firmly on his dark head and his travel hold-all, packed to
bursting by the look of it, sitting on the floor beside him,
while one little fist had a death grip on the bag's thick strap.

If he'd already been aware that his father was here, then
the complete lack of expression on his solemn little face
would have been understandable. But he hadn't known;
Catherine was sure of it. Their home was old and the walls
were thick. And no matter how heated their verbal ex-
changes had grown on occasion, neither of them had raised
their voices enough for the sound to filter out of this room.

So her heart stopped aching for the father to begin aching
for the son as Santo completely ignored Vito's presence in
the room to level his defiant dark brown eyes on his mother.

'I'm running away,' he announced. 'And you're not to
follow.'

It could have been comical. Santo certainly looked and
sounded comical standing there like that and making such
a fantastic announcement.

But Catherine had never felt less like laughing in her
life. For he meant it. He truly meant to run away because
he believed that nobody loved him.

And if Marietta had done Catherine the favour of walking in here right now she would have scratched her wicked
eyes out.

She went to go to him, needed to go to him and simply
hug him to her, wrap him in as much love as she could
possibly muster.

Only Vito was there before her—and he was wiser. He
didn't so much as attempt to touch the little boy as he

hunkered down on his haunches in front of him. Instead, he began talking in a deep and soft husky Italian.

Santo responded by allowing himself brief—very brief—eye to eye contact with his *papà*. 'English,' he commanded. 'I don't speak Italian any more.'

To Vito's deserving credit, he switched languages without hesitation, though the significance of his son's rejection must have pierced him like a knife.

'But where will you go?' he was asking gently. 'Have you money for your trip? Would you like me to lend you some?' he offered when the little boy's eyes flickered in sudden confusion because something as unimportant as money hadn't entered into his thoughts while he had been drawing up his plans to run away.

What was in his bag didn't bear thinking about unless Catherine wanted to weep. But she could hazard a fairly accurate guess at several treasured toys, a couple of his favourite tee shirts and his new trainers, since he didn't have them on. And tucked away hidden at the bottom of the bag would be a piece of tatty cotton that the experts would euphemistically call his comforter, though only she was supposed to know about it and he would rather die than let his *papà* find it.

'I don't want your money.' Vito's son proudly refused the offer.

'Breakfast, then,' Catherine suggested, coming to squat down beside Vito, her eyes the compassionate eyes of a mother who understood exactly what a small boy's priorities would be. 'No one should run away without eating a good breakfast first,' she told him. 'Come and sit down at the table,' she urged, holding out an inviting hand to him, 'and I'll get you some juice and a bowl of that new cereal you like.'

He ignored the hand. Instead his fiercely guarded brown eyes began flicking from one adult face to the other, and a confused frown began to pucker at his brow. Vito uttered a soft curse beneath his breath as understanding hit him. Catherine was a second behind him before she realised what it was that was holding Santo's attention so.

And now the tears really did flood her eyes, because it wasn't Santo's fault that this had to be the first time in his young memory that his parents' two faces had appeared in the same living frame in front of him!

An arm suddenly arrived around her shoulders. Warm and strong, the attached hand gave her arm a warning squeeze. As a razor-sharp tactician, famed for thinking on his feet, Vito had few rivals; she knew that. But the way he had quickly assessed the situation and decided on expanding on the little boy's absorption in their novel togetherness was impressive even to her.

'We don't want you to leave us, son…' As slick as that Vito compounded on the 'togetherness'.

Santos's eyes fixed on Catherine. 'Do you want me to stay?' he asked, so pathetically in need of reassurance that she had to clench her fists to stop herself from reaching out for him.

'Of course I do. I love you.' She stated it simply. She then extended that claim to include Vito. 'We *both* love you.'

But Santo was having none of it. 'Marietta says you don't,' he told his father accusingly. 'Marietta said I was a mistake that just gets in the way.'

'You must have misunderstood her,' Vito said grimly.

The son's eyes flicked into insolence. 'Marietta said that you hate my mummy because she made you have me,' he said. 'She said that's why you live in Naples and I live here in London, out of your way.'

Vito's fingers began to dig into Catherine's shoulder. Did he honestly believe that *she* would feed her own son this kind of poison when anyone with eyes could see that Santo was tearing himself up with it all?

'What Marietta says is not important, Santo,' she inserted firmly. 'It's what Papà says and I say that really matters to you. And we *both* love you very much,' she repeated forcefully. 'Would Papà have gone without his sleep to fly himself here through the night just to come and see you if he didn't love you?'

The remark hit a nerve. Catherine saw the tiny flicker of doubt enter her son's eyes as he turned them on his father. 'Why did you come?' he demanded of Vito outright.

'Because you would not come to me,' Vito answered simply. 'And I miss you when you are not there...'

I miss you when you are not there... For Catherine those few words held such a wealth of love in them that she wanted to weep all over again. Not for Santo this time, but for another little person, one who would always be missed even though he could never be here.

Maybe Vito realised what kind of memory his words had evoked, maybe he was merely responding to the tiny quiver she gave as she tried to contain what was suddenly hurting inside her. But his arm grew heavier across her shoulders and gently he drew her closer to his side.

With no idea what was passing through his mother's heart, Santo too was responding to all of that love placed into his father's statement. The small boy let out a sigh that shook mournfully as it left him, but at last some of the stiffness left his body—though he still wasn't ready to drop his guard. Marietta had hurt him much too deeply for her wicked words to be wiped out by a couple of quick reassurances.

'Where's Nonna?' he asked, clearly deciding it was time to change the subject.

His father refused to let him. 'I promised her I would

bring you back to Naples with me, if I could convince you to come,' Vito said.

'I don't like Naples any more,' Santo responded instantly. 'I don't ever—ever—want to go there again.'

'I am very sorry to hear that, Santo,' Vito responded very gently. 'For your sudden dislike of Naples rather spoils the surprise your *mamma* and I had planned for you.'

'What surprise?' the boy quizzed warily.

Surprise? Catherine was repeating to herself, her head twisting to look at Vito with a question in her eyes, wondering just where he was attempting to lead Santo with this.

'I'm not going to live with you in Naples!' Santo suddenly shouted as his busy mind drew its own conclusions. 'I won't live anywhere where Marietta is going to live!' he stated forcefully.

Vito frowned. 'Marietta does not live in my house,' he pointed out.

'But she will when you marry her! I hate Marietta!'

In response, Vito turned to Catherine with a look meant to turn her to stone. He still thought it was she who had been feeding his son all this poison against his precious Marietta!

I'll make you pay for this! those eyes were promising. And as Catherine's emotions began the see-sawing tilt from pain to bitterness, her green eyes fired back a spitting volley of challenges, all of which were telling him to go ahead and try it—then go to hell for all she cared!

He even understood that. 'Then hell it is,' he hissed in a soft undertone that stopped the threat from reaching their son's ears.

Then he was turning back to Santo, all smooth-faced and impressive puzzlement. 'But how can I marry Marietta when I am married to your *mamma*?' he posed, and watched the small boy's scowl alter to an uncertain frown—then delivered with a silken accuracy the dart aimed to pierce dead centre of his son's vulnerability. 'And your *mamma* and I want to stay married, Santino. We love each other just as much as we love you. We are even going to live in the same house together.'

It was the ultimate *coup de grâce*, delivered with the perfect timing of a master of the art.

And through the burning red mists that flooded her brain cells Catherine watched Vito's head turn so he could send her the kind of smile that turned men into devils. Deny it, if you dare, that smile challenged.

She couldn't. And he knew she couldn't, because already their son's face was lighting up as if someone had just switched his life back on. So she had to squat there, seething but silent, as Vito then pressed a clinging kiss to her frozen lips as still he continued to build relentlessly on the little boy's new store of 'togetherness' images.

Then all she could do was watch, rendered surplus to requirements by his machiavellian intellect, as he turned his attention back to their little witness and proceeded to add the finishing touches with an expertise that was positively lethal.

'Will you come too, Santo?' he murmured invitingly. 'Help us to be a proper family?'

A proper family, Catherine repeated silently. The magic words to any child from a broken home.

'You mean live in the same house—you, me and mummy?' Already Santo's voice was shaky with enchantment.

Vito nodded. 'And Nonna,' he added. 'Because it has to be Naples,' he warned solemnly. 'For it is where I work. I *have* to live there, you understand?'

Understand? The little boy was more than ready to understand anything so long as Vito kept this dream scenario flowing. 'Mummy likes Naples,' he said eagerly. 'I know she does because she likes to listen to all the places we've visited and all the things that we do there.'

'Well, from now on we can do those things together, as a family.' His *papà* smoothly placed yet another perfect image into his son's mental picture book.

At which point Catherine resisted the power of the arm restraining her and got up, deciding that she was most definitely surplus to requirements since the whole situation was out of her control now.

'I'm going to get dressed,' she said. They didn't seem to hear her. And as she stepped around Santo he was already moving towards his darling *papà*. Arms up, eyes shining, he landed in Vito's lap with all the enthusiasm of a well-loved puppy…

'If you still possess a healthy respect for your health, then I advise you to keep your distance,' Catherine warned as Vito's tall, lean figure appeared on the periphery of her vision.

She was in her small but sunny back garden hanging out washing, in the vague hopes that the humdrum chore would help ease some the angst that had built up in her system after having a great morning playing happy families.

Together, they had eaten a delightful breakfast where the plans had flown thick and fast on what to do in Naples during a long hot summer. And she'd smiled and she'd enthused and she'd made suggestions of her own to keep it all absolutely super. Then Santo had taken Vito off to show him his bedroom with all the excitement of a boy who felt as if he was living in seventh heaven.

Now Santo was at his best friend's house, several doors away, where he was excitedly relaying all his wonderful news to a captivated audience, who would no doubt be seeing Santo's change in fortune in the same guise as the child equivalent to winning the lottery.

Which clearly left Vito free to come in search of her, which was, in Catherine's view, him just begging for trouble.

He knew she was angry. He knew she was barely managing to contain the mass of burning emotion which was busily choking up her system at the cavalier way he had decided her life for her.

'Don't you have an electric dryer for those?' he questioned frowningly.

For a man she'd believed had no concept of what a tumble dryer was, the question came as a surprise to her. But as for answering it—she was in no mood to stand here explaining that shoving the clothes into a tumble dryer was no therapy at all for easing what was screaming to escape from her at this moment.

So instead she bent down to pluck one of Santo's tee shirts out of the washing basket, then straightened to peg it to the line, unaware of the way the sunlight played across the top of her neatly tied hair as she moved, picking out the red strands from the gold strands in a fascinating dance of glistening colour.

Nor was she aware of the way the simple straight skirt she was wearing stretched tight across the neat curve of her behind as she bent, or that her tiny white vest top gave tantalising glimpses of her breasts cupped inside her white bra.

But Vito Giordani was certainly aware as he stood there in the shade thrown by the house, leisurely taking it all in.

And a lack of sun didn't detract from his own dark attraction—as Catherine was reluctantly aware. Though you would be hard put to tell when she had actually looked at him long enough to note anything about him.

A sigh whispered from her, and her fingers got busier as a whole new set of feelings began to fizz into life.

'Could you leave that?' Vito asked suddenly. 'We need to talk while we have the chance to do so.'

'I think I've talked myself out today,' Catherine answered satirically.

'You're angry,' he allowed.

'I am?' With a deft flick she sent the rotating line turning, so she could gain access to the next free bit of washing line. 'And here was I thinking I was deliriously ecstatic,' she drawled.

His brows snapped together as her sarcastic tone carried on the crystal-clear morning air. Out there, beyond the low fencing that formed the boundaries between each garden, children's voices could be heard. Any one of them could be Santo, and Vito, it seemed, was very aware of that, because he started walking towards her, closing the gap between them so that their voices wouldn't carry.

'You must see that I really had no alternative but to say what I did,' he said grimly.

'The troubleshooter at work, thinking on his feet and with his mouth.' She nodded, fingers busy with pegs and damp fabric. 'I was very impressed, Vito,' she assured him. 'How could I not be?'

'I would say that you are most unimpressed.' He sighed, stooping to pick up the next piece of washing for her.

Another first, Catherine mused ruefully. Vittorio Giordani helping to hang out washing. For some stupid reason the apparition set her lower abdomen tingling.

'I have a life here, Vito,' she replied, ignoring the sensation. 'I have a job I love doing and commitments I have no wish to renege on.' Carefully, so she didn't have to make contact with his fingers, she took Santo's little school shirt from him.

'With your language and secretarial qualifications you could get a job anywhere.' He dismissed that line of argument. 'Templeton and Lang are not the only legal firm that specialise in European law.'

'You know where I work?' Surprise sent her gaze up to his face. He was smiling wryly—but even that kind of smile was a sexy smile. She looked away again quickly before it got a hold on her.

'Santo has been very vocal about how busy his *mamma's* important job keeps her.'

'You don't approve,' Catherine assumed by his tone.

'Of you working?' Bending again, he selected the next piece of washing. 'I would rather you had been here at home for Santo,' he said, with no apology for his chauvinistic outlook.

'Needs must,' was all she said, not willing to get into that particular argument. They'd had it before, after all, when she'd insisted on continuing to work after they married. Then it had been easy for her, because her multilingual expertise had been well sought after in many fields of modern business. In Naples, for instance, she had managed to pick up a job working for the local Tourist Information Board. Vito had been furious, his manly ego coming out for an airing when he'd wanted to know what the hell people would think of him allowing his pregnant wife to work!

Just another heated row they'd had amongst many rows.

'But the *devil* in this case is definitely not me,' Vito said dryly. 'It is you who refused any financial support when you left me,' he reminded her.

'I can support myself.' Which she always had done, even while she'd been living with Vito in his big house with its flashy cars and its even flashier lifestyle.

She had never been destitute. Her father had seen to that. Having brought her up himself from her birth, he had naturally made adequate provision for the unfortunate chance of his own demise. She owned this little house in middle-class suburbia outright, had no outstanding debts and still had money put away for the rainy days in life. And being reared in a single-parent professional house meant she'd grown up fiercely independent and self-confident. Marrying an arrogant Italian steeped in old-fashioned values had been a test on both qualities from the very start.

But the only time her belief in herself had faltered had been when she was pregnant for a second time and too sick and weakened to fight for anything—and that had included her husband's waning affections.

An old hurt began to ache again, the kind of hurt that suddenly rendered her totally, utterly, helplessly desolate.

'I can't live with you again, Vito,' she said, turning eyes darkened by a deep sadness on him. 'I can't…' she repeated huskily.

The sudden glint of pain in his own eyes told her that he knew exactly what had brought that little outburst on, but where compassion and understanding would have been better, instead anger slashed to life across his lean, dark features.

'Too late,' he clipped. 'The luxury of choice has been denied to you. This is not about what *you* want any more, Catherine,' he stated harshly. 'Or even what I want. It is what our son wants.'

'Our surviving son,' she whispered tragically.

Again the anger pulsed. 'We mourn the dead but we celebrate the living,' he ruthlessly declared. 'I will not allow Santo to pay the price of his brother's tragic ending any longer!'

Or maybe his tactics were the right ones, Catherine conceded as she felt his anger ignite her anger, which sent the pain fleeing. 'You truly believe that's what I've been doing?' she gasped.

His broad shoulders flexed. 'I do not know what motivates you, Catherine,' he growled. 'I never did, and now I have no wish to know. But the future for both of us is now set in stone. Accept it and leave the past where it belongs.

because it has outplayed its strength and no longer has any bearing on what we do now.'

With that, he turned away, his black scowl enough to put the sun out.

'Does that include Marietta?' she demanded of his back.

He'd already stopped listening—his attention suddenly fixing on something neither of them had noticed while they'd been so busy arguing. But they certainly noticed now the rows of boundary hedges with varying adult heads peering over the top of them, all of them looking curiously in their direction.

'Oh, damn,' Catherine cursed. At which point, the sound of the telephone ringing inside the house was a diversion she was more than grateful for. Smiling through tingling teeth, she excused herself and went inside, leaving him to be charming to the neighbours, because that was really all he was fit for!

Snatching up the phone from its kitchen wall extension, she almost shot her name down the line.

'Careful, darling, I have delicate eardrums,' a deeply teasing voice protested.

It was like receiving manna from heaven after a fall-out of rats. 'Marcus,' she greeted softly, and leaned back against the kitchen unit with her face softened by its first warm smile of the day. 'What are you doing calling so early in the morning?'

'It's such a beautiful morning, though. So I had this sudden yen to spend it with my favourite person,' he explained, unaware that he had already lost Catherine's attention.

For that was fixed on her kitchen doorway, where Vito was standing utterly frozen, and a hot blast of vengeful pleasure went skating through her when she realised he had overheard her words—and, more importantly, the soft intimacy with which she had spoken them.

'So when I remembered that this was also the day that

your son goes to Italy,' Marcus was saying, 'I thought, Why not drag Catherine out for a leisurely lunch by the river, since she will be free of her usual commitments?'

But 'free' was the very last word that Catherine would use to describe her situation right now. In truth she felt trapped, held prisoner by a pair of gold-shot eyes that were threatening retribution.

CHAPTER FOUR

THE fine hairs all over her body began to prickle as they stood on end in sheer response. 'I'm so sorry, Marcus,' she murmured apologetically, but the way her lungs had ceased to function made every syllable sound soft and breathless and disturbingly sensual. 'But Santo's trip has been—delayed,' she said, for want of a less complicated way of putting it.

'Oh.' He sounded so disappointed.

'Can I call you back?' she requested. 'When I have a clearer idea of when I will be free? Only it isn't—convenient to talk right now...'

'There is someone there,' Marcus realised, the sharp-minded lawyer in him quick to read the subtle intonations in her voice.

'Yes, that's right,' Catherine confirmed with a swift smile.

'Man, woman or child?' he enquired with sardonic humour.

More like frozen beast about to defrost, Catherine thought nervously, but kept that observation to herself. 'Thanks for being so understanding,' she murmured instead. 'I'll—I'll call you,' she promised. 'Just as soon as I can.' And said a hurried farewell before ringing off.

The phone went back on its cradle with the neat precision required of fingers that were trembling badly. 'That was Marcus,' she said, turning a flat-edged smile on Vito meant to hide the flurry of nervous excitement that had taken up residence inside her stomach.

'And?' he prompted, arching an imperious brow at her

57

when she didn't bother to extend on that. 'I presume this—Marcus has a role to play here?'

A role? A strange way of putting it, Catherine mused. Especially when they both knew exactly the *role* Marcus was supposed to be playing. Still…

'That is none of your business,' she told him, provoking him even though she knew it was a dangerous thing to do. But she was too busy enjoying herself, giving him back what he usually gave to her, to care about the consequences.

And body language is such a rotten tale-teller she thought ruefully when she noticed the way she had folded her arms beneath her breasts in a way that could only be described as defiant.

The back door slammed shut, making her jump. A different kind of body language, she noted warily.

'He's your lover,' Vito bit out condemningly.

'But why look so shocked?' she asked, refusing to deny the charge. 'What's the matter, Vito?' she then taunted goadingly. 'Hadn't it occurred to you before that I might well have a personal life beyond Santo?'

A telling little nerve flicked in his jaw. Catherine enjoyed watching it happen. Did he honestly believe that she'd spent the last three years in social seclusion while he hadn't been around to give her life meaning? The man was too arrogant and conceited for his own good sometimes, she decided. It wouldn't hurt him one bit to discover that he wasn't the be-all and end-all of her existence!

'Or is it your colossal ego that's troubling you?' she said continuing her thought patterns out loud and with derision. 'Because it prefers to think me incapable of being with another man after having known you? Well, I'm sorry to disappoint your precious ego, but I have a healthy sex drive—as you very well know,' she added before he decided to say it. 'And I can be as discreet as you—if no more so, since it's clear by your face that you knew nothing about Marcus, whereas I've had Marietta flung into my face for what feels like for ever!'

'Leave Marietta out of this,' he warned tightly.

'Not while she remains a threat to my son,' she refused.

'The most immediate threat here, Catherine, is to yourself.' He didn't move a single muscle but she was suddenly aware of danger. 'I want this man out of your life as of now!'

'When Marietta is out of your life,' she threw back promptly. 'And not before.'

'When are you going to accept that I cannot dismiss Marietta from my life!' he said angrily. 'Her husband was my best friend! She holds shares in my company! She works alongside me almost as my equal! She is my mother's only godchild!' Grimly, precisely, he counted off all the old excuses that gave Marietta power over them.

So Catherine added to it. 'She sleeps in your bed,' she mimicked him tauntingly. 'She slips poison into your son's food.'

'You are the poisonous one,' he sighed.

'And you, Vito, are the fool.'

He took a step towards her. Catherine's chin came up, green eyes clashing fearlessly with his. And the atmosphere couldn't get any more fraught if someone had wired the room up with high-voltage cable. He looked as if he would like to shake her—and Catherine was angry enough to wish he would just try!

What he actually did try to do was put the brakes on what was bubbling dangerously between them. 'Let's get this discussion back where it should be,' he gritted. 'Which is on the question of your love-life, not mine!'

'My love-life is flourishing very nicely, thank you,' she answered flippantly.

It was the wrong thing to say. Catherine should have seen

the signs—and maybe she had done. Afterwards she couldn't quite say she hadn't deliberately provoked him into action.

Whatever. She suddenly found herself being grabbed by hands that were hell-bent on punishment. 'You hypocrite,' he gritted. 'You have the damned cheek to stand in judgement over my morals when your own are no better!'

'Why should it bother you so much what I do in my private life?' Catherine threw back furiously.

'Because you belong to me!' he barked.

She couldn't believe she was hearing this! 'Which makes you the hypocrite, Vito,' she told him. 'You want me—yet you don't want me,' she mocked him bitterly. 'You like to play around—but can't deal with the idea that I might play around!'

With a push, she put enough space between them to slide sideways and right away from him. But inside she was shaking. Shaking with anger or shaking with something far more basic. She wasn't really sure.

'Until last night—' Was it only last night? She paused to consider. 'We hadn't even exchanged a single word with each other for the past three years! Then you suddenly walk in through my front door this morning and start behaving as if you've never been away from it!' The way the air hissed from her lungs was self-explanatory. 'Well, I've got news for you,' she informed him grimly. 'I have a life all right. A good one and a happy one. Which means I resent the hell out of you coming here and messing with it!'

'Do you think that I am looking forward to having you running riot through *my* life a second time?' he responded. 'But you *are* my wife! Mine!' he repeated. 'And—'

'What a joke!' Catherine interrupted scornfully. 'You only married me because you had to! Now you are taking me back because you have to! Well, hear this,' she announced. 'You may have walked me into a steel trap b saying what you did to Santo. But that doesn't mean I am willing to stay meekly inside it! Anything you can do I can do,' she warned him. 'So if Marietta stays then Marcus stays!'

'In your bed,' he gritted, still fixed, it seemed, on getting her to admit the full truth about her relationship with Marcus.

'In my bed,' she confirmed, thinking, What the hell— why not let him believe that? 'In my arms and in my body,' she tagged on outrageously. 'And so long as my son doesn't know about it, who actually cares, Vito?' she challenged. 'You?' she suggested as she watched his face darken with contempt for her. 'Well, in case you haven't realised it yet, I don't care what you think. The same way that you didn't care about me when you went from my arms to Marietta's arms the day I lost our baby!'

Seven o'clock, and Vito still hadn't come back.

Catherine stood by her bedroom window staring down at the street below and wondered anxiously whether she had finally managed to finish it for them.

She shouldn't have said it, she acknowledged uncomfortably. True though it might have been, those kind of bitter words were best kept hidden within the dark recesses of one's own mind. For it served no useful purpose to drag them all out, and if anything only added more pain where there was already enough pain to be felt.

She knew that he had felt the loss of their second child just as deeply as she had done. And had suffered guilt in knowing that she had known exactly where he had been and with whom he had been when she'd needed him. But in the thrumming silence which had followed her outburst, while she'd stood there sizzling in her own corrosive bitterness, she'd had to watch that tall, dark, proudly arrogant man diminish before her very eyes.

His skin had slowly leached of its colour, his mouth began to shake, and with a sharp jerk of his head he wrenched his eyes from her—but not before she'd seen the look of hell written in them.

'Oh, God, Vito.' On a wave of instant remorse she'd taken a step towards him. 'I'm so…'

'Sorry,' she had been going to say. But he didn't give her the chance to, because he'd just spun on his heel and walked out of the house.

And if the kitchen floor had opened up and swallowed her whole at that moment, she would have welcomed the punishment. For no man deserved to be demolished quite so thoroughly as she had demolished Vito.

Par for the course, she thought wearily now, as she stood there in the window. For when had she and Vito *not* been hell-bent on demolishing each other? They seemed to have been at loggerheads from day one of their marriage— mostly over Marietta. And the final straw had been her miscarriage.

In the ensuing dreadful hours after being rushed into hospital she had almost lost her own life. She'd certainly lost the will to live for several long black months afterwards. She felt she had failed—failed her baby, failed in her marriage and failed as a woman. And the only thing that had kept her going through those months was Santino, and driven need to wage war on Vito for coming to her hospital bed straight from Marietta's arms.

But that was three years ago, and she had truly believed that she had put all of that anger and bitterness behind her. Now she knew differently, and didn't like herself much for it. Especially when she knew that downstairs in the sitting room, already fed and bathed and in his pyjamas, was their son, kneeling on the windowsill doing exactly the same as his mother was doing. Staring out of the window anxiously waiting for his father's return even though she'd assured him that his *papà* had merely rushed off to keep an appointment in the City and would be back as soon as he was able.

The throaty roar of a powerful engine reached her ears just before she saw the sports car turn the corner and start heading down the street towards them.

And Catherine's hand shot up to cover her mouth as tears of relief, of aching gratitude, set her tense mouth quivering.

From the excited whoop she heard from her son, Santo had heard the sound and recognised it instantly.

Low, long, black and intimidating, Vito's car hadn't even come to a halt when she heard the front door open then saw her son racing down the path towards him. As he climbed out on the roadside, Vito's face broke into a slashing grin as he watched his son scramble up and over the gate without bothering to open it.

He must have gone back to his London home as he had changed his clothes, she noticed. The creased suit and shirt swapped for crease-free and stylishly casual black linen trousers and a dark red shirt that moulded the muscular structure of his torso. And his face was clean shaven, the roguish look wiped away so only the smooth, dark, sleek Italian man of means was visible.

Coming around the long bonnet of the car, Vito only had time to open his arms as his son leapt into them. Leaning back against the passenger door of the car, he then proceeded to listen as Santo rattled on to him in a jumble of words that probably didn't make much sense he was so excited. But that didn't matter.

What Santo was really saying was all too clear enough. 've got my *papà* back. I'm happy!

Glancing up, Vito saw her standing there watching them, and his eyes froze in that instant. Take this away from me f you dare, he seemed to be challenging.

But Catherine didn't dare—she didn't even *want* o dare.

Turning away from the window, she left them to it and went to sink weakly down on her bed while she tried to decide where they went from here.

To Naples, of course, a dryly mocking voice inside her head informed her. Where you will toe the line that Vito will draw for you.

And why will you do that? she asked herself starkly.

Because when you brutally demolished him today, what you actually did was demolish your will to fight him.

Getting wearily to her feet, she grimly braced herself, ready to go down and face Vito. She found them in the sitting room and paused on the threshold to witness the easy intimacy with which Santo sat on Vito's lap with his latest reading book open. Between them they were reading it in English then translating into Italian in a way that told Catherine that they did this a lot back in Naples.

And still she didn't know what her place was going to be in this new order of things. But when Vito glanced up at her and she saw the residue of pallor that told her he still had not recovered from all of that ugliness earlier, she knew one thing for an absolute certainty as shame went riddling through her.

Vito might be feeling the weight of his own guilt but he would never forgive her for making him remember it.

'I'm sorry,' she murmured, because it had to be said now or never, even if their son was there to hear it. 'I didn' mean to—'

'Santo and I are going to spend the day out tomorrow,' Vito coolly cut in. 'To give you chance to close up you life here. We fly back to Naples the day after…'

'Damn…' Catherine muttered as she lost the end to the rol of sticky tape—again. 'Damn, damn, blasted damn…'

With an elbow trying to keep the cardboard box lid shut

she used a fingernail to pick carefully at the tape while her teeth literally tingled with frustration.

She'd had a lousy day and this stupid sticky tape was just about finishing it. First of all she'd had a row with Santo just before he'd gone off with his father and she'd walked into his bedroom to find it in complete upheaval.

'Santino—get up here and clean this mess up!' she'd yelled at him down the stairwell.

He'd come, but reluctantly. 'Can't you do it, this once?' he'd asked her sulkily. 'Papà is ready to go now!'

'No, I cannot,' she refused. 'And Papà can wait.'

'I never have to do this in Naples,' her son muttered complainingly as he slouched passed her.

In the mood she was in, mentioning Naples was the equivalent of waving a red flag at a bull.

'Well, in this house we clean up after ourselves, and *before* we get treats out!' Catherine fired back. 'And guess what, sweetie?' she added for good measure. 'From now on Mummy is going to be in Naples to make sure you don't get away with such disgraceful behaviour!'

'Maybe you should stay here, then,' the little terror responded.

'Santino!'

Catherine hadn't realised that Vito called his son Santino, as she did, when the boy was in trouble. And it had a funny little effect on her to hear him doing it this morning.

'Apologise to your mother and do as she tells you!'

The apology was instant. And Catherine sighed, and seethed, and resented the hell out of Vito for getting from her son what she had been about to get from him herself.

But then that was just another little thing about herself she'd learned that she didn't like. She was jealous of Santo's close relationship with his father. It had shown its ugly green head when Santo had insisted Vito take him to bed last night, leaving her feeling pathetically rejected.

And the pendulum had swung back the other way, just like that, putting her right on the attack again. So when Vito had come down half an hour later and coolly informed her that their son was expecting him to stay the night—she exploded.

'You've got your own house only two miles up the road. Use it!' she'd exclaimed. 'I don't want you staying here.'

'I didn't say that *I* wanted to stay,' he'd drawled. 'Only that our son expects it.'

'Well, I expect you to leave,' she'd countered. 'Now, if possible. I've got things to do and you—'

'Or people to see?' he'd silkily suggested. 'Like your lover, for instance?'

So, they were back to that already, she'd noted angrily, realising that neither seemed to have learned much from their row that morning. 'I do not bring my lovers into this house,' she'd informed him haughtily. 'Behaviour like that might be acceptable in Italy but it certainly isn't here!'

As a poke at Marietta without actually saying her name, it had certainly hit its mark. His hard face had shut down completely. 'Then where do you meet him? In a motel under assumed names?'

'Better that than allocating him the room next to my room,' she'd said.

The remark had sent his eyes black. 'Marietta never occupied a room within ten of ours, Catherine,' he'd censured harshly.

But at least he had voiced whom it was they were talking about. 'Well, rest assured she won't be occupying *any* room when I move back in,' she'd informed him. 'And if I see her with so much as a toothbrush in her hand, I'll chuck her through the nearest window.'

To her annoyance he'd laughed. 'Now that I would like to see,' he'd murmured. 'After all, Marietta stands a good two inches taller than you and there is a little bit more of her—in every way.'

'Well, you should know,' she'd drawled, in a tone that had wiped that grin right off his face!

He'd left soon after that, stiffly promising to return before Santo woke up the next morning. He'd left soon after her argument with Santo this morning too, she recalled now, with a grimace. One glance at her face as she'd walked down the stairs must have told him she was gunning for yet another round with him.

Next she'd had to beg an immediate release from her contract, which Robert Lang had not taken kindly. Then she'd had to say her goodbyes to people she had been working with for over two years, and that had been pretty wretched. Then—surprise, surprise—something nice had happened! One of the new recruits at the company had come to search her out because he'd heard she was leaving London and wanted to know if he could lease her house from her.

Why not? she'd thought. It was better than leaving it unlived in, and she liked the idea of him and his small family looking after the place for her.

But she hadn't bargained on the extra work it would entail to leave the house fit for strangers. Instead of just doing the usual preparations, then shutting the front door on everything as she left it, she'd had to go hunting round for anything and everything of a personal nature and box up ready to go into storage, arrange for that darned storage, and also arrange for a company of professional cleaners to come in and get the place ready for her new tenants.

Now she was tired and fed-up and harassed, and all she wanted to do was sit down and have a good weep because everything she'd grown to rely on for security in her life had been effectively dismantled today!

But she couldn't weep because Vito and her son were

due back at any minute, and she would rather die than let Vito catch her weeping!

But none of that—or even all of that put together—compared with the awful lunch she had endured with Marcus Templeton.

Okay, she reasoned, so their relationship was not quite on the footing that she had led Vito to believe. But it had been getting there—slowly. And she liked Marcus—she really did! He was the first man she had allowed to get close to her after the disastrous time she'd had with Vito.

He was good and kind and treated her as an intellectual equal rather than a potential lover. And she liked what they'd had together. It was so much calmer and more mature than the relationship she'd had with Vito.

No fire. No passion to fog up reality.

Marcus was tall, he was dark—though not the romantically uncompromising dark that was Vito's main weapon of destruction. And he was very good-looking—in a purely British kind of way.

She'd wanted to want him. She'd wanted to stop comparing every other man she met with Vito and actually take a chance on Marcus being the one to help her remove Vito's brand of hot possession from her soul for ever. But had she been in love with Marcus? She asked herself. And the answer came back in the form of a dark shadow. For no, she had not fallen in love with him nor even been close to falling, she realised now.

But what really hurt, what really shocked and shamed and appalled her, was that she hadn't realised just how seriously Marcus had fallen in love with her—until she'd broken her news to him today.

With a heavy sigh she sat back against the wall behind her, her packing forgotten for the moment while she let herself dwell on the biggest crime of blindness she had ever been guilty of.

She had stunned Marcus with her announcement that she was going back to Naples and to her husband. She had knocked the stuffing right out of him. So much so, in fact, that he hadn't moved, hadn't breathed, hadn't done anything for the space of thirty long wretched seconds but stare blankly into space.

The threatened tears arrived. Catherine felt them trickle down her dusty cheeks but didn't bother to stop them.

Because Marcus loved her—and she'd always wanted to be loved like that—for herself and not just the heat of her passion!

Oh, he'd pulled himself together eventually, she recalled with bittersweet misery. Then he'd said all the nice, kind gentlemanly things aimed to make her feel better when really it should have been the other way around and her consoling him.

But how do you console someone you know you've hurt more than you would ever want to be hurt yourself?

'Mummy?' The concerned sound of her son's voice reached deep inside to where she'd sunk in, and brought her shuddering back to a sense of where she was. She opened her eyes to find him squatting beside her with a gentle hand resting on her shoulder and his brown eyes looking terribly anxious. 'What's the matter?' he asked worriedly.

'Oh,' she choked, hurriedly pulling herself together. 'Nothing,' she said huskily. 'Just some dust in my eye. How…?' She rubbed at the offending evidence. 'How did you get in?' she asked.

'The front door was open,' another deeper and very protracted voice grimly informed her.

Vito. Her heart sank. And now she felt thoroughly stupid.

'You left it on the latch.' Her small son took up the censure. 'And we couldn't find you anywhere so we thought something might have happened to you.'

Couldn't find her? Why, where was she? she asked herself with a blank stare at her immediate surroundings.

She was in her bedroom, she realised. Sitting on the floor between the chest of drawers and the wardrobe while the space around her was piled with hastily filled cardboard boxes.

Boxes in which to pack her life away, she thought tragically. And without any warning the floodgates swung wide open. It was terrible—the lowest moment of her whole rotten day, in fact.

So the tears flowed in abundance and she couldn't stop them, and beside her Santo began crying too. He tried to hug her and she tried to comfort him by hugging him back and mumbling silly words about his mother being silly, and somewhere in the background she could hear things being shifted and someone cursing, but didn't even remember who that someone was until her son was plucked away from her and put somewhere so a pair of strong arms could reach down and gather her up.

She simply curled up against a big, firm male body and continued weeping into its shoulder. Oh, she knew it was Vito, but to admit that to herself meant fighting him again, and she didn't want to fight right now. She wanted to cry and be weak and pathetic and vulnerable. She wanted to be held and clucked over and made to feel safe.

He sat down on the bed with her cradled against him and beside them Santo came to put his arms back around her; he was still sobbing.

'Santino, *caro*,' Vito was murmuring with husky firmness. 'Please stop that crying. Your *mamma* is merely sad at having to leave here, that is all. Females do this; you must learn to expect it.'

The voice of experience, Catherine mocked within her own little nightmare. Yet she'd never cried on him like this—ever. So where had he acquired that experience?

'I hate you,' she whispered thickly.

'No, you don't. Your *mamma* did not mean that, Santo,' Vito coolly informed his son. 'She merely hates having to leave this house, that is all.'

In other words, Remember who is listening.

'We'll have to stay here, then,' his young son wailed, his arms tightening protectively around Catherine.

'We will not.' His father vetoed that suggestion. 'Your *mamma* loves Naples too; she is just determined to forget that for now.' The man had no heart, Catherine decided miserably. 'Now be of use,' he instructed his son sternly, 'and go and get your mother a glass of water from the kitchen.'

The sheer importance of the task diverted Santo enough to stop his tears and send him scrambling quickly from the bed.

'Now, try to control yourself before he comes back.' Vito turned his grimness onto Catherine next. 'You are frightening him with all of this.'

She didn't need telling twice to realise that Vito was only being truthful and she had frightened Santo by breaking down. So she made a concerted effort to stem the tears, then pulled herself free of his arms and crawled off his lap and beneath the duvet without uttering a single word.

What could she say, after all? she pondered bleakly. I'm crying because I hurt the man I wanted to replace you with? Vito would really love to know that!

By the time Santo came back, carefully carrying the glass of water in front of him, her tears had been reduced to the occasional sniffle. Smiling him a watery smile, she accepted his offering and added a nasal-sounding thank you that didn't alter his solemn stare.'

'I don't like to see you upset, Mummy,' he confessed.

'I'm sorry, darling,' she apologised gently, and pressed a reassuring kiss to his cheek. 'I promise I won't do it again.'

And to think, she slayed herself guiltily, only this morning she had been shouting at him, and here he was being so excruciatingly nice to her! It was enough to make her want to start crying all over again.

Maybe Vito saw it coming, because as quick as a flash he was ushering Santo out of the room with murmured phrases about Catherine needing to rest now.

Oddly enough she did rest. Lying there, huddled beneath the duvet, she started out by thinking about Marcus and Santo and herself and ended up falling asleep, to dream about Vito coming back into the bedroom, she didn't how much later, and silently but gently undressing her before slipping the duvet back over her boneless figure. She could remember dreaming that she had a one-sided conversation with him, but before she could remember what that conversation was about sleep claimed her yet again.

The next time she awoke she knew it was the middle of the night simply by the hushed silence beyond the closed curtains. She lay there for a while, feeling relaxed and comfortable—until something moved in the bed beside her that had her shimmying over on a gasp of alarm.

She found Vito asleep in the bed beside her. Lying flat on his back, with an arm thrown in relaxed abandon on the pillow behind his head, he looked as if he had been there for hours!

But that wasn't all—not by a long shot. Because from what she could see of his bronze muscled torso, he had also climbed into her bed naked!

CHAPTER FIVE

'VITO!' she cried in whispering protest, and issued an angry push to his warm satin shoulder.

'Hmm?' he mumbled, black-lashed eyelids flickering upwards to reveal slumberous eyes that were not quite in focus.

'What do you think you are doing here?' Catherine demanded.

'Sleeping,' he murmured, and lowered his eyelids again. 'I suggest that you do the same thing.'

'But I don't want you in my bed!'

'Tough,' he replied. 'Because I am staying. You could not be left alone here in the state you were in, and Santo needed the reassurance of my presence. So be wise, *cara*,' he advised. 'Accept a situation you brought upon yourself. Shut up and go to sleep before I awaken properly and begin thinking of other things we can do to use up what is left of the night.'

'Well, of all the—' She couldn't believe she was hearing this. 'What makes you think that all of that gives you the right to climb into bed with me?'

'Arrogance,' he replied, so blandly that Catherine almost choked on the sudden urge to laugh!

Only this was no laughing matter. 'Just get out of here,' she hissed, giving his rock-solid shoulder yet another prompting push.

'If I open my eyes, Catherine, you will intensely regret it,' he warned very grimly.

She was no fool; she recognised that tone. On an angry

73

flurry of naked flesh, she flung herself onto her back, to lie seething in silence.

Naked. Her heart stopped beating as a new kind of shock went rampaging through her.

So it had not been a dream and Vito *had* undressed her! The man's self-confessed arrogance knew no bounds! she decided as she sent one of her hands on a quick foray of her own body to discover just how naked she was.

She was very—very naked.

'Did you know you have developed a habit of talking in your sleep?' he said suddenly.

Catherine froze beside him. She heard a very muddled and very disjointed echo of words being spoken by her that should have taken place in the privacy of her head.

Regretful words about Marcus.

'Shut up,' she gasped, terrified of what was coming. 'He must be quite something, this man you weep for.' He ignored her advice in the dulcet tones of one readying for battle. 'To reach the frozen wastelands where your heart lies hidden. Maybe I should take the trouble to meet him, see what he's got that I never had.'

'Why bother?' she slashed back. 'When you would never find the same qualities inside yourself if you searched for ever.'

'Is he good in bed?'

Her next gasp almost strangled her. 'Go to hell,' she replied, turning her back towards him.

As an act of dismissal it had entirely the opposite effect, because Vito's arm had scooped around her and rolled her back before she even knew what was happening.

And suddenly he was leaning right over her, all glinting eyes and primitive male aggression. 'I asked you a question,' he prompted darkly.

Her mouth ran dry, the tip of her tongue slinking out to moisten parted lips that were remaining stubbornly silent

because she was damned if she was going to tell the truth—
that she had never even been tempted to go to bed with
Marcus—just to soothe Vito's ruffled ego! Luxurious dark
eyelashes curled down over shimmering eyes as he lowered
his gaze to observe the nervous action—and completely
froze it as an old, old sensation went snaking through her.

He was going to kiss her. 'No, Vito,' she breathed, but
even she heard the weakness in that pathetic little protest.

It was already too late. His mouth claimed hers with the
kind of deeply sensual kiss that could only be issued by
this wretched man. It was like drowning in the most exquisite substance ever created, she likened dazedly as she
began to sink on a long, spiralling dive through silken liquid kept exactly at body heat so it was impossible to tell
what part of the kiss was hers and what part was his.

The man, his closeness, even the antipathy that was pulsing between them, was so sexual that she found herself
thinking fancifully of lions again. Her skin came alive, each
tiny pore beginning to vibrate with an awareness that held
her trapped by its power and its intensity.

Whether it was she who began to touch him first or
whether Vito was the one to begin their gentle caresses, she
didn't know—didn't really care. Because the heat of his
flesh felt so exquisitely wonderful to her starved fingertips,
and where he touched she burned, and where he didn't she
ached.

She tried to drag some air into lungs that had ceased
working, felt the tips of her breasts briefly touch his hair-
roughened breastplate, felt her nipples sting as they responded to the contact and moaned luxuriously against his
mouth.

With a sensual flick of his tongue, Vito caught that little
moan, took possession of it as if it belonged to him. And
as his hands worked their old magic on her flesh with the

sensual expertise of a master, he watched in grim triumph as, bit by bit, she surrendered herself to him.

'Does he make you feel like this, *cara*?' he grated with electric timing across the erect tip of one pouting nipple. 'Can he send you this far, this fast?' he demanded as his fingers, so excruciatingly knowing, slid a delicate caress over her sex.

She shuddered, moaned again, flexed and unflexed muscles that were moving to their own rhythm. 'Vito,' she breathed, as if her very life depended on her saying that name.

'Yes,' he hissed. 'Vito,' he repeated in rough-toned satisfaction. 'Who touches you—here—and you go up in flames for me.'

She went wild then. Three years of abstinence was no defence against what he could do for her. She moved for him, breathed for him, writhed and begged for him.

His laugh of black triumph accompanied the first deep penetrating thrust of his body. But Catherine was too busy exalting in the power of his passion to care that he seemed to be taunting her surrender. And as Vito gritted his teeth and began to ride her his eyes remained fixed on her shuttered eyelids, because he knew her so well and did not want to miss that moment when those eyelids flicked upwards just before she shot into violent orgasm.

Then let him see if she was shocked to find *his* dark face bearing down on her instead of her damned lover's face! 'Me,' he muttered tautly as he grappled with his own soaring need to surrender. 'Vito,' he gritted.

Why? Because despite what he was telling himself the very last thing he needed right now was Catherine shattering his ego by expecting it to be another man making her feel this good!

So he repeated his name. 'Vito, *cara*.' And kept on repeating it with each powerful thrust of his powerful frame,

'Vittorio—Adriano—Lucio—Giordani,' in the most seductive accent ever created.

Her answering whimper caught him in mid-thrust. Her eyes flicked open. She looked straight at him. *'Pidoccio,'* she said, then shot into a flailing orgasm.

They lay there afterwards, sweat-soaked, panting, utterly spent. He on his back, with his arm covering his face, she on her side, curled right away from him. 'Louse,' she whispered again—in English this time.

She was right and he was. So he didn't deny it. 'You are *my* wife,' Vito stated flatly. 'Our separation is now officially over. So take my advice and be careful, *cara*, who you dream about in future.'

That was all. Nothing else needed to be added to that. Catherine had unwittingly struck at the very centre of his pride when she'd mumbled mixed-up words about Marcus in her sleep. The experience just now had not been performed for mere sexual gratification's sake, but in sheer revenge.

Naples was shimmering beneath a haze of heat that made Catherine glad they were taking the coast road towards Mergellina then on to Capo Posillipo, where most of the upper echelons of Neapolitan society had their residences.

Vito was driving them in an open-top red Mercedes Cabriolet that must be a recent buy judging by the newness of the cream leather. And driving alfresco like this beat air-conditioned luxury any day, to Catherine's way of thinking. She could feel the breeze in her hair and the sun on her skin, and if it hadn't been for the man beside her she would have been enjoying this. The views were every bit as spectacular as she'd remembered them to be. And Santo was safely strapped into the rear seat, happily singing away to himself in whichever language took his fancy.

The three of them must look the perfect family, she mused. But they weren't.

In fact she and Vito had hardly swapped three words with each other since they got up this morning. He'd risen first, rolling out of the bed and striding off to the bathroom very early—but then he always had been an early riser. Catherine had stayed huddled where she was, listening until she'd heard Santo go down the stairs before she made any attempt to stir herself.

She'd needed her son as a buffer. Catherine freely acknowledged that. At least with Santo there she could try to behave with some normality. But Vito had been as withdrawn and reticent as she had been, as if his behaviour last night had pleased him as little as it had done Catherine.

'...sunglasses in the glove compartment.'

Catching only the tail end of Vito's blunt-edged comment brought her face automatically swinging around from the view to find him looking directly at her. Blinking uncomfortably, she turned quickly away again.

It was all right for him, she thought as she leant forward to open the door to the glove box, his eyes were already hidden behind silver-framed dark lenses, but he hadn't been able to look at her before he'd put the darn things on!

Once through Mergellina the car began the serpentine climb on the Via Posillipo. As Catherine turned her attention to enjoying the spectacular view now unfolding beneath them, a flash of gold caught her eye.

It was Vito's wedding ring, gleaming in the sunlight where his fingers were hooked loosely around the steering wheel. Glancing down at her lap, she saw her own slender white fingers suddenly looked distinctly bare. In what had been meant to be a dramatically expressive gesture she had left her rings behind when she left Vito all those years ago.

But now she shifted uncomfortably, a sudden wistfulness

sending her thumbpad on a stroke of the empty space where her rings should be.

'Do you want them back?'

Catherine jumped, severely jolted by the fact that he wasn't only looking at her now, but was doing it enough to miss nothing!

'It seems—practical,' she said, using the same flat tone as he. 'To avoid any—speculation. For Santo's sake.'

For Santo's sake. She grimaced at the weakness of her excuse, and even though she didn't check she knew that Vito was grimacing too. Because they both knew that if she put her rings back on she would be doing it for her own sake.

Pride being another sin they were all victim to in different ways. And her pride wanted her to wear the traditional seal of office that stated clearly her position in Vito's life. That way she could hold her head up and outface her critics—of which she expected to meet many—and feel no need to explain her arrival back to those people who probably believed their marriage had been dissolved long ago.

The car moved on up the hillside, and the higher it went the bigger the residential properties became and the more extensive and secluded became the land surrounding them. As they reached a pair of lattice iron gates that automatically swung open as they approached them, Catherine's attention turned outwards again, her interest picking up as she viewed the familiar tree-lined approach to her old home and found herself watching breathlessly for the house itself to come into view.

The gardens were a delight of wide terraces, set out in typically Italian formality, with neat pathways and hedgerows and elegant stone steps leading down to the next terrace and so on. There were several tiny courtyard areas fashioned around tinkling fountains framed by neatly

clipped box hedgerows of jasmine and bougainvillea that
were a blaze of colour right now.

As they rounded a bend in the driveway the house suddenly came into view. The Villa Giordani had been standing here for centuries, being improved on and added to until
it had become the most desired property in the area.

Bright white walls as thick as four feet in places stood
guarding an inner sanctum. Good taste and an eye for
beauty had always been present in the Giordani genes.
There was no upper floor terrace exactly, but each suite of
rooms had its own balcony set flat against the outer wall
and marked by a thick stone arch and balustrade supported
on turned stone supports. The balconies went deep—deep
into the house itself—in an effort to offer shade to their
occupants, who might want to sit there and enjoy the view
over the Bay of Naples, which was nothing short of breath-
taking from this high on the hill.

In keeping with the upper floor, the ground floor kept to
the same arched theme, only the low stone balustrades had
been extended out to the edge of the wide terrace which
circumvented the whole house.

Nothing had ever been skimped on in the creating of the
Giordani residence. Even the four deep steps leading up to
the terrace had been designed to add to the overall grandeur
of the place.

The driveway continued on to curve round towards the
back of the house, where Catherine knew the garages lay
along with a stable block, two tennis courts and a swimming pool tucked away in a natural bowl in the landscape.
But Vito brought the car to a halt at the front steps and
shut down the engine.

Santo was already scrambling at the back of Catherine's
seat in an effort to get out. 'Hurry up, Mummy!' he commanded impatiently. 'I want to go and surprise Nonna before she knows we're here!'

Climbing out of the car, Catherine unlocked the back of her seat to set her impatient son free, then stood watching as he raced off towards the house, bursting in through the front doors with a, 'Nonna, where are you?' at the top of his voice. 'It's me, Santo! I'm home!'

I'm home... Catherine felt her mouth twist in bitter rueful acknowledgement at just how much 'at home' her son had looked and sounded as his dark-eyed, dark-haired little body had shot him through those doors without a thought given to knocking first. And the words had burst from him in free-flowing Italian, as if it was the only language he knew how to speak.

As if he belonged here.

On the other side of the car, Vito stood watching also. And as her top lip gave a quiver in response to an unacceptable hurt she was suddenly feeling, he murmured, 'Here...' and Catherine turned only just in time to catch what it was he was tossing to her. 'A sweet to follow the bitter pill,' he drawled sardonically.

Frowning slightly, puzzled by both the cryptic remark and what he had tossed to her, she looked down to find that she was holding the keys to the Mercedes in her hand.

Her frown deepened, and for a confused moment she actually wondered if he was ordering her to go and garage the car! Then enlightenment struck. The sardonic words began to make sense.

He had not been watching their son; he had been watching her. And the sweetener remark had been a sarcastic reference to her reaction to the confidence with which Santo knew his place here!

But, worse than that, the keys had not been tossed to her to use to garage anything.

Vito was making her a gift of this beautiful Mercedes!

Her eyes shot up to clash with his, shaded lenses trying to probe through shaded lenses in an effort to try and discover before she responded if this was some kind of joke! Out here beneath his native skies he looked more the arrogant Italian than he had ever done. The darkness of his hair, the richness of his skin and the proud angle at which he held his head all sent the kind of tingling messages running through her that she did not like to feel.

Sexual messages. Without her being able to do a single thing to control it, the soft, springy cluster of curls nestling at the crown of her thighs began to tingle and stir beneath the covering of her thin jade summer dress. And her nipples gave a couple of sharp pricking stings in response.

It was awful, like being bewitched. She even found it shamefully sexy to note the way he had rolled up the sleeves on his pale blue shirt—as if it came as supremely natural for him to have them settle at just the right place to draw attention to the hair-peppered strength in his forearms.

'I can't accept this!' she burst out shrilly—and secretly wondered if it was the car or the man's sexual pull that she was refusing to accept. 'It's too much, Vito,' she tagged on hurriedly. 'And I have a car tucked away here somewhere,' she remembered, glancing around her as if she expected her little Fiat runabout to suddenly appear of its own volition.

'It lost the will to live over a year ago,' he informed her with yet more dry sarcasm. 'When no one else bothered to use it.'

And when she still hovered there in the sunlight, so conditioned to accepting nothing from Vito that she couldn't bring herself to accept this gift now, she heard him release a small sigh. 'Just bite the bullet and say thank you graciously,' he grimly suggested.

'As gracious as you were in offering the car to me?' she couldn't resist flashing back.

His grimace acknowledged her thrust as a hit. And he

opened his mouth to say something, but whatever it was stalled by the sudden appearance of his mother on the terrace.

In her sixties now, Luisa was still a truly beautiful woman. Only slightly smaller than Catherine, and naturally slender, she was a walking advert for eternal youth. Her skin was as smooth as any twenty-year-old's, and her hair kept its blackness with only the occasional help from her talented hairdresser.

But it was the inner Luisa that drew people to her like bees to the sweetest honeypot ever found. There wasn't a selfish bone in her body. She was good, she was kind, she was instinctively loving. And if she had one teeny-teeny fault, then it was an almost painful refusal to see bad in anyone.

And that included her daughter-in-law, most definitely her son, and of course her goddaughter—Marietta.

'Darling, I cannot tell you how wonderful it is to see you standing here!' Luisa murmured sincerely as she walked down the steps and right into Catherine's open embrace. 'And you look so lovely!' she declared as she drew away again. 'Vittorio, the Giordani eye for true beauty did not escape you,' his mother informed him. 'This woman will still be a source of pride to you when you are both old and grey.'

Off with the old, on with the new, Catherine wryly chanted to herself. In true Luisa form she was discarding the last three intensely hostile years as if they'd never happened.

'Come,' Luisa said, linking her arm through Catherine's and turning them both towards the house. 'Santo is already raiding the kitchen for snacks, and I have a light tea prepared in the summer room. The special carrier bringing your luggage will not be here for another couple of hours, so we have time to sit and have a long chat before you need worry about overseeing your unpacking…'

Behind her, Catherine was aware of Vito's shaded gaze following them as arm in arm they mounted the steps. And there was an unexpected urge in her to turn round and invite him to come and join them. But somehow she couldn't bring herself to do it. That kind of gesture had no place in what they had with each other.

Yet…

With her fingers curling around the bunch of keys she still held in her palm, she paused on the top step that formed the beginning of the wide terrace.

'Wait,' she murmured to Luisa. And on impulse turned and strode back down the steps to where Vito was still standing where they had left him.

An excuse? she asked herself as she drew to a stop in front of him. Had she needed an excuse to justify coming back to him? Yes, it was an excuse, she answered her own question. And, yes, she needed one to approach Vito in any way shape or form.

'Thank you for the car,' she murmured politely.

He was gazing down at her through those dratted glasses, though in a way she was glad they were there so she didn't have to read his expression.

She saw his mouth twitch. 'My pleasure,' he drawled with super-silken sardonicism.

It put her set teeth on edge. 'I really do appreciate the thought,' she added through them.

'My heart is gladdened by your sincerity,' he replied with taunting whimsy.

Her eyes began to flash behind the glasses. Maybe he caught a glimpse of it, because his hand suddenly shot up and in the next moment both pairs of sunglasses had been whipped away and tossed casually onto the back seat of the car.

Stripped bare of her hiding place, Catherine didn't know what to do other than release a stifled gasp. Then, on another move that left her utterly floundering, he dipped his head and caught her parted mouth with his own.

His kiss was deep and very intimate, and his body heat was stifling. The way his fingertips were sliding feather-light caresses up and down her arms was just another distraction she would have preferred to do without.

But her lips softened beneath his, and she swayed even closer to the source of heat, and the shaky sigh that escaped from her was really a shiver of pleasure at what his fingers were doing to her.

'Now I feel thanked,' he murmured as he drew away again. 'And my mother is enchanted. That is two birds killed with one small stone, Catherine. You may commend yourself.'

'You sarcastic rat,' she hissed at him, stepping away from him with a sudden flush to her cheeks that had nothing whatsoever to do with pleasure.

'I know,' he agreed, still smiling that sardonic smile as he leant back against the car and folded his arms across his pale-blue-covered chest. 'But it was either sarcasm or ravish you,' he said, and when she blinked, he grimaced. 'You turn me on, hard and fast, Catherine. I thought you were aware of that. Watching you walk up the steps to my house was, in fact, the biggest turn-on I've experienced in a long—long time.'

'You're over-sexed,' she snapped, turning away from him.

'And under-used,' he tagged on dryly.

Catherine walked off back to his waiting mother with her chin up and her expression a comical mix of angst and sweetness. The angst was for Vito, the sweetness a sad attempt to show Luisa that everything was fine! But she dropped the Mercedes car keys on the nearest flat surface

she passed as she entered the elegant Giordani hallway—
and gained a whole lot of satisfaction from knowing that
Vito had arrived at the front door in time to see her doing
it.

He knew why she had done it. He knew she was discarding both him and his sex appeal—and the darn gift—
with that one small gesture. But, in usual arrogant Vito
form, he ignored it all, politely declined to join them for
refreshment and went off instead to find his son—which
was all that really mattered to him anyway.

Afternoon tea was surprisingly pleasant, mainly because
both Luisa and Catherine were careful not to broach any
tricky subjects. Afterwards Santo came looking for his
mother, so he could take her up to show her his bedroom.
They spent a while in there together, looking at and discussing all the surprisingly well-used things he had in there.
There was a nice informality about the place that touched
her a little, because it was really only a bigger version of
Santos's bedroom at home.

Home. Once again the word brought her up short. Home
is here now, she told herself sternly. Home is here…

After that Santo was taken by his grandmother to visit
friends he had in the area, and after watching them stroll
away hand in hand down one of the pathways towards the
lowest part of their huge garden, where Catherine remembered there was a small gate which led out onto the road,
she decided to fill in her time by making a tour of the
house, to reacquaint herself with all of its hidden treasures.

Nothing had changed much, she noted as she strolled
from elegantly appointed room to room. But then, why
mess with perfection once you'd achieved it? Most of the
rooms were furnished with the kind of things which had
been collected through several centuries, by Giordanis adding to rather than discarding anything, so the finished result

was a tasteful blending of periods that gave an impressive picture of the family's successful history.

Vito was proud of his heritage. And it meant a lot to him to have a son to follow after him. Coming here for the first time, Catherine had admitted to feeling rather in awe of the kind of rarefied world she was being drawn in to. But by then it had already been too late to have second thoughts about whether she wanted to marry a man who in name alone was a legend in his own country. Already heart and soul in love with Vito, *and* pregnant with the next Giordani heir, she'd had her freedom of choice taken away from her.

And there had been so many people very eager to remind her of just how lucky she was to be marrying Vito. He was special, and being treated as special had also made him arrogant, she thought dryly, as she stood gazing around the huge ballroom which still looked exactly as it had done in the early eighteenth century when it had been constructed. To her knowledge it was still used for formal occasions.

Her own wedding ball had taken place here, she recalled. It had been a wonderful extravagant night, when the house had been filled with light and music and laughter, and the gardens hung with romantic lanterns so their guests could take the air if they felt like it. A reminiscent smile touched her lips as she watched herself being danced around the vast polished floor in the arms of her new husband in her flowing gown of gold which had been specially designed for her.

'Have I told you today how beautiful you are?' Vito's softly seductive voice echoed back to her through a trail of memories. 'You outshine every woman here tonight.'

'You're only saying that because it flatters your own ego,' she'd mocked him.

She could still hear the sound of his burst of appreciative laughter ringing around this room even as she drew the doors shut on the ballroom. And she was smiling wryly to herself as she turned to make her way to the elegant central stairway. For Vito had laughed like that because the man *was* conceited enough to know that having a beautiful wife flattered his ego for choosing her, not her ego for *being* her.

That was the way it was with a Giordani, she mused whimsically as she strode along the upper mezzanine and in through one of the many doors that lined the elegant two-winged landing. To them, other people were the satellites which revolved around *their* rich and compellingly seductive world. It was supposed to be a privilege to be invited to enter it.

Enter where? she then thought suddenly, and brought her wayward attention to an abrupt standstill along with her feet, when she realised just where it was she was standing.

A bedroom. *Their* bedroom. The one she'd used to share with Vito before she ran away.

Her heart began to thud, her throat closing over as she took on board just what she had done while her mind had been elsewhere.

She had walked herself right into the one room in the house she had been meaning to steer well clear of.

Her first instinct was to get out of there again as quickly as she could! Her second instinct had her pausing instead, though, giving in to an irresistible urge to check out the one place where she and Vito had always managed to be in harmony.

The bedroom. The bed, still standing there like a huge snow sleigh, made of the richest mahogany and polished to within an inch of its life. The width of three singles, it still had the same hand-embroidered pure white counterpane covering its fine white linen, still had its mound of fluffy white pillows they'd used to toss to the floor before retiring each night.

Then she recalled why they'd used to toss those pillows

away so carelessly, and felt the tight sting of that memory attack the very centre of her sexuality.

Was that all to begin again? she asked herself tensely. All the rowing and fighting, followed by the kind of sexual combat that used to leave them both a little shell-shocked afterwards?

It has already started again, she reminded herself. And on that grim acknowledgement let her eyes drift around the rest of the room to discover that not a single thing had been changed since she'd last stepped into it.

Yet, *she* had changed. She wasn't the same person she had been three years ago. In fact, at this precise moment she felt rather like a lost penny that had found itself being tossed back, only to land in the wrong place entirely.

She didn't want to be here, didn't think she *should* be here, even though she knew without a single doubt that this was the room Vito would be expecting her to share with him again.

Not that she'd asked the question, and would not be doing when she knew it would only give Vito the chance to taunt her with the fact that she had been brought back here to provide him with sex.

Sex, lies and pretence—the status quo re-established for Santo's sake—and to slake Vito's thirst for revenge. She was about to turn back to the door when—without any warning at all—the bathroom door suddenly flew open and Vito appeared in its aperture. He must have come directly from the shower, because all he had on was a white towel slung around his lean hips and he was rubbing briskly at his wet hair with another towel.

His arrival froze her to the carpet. And seeing her standing there had the same effect on him. So for the next few pulsing seconds neither seemed able to move another muscle as shocked surprise held them utterly transfixed.

CHAPTER SIX

WAS he seeing her like a lost penny that really shouldn't be where it was standing? she wondered as she watched those lush dark sensual lashes slowly lower over eyes that were determinedly giving nothing away.

The silence between them stretched into tension, and within it Catherine tried to stop her gaze from drifting over him. But it was no use. She had been drawn to this man's physical attraction from the first moment she ever set eyes on him. And nothing had changed, she realised sadly as, dry-mouthed, she watched crystal droplets of water drip from his hair onto his wide tanned shoulders then begin trailing into the crisp dark hair covering his chest.

He was male beauty personified, his face, his body, the long lean muscular strength in his deeply tanned legs.

'Have your things arrived yet?' Deep and dark, and unusually sedate for him in this kind of situation, Vito's voice held no hint of anything but casual enquiry.

Yet her skin flinched as if he'd reached out and touched it with the end of an electric live wire. 'I...n-not that I know of,' she replied, eyelashes fluttering as she dragged her gaze away from him. 'I've been—showing myself around,' she then added on a failed attempt at sounding casual.

'No surprises?' he asked, drawing her eyes back to him as he began to rub at his wet hair with the towel again.

She watched his biceps flex and his pectorals begin to tremble at the vigorous activity. 'Only Santo's room,' she murmured, and wished she knew how to cure herself of wanting this man. 'It's nice,' she tagged on diffidently.

'Glad you think so.' There should have been a hint of sarcasm when he said that, but there wasn't. In fact he was playing this all very casual—as if the last three years had never happened and they shared this kind of conversation in this room all the time.

But then, wasn't she trying to treat it the same way herself?

The towel was lowered and cast aside. Catherine bit her inner lip and tried desperately to come up with some excuse to leave that wouldn't make her appear a total coward.

In the end it was Vito who solved the dilemma for her. 'Sorry,' he apologised suddenly, and took a step sideways. 'Did you come here to…?'

He was asking if she needed to use the bathroom. 'N-No,' she murmured. Then, 'Yes!' she amended that, seeing the bathroom, with the lock it had on its door, as the ideal place to escape to.

But it was only as she pushed her tense body into movement that she realised she was going to have to pass very close by him to gain that escape. And Vito didn't move another muscle as he watched her come towards him. So her tension grew with each step that she took, and by the time she reached him her heart was thumping, and her breathing was so fragile that it was all she could do to murmur a frail, 'Thank you,' as she went to pass by him.

'Are you going to take a shower?'

Her senses were lost to a medley of tingles, all of which were set on high red alert. 'Y-Yes,' she heard herself answer, seeing yes as good as no at this precise moment, when she had absolutely no idea what she was intending to do in there! She didn't even need to use the bathroom!

'Then allow me…' his smooth voice offered.

At which point she found herself freezing yet again as his hands came to rest upon her shoulders. Then his fingers began trailing downwards over her pale skin until they reached the scooped edge of her jade linen dress where the long zip lay.

Gritting her teeth, Catherine prayed for deliverance. He was standing so close she could actually feel his lightly scented dampness eddying in the air surrounding her. It was incredibly alluring, the kind of scent that conjured up evocative pictures of warm, naked bodies tangled in loving.

She shivered delicately when, with a deftness that had always been his, he sent the zip of her dress skimming downwards. By the time the fabric parted her shivers had become tremors, and she had to close her eyes and grit her teeth harder while she waited for the ordeal to be over.

But Vito didn't stop there. Next his fingers were unclipping the catches on her bra and her breasts were suddenly free to swing unsupported. And in all of their long and intimate association she had never felt so wary and unsure of his intentions.

Even the way he ran the back of one long finger down the rigid length of her spine was telling her one thing while his voice, as cool as a mountain spring, was telling her another when he suggested levelly, 'Make it a long shower, Catherine, you are as tense as a bowstring.'

Make it a long shower, she repeated to herself. Make it a long, *cold* shower, she helplessly extended.

'But of course,' he then added, and suddenly his voice was as silken as his wretched voice ever could be, 'there are other, much more pleasurable ways to cure your tension.'

And before she could react his mouth landed against the side of her neck and, like a vampire swooping on its chosen prey, he bit sensually into the pulsing nerve there that lay alongside her jugular. At the same time his hands slid inside her dress and took possession of her recently freed breast.

Sensation went streaking through her. After the day-long build-up of sexual tension, it was like being sprung free from the unbearable restraints that had been binding her, though she did at least try to put up some kind of protest.

'Vito, no,' she groaned. 'I need a shower—'

'I like you just the way you are,' he huskily countermanded. 'Smelling of you, and tasting of you.'

He was already urging her dress to slither down her body, and in seconds she was standing there in just her panties. As those long, knowing fingers moulded her breasts so his thumbpads could begin drawing circles around their tips to encourage them to peak for him, his mouth continued to suck sensually on her neck.

It was all so exquisite, the caress of his hands, the wetness of his mouth, the way he was pressing her back against him. When he stroked one hand down the flat wall of her stomach and beneath the fabric of her briefs she simply gave up trying to fight it. On a shaky little sigh that heralded her complete surrender her eyes drifted shut, and, tilting her head back against his shoulder, she allowed him to arouse her in a way only a deeply familiar lover would arouse a woman.

But not enough—not enough. Her hands reached behind him to rip away the towel so she could press him against her, and her head turned against his shoulder, searching out his mouth so she could join her own with it. 'Kiss me properly,' she commanded, no shrinking violet when it came to her body's pleasures.

On an answering growl he swung her around, lifted her up his body until she was off her feet—then kissed her hard and hot and deeply. The wall not far away was a godsend as he pressed her back against it and let her feet find solid ground again. Catherine parted her thighs and pressed him even closer, then tightened herself around him.

He was very aroused, and with the towel gone it left him free to use other, far more invigorating methods to keep her riding high on the crested wave of pleasure. Dragging her mouth free from his, she tilted her head back and simply let herself concentrate on the stroke of his body.

'You're wearing too much,' he murmured sensually.

'I'll never wear panties again,' she agreed with him.

Vito laughed, but it was a hard, tense, very male laugh, and it set fires alight inside her that did nothing for her self-control as he caught her mouth again and began kissing her greedily.

'I need the bed,' she groaned, when things began to get too much for her and her legs threatened to completely give away.

'I'm way ahead of you, *cara*,' he murmured raspingly.

Opening her eyes, Catherine found herself looking directly into two hot, hard golden points of passion that were doing nothing to hide the intensity of what he too was experiencing.

And they were moving. Catherine hadn't even noticed until that moment that he was actually carrying her. They arrived at the bed. With a complete lack of ceremony he dropped her to her feet, then bent to get rid of her last piece of clothing.

As he buried his mouth into this newly exposed part of her body, she stretched out an arm behind her and began tossing away pillows, raking back bedcovers. It was all very urgent, very hectic, very fevered. No time for lazy foreplay, no hint of romance. She wanted him now, and it was patently obvious that he was the same.

As she lowered herself onto the bed, then began sliding backwards so she could lie down flat, she remembered the door. 'Lock us in first,' she whispered.

'To hell with the door,' he refused, following her onto the bed as if they were joined at the hip. 'I'm not stopping this if the whole house walks in to watch.'

With that he entered her, sure and swift, and as she cried out in sheer surprise he laughed again, the same very male laugh, caught her face between his hands then made her look at him.

'Hi.' He grinned, as her lashes flickered upwards. 'Remember me? I am your fantastic lover.'

He wasn't even moving. He was playing with her, toying with her. He had fired her up until she didn't know her own name any more. Now he was trying to lighten the whole thing!

With a flash from vengeful green eyes, she tightened the muscles around her abdomen. The motion made him suck in his breath. 'Want to play, Vito?' she taunted, and raked her fingernails along his lean flanks where some of this man's most vulnerable erogenous zones were situated.

The breath left his lungs on a driven hiss. Catherine put out her tongue and licked the sound right off his warm, moist, pulsing lips. He began cursing in Italian, and there was no hint of humour left in him when he began moving on her with a fierceness that sent her reeling away into a pool of hot sensation.

When she shattered her arms flew out, wide, like a swimmer floating on its back. Vito slid his hand beneath her head to her nape, then lifted her towards him. It was a need he'd always had, to capture her desperate little gasps as she went into orgasm, and Catherine didn't deny him them now as she breathed those helpless little sounds into his mouth and felt his body quicken as he too came nearer to his peak.

After that she remembered nothing. Not his own intense climax, not the swirling aftermath, not even the way he slid away from her, then lay fighting for recovery.

Outside it was still daylight. Inside the air-conditioning was keeping the room temperature at a constant liveable level. But Catherine was bathed in sweat from tingling toes to hairline. And beside her she could see the same film of sweat glistening on Vito's skin.

She watched him for a little while, enjoying the way he

was just lying there, heavy-limbed and utterly spent. Yet, even spent, Vito was physically imposing. A man with the normal potency of ten.

Potent…

Catherine stiffened—then went perfectly still, the sweat slowly chilling her flesh as she lay there, held by a sudden thought so terrible that her mind literally froze rather than dare let her face it. Beside her, sensing the change in her, Vito turned his dark head, then began frowning as he watched her steadily draining pallor.

But before he had a chance to say anything she sat up with a jerk, then began sliding frantically for the edge of the wide bed. Her long legs hit the ground at a run, her hair flying out behind her as she streaked like a sprinter for the bathroom.

Whatever she was looking for wasn't there, because she appeared again almost immediately. To say she was in shock was an understatement. White-faced, and shaking so badly that her teeth chattered, she looked at Vito, who was only just pulling himself into a sitting position.

'My things,' she shot out in a taut staccato. 'Where are my things?'

Still frowning in complete bewilderment as to what was going on, he shrugged. 'They have not arrived yet, remember?'

'Not arrived,' she repeated, then her eyes went blank and Vito shot off that bed like a bullet from a gun because he thought she was actually going to pass out where she stood!

'For goodness' sake, *cara*,' he rasped. 'What is wrong with you?'

'M-my bag, then,' she whispered shakily, and when all he did was come striding towards her without bothering to answer she hit the hysteria button. 'My *handbag*, Vito!' she actually screamed at him. 'Where is it? My handbag—*my handbag*!'

It brought him to a stop in sheer astonishment. 'Catherine—what the hell is this?' he demanded, beginning to sound shaken himself.

She didn't answer, instead she suddenly burst into action again. Darting down to snatch up her dress, she began to pull it on. She was trembling so badly she could barely manage the simple task, but when he attempted to help her she slapped him away.

'I can't believe I let you do this!' she launched at him shrilly. 'I can't believe I let myself!'

'Do what, for God's sake?' he shouted back angrily. 'Make love?' He decided that was the only answer. 'Well, that's rich coming from the woman who just ravished me!'

If anything, her face went even whiter, though it didn't seem possible. And, on a pained whimper that did nothing for his temper, she turned and ran for the bedroom door with her fingers still grappling with the zip on her dress and the rest of her still completely naked.

'Catherine!' Vito barked at her in a command meant to stop her leaving the room.

But Catherine was already out of it and running down the stairs. Outside in the late-afternoon sunshine she found her handbag, still lying where she had left it on the floor of the red Mercedes.

By the time Vito had pulled some clothes on and followed her Catherine was just sitting there on the bottom step in front of the house, with the bag and its spilled contents lying beside her.

And there was such an air of fragility about her that he made his approach with extreme caution, walking down the steps to come and squat down in front of her. 'Are you going to tell me what that was all about now?' he requested carefully.

She shook her head and there were tears in her eyes. He sighed, his mouth tightening as he began flicking his gaze across the contents of her bag as if the answer would show itself there.

But it didn't. All he saw was the usual clutter of personal things women tended to carry around with them. Lipstick, wallet, the passport she'd needed to get her into the country. A packet of paper tissues, a couple of spare clips she used to hold back her hair sometimes, and a hair comb. He looked back at Catherine, looked at the way she was staring out at nothing, and automatically looked down, expecting to find the cause of all of this—trauma clutched in her hands. But her hands were empty, their palms pressed together and trapped between her clenched knees.

It was then that he spied it, lying on the ground between her bare feet, and slowly, warily, he reached out and picked it up.

It took him about five seconds after that to realise what was wrong with her. Then the cursing started. Hard words, hoarse words, words that had him lurching to his feet and swinging around to slam his clenched fist into the shiny bodywork of the Mercedes.

After that, he too went perfectly still, frozen by the same sense of numbing horror that was holding Catherine. And the ensuing silence throbbed and punched and kicked at the both of them.

Until a sound in the distance grabbed Vito's attention. His dark head went up, swinging round on his shoulders so he could scan the furthest corner of the garden, where a gate out onto the road served as a short cut to their nearest neighbours.

Then suddenly he was bursting into action again, spinning back to Catherine and stooping down to gather her into his arms before turning to dump her into the passenger seat of the Mercedes.

'What—?' she choked, coming out of her stunned stupor on a gasp of surprise.

'Stay put,' he gritted, then turned back to the house and disappeared inside it, only to come back seconds later with a bunch of keys in his hands. On his way past her bag he bent to gather in its contents; it landed on the back seat beside two pairs of sunglasses as he climbed behind the wheel.

The engine fired first time, and with the efficiency of a born driver he turned the car around and took off at speed down the driveway.

'Santo and my mother are on their way back.' He grimly explained his odd behaviour. 'I did not think you would want them to see you looking like this.'

Like this... Catherine repeated to herself, looking down at herself with the kind of blank eyes that said she couldn't see, as he could see, the changes that had come over her in a few short, devastating minutes.

Stopping at the end of the drive, Vito Giordani looked at this woman who had known more than her fair share of pain, heartache and grief in her life, and felt the air leave his lungs on a constricted hiss.

'How many have you missed?' he questioned flatly.

Catherine lifted those wretched dull grey eyes to him and a nerve began ticking along his jawline as he set the car going again, taking them not down the hillside but up it, out into open country.

'You can count as well as I can,' she answered dully.

Vito grimaced. 'I am afraid my eyes glazed over when I noticed that yesterday's was still there.'

Yesterday's, the day before—and the day before, Catherine counted out bleakly. A contraceptive pill for each day since Vito had come back into her life, in fact.

'I hate you,' she whispered. 'You've been messing up

my life since I was twenty-three years old, and here you
are, six years on, still messing it up.'

About to remind her that it wasn't him who'd forgotten
to take the damn pills, Vito bit the words back again. 'Getting embroiled in a fight about whose fault it is is not going
to solve the problem,' he threw at her instead.

'Nothing can solve it,' Catherine countered hopelessly
'The damage has already been done.'

Mouth set in a straight line, Vito said not another word
as he drove them higher and higher, until eventually he
pulled the car off the road and onto a piece of scrub land
that overlooked the kind of views people paid fortunes to
see.

They didn't see the beauty in it, though. There could
have been pitch-blackness out there in front of them for all
they knew. And they were surrounded by perfect silence
Not a bird, not a house, not another car, not even a breeze
to rustle the dry undergrowth. In fact they could have been
the only two people left in the world, which suited exactly
how they were both feeling.

Two people alone with the kind of problem that shut out
the rest of the world.

'I'm sorry,' Vito murmured.

Maybe he felt he needed to say it, but Catherine
shrugged. 'Not your fault,' she absolved him. 'It's me
who's been unforgivably stupid.'

'Maybe we will get lucky and nothing will come of it,'
he suggested, in an attempt to place a glimmer of light in
their darkness.

'Don't count on it,' Catherine replied heavily. 'Twice
before we've taken risks, and twice I got pregnant. Why
should this time be any different?'

Why indeed? was the echo that came back from the next
drumming silence.

'There has to be something we can do!' he muttered

harshly. And on a sudden flash of inspiration said, 'We will drive to the doctor's. Get that—morning-after pill—or whatever it is they call it…'

Catherine flinched as if he had plunged a knife in her. 'Do you know what they call those pills, Vito?' she whispered painfully. 'Little abortions,' she informed him starkly. 'Because that's what they do. They abort the egg whether it is fertilised or not.'

'But you also know what they told you,' he reminded her. 'Another pregnancy like the last one could be dangerous.'

Her tear-washed eyes shimmered in the sunlight. 'So I abort one life to safeguard my own life?'

The anguish she saw in his eyes was for her; Catherine knew that. But she couldn't deal with it. And on the dire need to escape from both him and the whole wretched scenario, she opened the car door and climbed out.

Leaving Vito sitting there staring ahead of him, she walked, barefooted, across the dusty ground to a lonely cypress tree and leaned against its dry old trunk.

First she had almost lost Santo, due to mid-term complications. She had managed to hold onto him until he was big enough to cope outside his mother's womb, and the doctors had assured her that the same condition rarely struck twice in the same woman. But they had been wrong. And the next time it had happened she'd almost lost her own life along with her baby.

'No more babies,' they had announced. 'Your body won't take the physical trauma.'

No more babies…

A movement beside her made her aware that Vito had come to lean a shoulder on the other side of the tree. For a man who had only had enough time to drag on the first clothes that came to hand he looked remarkably stylish in his light chinos and a plain white tee shirt. But then, that was Vito, she mused hollowly. A man so inherently special that no one in the world would believe that anything in his life would ever go wrong for him.

His marriage had. From its unfortunate beginning to its tragic ending.

Catherine didn't count this latest encounter. Because in truth she no longer felt married to Vito; if anything, she felt more as she had done when she first met him: alive, excited, electrifyingly stimulated. Which was why they'd ended up in bed making love like there was no tomorrow. It was a taste of the old days—irresistible.

And now the piper demands his payment, she concluded dully.

'Santo needs his mother, Catherine,' Vito stated levelly—nothing more. He didn't need to elaborate. Catherine knew exactly what he was telling her here.

They were back to celebrating the living, she supposed. Santo needs his mother alive and well and very much kicking. Tears burned her eyes again. She blinked them away. 'I'll take the pill,' she said.

He didn't say anything. Instead he just continued to lean there, staring out at his homeland as if he was watching Naples sink beneath a sea of lava and was as helpless to stop that from happening as he was to stop Catherine from having to make that decision.

Without another word, she walked back to the car and climbed into it. Vito followed her, got in, fired the engine and drove them away, down the hillside this time, and into Naples proper, where he took grim pleasure in fighting with the unremitting flood of traffic before eventually turning into an arched alleyway which led through to a private courtyard belonging to his offices.

Climbing out of the car, he came around to Catherine's side, opened her door and helped her to alight. She didn't put up any protest, not even when he silently turned her around and did up the rest of her zip before leading the way into the building. His concierge took one look at his face and with only a brief nod of his head backed warily away, but his glance swept curiously over Catherine's dusty bare feet and tangled mane of bright hair as the lift doors shut them away.

It was getting late by now. The working day was over so the place was empty of people. Leading the way to his own office suite, Vito pointed to a door. 'Take a shower,' he instructed, and walked off to his desk to pick up the telephone.

As she stepped into the bathroom she heard him talking to his mother, making some excuse about them going shopping on impulse and forgetting to tell anyone before leaving.

It was as good an excuse as any, she supposed, so long as no one had thought to check their bedroom, where the evidence of what they had been doing before they went out was painfully clear to see.

The next call Vito made was out of her hearing. It was curt, it was tight, and it didn't improve his temper as he began his third call, instructing a fashion boutique a short block from here, that knew him through his mother, to deliver the full range of whatever they had in stock to fit a British size ten, including shoes and underwear.

Catherine still hadn't emerged from the bathroom by the time the concierge came in, laden down with the boutique's delivery. In any other mood Vito might have been interested in what he had got for his money, but since most of the items were simply a bluff to fool his mother, he merely told the man to place the purchases on the low leather sofa beneath the window, then dismissed him.

But before he went the concierge handed him a different kind of purchase entirely. It was small, it was light, and it bore the name of a well-respected medical practice in Naples.

Vito was still staring grimly down at it when Catherine emerged from the bathroom, wrapped in his own short white towelling robe that was way too big for her. She looked wet, she looked clean—and utterly miserable.

'I couldn't find a hairdryer,' she said, indicating her head, where her hair hung straight and at least five shades darker against the whiteness of her face.

'I'll find it in a minute,' he replied, walking towards her.

She wasn't looking at him, but then she hadn't done so since they'd made love earlier—not with eyes that could see him anyway.

'Here,' he said gruffly, and handed her the small package.

She knew what it was the moment she looked at it, even though her eyes couldn't focus on the writing. 'Two now, two more in twelve hours,' he instructed.

A cold chill went sweeping through her, turning her fingers to ice as she reached out and took the packet from him.

'I need a drink,' she said.

He nodded briskly and moved away. 'Tea, coffee, ice water?' he enquired, opening the doors to a huge drink cabinet equipped with everything from kettle to cocktail shaker.

'Water,' she chose, then slid her hands into the cavernous pockets of the robe before lifting herself to take a forced interest in her surroundings.

This place hadn't changed much since she'd last been here either, she saw. Same classic trappings of a well-to-do businessman, same hi-tech equipment, only a lot more of it.

He turned with the glass of water. 'Catherine—'

'Shut up,' she said flatly, and, ignoring the grim tension

in his stance, she made herself walk over to the sofa where the concierge had placed Vito's purchases. 'For me?' she asked.

'Take your pick,' he replied. 'There should be a selection of everything you will require.'

'The man thinks of everything,' she dryly mocked as her fingers flicked open boxes and checked out bags with about as much interest as a hungry dog being offered a plastic bone to eat. 'Troubleshooter extraordinaire.'

He didn't answer, but then, why should he bother? It was only the truth after all. For who else did she know who could achieve so much in the time it took her to have a shower?

'I'll take these,' she said, choosing at random a teal blue silk dinner dress and some matching underwear. Going back towards the bathroom, she paused in the doorway. 'The hairdryer?' she prompted him.

He walked over to her, then stopped to silently hand her the requested glass of water that she seemed to have had already forgotten about, before he slid past her into the bathroom and unearthed a hairdryer from the back of a vanity unit.

Grimly plugging it in, he left it ready for her on the marble top, then turned to leave her to it. In her hand was the glass of water. The water was to help her swallow the medication he had given to her. He walked past her, then stopped, tensely swung back. 'Catherine—'

She shut the door in his face.

Fifteen minutes later she came out again, hair dried into some semblance of a style, her clothes looking unexpectedly fantastic, considering the way they had been chosen. The dress was short, slim, and edged with a layer of fine black lace. Standing staring out of the window, Vito turned when he heard her, then went still, his sombre eyes hooding over as they slid down her.

'Shoes,' was all he said, though, pointing to a pair of

teal-blue strappy sandals standing neatly by the sofa. Everything else had gone—where to Catherine didn't know, nor care.

She found out when they arrived back at the car and saw the back seat was full of packages. The car's roof had been raised, and as they climbed inside she felt the difference as a humid heat quickly enveloped her. Vito started the car and switched on the air-conditioning system, then they drove off, back home to their twisted version of normality.

It was growing quite dark by the time they arrived at the house. Lights were burning on the driveway, offering a warm welcome that didn't touch Catherine.

As they walked into the house Santo appeared, already dressed for bed in his pyjamas. With a delighted whoop he came running towards them. Whether it was deliberate, Catherine wasn't certain, but Vito took a small step backwards then slid stealthily behind her, as if he was trying to reduce Santo's options so he would run into his mother's arms and not his father's.

If it was deliberate then it was a very selfless gesture, one that showed a deep sensitivity to her needs right now. And an understanding that her emotions had taken a big enough battering today without having her son giving it a further knock by choosing to hug his father before hugging her.

So she received her warm bundle of love and hugged him to her as if her life depended on holding this precious child of theirs. And with his arms around her neck and his legs around her waist Santo chatted away about what he had been doing, with absolutely no idea that his mother was frantically fighting a battle with tears again.

It was only when she eventually set her son down again so he could go to his father, and she saw the way Vito held Santo to him in much the same way that she had done, that she allowed herself to acknowledge that he too was suffering.

It was too much—much too much for her to cope with right now, when she could barely cope with her own inner agony. So she walked away, wishing she could just go and crawl into bed, pull the covers over her head and stay there for ever.

But she couldn't do that, because Luisa was waiting for them and expected bright smiles and conversation. Catherine played the game to the best of her ability, and even managed to smile at Luisa teasing Vito about the new wardrobe of clothes he had just bought Catherine because her own luggage hadn't arrived.

'But it came while you were out!' her mother-in-law laughingly informed them. 'How terribly impatient and extravagant of you, darling!' Her eyes twinkled teasingly at her son, and why were they twinkling? Because Luisa was seeing the gesture as a demonstration of how wonderfully romantic things must be between her son and his wife— when really things couldn't be more wretched. 'And what a lovely treat for you, Catherine…!'

Dinner that night was just another ordeal she had to force herself to get through. She had to eat when she didn't want to, smile when she didn't want to, had to make pleasant innocuous conversation when she didn't want to. And through it all she had to watch Vito watch her from beneath heavily veiled eyes, as if he was expecting her at any moment to jump up and start screaming the place down.

She didn't really blame him, for she knew that beneath her relaxed exterior she was so uptight it was actually beginning to hurt. She had been avoiding him like the plague since they got back. If he walked into a room then she walked out of it; if he went to speak to her she pretended she didn't hear. Now, across the dinner table, if she found herself being forced into making eye contact with him she did it from behind a frosted veil, which thankfully kept him out of focus.

But that didn't mean that she wasn't aware of *his* tension, or of the greyish pallor sitting just beneath the surface of his golden skin that had been there ever since he had handed her that packet in his office.

'…Marietta…'

Suddenly feeling as though a thousand sharp needles were embedding themselves into her flesh, Catherine blinked her mind back into focus on the conversation at the table.

'She was sorry she couldn't be here to welcome you home today,' Luisa was saying innocently. 'But Vito saw fit to send her off to New York on some wild-goose chase she insists did not really warrant her attention.' A censorious glance at her son gained no response whatsoever. 'Still, since Vito's priority had to be here with you and Santo, one of them had to go, I suppose,' Luisa allowed, with a little shrug meant, Catherine presumed, to dismiss her son's silence. 'She will be back by the weekend, though, so maybe we could all get together then for a celebratory dinner—which would be nice, don't you think, Catherine? The two of you were such good friends once upon a time. I'm sure you must be looking forward to reviving the friendship.'

'Excuse me.' She stood up with an abruptness that surprised everyone. 'Forgive me, Luisa, but I'm afraid I can't sit here any longer—'

'Aren't you well, Catherine?' It was a logical conclusion to make, bearing in mind that her dinner plate was sitting untouched, right in front of her. And at last Luisa seemed to notice Catherine's strained pallor, while, with the kind of good manners that had been bred into him, Vito rose gracefully to his feet also. But he was still watching her like a hawk, and Catherine wanted to scratch his blasted eyes out because he knew his mother had just advantageously stopped her from saying something she would have regretted later about Luisa's precious Marietta!

'Just tired, that's all.' She smiled a weak smile that was

really an acknowledgement of her own sense of relief at Luisa's interruption. For hadn't it always been easier to leave Luisa with her rose-tinted glasses in place than be the one to rip them from her? 'It has been a long day in one way or another.'

'Of course, dear,' Luisa murmured understandingly. 'And you are not used to our late dining habits—which probably accounts for your lack of appetite tonight...'

'Yes.' Catherine kept on smiling the wretched smile and bent to brush a kiss across Luisa's cheek before mumbling some incoherent remark about seeing Vito later as she stumbled wearily from the table.

By the time she had prepared for bed and carried out her most dearest wish by crawling beneath the sheets and pulling them right over her, she had hardly any energy left to do much more than switch her brain off.

So she was completely lost to a blessed oblivion when a pair of arms firmly gathering her in brought her swimming back to consciousness.

'No.' Her response was instant rejection.

'Be still,' Vito's deep voice flatly countered, and, drawing her into the warm curve of his body, he firmly clamped her there. 'You may wish to pretend that I do not exist right now, but I do, and I am here—'

'While your lover is several thousand miles away,' she tagged on waspishly.

'Marietta is your obsession, not mine,' he replied. 'But since you have decided to bring her into this bed with us, may I remind you that you are here to replace her? So stop fighting me, Catherine.' Once again his arms tightened to subdue her wriggling struggles. 'You may like to believe that you are the only miserable one in this bed, but you are not. And I need to hold you as much as you need to be held like this.'

He wasn't talking about Marietta now, she realised. He was talking about something far more emotive. Impulsively she opened her mouth to say something about that—then changed her mind, for her emotions were in such a dreadful mess that remaining silent seemed wiser at this moment than saying anything that could well start another quarrel.

So she subsided, reluctantly, into the warmth of his embrace, felt his muscles relax when he recognised her surrender. And as she began taking on board other things, like his nakedness against her thin cotton pyjamas, she bitterly wished that the man wasn't so physically alluring.

Wished to God that she wasn't so useless as a woman. She wished her heart didn't hurt so much and her brain was more able to make a clear-cut decision between what was right and what was wrong.

And she wished so very sincerely that the world would stop turning, so that she could get off it and never come back to it again!

'Cry if you want to,' his rusty voice encouraged.

'No,' she refused, but her body was already trembling with the effort it was costing her not to.

'It was the right thing to do, Catherine. The only thing to do.' Vito's mouth pressed a kiss to the back of her head. 'But that does not mean you must not mourn the decision.'

But it did—it did! And Vito was never going to understand what that decision was costing her because she was not going to tell him—or tell anyone for that matter.

'I just want to go to sleep and forget all about it,' she whispered thickly.

'Then do so,' he allowed. 'But I will be here if you change your mind, *cara*. Right here beside you.'

Was this his way of making up for the time when he hadn't been there for her? If it was then Catherine was not going to taunt him with it. Because she might be absorbed by her own torment right now, but she could feel the way his hands were tensely gripping her hands, that Vito was no less tormented.

CHAPTER SEVEN

His arms stayed wrapped around her throughout the long night. Each time Catherine swam up from the dark well of sleep towards reality she felt him there, and drew enough comfort from that to help sink her back into oblivion once again.

The next morning he woke her up very early and gently reminded her to take her second set of pills. Without a word she dragged herself out of the bed and disappeared into the bathroom. But it was only as she stood there in the middle of the bathroom floor, feeling a bit like a spare part that had no useful function, that the sudden realisation that something was different had her glancing down at her left hand—then going perfectly still when she saw her rings winking up at her.

The first one—an exquisite square-cut diamond set to stand on its own—she'd received a week after she'd told Vito she was pregnant with Santo. The second was the plain gold band given to her on her wedding day that matched the one Vito wore on his finger. And the third—a diamond-encrusted eternity ring—arrived the day after she'd announced the coming of their second baby.

When had he done this? she wondered frowningly, remembering that there hadn't seemed to be a single moment during the night when she hadn't been aware of him right there beside her. Yet he must have left her at some point and gone downstairs to his safe in the study, where she presumed he had placed her rings when she'd left them behind her, then come back upstairs to slide the rings on her finger—carefully, so as not to waken her.

111

But *why* had he done it? That was the much more disturbing question. And why last night, of all nights, when she couldn't have felt less deserving of these rings if she'd tried?

What kind of message was he trying to convey to her? There had to be some significance in him replacing these rings on her finger last night when things could not have been more pitiable between them.

A statement of intent? 'I am here for you, Catherine,' he had told her. And the appearance of her rings seemed to be telling her that he wanted her to know he was seriously committing himself to this ailing marriage of theirs, when really what had happened yesterday could not have been a better reminder as to why he was better off without her!

Guilt riddled through her. The guilt of a woman who knew she wasn't being entirely truthful with him.

But then, she asked herself, when had she ever felt that she could be? She had always only ever felt like a means to an end for Vito. First as a very compatible lover, then as the mother of his future child, and now as a necessary means of making his son happy. You couldn't build trust and honesty on foundations as shaky as theirs were.

Rings or no rings, none of that had changed since yesterday. She still felt as alone now as she had done on the day she'd lost their baby three years ago.

'Forgive me, Catherine,' he had pleaded at that time. 'If there was anything I could do to make the last twenty-four hours go away then I would do it. You have to believe me.'

But no one, not even Vito, was able to turn back time. It had already been too late for them by then. Just as it was also too late to change the consequences of the last twenty-four hours now.

And right now as she stood here, staring at these rings which seemed to be making such an important statement, she wished he hadn't done it when it only complicated a situation that was complicated enough already. Because he didn't know.

He didn't know...

A point which made her manner awkward when she returned to the bedroom a few minutes later. 'Thank you,' she mumbled, making a gesture with the hand bearing the rings.

He smiled a brief, tight smile. 'I missed them last night,' he explained. 'Then could not go to sleep without putting them back where they belonged.'

That word 'belonged' made her aching heart flinch. And for the life of her she couldn't think of a single thing to say in reply. So a tension built between them, a different kind of tension that lacked the old hostility that usually helped to keep them going.

Vito eventually filled it. 'So—what would you like to do today?' he asked briskly. 'I usually take Santo on a short horse-ride on his first day here, to brush up on his riding skills.'

'Fine.' It was her turn to flash a brief, brisk smile. 'I'll come too, if I may.'

But her light reply sent his eyes dark. 'That was the idea, Catherine,' he said soberly. 'That we do things together as a family.'

'I thought I just agreed to that,' she countered blankly.

'It was the way that you said it,' Vito grimly replied. 'As if you were afraid you may be an intrusion.'

This time Catherine's smile was wry to say the least. 'Let's face it, Vito. I wouldn't be here at all if Santino hadn't backed you into a corner.'

His eyes began to flash. And, snap—just like that the antagonism was back. 'Well, you are here,' he grated. 'And this is your home. We are your family and the sooner you come to terms with that, the sooner you will stop being an intrusion!'

With that, Catherine watched him slam himself into the bathroom, leaving her to wonder what the hell had motivated it.

Going back over the conversation, the only thing she could come up with that could have ignited his temper was her silence after he had explained about her rings.

Had he been expecting a whole lot more than a blank stare? A declaration of mutual intent, maybe? But why he should expect or even want that baffled her. He had never looked for those kind of declarations before when—marginally—they'd had something more substantial to work with than they had now.

And anyway, she concluded as she went to find something suitable to wear to go riding in, she felt more comfortable with antagonism than she did with the terrible lost and vulnerable feeling that she'd woken up with this morning. So let him stew, she decided. Let him bash his ego against the brick wall of her defences if that was what he wanted to do. Because there was no way that even Vittorio Giordani could really believe he had a right to expect more from her than he was willing to give out himself!

Yet something fundamental had altered inside him, Catherine had to admit as her first week in Naples drew to a close. For after that one show of his Italian temperament Vito had never uttered another harsh word to her, and seemed to be very careful not to give her the opportunity to flash hers at him.

He had allotted this week to spend with Santo, and work had been set to one side so he could play the loving family game their son had been promised. So they'd filled in their days by riding and swimming, and with trips out around Naples. And their nights had been spent in each other's arms, without even the slightest question of sex rearing its emotive head between them.

And slowly—slowly—Catherine had begun to relax her

guard a little, begun to cautiously enjoy herself. And without the sex to complicate matters, they had actually managed to achieve a kind of harmony that was almost as seductive as the sex used to be.

But it couldn't last. Did she honestly believe that it could? Catherine asked herself as she lay, supposedly relaxing with a book at the poolside, left entirely to her own devices for the first time since she had arrived back here. Luisa had announced her intention to take Santo and a group of his friends off to the beach for the day, and Vito had informed her that he planned to spend the day in his study, putting in some work for his neglected company.

Nothing particularly life-changing in those events, you would think, she mused to herself. But, for reasons she refused to let herself delve into, the book she was reading wouldn't hold her attention. After having pounded out a dozen or so laps of the pool, she had hoped she would just collapse on the sunbed in exhaustion, but she hadn't.

She felt tense and edgy, and kept glancing at the sky, as if she expected to find thunderclouds gathering on the horizon, which would explain this strange tension she was experiencing. But no hint of grey spoiled the perfect blue. In the end she gave up trying to be relaxed when she so obviously wasn't, and went back indoors to shower the suncream from her skin and get dressed with the vague intention of driving herself into Naples in an effort to kill some time.

She had rubbed herself dry, and was just in the process of smoothing body lotion into one of her long slender thighs when the bathroom door swung open. Standing there completely naked and with one foot lifted onto the bathroom stool to make her task easier, she glanced up, saw Vito filling the doorway—and knew in that instant that the storm she had been expecting all day had finally arrived.

It was a storm called desire. Pure and simple, hot and

hungry, tense and tight. It raged in the burning intensity of his eyes and pulsed in the tautness of his stance.

He was wearing a casual wine-red shirt and a pair of lightweight black linen trousers, but as his gaze glittered over her she saw his hand lift up and begin unfastening shirt buttons—and the frisson of response which went shimmering through her was electric.

She had to move. It was a point of necessity that she drop her raised foot to the floor so she could squeeze her pulsing thighs together. The shirt fell apart to reveal a wide bronzed breastplate covered in short, crisp devil-black hair.

'I w-was about to go out,' she heard herself stammer, really as a vehicle to break the raging tension now filling the space between them. 'Drive in-into Naples.'

'Later,' he murmured as the shirt landed on the bathroom floor. Then he half bent so he could slide off his shoes and socks before moving his attention to his trousers.

This was one hell of a strip show. Catherine clutched the bottle of lotion in one hand and felt her flesh begin to tingle. As the trousers parted to reveal that dark patch of body hair she knew thickened beneath the covering of his briefs panic erupted, though it was a very sexual kind of panic and had nothing to do with any dismay at what he was clearly intending.

Yet something made her put up a protest. Maybe it was the knowledge that the trousers were about to go, as she saw his fingers grip at the waistband in readiness to rake them down his legs.

'I… Vito, you—I—we c-can't,' she mumbled incoherently.

'Why not?' he countered.

'Y-your mother—Santo…'

But he shook his dark head. 'I've waited a full week for you to tell me it is okay for us to do this,' he said rawly.

'I am not waiting any longer, Catherine. I *cannot* wait any longer—'

Was that what had been holding him back for all of this time? Because he had assumed she would be rendered unavailable by the pill-induced menstrual cycle?

Chagrined heat blushed her skin from toes to hairline. Seeing it happen brought his strip show to a taut standstill. 'Is it okay?' he then demanded, and his consternation was so great that Catherine almost let out a giggle.

Except that this was no moment for humour. The man in front of her was suffering too badly to appreciate it—as his next gruff statement clearly illuminated. 'For goodness' sake, answer me, Catherine,' he commanded. 'The tension is starting to kill me, very slowly and very painfully.'

'It's okay,' she whispered.

Honey-gold eyes grew suddenly darker, their heat piercing her in all the right places. The trousers went the same way as the shirt, taking his underwear with them to leave only the man in his full and sexual glory to come walking towards her.

The tip of her tongue came out to moisten her lips as he took the bottle of lotion from her nerveless fingers then set it aside. And, without taking his eyes from her eyes, he bent his dark head to capture the tongue-tip between his own lips and draw it into his mouth in an act so inherently erotic that she whimpered in protest when he withdrew again almost immediately.

But his eyes continued to make love to her eyes as one of his hands slid around her waist while the other hand reached up to release her hair from the knot she had it twisted in for her shower. As her hair tumbled down over his fingers to brush sensually against her naked shoulders, he slowly drew her against him.

The contact was utterly scintillating, a fine brushing of warm flesh against flesh that set every nerve-end she possessed singing. Then he kissed her again, slowly and deeply, while stroking her with featherlight fingertips until she was breathless and trembling.

It was all too much for her to just stand there passive while he did this to her. With a sigh that was about as tactile as a sigh could be, she wound her arms around his shoulders, caught his head in her palms and began kissing him hungrily.

It was all the encouragement he needed to pick her up in his arms and carry her to the bed. The pillows went the way they usually did, to the floor, sent there by his urgent hands while Catherine dragged back the covers.

They came together in a tangle of limbs on the smooth, cool linen. It was all very deep, very unconstrained—very erotic, very definitely them at their most sensuously intense. Nothing was taboo, no means to give pleasure ignored—no words uttered. And their silence in itself was deeply seductive. Only the sounds of their breathing and their bodies moving in unison towards the kind of finale that stripped the soul.

Afterwards they lay just touching and kissing, communicating by all other means than talking, because words were dangerous, and neither of them wanted to spoil the special magic they had managed to create, that enclosed them in this wonderful bubble of tactile contentment. Of course they made love again several times during that long, quiet, lazy afternoon, then eventually slept in a possessive love-knot while the sun died slowly out of the room. This was fulfilment at its most sweetest.

Catherine came awake to find herself lying on the bed with a sheet draped strategically across her. Vito had gone from his sleeping place beside her, but her initial sense of loss was quickly replaced with a gasp of shock when she glanced at the bedside clock and actually saw what time it was!

Seven o'clock—Luisa and Santo would have been home for ages! What must they be thinking of her? What had Vito given as an excuse for her being so lazy? How could he just leave her to sleep like this?

'You rat, Vito,' she muttered to herself as she scrambled off the bed, then hurried to find some clothes to drag on.

The thin blue summer dress she had been intending to put on after her shower earlier still lay draped over a chair where she had left it. Scrambling into her underwear, then the dress, she was acutely aware of a series of deep inner aches that offered a good reason why she had slept so heavily. She had never been so thoroughly ravished!

She even felt herself begin to blush as she slid her bare feet into a pair of casual sandals, remembering just what they had done to each other. Or *for* each other, she then corrected, and on an agitated mix of pleasure and embarrassment she began finger-combing her tumbled hair as she made for the door.

The moment that she stepped out onto the landing she knew something was wrong, when the first thing that she heard was Santo's voice raised in anger.

What could be the matter? she wondered frowningly as she followed the sound of her son's angry voice down the stairs and into the main drawing room.

The sight that hit her eyes as she arrived in the doorway sent her still in dismay. Both Luisa and Vito were staring at a surly-faced Santo, who was standing there belligerently facing up to—none other than Marietta.

Of course it had to be Marietta causing all of this mayhem, Catherine grimly acknowledged as she watched the other woman bend at her slender waist to smile sweetly at Santo and say gently. 'But, darling, *you* told *me* that *you* would like your *papà* to marry me.'

'No, I didn't.' Santo angrily denied it. 'Why would I say that when I don't even like you?'

'Santino!' his father cautioned sternly. 'Apologise—now!'

If Catherine thought Santo had been difficult enough during the week before Vito arrived, when she'd endured some spectacular tantrums from him, she was now seeing he had not even got started.

For his face was hot, his eyes aflame, and his stance was more than ready for combat. Turning his glare on his father, he spat, 'No!' with enough force to make Vito stiffen. 'She's lying, and I won't let her!'

'Oh, please...' It was Luisa who tried to play peacemaker, by hurrying forward in an attempt to put herself between Santo and Vito. 'This is just a silly misunderstanding that has got out of hand,' she said anxiously. 'Please don't be alarmed by it, Vito.'

'Alarmed?' Vito bit out. 'Will you explain to me, then, why I walk in this room to the alarming sounds of my son being rude to a guest in this house?'

'A language thing, obviously,' his mother suggested. 'Marietta said something to Santo the last time he was here that he clearly misunderstood, and he said something to Marietta that she misunderstood. Such a silly thing to get fired up about.'

'I didn't misunderstand,' Santo insisted.

'Santino!' Vito turned his attention back to his son. Everyone had been talking in Italian until that point, but Vito's next sentence was delivered in clear, crisp English. 'You will apologise to Marietta now! Do you understand that?'

The little boy was close to tears; Catherine could see that even though he was determined to face the whole thing out with an intransigence that was promising to be his downfall.

'Oh, don't make him do that, Vito.' It was Marietta who came to Santo's rescue. Marietta sounding beautifully pla cating. 'He meant no offence. He's just a little angry because I corrected his Italian.'

'No, you didn't!' the little boy protested. 'You said I was a nuisance and that when *papà* married you he wouldn't want me any more! And I hate you, Papà!' he turned to shout at his father. 'And I won't say sorry! I won't—I won't—I won't!'

Shocked surprise at his son's vehemence hardened Vito's face. 'Then you—'

'Santo,' Catherine said quietly, over whatever Vito had been about to say to him, and brought all four pairs of eyes swinging around in her direction.

And if Catherine had never been made to feel like the poor relation in this house before, she was certainly feeling that way now, as she stood there in her scrap of cheap cotton and took in with one brief, cold glance Marietta, looking smooth and sleek and faultlessly exquisite in her shiny black dress and shiny black shoes and with her shiny black hair stroking over one shoulder.

'Oh, Catherine!' It was poor, anxious Luisa that burst into speech. 'What must you be thinking?'

'I am thinking that this—altercation seems to be very lopsided,' she answered, without taking her eyes from her belligerent son. Silently she held out a hand to him, and with that simple gesture brought him running to her.

Vito was glaring at her for overriding his authority. Luisa was wringing her hands because her peaceful little haven had been shattered and she never could cope with that. And Marietta watched sympathetically as Catherine knelt down so her face was at her son's level.

'Santo, were you rude to Marietta?' She quietly requested his opinion.

He dropped his eyes. 'Yes,' he mumbled truculently.

'And do you think that deserves an apology?'

The dark head shook, then came back up, and Catherine

could see that the tears were real now in big brown eyes. 'I never said what she said I did, Mummy,' he whispered pleadingly. 'I just wouldn't,' he added simply. 'I *like* Papà being married to you.'

Catherine nodded. As far as she was concerned Santo had stated it as honestly as he knew how and the conflict was now over, because she was not going to make her son apologise to a woman she knew from personal experience could twist any situation round to suit her own purposes.

'Then you go off to your room,' she told Santo. 'And I'll come and see you there in a few minutes.'

'Catherine—' Vito wanted to protest, seeing his influence being thoroughly undermined here, but Catherine continued to ignore him as she came upright and sent her son off without offering anyone the chance to do anything about it.

When she turned to face all of those that were left, she found three completely different expressions being aimed right back at her. Vito—angry. Luisa—upset. And Marietta—smiling like a cat who'd pinched the last of the cream.

And why not? Catherine allowed. Within minutes of arriving here she had managed to stir up trouble between every single one of them.

'Good grief, Catherine, what a temper your son has!' Marietta broke the silence with a mocking little laugh. 'Sadly, I seem to have a knack of inadvertently sparking it off! I shall attempt to stay out of his way while I am staying here,' she determined ruefully.

Staying here? Catherine turned to look at Vito, who was looking as puzzled as she was by the comment.

'Marietta arrived home from the States this morning to find her apartment under water,' Luisa jumped in hurriedly. 'A burst water pipe while she was away has ruined everything, so of course I invited her to stay here while the repair work is being done.'

Of course, Catherine parodied, feeling an old-remembered weariness begin to settle over her like a thick black cloud.

'I have just placed my things in the rooms next to Vito's rooms,' Marietta inserted sweetly. 'If you want to know where to find me.'

'No.'

The harsh negative did not come from Catherine's lips, though it very well could have done, since she was thinking the exact same thing as Vito obviously was by the way he had stiffened his stance. Was he remembering a conversation they'd had recently, where the question of which rooms Marietta used when she stayed here had been the one of too many points of conflict between the two of them?

The woman had a special knack of making other people out to be liars.

'Whoever put you there has made a mistake,' he said tersely. 'If you need to stay here, Marietta, then stay in my mother's wing of the house. Catherine and I desire our privacy.'

'Of course,' Marietta instantly conceded. 'I will move rooms immediately. And I apologise that Luisa and I did not take into consideration the—newness of your reconciliation when we chose my rooms.'

And the poison barbs fly thick and fast, Catherine observed as Luisa began to look anxious again, which made her wonder if her mother-in-law had had any say at all in which room Marietta had chosen to use.

On top of that, Vito was getting really touchy now, she noted, as his frown deepened into a real scowl. First his son had annoyed him, then his wife by interfering, and now his mother, by placing Marietta where he didn't want her to be.

In fact the only person he did not seem cross with was dear Marietta. Clever girl, Catherine silently commended her as Marietta deftly flipped the conversation over to business things and proceeded to dominate his attention to the exclusion of everyone else.

Catherine left them to it to go in search of her son, whom she found sitting slouched over a large box of building blocks from where he was picking one up at random then throwing it sullenly back into the pile.

Chivvying him up with a determined brightness aimed to overlay the ugliness of the scene downstairs, she helped him with his bath then curled up on the bed beside him to read a couple of his favourite stories to him. Then, when she saw his eyes begin to droop, she kissed him gently goodnight and got up to leave.

'I don't like Marietta,' he mumbled suddenly. 'She's always spoiling things.'

Out of the mouths of babes, Catherine thought dryly.

'Do you like her?' he shot at her.

Well, do I lie or tell the truth? she wondered ruefully. And on a deep breath admitted, 'No. But Nonna does. So for Nonna's sake we have to be nice to her, okay?'

'Okay,' he agreed, but very reluctantly. 'But will you tell Papà for me that I'm sorry I shouted at him? I don't think he likes me now.'

'You can tell me yourself,' a voice said from the doorway.

They both glanced around to find Vito leaning there looking as if he had been standing like that for ever—which probably meant he had overheard everything.

A quick glance at his face as she walked towards him told Catherine he didn't look pleased. But then, who did around here? she wondered grimly.

'We need to talk,' he murmured as she reached him.

'You just bet we do,' she replied. And once again the mutual antagonism was rife between them. Whatever they had managed to achieve in bed today had now been almost wiped away by one very clever lady.

They met in their bedroom when it was time to change for dinner. Catherine was already there, waiting for him when he came through the door with all guns blazing.

'Right,' he fired at her. 'What the hell did you think you were doing undermining my authority over Santo like that?'

'And what the hell did you think *you* were doing forcing him to take no other stand in front of everyone?' she shot right back.

'The boy was rude,' Vito gritted unapologetically.

'Our *son* was upset!' Catherine snapped. 'Have you any idea how it must have felt to him to have his own words twisted around like that?'

'Maybe he was the one who did the twisting, Catherine,' Vito grimly pointed out. 'Marietta was only trying to make pleasant conversation with him and...'

Catherine stopped listening. She'd heard more than enough as it was. On an angry twist of her heel she turned and walked out onto the balcony, leaving Vito talking to fresh air.

Out here the air was warm, after the air-conditioned coolness of the bedroom, and tiptoe quiet—soothing in its own way. Leaning her forearms on the stone balustrade, she tried breathing in some deep gulps of that warm air in an effort to dispel the angry frustration that was simmering inside her.

Because the hurt she felt, the disappointment and frustration at Vito's dogged championship of Marietta, only made her wonder why Vito had gone chasing all the way to London when it was so very clear to her that Santo came a poor second-best to dear Marietta.

Pulling the glass French door shut behind him, Vito came to lean beside her. He knew as well as she did that the earlier row was not over.

'You can be so aggravating sometimes,' he censured. 'Did no one ever tell you that it is rude to walk out when someone is speaking to you?'

'Which makes me rude and Santo rude all in one day,' she said tartly. 'My, but we must be hell to live with.'

His sigh was almost a laugh, his sense of humour touched by her sarcasm, which actually managed to cool some of the angry heat out of her. And for the next few moments neither said anything as they gazed out at the view.

It was fully dark outside, but a three-quarter moon was casting silver shadows on the silk-dark water, and Naples was sparkling like fairy dust on a blanket of black velvet.

A beautiful sight. A sensually soothing sight.

'Did you tell Santo off just now?' she asked eventually.

'No, of course not,' he denied. 'I apologised to him for losing my temper. I'm not a fool, Catherine,' he added gruffly. 'I know I behaved no better down there than Santo did.'

Well, that was something, she supposed. 'So you're both friends again?'

'Yes,' he said, but he wasn't comfortable with it all. 'Marietta's right,' he muttered frowningly. 'He does seem to have developed a temper—'

'Marietta can keep her opinion about my son to herself,' Catherine returned tightly. 'And while she's at it she can go and stay at a damned hotel!'

'Hell, don't start on that one, for goodness' sake,' Vito pleaded wearily. 'You know I can't stop her from staying here!'

'Well, either she goes or we go,' Catherine informed

him. 'And while we are on the subject of Marietta,' she added tightly, 'you lied to me about her.'

'I did?' he sighed wearily. 'When was that, exactly?'

'When you led me to believe that you would be marrying her after we divorced. But the question of marriage between you two was never an option, was it?'

'Ah.' Vito grimaced. 'Would you care to tell me how you came to that conclusion?'

'Marietta herself told me,' she replied. 'When she was forced into twisting Santo's words around to cover up her own lies.'

'Or corrected a misunderstanding between two people who naturally speak two different languages?' he smoothly suggested.

A shrug of her shoulders dismissed the difference. 'Whichever, it still means that our son upset himself badly over nothing, and you brought me back here under a threat that was a lie.'

'I did not lie,' he denied. 'In fact I told you quite plainly why I wanted you back here with me.'

'You mean the revenge for your hurt pride thing?' she said, turning to look at him.

He was already looking at her, and their eyes clashed with a heat that set her insides burning. 'Did what we shared today feel like revenge to you?' he countered very softly.

No, it hadn't. Catherine silently admitted it. But the only other alternative she could come up with for his motives was just too unreliable to contemplate.

So she changed the subject. 'But you did promise me that if I came back here, then Marietta would be kept out of our lives.'

'I never made that promise.' He denied that also. 'If you remember, Catherine, I told you that I *couldn't* make that kind of promise.'

She released a small sigh, anger coming to life on the wings of frustration. 'In the name of decency, Vito. A man does not keep his mistress under the same roof as his wife!'

'I'm not telling you again that she isn't my mistress,' he snapped.

'Ex-mistress, then. Whatever.' She shrugged. 'She should not be here and you know she should not be here!'

'I know that you are crazy, obsessed and just downright delusional,' he told her.

Catherine's chin came around, eyes flashing green in the darkness. 'Okay, so I'm crazy.' She freely admitted it. 'You have married yourself to an absolute lunatic with obsessive tendencies and paranoid delusions. Now deal with the lunatic's delusions before she does something about them herself!' she advised.

Despite himself, Vito laughed. 'Now I do know you are crazy, for admitting all of that,' he murmured ruefully.

'Comes with the hair and the green eyes,' she explained 'I believe I can cast spells too, and ride on a broomstick Which also means I can tell a fellow witch when I mee one.'

'Meaning?' He was still smiling, fooled by her light ton into thinking the other subject was over.

But the smile died when she said. 'Marietta. Wicke Witch of the North, complete with black hair, black eyes black heart—and a yen for other people's husbands.'

'She has been a close friend of this family for as far bac as I care to remember,' Vito reminded her. 'I will not, o that point alone, think of alienating Marietta simply becaus you cannot like her.'

And that, Catherine acknowledged, is telling me.

'What about doing it because your son cannot like her' she therefore suggested.

'He dislikes what you dislike.'

'Ah, so it's my fault,' she mused dryly. 'I should have expected it.'

But what really annoyed her was that he didn't deny it. 'I refuse to pander to unfounded prejudice,' he stated firmly instead.

Staring out across the bay, Catherine's eyes changed from flashing green to winter-grey, as if they were absorbing the bleakness in the moonlight. So he wanted sound proof of Marietta's prejudice towards them? she pondered. Well, she had that proof, circumstantial though it was.

The point was, did she tell him? For the last time she had brought up the subject she had demolished him so utterly that she'd vowed never to do that to him again.

Then she remembered their son, and the kind of depths Marietta's obsession with Vito had forced her to sink to—and with a sigh that told of a heaviness which went too deep for words, she made her decision. 'On the day I started to lose our baby,' she began, 'I rang around everywhere looking for you. I eventually tracked you down at Marietta's apartment.'

'I know that.' He was already stiffening. 'I have never denied to you where I was.'

Only *his* excuse for being there had been to get drunk and find oblivion from his nagging wife. Marietta's version had been very different.

'Why, then, if Marietta *woke* you immediately, did it take you six hours after that call to arrive at my hospital bed?' she asked. 'The traffic bad, was it?' she taunted softly as his face began to drain. 'Or maybe you ran out of petrol? That is another male euphemism for being busy in bed with someone else, I believe. Or maybe—just maybe,' she then added grimly, 'Marietta didn't bother to pass on my message until she felt like it, hmm? What does that tell you about your precious Marietta?' she demanded—only to instantly withdraw the question.

'No, don't tell me,' she said. 'Because in truth I don't really care what it tells you, when really there is no excuse you can offer as to why you went from me to her that day, or why you weren't there for me when I needed you to be. But from now on when I tell you that that woman is poison where I am concerned, you believe me,' she insisted. 'And you keep her away from both me and my son or we leave here. And if that is prejudice, then that's fine by me. But it is also a rock-solid promise.'

After that, the silence droned like the heavy pulse of a hammer drill while they both stood there watching Naples twinkle. How much of that Vito had already known and how much he had been stubbornly hiding from himself was impossible to tell. But Catherine knew one thing for sure, and that was if he still persisted in standing in Marietta's corner after what she'd just said, then it really was over for them.

Okay,' he said finally, deeply—flatly. 'I will see what I can do about the situation. There are a couple of new ventures on the planning table at the moment,' he murmured—thinking on his feet again, Catherine made note. 'One in New York, one in Paris. Marietta would be the ideal person to oversee either one of them. But it will take time for me to set it up,' he warned. 'She is going to need time to clear any outstanding projects from her desk before she can go anywhere. And my mother's birthday is coming up,' he then reminded her. 'It will be her sixty-fifth and she is planning a big party here to celebrate. She will expect Marietta to be here for it, Catherine, you must see that.'

Did she? she asked herself. No, actually, she didn't. But she could accept that Vito had a right to protect his mother from hurt just as Catherine had a right to protect herself and her son.

'Two weeks,' he repeated huskily. 'And I promise you that she will be gone from this house and gone from Naples…'

Two weeks, Catherine pondered. Can I live through two whole weeks of Marietta?

Do you really have a choice here? she then asked herself bleakly. For she could spout out threats about leaving until she was blue in the face, but she knew—probably as well as Vito knew—that she was trapped here no matter what the circumstances, so long as this was where Santo wanted to be.

'All right, you have your two weeks,' she agreed. 'But in the interim you keep her well away from both me and Santo,' she warned him. And with that she straightened away from the balcony, then turned to make her way back inside.

'I did not sleep with Marietta the day you lost our baby.' His deep voice followed her.

'"Sleep" being the operative word there, I suppose,' she derided.

The harsh hiss of air leaving his lungs had him spinning angrily round to glare at her. 'Did I ever call out Marietta's name in my sleep while you were lying beside me?' he rasped out bitterly.

About to open the French doors, Catherine went perfectly still, understanding exactly where he was going with this. 'No,' she admitted.

She heard him shift his tense stance a little, as if maybe relief had riddled through him.

'Unlike you and your Marcus. At least you were saved that bloody indignity.'

'I never slept with Marcus,' Catherine countered stiffly.

On the next balcony Marietta sat forward, the new name being inserted into the conversation sparking her back to life when only a moment before she had been almost defeated.

'Funny, that,' Vito drawled. 'But I don't believe you. So now what is left of trust?'

'We never really had any to begin with,' Catherine denounced. 'You married me because you had to. I accepted that because I felt I had to. You don't build trust on foundations like those.'

It seemed he didn't have an answer to that one, because the silence behind her deepened again. So, opening the French door, she stepped back into the bedroom. Vito didn't follow her. In fact he remained outside, leaning against the balcony for ages afterwards, thinking—she knew not what. But when he did eventually reappear, one brief glimpse of his closed, very grim expression was enough to tell her that his thoughts had not been pleasant ones.

And what bit of closeness they had managed to find in their bed that afternoon had now been well and truly obliterated.

CHAPTER EIGHT

SO DINNER that evening was a strained affair. Luisa clearly had not yet recovered from the angry scene with her grandson in her drawing room earlier. And the way she kept on looking anxiously from Vito to Catherine said she too was acutely aware that the fine peace they had all been enjoying since Catherine had come back here to live had been completely shattered.

Did she ever bother to ask herself why that was? Catherine wondered, and decided not, because to do so would mean Luisa seeing the faults in her wonderful family.

Even Marietta was unusually quiet for her. She spent most of the wretched meal seemingly lost in her own deep vein of thought.

Jet-lag, she called it when Luisa anxiously asked her if anything was the matter. But she did briefly raise herself to attempt polite conversation with Catherine. 'I believe you have been working for Templeton and Lang while living in London,' she remarked.

Go to hell, Catherine wanted to snap. But she smiled a civilised smile and answered cordially enough. 'Yes. I originally trained as a legal secretary, so it was nice to get back to it.'

'And your gift for languages must have been very useful to a firm which specialises in European law.' Marietta nodded in understanding. 'Have we ever used them, Vito?' she asked.

Busy glowering into his wine glass, Vito seemed to

stiffen infinitesimally, though why he did Catherine had no idea. 'Not that I recall,' he answered briefly.

'That is very odd.' Marietta frowned. 'For I am sure I know them. Marcus Lang is one of the senior partners, is he not?' she enquired of Catherine.

'No. *Robert* Lang and *Marcus* Templeton,' she corrected, feeling Vito's tension like a sting in her throat as she said Marcus's name.

'Ah. My mistake,' Marietta replied. 'Still…you are going to miss the stimulation, no doubt,' she murmured sympathetically. 'I know I would not like to go back to doing nothing again.'

'I have some work to do.' Vito rose so abruptly that everyone was taken aback. 'Marietta, I could do with going over a few things with you before you retire, if you are not too tired.'

'Of course,' Marietta agreed, but she was already talking to Vito's back, because he was striding from the dining room.

She followed very soon after him, which left Catherine to smooth out poor Luisa's ruffled feathers before she too could escape to the relative sanctuary of the bedroom. And by the time she had undressed and crawled into bed, she was ready—more than ready—to switch today off by dropping herself into the oblivion of sleep.

So having Vito arrive only minutes later was the last thing she needed.

Presuming he was coming to bed, she lay curled on her side with her eyes closed and pretended to be asleep. So when his finger gently touched her cheek only seconds later, her eyes flicked open in surprise to find him squatting down by the bed beside her.

'Something has come up,' he told her quietly. 'I need to go into Naples to my office for a while.'

'Alone?' The question shot from her lips without her

expecting it, never mind Vito. And instantly she wanted to kick herself as she watched his expression harden.

'Yes, alone,' he gritted. 'And if you don't watch out, Catherine, your mistrust is going to eat you alive!'

With that, he levered himself upright, turned and walked out of the room.

She didn't blame him. And he was right about her lack of trust eating her alive. Because it was already doing it.

'Oh damn,' she breathed, rolling onto her back to stare at the ceiling. 'What am I *doing* to myself?'

You know what you're doing, she immediately answered her own question. You are tearing yourself apart over the same man you have been tearing yourself apart over for the last six years.

Hearing the sound of a car engine firing into life, she got up and walked out onto the balcony to watch Vito leave. She arrived at the balcony rail just in time to see his red tail-lights gliding down the driveway.

'I love you,' she whispered after him. 'Even though I don't want to.'

And miserably she watched those tail-lights snake their way down the hillside until they became nothing but red dots among a million other red dots. She was about to go back inside when the sound of yet another car engine firing caught her attention. Turning back to the rail, she watched a black BMW come around from the back of the house where the garages were situated.

It was Marietta.

Even though it was too dark to see from up here who was driving, she just knew it was Marietta, and that she had to be following Vito to wherever they had arranged to meet.

So much for my paranoid delusions, she thought, and oddly didn't feel angry, or hurt, or even bitter any more.

But then she had a feeling that she had no more hurt left to feel about what Vito and Marietta did together.

She didn't sleep much that night. And was still awake when one car came back up the driveway at around four-thirty. The other she didn't hear, because she had eventually fallen into a heavy pre-dawn slumber.

Sounds in the bedroom eventually awoke her, and, opening her eyes, she found Vito quietly readying himself for the day. But a swift glance at his side of the bed told her it had not been slept in. On that observation alone, she shut her eyes again and pretended that she didn't know he was there.

An hour later she came downstairs in an outfit she'd had for years. The classic cut of the calf-length pin-straight cream skirt was timeless, the crocheted silk sleeveless top a soft coffee shade that went well with her warm autumn colouring.

Walking into the sunny breakfast room, she found Vito and Marietta there sharing a working breakfast. There was a scatter of paperwork lying on the table between them and Marietta was busily scribbling notes across one of them while Vito sat scanning the contents of another.

All very businesslike, Catherine dryly observed, very high-executive, with Marietta wearing her habitual black and Vito in tungsten-steel-grey. And, considering he was supposed to have been up working all night, he looked disgustingly well on it, she mocked as she watched his dark head come up at the sound of her step and his eyes narrow as they took in her own coolly composed demeanour today.

He knew the look. He knew the outfit. He even knew the neat way she had loosely tied back her hair with a large tortoiseshell clip at her nape that gave the red-gold thread chic without being too formal.

'Going somewhere?' he questioned, not pleased, by the sound of it.

Catherine smiled a bland smile. 'To re-establish links with some old contacts,' she replied, and walked towards one of the vacant chairs at the table as Marietta's dark head lifted and her eyes drifted over her.

'*Buon giorno,*' she greeted. 'So you mean to go back to work,' she observed, like Vito, recognising the outfit.

'Better than "doing nothing again", don't you think?' she answered sweetly as she sat herself down, then reached for the coffee pot.

'Did I draw blood when I said that?' the dark beauty said. 'I'm sorry, Catherine, it was not intentional.'

Of course it was, Catherine silently countered, while Marietta turned her attention back to the business presently in hand across the breakfast table and began discussing figures with Vito.

He, on the other hand, wasn't listening. His whole attention was arrowed on his wife, who was now calmly pouring herself a cup of coffee as if this was just any ordinary day. But there was nothing ordinary about it. He knew it—she knew it. Catherine was angry and she was in rebellion.

'Santino is with his grandmother,' he said, over the top of what Marietta was saying. 'They are spending the day at the beach again.'

'I know. I waved them off.' Catherine smiled serenely and reached for a slice of toast from the rack, then the bowl of thick, home-made orange marmalade.

'Vito, if you—'

'Shut up, Marietta,' he interrupted.

Her lovely eyes widened. 'Am I interrupting something?' she drawled.

'Not at all,' Catherine assured her, spreading marmalade on her toast.

'Yes!' Vito countered. 'Please leave us.'

Marietta's expression revealed no answering irritation as,

on her feet in an instant, she obediently gathered up her papers and left them alone.

Biting neatly into her slice of toast, Catherine watched her go. But Vito pushed back his chair and got to his feet. A few strides had him rounding the table, then he was lowering himself into the chair next to Catherine's.

'I don't want you to go out to work,' he said curtly.

'I wasn't aware that I was giving you a choice,' she replied.

His lean face snapped into irritation at her very dry tone. 'Rushing out there and taking the first job that is offered to you just because you are angry with me is childish,' he clipped.

'But I'm not angry with you,' she denied, taking another bite at her toast.

'Then for what reason are you doing this?' he demanded. 'You have not once mentioned going to work since you came back here!'

'Myself,' she explained. 'I am doing it for myself.'

It was a decision she had come to at some very low point during the night. That there was very little she could do to change the status quo, so she might as well just get on with it.

Which was the reason why she was dressed for the city this morning. Getting on with it meant getting a life. A life outside the suffocating confines of this house, anyway.

'What about Santino?' Vito tried another tack.

Catherine smile a rueful smile. 'Santino has more people eager to amuse him here in this house than a whole school of normal children have.'

'He prefers to have his *mamma* at home with him. I prefer to have his *mamma* at home with him. What is the use of my providing all of this,' he said, with a wave of a hand meant to encompass their luxury surroundings, 'if you will not let yourself appreciate its advantages?'

'That is a terribly arrogant thing to say,' Catherine replied.

'I don't feel arrogant,' he confessed. 'I feel damned annoyed that you did not discuss this with me before making your decision. It is so typical of you, Catherine,' he censured, unaware that her face had quite suddenly gone very pale. 'You are so stubbornly independent that you just go ahead and do whatever it is you want to do and to hell with what anyone else may think!'

'I'm sorry you think that,' she murmured, but her tone said she was not going to change her mind.

Vito released a driven sigh. 'Listen to me...' he urged, curling his fingers tensely around her fingers. 'I don't want to wage war with you every time that we speak. I want you to be happy here. I want *us* to be happy here!'

'With you as the family provider and me as the trophy you keep dusted in the corner?' she mocked. 'No, thank you, Vito. I'm not made of the right kind of stuff to play that particular role.'

'That woman should learn to curb her stupid tongue!' he muttered.

A criticism of Marietta? Catherine almost gasped at the shock of it—albeit sarcastically. 'Don't you have some work to do?' she prompted him.

As if on cue, the door suddenly opened. 'Have you two finished?' a cool voice questioned. 'Only we have a lot to get through, Vito, if we are to catch that noon flight to Paris today.'

The air in the sunny breakfast room suddenly began to crackle. Catherine glared at Vito. 'You're going to Paris today—with her?' she demanded.

He looked fit to wreak bloody murder. 'I—'

'Oh—didn't you know, Catherine?' Marietta inserted. 'I assumed Vito would have told you.'

'I was about to,' he gritted—at Catherine, not Marietta.

'No need now, though,' Catherine pointed out, raking her fingers from beneath his as she shot stiffly to her feet. 'Since your ever-efficient compatriot has done the job for you.'

'Catherine—' Vito's voice was harsh on a mixture of fury and frustration.

'Excuse me,' she spoke icily over him, 'I have some calls to make.' And she walked towards the door. 'Enjoying yourself?' she asked sweetly of Marietta as she passed by her.

The other girl's eyes widened in mock bewilderment. 'I don't know what you mean,' she lied.

Catherine just laughed—a hard, scoffing sound that jarred on the eardrums—and left the two of them to it, with Marietta's voice trailing after her. 'Vito, I am so sorry. I just thought…'

Vito followed her. Catherine would have been more surprised if he hadn't. He found her standing in their bedroom grimly pulling on the jacket to match her cream skirt.

'Don't you have a plane to catch?' she questioned sarcastically.

His angry face hardened. 'Don't do this, Catherine,' he warned. 'Don't rile me today when I've worked right through the night and am low on sleep and on patience.'

'And where were you *working* last night?' she challenged.

'You know where. The office,' he said heavily. 'I told you.'

'Alone?'

'Yes—alone!' he snapped.

'What time did you come home?'

'Around five—why the inquisition?' he asked dazedly.

'Marietta left here straight after you last night and arrived back half an hour before you say you got back,' she informed him. 'Is that the standard time-lapse for secret trysts these days? Only it's best to know the form when I start some trysts of my own.'

'You think I was with Marietta.' He began to catch on at last. *'Madre di Dio,'* he sighed. 'When are you going to try trusting me?'

Not in this lifetime, Catherine thought bitterly. 'How long will you be away?'

'About a week—' He went to say more, but Catherine beat him to it.

'Staying where?'

'The company apartment—where else?' he sighed out heavily. 'Catherine, it was you who told me to keep her out of the way,' he tagged on impatiently. 'And that is exactly what I am trying to do!'

'Enjoy yourself, then.'

Wrong thing to say, she realised as he suddenly leapt at her. She was trapped in his arms before she could gasp. And his mouth, when it found hers, was intent on taking no prisoners.

Yet—what did she do? She surrendered was what she did. Without a fight and without dignity she let her head tilt backwards, parted her lips—and let him do whatever it was that he wanted to do.

The slave for her master, she likened, not even bothering to be disgusted with herself as her fingers turned into claws that took a grip on his head and she let the power of his hungry, angry passion completely overwhelm her.

And his hands were everywhere, yanking off her little jacket, raking up her top, and the flimsy lace bra she was wearing beneath it, was no barrier at all against those magic fingers. She started whimpering with pleasure. He laughed into her mouth, then reached up to grab hold of one her hands and dragged it down to press it hard against his rising sex.

'Now this is what I call enjoying myself,' he muttered,

as he transferred his mouth to one of the breasts he had prepared for himself.

As he sucked, and sensation went rampaging through her, the telephone by the bed began to ring. His dark head came up. It would be Marietta, telling him to get a move on.

'Answer that and you're dead,' Catherine told him, and to state her point her fingers closed more tightly around him.

On a growl of sheer sensual torment he caught her mouth again, sent her mind spinning, drove her straight back out to where they'd both briefly emerged from, while the ring of the telephone acted like a spur to every single sense they possessed as she slowly eased her grip to begin sliding her palm along the full throbbing length of him with the intention of finding the tab to his trouser zip—

He stepped away from her so quickly she barely registered what was happening. And as her confused eyes focused on the wicked grin slashing his arrogant features she realised why he had stepped away as abruptly as he had.

Or he would not have escaped without injury. Vito was well aware that his wife could be a little hell-cat when she wanted to be, and the grin he was offering her was one of triumph, because he knew he had just stage-managed his own very lucky escape.

'Hold that thought,' he commanded. And with one flashing, gleaming dip at the way she was standing there—looking utterly ravaged without the ravaging—he had the damn audacity to wink! 'I will be back to collect the rest at the end of the week.'

He was gone before she could answer. And as she stood there blinking bemusedly at the back of the door, unable to believe she had let him do this to her, the telephone kept on ringing with a ruthless persistence that was Marietta.

Yet what did she find herself doing? She found herself standing there loving the sound of that ringing telephone, knowing that Marietta must be seething in frustration while she stubbornly hung on there, waiting for one of them to answer. And also knowing, by the length of time it took the ringing to stop, that Vito had needed to take time to compose himself before going to find Marietta.

It ended up being a strange week all told. A long week that made her feel a bit like a bride marking time before her big day—though she was truly annoyed with herself for feeling like that.

The man leaves one decidedly provocative taunt hanging in the air and you respond to it like this, she scolded herself crossly. But it didn't stop her from feeling pumped up with a waiting expectancy which had her almost floating hazily through the ensuing days until Vito's return.

The man was her weakness, his body a temple at which she worshipped whether she liked it or not. Control was a no-word where he was concerned. It always had been. Weak of the mind, weak of the flesh and weak of the spirit was what she was.

So she tried very hard to combat all of that by throwing herself into a whirl of activity that didn't seem to achieve anything. She had lunch each day with old acquaintances, put out feelers about a job, then found herself in no rush to take one—though she didn't understand it, since she had thought a job was her number one priority if she was going to make her life bearable here.

Another thing she learned was that Luisa was no part-time grandmother. She adored Santo. In fact she loved nothing better than to have her grandson with her all day and every day. She *did* things with him, took him places with her, was always interested in everything he had to say. And Santo blossomed under her loving attention. Not that he hadn't been happy with just Catherine back in London, because he had been—very happy. It was just that watching from the sidelines how Luisa treated Santo made Catherine realise why Vito was the man he was. Luisa seemed to instinctively instill confidence and self-belief into Santo, and she would have done the same for her own son.

A son who rang home every evening religiously. Spoke to his mother, spoke to his son—and spoke to Catherine.

Neither of them mentioned Marietta during those telephone calls. Catherine wouldn't in case the wretched woman was there in the room with him and would therefore know that her existence worried Catherine. And Vito didn't mention her because, Catherine presumed, Marietta *was* right there with him and he didn't want *Catherine* to know.

Oh, the evils involved in feeling no trust, she mused grimly one afternoon while she was standing beneath the shower attempting to cool herself, because Naples had been hit by the kind of heatwave that even the air-conditioning system was struggling to cope with.

But it wasn't just the heatwave that had forced her into taking her second shower of the day. The real culprit for that was Vito. He had left her hungry, and hungry she had stayed. So much so that even standing here like this, with a cold jet of water pouring all over her, she couldn't stop her body from responding to the knowledge that he was coming home today. Her breasts were tingling, their sensitive tips tightly peaked, and a permanent throb had taken up residence deep down in her abdomen. And if she kept her eyes closed she could even imagine him stripping off his clothes to come and join her here.

So when a naked, very male body slid in behind her she thought for a moment that she was fantasising his presence.

'Vito!' she gasped, almost slipping on the wet tiles in shocked consternation. His arms wound around her, to hold her steady. 'You frightened the life out of me!' she protested.

'My apologies,' he murmured. 'But hearing you in here was an irresistible temptation.'

'I thought you weren't due back until this evening,' she said, trying desperately to steady her racing heartbeat.

'I caught an earlier flight.' He was already bending his dark head so that he could press his open mouth to the side of her throat. 'Mmm, you taste delicious.'

And you feel delicious, Catherine silently countered.

'The water is a bit cold, though,' he complained, reaching over her shoulder to alter the temperature gauge slightly. 'What are you trying to do—freeze yourself?'

'It's so hot,' she murmured in idiot-like explanation. But the blush that suffused her skin told its own wretched story.

He knew it too. 'Ah,' he drawled. 'Missed me, hmm?'

'I have hardly given you a second thought,' she lied.

'Well, I missed you,' he murmured as he turned her round to face him. 'And please do note that *I* am not too proud to admit it.'

'Only because you want something,' she mocked.

But he just laughed softly, then proceeded to show her exactly what he wanted. And as she wound her long legs around his body, while Vito loved her into ecstasy, she let herself smile. Because a man couldn't be this hungry if he had spent the whole week doing this with someone else, could he?

Because even though it was her mouth that was gasping out its little sounds of pleasure, she wasn't so mindless with sensation that she wasn't aware that Vito was trembling, that despite the rhythmic power of his thrusts he was struggling to hang onto control here.

'Kiss me,' she groaned, as if in agony. 'I need you to kiss me!'

On a growl, he did so, felt her begin to quicken as his

mouth fused with her mouth and sent her spinning into orgasm, and almost instantly joined her, their mutual gasps mingling with the sound of the shower spray.

Afterwards he carried her out of the shower before letting her stand on her own shaky legs again. She leaned weakly against him while he set about drying her, her mouth laying lazy kisses across his hair-roughened chest while her arms rested limply against his lean hipline.

They didn't speak. It didn't seem necessary—or maybe they were both too aware that words tended to ruin everything. So when he made her stand up properly, so he could dry her front, Catherine stood staring wistfully up at his beautiful face and wished she could dare love him again.

Wished it with all she had in her to wish.

'Keep looking at me like that…' his smile was rueful '…and you will be spending the rest of the day in the bedroom.'

'Santo is spending the day with his friend Paolo,' she murmured.

A sleek eyebrow arched. 'Is that your way of telling me that you don't mind spending the day in the bedroom with me?' he asked.

'Got any better ideas?' she softly queried.

It was Luisa who asked about Marietta over dinner that night.

'She remained in Paris,' Vito replied. 'But she will be back in time for your birthday party next week.'

No Marietta for another whole week. Catherine's mood suddenly felt positively buoyant. And remained like that throughout the next few days as their life returned to the same routine it had developed before Vito had taken Marietta to Paris. He spent his mornings in his study and his afternoons with his wife and son while his mother became deeply involved in the preparations for her party at the weekend.

In fact, life could almost be described as happy. They swam in the pool and took drives into the mountains in an attempt to escape the oppressive heat. And Vito took Santo and a small group of his friends out for the day so that Catherine could help Luisa. Then a job cropped up that Catherine quite fancied, because it involved working freelance from home, translating manuscripts for a publishing company.

'I must be getting lazy,' she confessed to Vito that evening as they lay stretched out on the bed together.

'It could not be, I suppose, that you are merely contented?' he suggested.

Is that why I've been working so hard through the last few years? she asked herself. Because I was so discontented with my life?

It could be, she had to admit, because she certainly hadn't felt this relaxed with herself in a very long time.

'Well, I am going to have to commandeer the library to use as my workplace,' she warned him. 'It's either there or your study, and I don't think you would like it if I moved in there with you.'

'We would neither of us get much work done,' he agreed. Then, 'Mmm,' he groaned. 'You are very good at this.'

He was lying stretched out on his stomach and Catherine was running her nails down the muscle-cushioned tautness of gold satin skin covering his long back while he enjoyed the sensation with all the self-indulgence of a true hedonist.

'I know,' she replied with a bland conceit. 'I've had loads of practice, you see.'

She'd meant with him, because once upon a time they'd used to lie for ages just doing this. But from the way his muscles tensed Catherine knew he had misunderstood her.

'How much practice?' he demanded.

Sighing, she sat up and away from him.

He moved too, rolling onto his back to glare up at her. 'How many lovers have there been, Catherine?' He insisted on an answer.

'You know there was no one before you,' she reminded him. 'So why start asking questions like that now, all of these years later?'

'I meant *since* we married.'

Turning her head, she looked down at this man who was lying beside her in all his naked arrogance, with the power of his virility on blatant display, and wished she knew what made his mind tick as well as she knew his body.

'How many for you?' she counter-challenged.

'None,' he answered unhesitatingly.

'Same here,' she replied, and knew they both thought the other was lying. 'Does it matter?' she asked.

'No.' He grimaced, and she knew that was a lie also.

Her hand reached out to lightly stroke him. Releasing a small sigh, he closed his eyes. 'Okay,' he said. 'I can take a hint. You can ravish me.'

Coming on top of him, Catherine eased him inside her then sighed herself. 'Talking never did us any favours, Vito,' she murmured sombrely. 'Let's make a pact not to do it more than is absolutely necessary.'

Then, before he could answer, she closed her own eyes and began to move over him. And she rode him with a muscular co-ordination that soon sent any arguments he might have been about to voice fleeing in favour of more pleasurable pursuits.

CHAPTER NINE

THE house was on show tonight, lit by strategically placed halogens that turned its white walls a seductive gold, and its many garden features were subtly lit from within the shrubbery that lined its many pathways. Inside, everything had been cleaned or swept or dusted or polished, and in the large formal dining room attached to the ballroom a buffet banquet fit for kings had been laid.

Which left only the house occupants to dress themselves up in the kind of clothes that would complement the house. Catherine had achieved this by deciding to wear a striking long red silk gown with a strapless and boned basque-style bodice that was as bold as it was stunning with her colouring. She had dressed her hair into an elegant twist held in place by a diamond clasp that allowed a few stray tendrils to curl around her nape and around the diamond earrings she had dangling from her earlobes. And on her feet she wore very high, very strappy, shiny red shoes that forced her to move in a way that set men's pulses racing.

It certainly set Vito's pulses racing as he watched her come gliding down the stairs towards him. He had just returned from delivering Santo into the care of Paolo's *mamma*, where he was to enjoy his first sleep-over.

Which did not mean he had missed out on the fun. Luisa had been all for thoroughly enjoying her whole day, so when Santo decided that she should have a special birthday tea party with him and his friends, his *nonna* had been more than willing to play along. So it had been a balloons and red jelly party, with a novelty cake and the kind of games children believed a prerequisite for birthdays.

It had been fun. Probably would turn out to have been more fun than the grown up party that was about to follow, Catherine mused wryly as she watched Vito watch her come towards him. And the dark gleam in his eyes was telling her everything she wanted to know. Pride and appreciation were the words that came to mind, underpinned by the ever-present sexual vibrations that were such an integral part of what they had always shared.

'You look as if you have just stepped out of one of my father's Pre-Raphaelites,' he murmured deeply as she reached him, then frowned. 'But something is missing...'

'Jewellery,' Catherine agreed, touching her bare throat. 'You have most of it locked away in your safe, if you remember.'

'Then lead the way to my study,' he commanded, 'and we will rectify the situation immediately.'

Walking off in the direction of his study, she could feel the heat of his eyes as he followed behind her, and her ruby-painted mouth gave a rueful twitch because she was aware that he was now able to see how her gown dipped at the back in an audaciously deep V to her slender waistline.

'Very provocative,' he drawled.

Casting him a flirtatious glance over her shoulder, she replied, 'I *like* being provocative.'

His answering laugh was low and husky as they entered his study. And he was still smiling when he turned back to her after extracting something from the safe. Expecting him to come towards her with her old jewellery box in his hands, she was surprised, therefore, when he held only a flat black velvet case. 'Don't I get to choose?' she asked.

'No,' he replied. 'And that dress is most definitely an outright provocation,' he added, again eyeing censoriously the amount of naked back she had on show. 'Make sure I vet every man you dance with tonight.'

Catherine mocked him with a look as he came to stand behind her. 'You're being very imperious,' she complained. 'Choosing my dance partners and choosing my jewellery. What if I don't like your choice—like what you have in that box, for instance?'

'Tell me, then, what you think,' he said, and with that deftness that was his, something cool and heavy landed against her chest.

She transferred her eyes from him to herself, and an instant gasp of surprise whispered from her as she stared at the most exquisite diamond-encrusted heart resting just above the valley between the creamy slopes of her breasts.

'Oh, but this is beautiful,' she breathed, lifting slender fingers to gently touch the heart.

'Don't sound so surprised,' he drawled as he concentrated on fastening the intricate clasp which would lock the necklace safely in place. 'I may be imperious, but my taste is usually faultless.'

'It's a locket,' she realised, ignoring his conceit. 'If I look inside will I find your arrogant face looking out at me?'

'No,' he laughed. 'It is for you to decide who you carry around in there.'

You, Catherine thought. It would only ever be his image she would find nestling in any heart she possessed.

'Well, thank you.' She smiled up at him, keeping the tone as light as it had been between them despite the sudden wistfulness she was feeling inside. 'Now I feel properly decked out to grace the arm of the imperious Italian with the faultless taste.'

She knew the moment she saw his eyes cloud over that her response had disappointed him. 'You've always been fit to grace the arm of any man, Catherine,' he informed her deeply. 'I just happen to be the lucky one who claims the right to have you there.'

It was too much, too intense. They just didn't share these kind of deep and meaningful discussions. Never had done, never would do. It was the way of their relationship.

Shallow, she wanted to call it, but shallow didn't really say it either. Because there had never been anything shallow in the way she and Vito responded to each other.

What they really did was muddle on, never knowing what the other felt inside, because it was safer not knowing than finding out and being mortally wounded. So instead they used their love for their son as the common denominator to justify their being together—and the sex, of course, which had never been a problem where they were concerned.

And maybe her own clouding expression reminded him of all of that, because in the next moment Vito was smiling again, and the mockery was back when he ran a long finger down her spine and allowed it to settle low in the hollow of her back where the deep V in her dress finished.

'I have this terrible archaic urge to send you back to your room to change,' he admitted.

Turning to face him, Catherine baited him with a look 'Just remember who gets to remove it himself later,' she softly suggested.

Luisa appeared then, saving Catherine from a rather delicious bit of punishing ravishment for that piece of seduction. 'Oh, Catherine, what a lovely necklace!' she exclaimed when she saw it.

'I am reliably informed by the man who gave it to me that his taste is faultless,' Catherine replied mock solemnly

'Vittorio, your conceit will one day be your downfall,' his mother scolded.

'And there was I about to say that I get my faultless good taste from you,' Vito sighed—then, quite seriously 'You look beautiful, *mi amore*. How can a man be so lucky to have a *mamma* like you?'

'Now he is trying to use his charm on me to get him out of trouble,' Luisa confided to a smiling Catherine. 'It was always the same, even when he was as small as Santino.'

But she did look beautiful. A beautiful person dressed in shimmering gold satin who, two hours later, was wearing the soft flush of pleasure from the wealth of compliments that had flooded her way about her looking not a day over forty.

'She's enjoying this,' Catherine murmured to Vito as she caught sight of no less than three gentlemen gallantly vying for his mother's hand for the next dance.

'More than you are, I think,' he replied quietly.

But then, she'd had to outface a lot of curiosity from people she'd used to know three years ago. Not that any of them had been allowed to quench their curiosity about the present state of her marriage, because Vito had remained steadfastly at her side throughout the whole evening, as if to act as a shield to that kind of intrusion.

And with a hand lightly resting on the curve of her hip, so his thumb could make the occasional caressing stroke across the skin left exposed at the base of her spine, if she moved he moved with her; if she was invited to dance he politely refused for her. It was all very possessive, and deliciously seductive.

So the evening wore on, the champagne flowed freely, and the hired eight-piece orchestra played while some people danced and others went to help themselves to the buffet. And the only thing that seemed to be missing was— Marietta.

'Where is she?' she asked Vito.

'Delayed, so I believe,' he answered briefly.

'But your mother will be disappointed if she isn't here to toast her birthday.'

'Oh, don't worry,' he said dryly. 'I would say that you

can virtually count on her being here at some point or other.'

Catherine frowned, not liking the abrasion she had caught in his tone when he'd said that. In fact, when she thought about it, Vito's tone had been distinctly abrasive whenever Marietta's name had come up since their trip to Paris.

Had they had a row? she wondered. Then felt something disturbingly like hope curl her stomach. Had Vito actually come to accept that if he wanted his marriage to succeed this time then it had to be without Marietta in its shadows, and had he already called the parting of the ways he had promised?

Hope was a seed that could bloom all too quickly when its host was so eager to feed it. And Catherine was more than ready to do that tonight, with her man behaving so very possessively and with his diamond heart lying against the warm skin just above her breasts.

Good or bad timing on his part that he sent that intrusive thumbpad of his skating across the triangle of flesh exposed by the V of her gown? Whatever, she quivered, and she quivered violently enough to make Vito utter a soft curse beneath his breath.

'Let's dance,' he determined huskily.

It was an excuse to hold her closer. Catherine knew that as she let him guide her out onto the dance floor. His palm flattened against the silk-smooth skin of her back as his other hand closed around her fingers, and as she rested her free hand against his lapel he set them moving to one of those soulful melodies that had a nasty habit of touching the heartstrings. The usual vibrations that erupted between the two of them the moment their bodies were in touch with each other began to pulse all around them.

It was dangerously seductive, wholly mesmerising. They didn't attempt to talk, and the silence itself added fuel to their growing awareness of each other. When his lips touched her brow it was like being bathed in static. When his thigh brushed her thighs it set the soft curls of hair around her sex stinging in reaction.

And, in response to it all, she felt Vito's inner self quicken, felt his heart pick up pace beneath her resting hand and that familiar tension enter his body. Unable to resist the urge, she lifted her chin to look at him at the same moment that his lush, long curling lashes gave a flicker as he lowered his gaze and looked at her.

Their eyes suddenly locked. And for a short, stunning moment it was as if everything going on around them faded into the ether. It was seduction at its most torturously exquisite. He held her captive with eyes that were saturating her in the liquid gold heat they were pouring into her.

It was total absorption. Utterly enthralling. Because right there in the middle of a hundred other people she was sure she could feel love come beating down upon her from the one place she had never expected to find it.

'Vito…' she heard herself whisper, though she didn't know why.

'Catherine,' he said tensely. 'We have to—'

'Luisa. Happy birthday, darling!' a beautifully rich female voice called out in its warmest Italian and—snap—the link between them was broken.

Marietta had arrived. Dear Marietta. Even the music came to an abrupt standstill.

But then, if anyone could make a perfectly timed entrance, it was Marietta, Catherine mused cynically as she turned within Vito's slackened grasp to view her worst enemy.

At which point everything alive inside her froze to a complete cessation.

For there, framed by the open glass doors of the glittering ballroom, stood Marietta, dressed in a silver sequinned creation that was as bold as it was beautiful and did tremendous things for her wonderful figure.

But it wasn't what Marietta was wearing that was paralysing Catherine. That achievement was down to the man who was standing at Marietta's elbow. Tall, dark, extremely attractive in a very British kind of way, he was looking distinctly uncomfortable with his own presence here...

'Marcus,' she breathed, too shocked to even think of holding the name back.

So the tensing she felt taking place behind her sent her heart plummeting in a sinking dive to her stomach as she watched Marcus give a tense tug at his shirt collar before offering the hand and a stiff smile to Luisa, who was being formally introduced to him.

Marietta was smiling serenely while Luisa attempted to put Marcus at his ease, as you would expect from Luisa. But Marcus was beyond being put at his ease. It was so obvious he did not want to be here that Catherine could not understand why he was!

Confusion began to replace the numbing sense of surprised horror. 'But what is he doing here?' she murmured bewildered.

'You mean you cannot guess?' Vito taunted grimly.

'It has nothing to do with me, if that's what you're thinking!' she protested.

'No? I would say that his being here has everything to do with you,' he coolly informed her.

As if to confirm that, Marcus's restless eyes suddenly alighted on her standing there, with Vito tall and grim behind her. And colour rushed into the other man's face. It was awful. Like watching, helplessly from the sidelines someone slowly drown without being able to do a single thing to help him.

Then she caught the flash from a pair of malevolent eyes and suddenly realised that this was all Marietta's doing

Marietta had somehow managed to find out about Catherine's more personal association with Marcus and she had brought him here with the single intention of using that information to cause trouble.

But who could have told her? Her mind quickly tried to assess the situation. Certainly not Marcus himself. Besides his clear discomfort with his present position, he was not the kind of man who told kiss and tell stories.

And what was even more worrying was how Marietta was no longer attempting to hide her malevolence. It was out of the closet and on show for anyone to see—including Vito, if he wanted to.

Determined to find out just what was going on, Catherine went to break free from Vito. But his steely grip held her.

'No,' he refused. 'This is Marietta's game. We will let her play it.'

And he wasn't shocked. He wasn't even angry! 'You knew he was coming,' she realised shakily.

'It is very rare that anyone enters my home without my prior knowledge,' Vito replied smoothly.

Beneath his resting hands her stomach gave a quiver of dismay as a brand-new suspicion began to form like a monster, and she spun around angrily. 'This is all your doing,' she accused him. 'You told Marietta about Marcus and me. You helped her to arrange this!'

He didn't answer, and his expression was so coldly implacable that for Catherine it was an answer in itself.

Contempt turned her green eyes grey. 'I despise you,' she breathed, and turned back to look at the trio by the doorway just in time to see Marcus excuse himself to Luisa so he could come striding purposefully towards them.

He looked angry, he looked tense, and his eyes were filled with a mute plea for understanding even before he spoke. 'Catherine...' he said as he reached them. 'My sin-

cere apologies, but I had no idea whose party this was un
I was introduced to your mother-in-law just now.'

'It is called being set up,' Vito dryly inserted.

As Marcus glanced warily at him, Catherine took h
moment to break free from his grasp and stepped towar
Marcus. 'Dance with me,' she said, and before he cou
protest she had pulled him into the middle of the dan
floor and placed herself firmly in his arms.

'I don't think your husband is pleased that we are doir
this,' Marcus said uneasily.

Well, I'm not pleased with him, Catherine countered s
lently. 'Just smile, for goodness' sake,' she told him. 'A
tell me what you are doing here.'

On a low groan that was packed full of contempt for h
own gullibility, he explained about Marietta turning up
his offices that week, asking specifically for him. 'Havi
never heard of a Signora Savino before, I had no idea
all about her connection to the Giordani family.'

'She is my mother-in-law's goddaughter,' Catherine i
formed him.

'So I've just discovered.' Marcus nodded. 'She seems
nice lady, your mother-in-law,'

'She is,' Catherine confirmed. Shame about the rest
her family.

'But the goddaughter doesn't seem quite so nice.'

Catherine's eyes turned arctic grey. 'How did she get y
here?' She prompted him to continue.

'With that magical word *business*,' he replied. 'And c
we go somewhere less public, do you think?' he pleade
'Only I am beginning to feel distinctly *de trop* here…'

'Sure,' Catherine agreed, and stopped dancing to lead t
way out through the open French doors which led into t
lantern-lit garden, without even bothering to check wh
Vito was doing. She wasn't interested. In fact, she did

care at this moment if she never set eyes on the manipulative, vengeful swine ever again!

The air out here was warm and silken on the flesh. Catherine breathed in a couple of deep breaths of it, then said, 'Let's walk,' and began strolling down one of the pathways with Marcus pacing grimly beside her. 'Go on with your story,' she instructed.

'She lured me to Naples on the information that a well-known investment bank was looking for a new legal firm that specialises in European law,' he explained. 'When I asked her the name of the company she said she wasn't at liberty to give it until she had the go-ahead to make an official approach, but invited me over here this weekend— to meet some people—was the way she baited it. She sounded very plausible,' he added in his own defence. 'Extremely knowledgeable about what kind of legal expertise is required in the investment field.'

'She is,' Catherine confirmed. 'She owns stock in Giordani's, has a place on the board, holds some of their most lucrative portfolios.'

'Then she wasn't lying.' He frowned thoughtfully.

'About Girodani's wanting to change lawyers? I don't know, is the honest answer,' she replied. 'All I do know is that Marietta was one of the main causes for my marriage break-up three years ago. And since I came back here I have been expecting her to try the same thing again.'

'She's in love with your husband,' Marcus assumed from that.

Catherine didn't deny it, though she would probably use the word 'obsessed' instead of love. 'They work very closely together,' she murmured. 'Marietta is a natural charmer and Vito is—'

'Renowned for his troubleshooting qualities.' Marcus nodded. 'He turned Stamford Amalgamates round from bankruptcy in weeks only last year.'

'I didn't know that!' Catherine admitted, impressed without wanting to be, since most people knew that Stamford Amalgamates was about as big as a giant conglomerate could get.

'The fact that they were in trouble was kept secret to save the stock price,' Marcus explained. 'It was only after your husband had been in and waved his magic wand that those in the know discovered just how close things had been to collapse. He impresses me,' he added. 'Even though I don't want him to.'

'I know the feeling,' Catherine said grimly.

'Which means he's a dangerous man to cross.'

'I know that too.' She nodded.

'So why is Marietta attempting to cross him?'

'Because she is one of the only people Vito lets get away with it.' Catherine's smile was bitter.

'And the reason he does that?'

'Now there is the big question,' she mocked. 'I can give you a dozen maybes, Marcus. But no absolute certainties.'

'Okay,' he said. ' So give me the maybes.'

He was frowning thoughtfully—thinking on his feet just like Vito, Catherine likened wryly.

Which was probably why she liked him so much, she then realised, and didn't like the feel of that, since it also probably meant that she had always been looking for Vito-type qualities in every man she had come into contact with over the last three years.

'Because she is his mother's beloved goddaughter?' she suggested. 'Or because she was married to his best friend? Or maybe it could have something to do with the fact they are lovers?'

'Lovers in the past tense or the present?' Marcus asked sharply.

Catherine shrugged a slender shoulder. 'Both,' she replied.

'Rubbish,' Marcus denounced. 'That man has too much *nous* to play around with another woman when he's got you to come home to.'

Turning towards him, Catherine let her eyes soften. 'That was sweet of you,' she murmured softly.

But Marcus gave an impatient shake of his head. 'I wasn't being sweet, I was being truthful. I know men, Catherine. I am one myself, after all, so I should do. And I am telling you as a man that your husband is married to the only woman he wants to share his body with.'

Catherine stopped walking to turn sombre eyes on him. 'Then you tell me why you think you were brought here tonight?' she prompted gently.

He frowned, not understanding the question. 'It was Signora Savino who brought me here, in her quest to stir up trouble between you and your husband,' he replied.

'But who gave her the idea to use you as a weapon?' she posed. 'Who, in other words, told Marietta that you and I were more intimately involved than mere employer and employee?' she asked. 'Was it you who told her?'

'No!' he denied.

'And it wasn't me,' she said. 'Which leaves only one other person who knew about us.'

'Your husband?' Marcus stared at her in complete disbelief. 'You think your husband confided in that bitch about you and me?'

'Vito knew you were coming here tonight.' Catherine shrugged. 'He told me himself.'

'Then none of this makes any sense.' Marcus was frowning again. 'Because I can't see what either of them aimed to gain by bringing me face to face with you again. It served no useful purpose except to give us both a couple of embarrassing moments.'

He was right, and it hadn't. And they fell into a puzzled silence as their feet set them moving again—only to come to an immediate stop when the angry sounds of a familiar voice suddenly ripped through the air.

'You think you are so very clever, Marietta,' Vito rasped out. 'But what the hell do you think you have gained by bringing him here with you tonight?'

'Vengeance,' Marietta replied, and Catherine turned in time to see the metallic flash of Marietta's dress as it caught the light from one of the many hidden halogens. They were standing facing up to each other on the path that ran parallel with the one Catherine and Marcus were walking along. A neat boxed hedge surrounding a bed of pink roses was separating them. But that didn't mean Catherine couldn't see the malice in Marietta's face when she tagged on contemptuously, 'You have been flaunting Catherine at me since the day you married her—why the hell should I not flaunt her lover at you?'

'They were never lovers,' Vito denied as, beside Catherine, Marcus released a protesting gasp.

'They were lovers,' Marietta insisted. 'The same as we were once lovers! And when she tells you otherwise you know she is lying, Vito,' she added slyly. 'In the same way that she knows you lie every time you deny ever making love to me!'

'No,' Catherine murmured, closing her eyes as she waited tensely for Vito to deny the charge—now—when she could then let herself believe him at last!

But he didn't. 'That was a long time ago,' he bit out dismissively. 'Before I ever met Catherine—and therefore has no place in our lives today.'

Catherine felt Marcus's arm come around her shoulder when she must have swayed dizzily.

'It does to me!' Marietta insisted. 'Because you loved me then, Vito! You were supposed to have married me! Everyone expected it. I expected it! But what did you do?' she said bitterly. 'You settled for a short affair with me then dropped me. And I had to settle for second best and marry Rocco—'

'Rocco was not second best, Marietta,' Vito denied. 'And he loved you—genuinely loved you! Which from the sound of it was more than you deserved from him!'

'Is that why you did it?' she asked curiously. 'Because Rocco loved me, did you step gallantly to one side and let him have me?'

'No. I stepped gallantly to one side because *I* didn't want you.' Vito stated it brutally.

'Shame you didn't let Rocco know that,' Marietta threw back. 'For he died believing he had come between the two of us.'

'Oh, my God.' Catherine breathed out painfully, remembering that bright shining star that had always been Rocco, scintillating the world while inside he must have been feeling wretched.

As wretched as she was feeling right now, she likened bleakly.

'When you brought Catherine here and made her your wife he actually apologised to me,' Marietta told Vito.

'Not on my behalf,' Vito rejected. 'Rocco knew exactly how I felt about Catherine.'

'Are you suggesting that you married her for love?' Marietta mocked. 'Don't take me for a fool, Vito,' she scoffed. 'Like everyone else around here, we all know you married her because you had to if you wanted to uphold family tradition and make Santo legitimate. If I had known that getting pregnant was what it would have taken to get you to marry me I would have used the tactic myself! But such a sneaky manipulation didn't occur to me—unlike her,' she added witheringly. 'With her cool English ways and clever independent streak that kept you dancing on your toes in sheer fear that she was going to do something stupid enough to risk your precious son and heir!'

'I think you've said enough,' Vito gritted.

'No, I haven't,' Marietta denied. 'In fact I haven't even got started,' she pronounced. 'You had the arrogance to think that all you needed to do was banish me to Paris and all your marital problems would be over. Well, they will never be over while I still have a brain in my head to thwart you with!'

'So you intend to do—what?' Vito challenged. 'Lurk in some more dark corners listening in on private conversations in the hopes that you can discover some more dirt to throw?'

'Ah,' Marietta drawled. 'So you knew I was there.'

'On the balcony next to ours? Yes,' Vito confirmed, unwittingly answering one question that had been burning a hole in Catherine's brain. 'When you later began quizzing Catherine about Marcus Templeton, I then found it a simple step to put two and two together and realise that you were planning to do something as—crass as this. But what I still don't understand is what you aim to gain by it?'

'That is quite simple. I mean to bring about the absolute ruin of your precious marriage,' Marietta coolly informed him.

'By bringing Marcus Templeton here?' It was Vito's turn to scoff. 'Do you really think that my feelings for Catherine are so fickle that I would throw her out because you brought me face to face with her supposed ex-lover?'

'No. But by having him here Catherine will have someone to fall upon when I tell her that I am pregnant with your baby.'

'That's a filthy lie!' Vito raked out harshly as Catherine swayed in the curve of Marcus's arm.

'But Catherine doesn't know that,' Marietta pointed out. 'She believes we have been lovers since before she lost your second baby. For a woman like Catherine, who cannot have more children, believing that I am pregnant with your child will finish her, believe me,' she advised. 'And I am going to enjoy watching her walk away from you with her darling Marcus after I break the news to her.'

'But why should you want to hurt her like that?' Vito demanded hoarsely.

'I couldn't care less about Catherine's feelings,' Marietta stated carelessly. 'But I do care about hurting you, Vito,' she told him. 'Just as you made me hurt when you passed me on to Rocco like a piece of used baggage!'

'You were lucky to have him!' Vito rasped out painfully. 'He was a good man! A caring man!'

'But not a Giordani.'

'My God,' Vito breathed, sounding truly shaken. 'Catherine was right. You are poison to whatever you come into contact with.'

'And, being so, I really do think, Marietta, that it is time for you to leave now.' Another voice arrived through the darkness.

Four people started in surprise, then watched with varying expressions as Luisa moved out from the shadows of yet another pathway. And the moment that she could see her face clearly Catherine felt her heart sink in sorrow. She looked so dreadfully—painfully wounded.

Yet what did Luisa do? She looked towards Catherine and murmured anxiously, 'Catherine, are you all right, darling? I would have given anything for you not to have witnessed this.'

It was almost worth having her cover exposed just to see the look of stark, staring dismay that was Marietta's face when she spun round to face her. But if it hadn't been for Marcus's arm grimly supporting her, she knew she wouldn't still be standing on her own feet, right now.

'Catherine—you heard...' Vito murmured, and sounded so relieved that it was almost painful.

'Well, well,' Marietta drawled. 'None of us are above lurking in dark corners to eavesdrop, it seems.'

But they were the satirical words of a woman who knew she was staring right into the face of her own ruin...

CHAPTER TEN

CATHERINE stood on the balcony watching the red tail-lights from the final few stragglers snake stealthily down the hillside.

The party was well and truly over at last, though it had gone on for another few nerve-stretching hours after Marietta had left here.

Marcus had taken on the responsibility of her removal, and the way he had guided her away without uttering a single word in anger to her Catherine had, in a strange way, found vaguely comforting. Because she was not the kind of person that liked to watch someone being kicked when they were already down, and Marietta had certainly been right down by the time that she had left.

It had been Luisa's icy contempt that had finally demolished her. Luisa who could usually be relied upon to find some good somewhere in any situation. But for once she had chosen not to, and watching a relationship that was as old as Marietta herself wither and die, as it had done out there in the garden, had been terrible.

Luisa had wept a little, which had helped to fill in an awkward moment between Catherine and Vito while they attempted to comfort her. And then there had been a house full of guests to sparkle for, plus questions to field about Marietta's whereabouts and…

She released a small sigh that sounded too weary for words, because she knew that this wretched night was still far from over.

'Quite an evening, hmm?' a deep voice murmured lightly behind her.

Too light, Catherine noted. Light enough for the true tension to come seeping through it. Vito knew as well as she did that, no matter what had been cleared up during that ugly scene in his garden, the two of them had not even got started yet.

'How is your mother?' she asked, without bothering to turn and look at him.

'She is still upset, naturally,' he replied. 'But you know what she is like,' he added heavily. 'She never could cope well with discord.'

'She loved Marietta.' Catherine stated it quietly. 'Discovering that someone you love is not the person you thought they were can be shattering.'

There was a moment of stillness behind her, then, 'Was that a veiled prod at me?' Vito asked.

Was it? Catherine asked herself. And shrugged her creamy shoulders because, yes, it had been a prod at him. 'You lied to me,' she said. 'About your previous relationship with Marietta.'

His answering sigh was heavy. 'Yes,' he finally admitted. And as that little truth came right out into the open he walked forwards, to come and lean against the rail beside her. 'But it happened a long time ago, and—arrogant as I am,' he acknowledged wryly, 'I did not think you had any right questioning me about my life before you came into it.'

'It gave Marietta power,' Catherine explained. 'With you persistently denying you'd ever been her lover, it left her free to drop nasty hints all over the place. When you insisted you were doing one thing she insisted you were doing another. And she…' Turning to look at him, she felt her soft mouth give a telling little quiver. 'She—knew things about you that only a lover would know.'

Wincing at the implication, he reached out to touch

gentle fingertip to that telling little quiver. 'I'm sorry,' he said huskily.

It didn't seem enough somehow. And Catherine turned away from him to stare bleakly out across a now dark and very silent garden while beside her Vito did the same thing, their minds in tune to the heaviness Marietta had left behind her.

'She was out here that night, sitting on the next balcony listening to us bash out the same old arguments that we always used to share,' Vito said eventually. 'She must have lapped it all up. My continued lying, our lack of trust in each other, the mention of Marcus that must have seemed like a heaven-sent gift to her to use as yet another weapon.'

Standing in more or less the same place they had been standing that night, Catherine felt her skin begin to crawl at the mere prospect of anyone—worst of all Marietta—sitting there on the next balcony, eavesdropping on what should have been a very private conversation.

'How did you know she was there?' Catherine murmured.

'After you had gone back inside I remained out here, if you remember,' Vito explained. 'I was thinking—trying to come to terms with the very unpalatable fact that if your version of what happened the day you lost the baby was true, then a lot of other things you had said to me could also be true,' he admitted grimacingly. 'At which point I heard a movement on the next balcony—a chair scraping over the tiles, then a sigh I recognised, followed by the waft of a very distinctive perfume. Then I heard her murmur *"Grazie Caterina,"* and the way she said it made my blood run cold.'

He even shuddered. So did Catherine. Then, on a sigh that hissed almost painfully from him, he hit the stone balustrade with a clenched fist. 'How can you *know* someone as well as you think you know them—yet not really know them at all?' he thrust out tragically.

'She loved you.' To Catherine it seemed to explain everything.

But not for Vito. 'That is not love, it is sick obsession,' he denounced. And his golden eyes flashed and his grim mouth hardened. 'I decided she was out of my house by the morning and I didn't care what it took to achieve it,' he went on. 'So I went in to the office, worked all night clearing *her* desk, not my desk, and the rest you know—except that I used that week in Paris with her to let her know that her place in this family was over.'

'What did she say to that?' Catherine asked curiously.

'She reminded me that my mother may not like to hear me say that,' he dryly responded. 'So I countered that piece of blatant blackmail—by sacking her from the bank.'

Catherine stared at him in stunned disbelief. 'Can you do that?' she gasped.

His answering smile wasn't pleasant. 'She may own a good-size block of stock in the bank, but not enough to sway the seat of power there. And, although this is going to confirm your opinion about my conceit, I am the main force that drives Giordani's. If I say she is out, then the board will support me.'

'But what about her client list—won't you lose a lot of very lucrative business?'

'Given the option between going elsewhere with their investment portfolios or transferring them to me, her client list, to the last one, transferred to me,' Vito smoothly informed her.

'No wonder she was out for revenge tonight,' Catherine breathed, feeling rather stunned by the depths of his ruthlessness. 'You frighten me sometimes,' she told him shakily.

Catching hold of her shoulders, he turned her to face

him. 'And you frighten me,' he returned very gently. 'Why else do you think we fight so much?'

Because I love you and I still daren't tell you, Catherine silently answered the question. 'We married for all the wrong reasons,' she said instead. 'You resented my presence in your life and I resented being there.'

'That is not entirely true, Catherine,' he argued. 'At the time I truly believed we were marrying because we could not bear to be apart from one another. '

'The sex has always been good.' She nodded.

His fingers tightened. 'Don't be flippant,' he scolded. 'You know we have always had much more than that.'

Did she? Catherine smiled a wry smile that made his eyes flash with anger.

'Is it too much to ask of you to give an inch?' he rasped out. 'Just a single small inch and I promise you I will repay you with a whole mile!'

'Meaning what?' she demanded, stiffening defensively in his grasp.

A nerve began to tick along his jaw. 'Meaning I married you because I was, and still am, head over heels in love with you,' he raked out. 'Will that help you to respond in kind?'

'Don't,' she protested, trying to turn away from him, knowing it wasn't true. 'You don't have to say things like that to make me stay here. Marietta didn't do that kind of damage.'

'It is the truth!' he insisted. 'And it should have been said a long time ago—I know that,' he admitted tightly. 'But now it has been said you could at least do me the honour of believing me!'

Staring up into those swirling dark gold burning eyes of his, Catherine wished—*wished* she dared let herself do just that. But...

Lifting her shoulders in a helplessly vulnerable gesture,

she murmured dully, 'A man in love doesn't go from the arms of a woman he loves straight into the arms of another.'

He went white in instant understanding, and she felt like crying for bringing it all up again. But it had to be said. It had to be dealt with.

His heavy sigh as he dropped his hands away from her seemed to be acknowledging that.

'I did *not* sleep with Marietta on the night you lost our baby,' he denied. 'Though after tonight's little revelations I can understand why you may choose not to believe that.' Glancing at her, Vito searched her face for a hint of softening, only to grimace when he didn't find it. 'You used to drive me crazy,' he confessed. 'From day one of our marriage you made sure I knew that you were not so content with your lot as my wife. You were stubborn, fiercely protective of your independence and so bloody steadfast in your refusal to let me feel needed by you—except in our bed, of course.'

'I needed you,' she whispered.

He didn't seem to hear her. 'As hot as Vesuveus in it and as cold as Everest out of it.' He sighed. 'I began to feel like a damned gigolo, useful to you for only one purpose...'

And I felt like your sex slave. Catherine silently made the bleak comparison.

'But at least I *could* reach you there,' he went on heavily. 'So I didn't take it kindly when you fell pregnant once again and were so sick with it that the doctors were insisting on no exertion—and suddenly I found myself robbed of my only excuse to be close to you when making love was banned also.'

'We made love!' she protested.

His eyes flashed darkly over her. 'Not the grit your teeth, feel the burn, all-out physical love we had always indulged in.'

'Life can't always be perfect, Vito!' she cried, shifting uncomfortably at his oh, so accurate description of their love-life.

'The sex between us was perfect,' he responded. 'We blended like two halves coming together in the fiery furnace. And I missed it when I wasn't allowed to merge like that any more, and I found the—other stuff,' he described it with a contemptuous flick of his hand, 'bloody frustrating, if you want to know.'

Listening to him so accurately describe how she had been feeling herself, Catherine stared at his grim face and wondered how two people could be so wonderfully in tune with each other—and yet not know it!

'So I grew more frustrated and resentful of what you did to me week by wretched week,' he went on. 'Until it all exploded in one huge row, followed by the most glorious coming together.'

'Then you stormed off.' She nodded, bringing this whole thing painfully back to where it had started. 'To Marietta, in search of consolation.'

'I stormed off feeling sick with my lack of self-control,' he brusquely corrected. 'But I did not start out at Marietta's apartment. I started out at the office—where she found me too drunk to do much more than let her take me home with her while I attempted to sober up before coming back to make my peace with you. Only it didn't work out like that,' he sighed. 'Because I fell into a drunken stupor on her sofa, muttering your name and pleading for your forgiveness. And the next thing I know I wake up, too many hours later to even count, to find myself in hell, where everything I held dear in my life was being wrenched away from me. By the time I stopped spinning round like a mad dog trying to catch its own tail, months later, I realised that I deserved what I had got from you—which only made me resent you all the more.'

'I felt the same,' Catherine confessed.

'But never, since the day I set eyes on you, have I so much as *wanted* to sleep with another woman—and that includes Marietta!' he vowed. 'In fact,' he then added reluctantly, 'the three years without you were the most miserable of my life, if you want to know the truth.'

Catherine smiled in wry understanding, and felt herself beginning to let herself believe him. Maybe he saw it, because he reached out to gently touch her cheek. 'But I never knew just how miserable until the night I picked up the phone and heard your voice...' he told her softly. 'It was as if someone threw a switch inside me to light me up.' He smiled.

'You were as cold as ice with me!' she charged.

'Not beneath the surface,' he denied. 'Beneath the ice I felt very hot and very angry—it was marvellous! Even fighting with you was wonderful,' he confessed as the hand moved to her throat, while the other slid stealthily around her waist to draw her up against him.

She didn't fight—didn't want to fight. She was too busy loving what he was saying here, with his eyes so dark and intense and so beautifully sincere.

'I was not in your home for five short minutes before I knew without a doubt that I was going to get you back in my life, no matter what it took to do it.' He stated it huskily. 'Because I want you here. I want you to *know* I want you here. I want to wake up every morning to see your face on the pillow beside me and I want to go to sleep every night with you cradled in my arms.'

Bending his head, he brushed his mouth against her own. 'In short, I want us to be a warm, close, loving family,' he said as he drew away again. 'Just me, you, Santo and Mamma, in a small tight unit of four with no lies to cloud our horizon and no— What?' he said, cutting off to frown at her as Catherine's softened expression took on such a radical change that he couldn't miss it. 'What did I just say? Why are you looking like that?'

She was already trying to get away from him. 'I…'

'Don't you dare claim that you don't want these things also!' he exploded angrily, completely misreading the reason for the sudden way she had just shut him out again. 'Because I know that you do! I *know* you love me, Catherine!' he insisted forcefully. 'As much as I love you!'

Oh, God help me! she prayed as his angry declaration shuddered through her. 'Please, Vito!' she begged. 'Don't be angry. But—'

'But nothing!' he growled, and took ruthless possession of her mouth in a blatant act meant to stop her from speaking.

It was hard and it was urgent, and she loved him for it. But in all her life Catherine had never felt so wickedly wretched—because he was trembling—all of him! His mouth where it crushed her mouth, his arms where they bound her tightly to him. She could even feel his heart trembling where her hand lay trapped against the wall of his chest.

And if she had never believed a single word he had said to her before this moment, then she suddenly knew that she had to believe that any man who could be as affected as this must truly love her!

'Y-You don't understand,' she groaned as she wrenched her mouth free of him. 'I need to—'

'I have no *wish* to understand,' was his arrogant reply. But it was hoarsely said, and the look on his face was the one Luisa would call his frightened expression. 'You are mine! You *know* you are!' And on that he picked her up and began striding inside with the grim-faced, hard-eyed, burning intention of ravishing her—Catherine knew that.

'You just said that you wanted no more lies between us!' She tried to plead with him for reason. 'Well, at least give me a chance to be as honest with you as you have just been with me!'

'No.' The refusal was blunt and uncompromising as he fell with her onto the bed.

'I do love you!' she cried—and effectively brought him to a stop just as his mouth was about to take hers prisoner.

'Say that again,' he commanded.

'I love you,' she responded obediently. 'But I have a terrible confession to make, Vito!' she hurried on anxiously. 'And I need you to listen before you—'

'If you are going to admit that you and Marcus Templeton were lovers,' he cut in, 'then believe me, Catherine, when I tell you that I do not want to hear it!'

'Marcus and I were never lovers,' she shakily assured him.

His eyes drew shut, long dark lashes curling over dark golden iris in an effort to hide his deep sense of relief. And Catherine's teeth pressed deep indentations into her lower lip as she waited while some of the fierce tension began to ease out of him.

She watched those eyelids rise up again slowly to show her the eyes of a man who was not quite as driven by fear any more, though still dark and dynamic, with the kind of inherent passions that curled around the soul.

'Okay,' he invited grimly. 'Make your damned confession and get it over with.'

'I *do* love you,' she repeated urgently. 'I always have! Wh-which—which is why I just couldn't do it!'

'Do what?' he frowned.

She lost courage, and with it the words to speak. So instead she kissed him gently, softly, tenderly. But her heart was beating like a hammer drill and, lying on top of her as he was, Vito had to be aware of it.

His head came up. 'For goodness' sake,' he breathed. 'It cannot be this bad, surely?'

The fear was filtering back into his eyes. She bit her bottom lip again. Then the tears began to flood her own eyes as she forced herself to say what had to be said.

'I didn't take the morning-after pills,' she confessed in a frightened little rush of words that had him staring down at her uncomprehendingly. 'I couldn't, you see, wh-when it came right down to it. I mean—how could I destroy the chance of a new life we may make between us? It was just too—'

'No,' he cut in as understanding finally began to dawn on him. 'You would not be so stupid.'

'I'm sorry,' she breathed. With trembling fingers Catherine reached up to gently cover the sudden white-ringed tension circling his mouth. 'But I couldn't do it. I just—couldn't do it…'

Rolling away from her, Vito jack-knifed to his feet, then just stood staring down at her as if he didn't know who she was. It was awful—much, much worse than she had expected it to be.

'What is it with you?' he demanded hoarsely. 'Do you harbour some kind of death-wish or something?'

Catherine sat up to hug her knees and murmured shakily, 'It was too late.'

He let out a laugh—only it wasn't a laugh but more a burst of something else entirely. 'No, it damn well wasn't!' he exploded. 'You had seventy-two hours to take the bloody things after we made love that day!'

'I meant it was too late for me!' she yelled back in pained rebuttal. 'What if we'd conceived, Vito?' She begged for understanding. 'It would have been like killing Santino!'

'That's just so much rot, Catherine, and you know it,' he denounced. 'You have been taking the contraceptive pill for years! What difference could a couple of extra hours be to what you do every single day?'

'Not then.' She shrugged. 'But the night before, when we…'

She didn't finish, but then she didn't need to. Vito was well ahead of her. 'That is no excuse,' he denounced, 'for putting your own life on the line!'

'We don't know if I have done yet,' she pointed out. 'But at least I can be sure that I didn't deliberately kill another baby.'

His face turned pure white. 'You didn't kill the last one!' he shouted furiously.

Catherine flinched at his anger. 'I don't want to talk about it,' she said, and buried her face in her knees.

'Well, you are going to talk about it!' he rasped, and a pair of hands gently took hold of her head to pull it upwards again. 'You are going to talk about the fact that once again you have made a decision that should have been mine to share with you!'

'You wanted me to take the pills!' she cried. 'That isn't sharing a decision; that's me bowing down to what you decide!'

'Well, that has to be better than this!' he said in a voice that shook, then removed his hands and turned right away from her.

'I'm sorry,' she whispered again, but he didn't acknowledge it. Instead he strode into the bathroom, slamming the door shut behind him.

And Catherine lowered her head again, allowing him the right to be so angry—which was why she had let him go on believing she had taken the damned—stupid—rotten pills!

And actually—she had meant to take them. It had only been when it had come to the point of actually putting them in her mouth that she'd discovered she just couldn't do it

Not to herself, not to the child that might already have been forming its tenuous grasp for life deep inside her. So she'd binned the pills right there in Vito's bathroom then continued the lie with a determined blank disregard of the consequences.

Maybe Vito was right and she did harbour a secret death wish, she mused hollowly. But she knew deep down inside that this had nothing to do with death but to do with a chance of life. The maternal instinct to protect that life was as strong in a woman as the natural need to keep drawing in breath.

She hadn't been able to fight it, and somehow she had to make Vito understand that, she decided as she dragged herself off the bed and walked on shaking limbs towards the bathroom.

It had to mean something that he hadn't bothered to lock the door, she told herself bracingly as she twisted the handle and stepped bravely inside.

The room was steamy. Vito was already in the shower and his clothes lay in an angrily discarded heap over in one corner. Not really sure that she was doing the right thing here, Catherine walked over to the shower cubicle and pulled open the door.

He was standing with his back to the shower spray. Hands on narrow hips, wide shoulders braced, dark head thrown back to receive the full blast of the hot water right on his grim face.

A truly dynamic sensual animal, she mused, then smiled wryly at letting herself think of such things at a dire moment such as this.

'Vito,' she prompted quietly. 'We need to talk about this…'

His dark head tilted forward, then turned towards her. And his utterly cold dark golden eyes ran slowly over her while the water sluiced down his bronze back.

'You will ruin that dress in this steam,' was all he said, then turned his face back up to the shower.

Catherine gritted her teeth as her old enemy anger began to raise its dangerous head. And without thinking twice about it she stepped into the shower with him, silk dress and all, and firmly pulled the door shut.

She'd surprised him, she noted with some satisfaction as his dark head shot forwards again to stare at her in disbelief. 'What the hell do you think you are doing?' he protested.

'You are going to have to listen some time.' She shrugged determinedly. 'So it might as well be now.'

Forever the man to think fast on his feet, Vito responded by taking a small step sideways. Doing so gave the water spray unrestricted passage towards her, and, with a grim intention that galled, he leaned his shoulders into the corner of the shower, folded his arms across his impressive chest, then watched uncaringly as the water turned her red silk dress almost transparent before his ruthless eyes.

Diamonds glittered at her throat, at her ears, and on her finger. Her chin was up, her eyes flashing green fire at him at his black-hearted retaliation. But she didn't so much as gasp as the hot water hit her.

'Okay,' he said coolly. 'Talk.'

'I am a woman,' she announced, earning herself the mocking arch of an arrogant brow in response. Gritting her teeth, she ignored it. 'Being a woman, the urge to nurture and protect new life is so deeply entrenched in my very psyche that I would probably find it easier to shoot myself than harm that new life.'

'This is not the Dark Ages,' he grimly derided. 'In case you have forgotten, your sex stopped being slaves to your hormones a long time ago.'

'I'm not talking about hormones,' Catherine refuted. 'I am talking about instinct—the same kind of instinct that gives your sex the desire to impregnate mine!'

'Once again, *my* sex stopped being slaves to our sperm banks with the advent of condoms.' He also derided that

'It is called free sex—enjoyed by millions for its pleasure, not its original function.'

'Since when have you ever thought of using a condom?' Catherine scoffed at that. 'I don't remember you considering protection, even when you knew it was dangerous for me to risk getting pregnant!'

His jaw clenched on a direct hit, and Catherine noted it with a nod in acknowledgement. 'You left the protecting up to me, Vito,' she reminded him. 'Which therefore gives me the right to call the shots when that protection is breached!'

'Not at the risk of your own life,' he denied.

'You said it,' she agreed. 'It *is* my life. I made a decision that might risk everything—but might also be risking absolutely nothing, depending on how my pregnancy goes. That's a fifty-fifty chance either way,' she told him. 'Fifty-fifty odds are just too even for me to justify stealing from any child the right to survive them!'

'For goodness' sake,' he rasped. 'Your own mother died in childbirth, Catherine! What does that tell you about the risk you are taking!'

Tears burst into her eyes, making them glint like the diamonds she was wearing. 'I didn't say I wasn't frightened,' she whispered shakily.

On the kind of curse that turned the air blue Vito snapped off the gushing water, then reached out to drag her against him.

'You stupid woman,' he condemned, but it was a darkly possessive and very needy condemnation. 'How could you do this to us now, when we are actually beginning to *know* each other?'

'I need you to be strong for me—not angry,' Catherine sobbed against his shoulder.

'I will be strong,' he promised gruffly. 'But not yet,

while I still cannot make up my mind whether I want to kill you for doing this to us!'

Despite the tears, Catherine lifted her face to smile wryly at him. 'That was a contradiction in terms if ever I heard one.'

He gave a muttered growl of frustration and bent to kiss her. Then, 'Turn around,' he commanded gruffly, and without waiting for her to comply he twisted her round himself, then began dealing with the sodden length of zip down one of her sides which helped hold the dress in place. With an efficiency that had always been his, he stripped her bare, and, leaving her clothes in a wet puddle on the shower floor, he led her out of the cubicle, found a towel and began drying her with all the grimness of a man still at war with himself.

Or with her, Catherine corrected as she gazed at the top of his dark head while he briskly dried her legs for her.

'It might never happen,' she huskily pointed out.

'With our past record?' His mouth took on a scornful grimace as he rose to his full height. 'You are pregnant, Catherine,' he announced as he wrapped the towel around her and neatly tucked the ends in between her breasts. 'You know it and I know it. We don't need to await the evidence to be that sure.'

'I'm sorry,' she murmured yet again, with a glum sense of utter inadequacy.

'But not regretful,' he said, clearly not very impressed by the apology.

Catherine gave a mute shake of her head. He reached for another towel, which he tucked around his own lean waist, then grabbed hold of her hand to lead her back into the bedroom.

The bed awaited. He trailed her directly to it, bent to toss back the covers—then paused. 'Your hair is wet,' he observed belatedly.

'Just the loose ends,' she dismissed, not in the least bit interested in her wet hair because she was too busy waiting for whatever it was he had damped down inside him to come bursting through the restraints of his control.

'I love you,' she said, and inadvertently helped it to explode when he turned on her, grabbed her by the shoulders and gave her an angry shake.

'You don't deserve me, Catherine,' he informed her darkly. 'You give me nothing but arguments, heartache and grief and yet I love you. You mistrust me, leave me, and make me go through the horror of fighting to see my own son, and still I continue to love you!'

'I didn't know that then,' she reminded him.

'Well, you damn well do now!' he grimly responded. 'So now what do I have?' he asked her. 'I have you back where you belong, is what I have. I have you back in my home, in my bed and in my life, and what do you do? You tell me I have to go through the worry and stress and fear of losing you all over again because you hold your own life in lower regard than I do.'

'It isn't that simple—'

'It is from where I stand,' he informed her. 'In fact it is elementary from where I stand! Because this time you are going to do as you are told. Do you understand me?'

His hands gave her another small shake. 'Yes,' she answered meekly.

'No more working for money we do not need. No more fights to establish your precious independence. You will rest when I tell you to, and eat when I tell you to, and sleep when I tell you to!'

'You're being very masterful,' she said.

'You think this is masterful?' he questioned darkly. 'Wait until you have lived for nine months with me as your jailer and you will be very intimate with just how masterful I am going to be!'

'Sounds exciting,' she said, her green eyes glinting up at him with the kind of suggestion that had him tensing.

'Well, that is just something else you are going to have to learn to do without,' he informed her deridingly. 'Because sex is out for the next nine months, if you recall.'

'Are you joking?' she flashed. 'I'm not giving up sex until I have to!'

'You will do as you are told,' he informed her coldly.

That's what you think, Catherine thought, with the light of battle burning in her eyes. On an act of rebellion she whipped both towels away, then, with a push to his arrogant chest, sent him toppling backwards onto the mattress.

'I want you now, while you are still wet from your shower and I am dripping in diamonds!' she informed him as she followed him down so she was stretched out down his full length. Then she kissed him so sensuously that he didn't stand a cat in hell's chance of arguing the point with her.

'You are right; you are a witch,' he muttered when she eventually released him.

'A happy witch, though,' she said. 'I love you. You love me. It makes me feel so wickedly aroused,' she confessed as she trailed the heart-shaped diamond locket across his kiss-warmed mouth. 'So, do you want to fight some more or make love?' she asked. 'Bearing in mind, of course, that you have just ordained that we are not allowed to fight any more…'

Eight months later, Catherine was relaxing on one of the sun loungers reading a book while Santo played around in the pool. It was April, and the weather had only just turned warm enough to indulge in this kind of lazy pastime. But she put her book aside when Vito suddenly appeared around the corner of the house and came to join her.

'You're home early,' she remarked, accepting his warm kiss as he bent over her.

'I have some news for you,' he explained. 'But first—how are my two precious females?'

Catherine smiled serenely as his hand reached out to lay a gentle stroke across her swollen stomach. Learning the sex of their baby had been a decision they had made together very early on in her pregnancy, when neither knew what the future was going to offer them. Catherine had wanted to know as much about her baby as she could know—just in case. And Vito had not demurred. So Abrianna Luisa had become a very real little person to all of them, and that included her brother and her grandmother. But in the end they needn't have worried, for she had sailed through this pregnancy without so much as a hiccup to spoil its calm, smooth development.

'We are fine,' she assured him. 'But—what is this?' She frowned as he dropped a very official-looking document with red seals and signatures on her lap.

'You can read Italian,' he reminded her lazily, then walked off to collect a red and white football that was lying beside the pool and toss it playfully at his son.

It was several minutes before he came back to her. By then Catherine had finished reading and was waiting for him. 'She sold out to you at last,' she said.

'Mmm,' was all he said, but his brief smile held a wealth of grim satisfaction. 'Once our daughter has arrived as safely as the doctors have assured us she will, I will have the stock transferred to her.'

'Not Santino?' Catherine queried.

Vito shook his dark head. 'He already has a similar block of my own stock placed in his name. So…' He bent down to touch a gentle hand to Catherine's stomach. 'Marietta's block will belong to my Abrianna Luisa,' he ordained. 'And we can now put Marietta out of our lives.'

With a sigh, Catherine gazed out in front of her and thought about Marietta, living in New York now and working for another investment bank of great repute. She was happier there, so they'd heard via the Neapolitan grapevine. Like any addict denied her fix, she had eventually learned to overcome her obsessive desire to be a Giordani. And, as Vito had just more or less said, her willingness to sell him her shares in the company was final proof of that. 'It's time Santo came out of the water before he catches a chill,' she murmured. And just like that Marietta was set aside.

Vito nodded. 'Santino!' he called. 'Come and help me heave Mamma off this lounger. It is time for her rest!'

'Rest,' Catherine mocked as she watched her son power his wiry little frame to the edge of the swimming pool. 'What else do I ever get to do but rest?'

'Ah,' Vito smiled. 'But this one will be different. For I shall be there to share it with you.'

And his eyes were gleaming, because he was talking about spending an hour or so loving her—not the sexual kind of loving, but the other kind, that nourished the soul...

Sara Craven was born in South Devon, and grew up surrounded by books, in a house by the sea. After leaving grammar school she worked as a local journalist, covering everything from flower shows to murders. She started writing for Mills & Boon® in 1975. Apart from writing, her passions include films, music, cooking and eating in good restaurants. She now lives in Somerset.

Sara Craven has appeared as a contestant on the Channel Four game show *Fifteen to One* and is also the latest (and last ever) winner of the 1997 *Mastermind of Great Britain championship.*

**Look out for Sara Craven's latest sexually
intense romance:
THE BEDROOM BARTER
On sale February 2004, in Modern Romance™!**

ULTIMATE TEMPTATION
by
Sara Craven

CHAPTER ONE

'LUCY—check out the guy on the end table. Have you ever seen anything so gorgeous?'

Lucy Winters felt herself shrivel inwardly as Nina's penetrating stage whisper reached her ears—and, presumably, those of everyone else around them at the pavement café. She stared down at the guide to Tuscany she was studying, wishing she could climb inside it, closing the covers behind her.

Her only hope was that this unknown Adonis was either tone-deaf or spoke no English. But one swift, embarrassed glance in his direction told her instantly that her optimism was unfounded.

She saw a profile that Michelangelo might have sculpted in bronze, etched now with lines of total disdain. A high-ridged, aristocratic nose complemented a firm mouth, curling in contempt and annoyance, and a strong chin jutted arrogantly as their owner signalled to the waiter for his bill. He turned to pick up a flat leather briefcase from the adjoining chair, and for a moment his eyes, cold as frozen amber, met Lucy's.

They said that ice could burn. And Lucy felt as if she'd been scorched from head to foot.

She muttered urgently, 'Nina—for heaven's sake. He heard you.'

'Well, what of it?' Nina was unrepentant. 'That's what these Italian studs live for—being looked at—admired. There he goes.' She leaned back in her chair, sighing gustily. 'God, look at the way he moves his hips. I bet he's a sensation in the sack.'

Lucy, wincing at her companion's crudity, watched the
tall figure's retreat with more clinical interest.

Yes, he was almost classically good-looking, although his
thick, waving black hair was worn rather too long for her
taste, she decided with detachment. And he moved with a
careless grace which was probably instinctive rather than
studied. But he'd clearly resented being the object of Nina's
blatant interest, and made no bones about it either. And who
could blame him?

Not, Lucy thought, a man to cross.

She said drily, 'I think there could be more to him than
that. He was wearing a designer suit—probably Armani.'

Nina giggled. 'I was more interested in what was underneath it,' she returned, unabashed. 'I'm beginning to like
Italy.'

She signalled to the waiter to bring two more cappuc-
cinos, and Lucy returned to her guidebook.

Not for the first time in the forty-eight hours since their
arrival, she found herself wondering if she'd done the right
thing.

It had been a total shot in the dark, agreeing to share a
villa in Tuscany with three other girls who were comparative strangers to her. But she'd been desperate to get away—
to have a break—a complete change of scene.

And when she'd heard Nina, who worked in the accounts
department, lamenting the fact that the fourth member of
their projected house party had let them down virtually at
the last minute, she'd heard herself, to her own astonishment, saying, 'I'll go with you.'

Three weeks of Tuscan sun would have been unthinkable
while she was with Philip. He liked action holidays—white
water rafting, orienteering in Scotland, rock-climbing in
Wales—and Lucy had masked her apprehension and tried
to join in. Flotilla sailing in the Greek islands had been the
nearest thing to relaxation he would agree to, but Lucy had
turned out to be not a very good sailor.

Maybe his open irritation and impatience with her during that last trip should have alerted her to the fact that all was not well with their relationship. Or maybe love really did make you blind, after all, she thought, trying not to look at the pale band on her finger where his ring had been.

When he'd told her, quite abruptly, that there was someone else, she'd been devastated. But, looking back, she realised the signs had been there for a while.

She'd watched numbly while he briskly packed his things, and moved out of the flat they'd been sharing. Hers, of course, to begin with, but that was through choice. Now she had to choose again—to decide whether to stay there with all her memories or find somewhere new.

'You can always camp out with us for a while,' her sister Jan had told her, her pretty face wrinkled with concern. 'Until you find your feet.'

Lucy loved Jan, and her enormous rugby-playing brother-in-law, and her pair of permanently mud-stained nephews, but she'd known that moving in with them all, however temporarily, was not the answer.

'That's one of the reasons I'm taking this holiday—to think—to get my life sorted.' She'd tried to smile. 'It takes time to adjust.'

'But is this the right way to do it?' Jan sprinkled sugar over the fruit in the pastry case in front of her. 'Sharing a house with a girl you hardly know, and two of her friends?' She shook her head. 'Sounds like a recipe for disaster to me.'

'Well, you stick to apple pies.' Lucy tried to sound cheerful. 'I've seen a photograph of the Villa Dante and it looks fantastic, besides being absurdly cheap. It belongs to a friend of the manager of the Italian restaurant that Sandie and Fee go to after their language class.'

'Not a proper holiday company?' Jan's frown deepened, and Lucy hugged her.

'Stop being a mother hen. It'll be marvellous. I might even get some painting done.'

'Well, if you're sure.' Jan sighed. 'Oh, damn Philip. I can't believe he's done this to you.' She paused, giving Lucy a wary glance. 'Who is this new lady?' she asked carefully. 'Do you know?'

Lucy ate a slice of apple to cover her grimace. 'Remember he changed his job a few months ago—went to a merchant bank in the City? Apparently she's the chairman's daughter.' She added stonily, 'He always was very ambitious.'

'That's not the word I'd choose,' Jan said grimly. 'Well you forget about the two-timing swine and have a great holiday.'

That had been Lucy's intention, but she'd been conscious of her misgivings even on the flight to Pisa, when the others had taken full advantage of the free drinks offered by the stewardesses, as well as engaging in a noisy and uninhibited flirtation with a group of young men across the aisle.

Lucy, staying off alcohol because it had occurred to her that someone had to drive the rented car awaiting them at Pisa, had seen some of the scathing looks directed toward them by other passengers. She'd also been aware that some of the men opposite had girls with them who were beginning to look downright hostile.

But her attempt to cool the situation had been treated with derision by her companions.

'What a drag,' she'd heard Sandie mutter to Fee. 'No wonder her boyfriend dumped her.'

Tommaso, their landlord, had been waiting at the airport with the car—a smart little Fiat—and the keys to the villa. He was younger than Lucy had expected, efficient and more than charming, but she hadn't warmed to him.

And one glance from his bold dark eyes had told her that neither her slender shape, her smoothly bobbed hair nor her wide, faintly slanting hazel eyes held the least appeal for

n. Her companions, in their skimpy sundresses, high on
oze and excitement, were far more to his taste, and he'd
led them shamelessly while conducting the necessary ne-
tiations.

Lucy had not expected to hand over her share of the rental
cash, there and then, but the others had seen nothing
ong in it, so she'd supposed she was being overly fussy.
'Isn't there an inventory we should see?' she asked doubt-
ly, but Tommaso waved that away with one of his wide
iles.

'Any problem—you tell the maid, Maddalena,' he de-
ed.

'And if she can't deal with it?' Lucy's voice was cool.
e'd come to Italy to relax, but this was altogether too
ual.

Tommaso shrugged. 'Then you come to me.' He gave her
log-eared card with a hand-written address on it. 'I live
e, in Montiverno.'

Lucy, struggling to accustom herself to the left-hand
ve, as well as the unfamiliar clutch, felt consumed by
simism about the whole enterprise, especially when her
rry companions insisted she make a detour so that they
ld glimpse the famous Leaning Tower before they left
a.

Bloody thing looks straight,' was Nina's slurred com-
nt from the back seat.

Lucy sighed under her breath as she edged carefully out
Pisa and headed south.

t was a wonderful day, the sun warm in a faultlessly blue
, the faint breeze redolent of pine and rosemary. She
nd herself driving past fields of sunflowers, through tiny
ages bright with flowers and shuttered against the heat,
always on the edge of her vision were the untamed
ing hills. The others had fallen asleep, so Lucy had it all
erself, and was content.

Following the sketch map Tommaso had given her, she

bypassed Montiverno—a small town clinging to its rocky hilltop, and dominated by a ruined fortress—and turned into a wide valley lined by terraces of vines and silvery olive groves.

And, as she rounded a sharp bend, there, somewhat to her surprise, was the Villa Dante, its name carved into one of the tall stone pillars which flanked the gateway.

An imposing entrance for a holiday let, Lucy thought as she steered the Fiat carefully through the high wrought-iron gates and up the long, winding drive where cypresses stood like dark sentinels.

And when the house came finally into view, standing proudly back from a broad gravel sweep, Lucy felt the breath catch in her throat.

It was love at first sight.

She braked gently and sat, drinking in ancient walls the colour of pale apricot, the faded terracotta roof, the wide stone steps leading up to the heavily timbered front door.

The photographs in London hadn't done it any kind of justice, she thought almost reverently. It was like some exquisite antique painting set in the matchless frame of the golden Tuscan landscape.

'Well, it'll do,' Fee remarked as she emerged from the Fiat. 'I hope to God the plumbing works.'

Maddalena was waiting to greet them. She was small, her black hair was liberally streaked with grey, and she was patently nervous. She barely spoke or smiled as she led them on a swift tour of inspection.

The villa had been built on three sides of a large courtyard, surrounded by a colonnaded veranda, with the usual shady loggia on the first floor. In the centre of the courtyard was a large stone fountain into which water poured eternally from a tilted urn upheld by a smiling nymph, while steps led down to a broad terrace with a swimming pool, and finally to a tumble of garden with tall hedges, gravel paths and banks of roses and flowering shrubs running riot beyond.

Inside, the rooms were spacious, and while not over-furnished they gave the impression that each item had been selected with great care.

Lucy's eyes widened as she assimilated the dining room, with its frescoed walls, massive polished dining table set off by ornately carved wooden candelabra and tall-backed formal chairs, and then went into the formal *salotto*, with its exquisite ceiling, elaborately patterned in coloured plaster, the wide stone fireplace, big enough to roast one of the wild boar for which the region was famous, and the cavernous but supremely comfortable leather sofas.

All this grandeur for the kind of rent we're paying? Lucy questioned silently, but the others seemed to take it in their stride.

'A bedroom each, and a couple over,' Nina exulted. 'Let's hope we get lucky.'

Lucy was hoping for nothing of the sort. That kind of encounter had never been her style, and she felt too raw and vulnerable to contemplate even the most casual of relationships.

The first couple of days passed tranquilly enough. They sunned themselves, bathed in the pool and enjoyed Maddalena's excellent cooking. Sandie and Fee spent a fair amount of time on the telephone, having low-voiced giggly conversations.

Lucy could only pray they weren't calling home to Britain, or the bill at the end of their stay would be horrendous, and her funds were strictly limited.

But she would worry about that when the time came. In the meantime, she could revel in the drowsy ambience of her surroundings, and the unusual luxury of having a maid to wait on them.

Except, this morning, Maddalena hadn't turned up.

'Perhaps it's her day off,' Nina commented crossly as she

wrestled with the coffee-machine. 'Did she say anything to you, Lucy?'

'She hardly says anything at all,' Lucy admitted wryly. 'She still seems scared to death of us.' She looked at Sandie. 'Why don't you go down to her cottage and see if she's all right?'

'Why me?' Sandie bridled.

'Because you and Fee have been to Italian classes,' Lucy reminded her patiently.

Fee pulled a face. 'And a lot of good it's done us so far. But I'll try and get some sense out of her,' she added, with the air of one making a great concession.

She was back almost at once. 'There's no one there,' she reported. 'I had a look through one of the windows and the place looks deserted, as if she's cleared out altogether.'

'Oh, Lord.' Nina was alarmed. 'Our money—our travellers' cheques…'

But all their personal possessions and valuables were still safely in place.

'She must have got fed up with the job,' Fee said discontentedly. 'But maid servce is included in the price Tommaso's charged, so he can bloody well provide someone else. We'll tell him after we've been to the *alimentari* this morning.'

Which was how Lucy now found herself sitting in Montiverno's main square drinking coffee with Nina, while the other two shopped for provisions—something they'd volunteered to do, to her surprise.

They came back laden, and smiling like cats with a saucer of cream.

'You'll never guess who we bumped into in the supermarket,' Sandie said airily as she sat down. 'Those guys we met on the flight over—Ben and Dave. Ben's parents have got a summer place just a couple of miles away at Lussione. Isn't that an amazing coincidence?'

Her face and voice were equally guileless, but Lucy spotted the wink she directed at Nina.

They'd clearly been in touch with each other from the start. That was what all the phone calls were about, she thought resignedly. And this morning's shopping trip had been a rendezvous.

'So tonight we're throwing a little party—a welcome to Tuscany bash for us all. They thought it was a great idea.' Fee adjusted her sunglasses nonchalantly.

Lucy stared at her. 'You're having this party at the villa?'

'Why not?' Sandie challenged.

They were all glaring at her suddenly, looking as if they were waiting for her to put a damper on everything. As she felt she must.

'It doesn't seem the right setting for that kind of thing.' She felt about one hundred and three. 'A lot of the furniture's old and very valuable. And Tommaso may not want a lot of strangers on his property.'

'Well, if you're so uptight about it, ask him,' Nina flung at her. 'Get his permission at the same time you tell him about Maddalena. Ask him to join us, if he fancies it.' She looked at her watch. 'I'm going to look in that little boutique down the road. We'll see you back here in an hour.'

Now I really am the outsider, Lucy thought as she climbed up through the maze of narrow cobbled streets towards the *rocca*. Party pooper par excellence.

She stopped to check the address Tommaso had given her, frowning slightly. She'd asked for directions at the café before setting off, but the houses in this area seemed far too shabby and run-down for the man who controlled the Villa Dante. The paint was peeling off many of them, and the roofs needed attention as well, their tiles either slipping or missing altogether.

A scrawny dog, lying in a patch of shade, lifted its head and growled at her as she went past, peering at the numbers on the doors.

Tommaso's house was in the middle of the street. Two cracked steps led to the front door, and a broken shutter hung at a crazy angle from the main ground-floor window.

When the bell didn't work, Lucy hammered on the door, but to no avail. There was no sound or movement in the house.

She stood on tiptoe, peering through the window. The room was totally bare. No furniture. No sign of life at all.

Lucy bit her lip as she stepped back onto the street. First Maddalena, she thought uneasily, now Tommaso. What on earth's going on?

She glanced round, uncertain what to do next. Her phrase book didn't equip her to deal with errant maids and missing landlords, and she had the uncanny feeling, anyway, that she was being watched from several adjoining houses, and not in any kindly spirit either.

I'd better find the others—tell them, she decided, and began to retrace her steps, glad to get away from the mean narrow street and its unseen eyes.

But she must have taken a wrong turning, because she found herself in a different square altogether. No bars or bustle but dominated by an elaborate Gothic church, and completely deserted apart from the statutory pigeons.

Lucy heard her own footsteps echoing as she crossed the cobbles and she paused, wondering which of the many alleys leading off the square would take her back to the town centre.

The silence was oppressive—threatening. Then suddenly it was shattered by the roar of a motorcycle coming from behind her.

The pigeons flew up in a flurry of alarmed wings. Lucy spun round, had a confused impression of two figures leather-clad and anonymous in helmets, and realised a gauntleted hand was reaching towards her as the bike swerved in her direction.

She cried out, and tried to jump back as the hand snatched

at the strap of her shoulder bag and tried to jerk it from her. But Lucy clung on grimly, refusing to let go. She heard the snarl of the throttle, warning her that the bike was about to accelerate away, and was pulled forward, falling painfully onto the cobbles. She was going to be dragged behind the bike if she didn't release her bag.

She screamed, 'No,' her voice cracking, half in fear, half in anger. Then she cried, 'Help me, someone,' and heard a man's voice shout in answer.

She saw a dark figure running towards her, felt another shoulder-wrenching jerk at her bag, and then suddenly the metal clips on the strap gave up the struggle and she was left lying on the ground, winded, bruised but free, her bag still clutched in both hands, while her assailants sped off with the dangling strap as their only prize.

It seemed safer to stay where she was. Her heart was pounding, she was shaking all over, and she felt deathly sick. She was dimly aware of someone bending over her, of a man's deep voice speaking urgently in Italian, of a hand touching her shoulder.

'No.' She was galvanised into panicky reaction, kicking out. 'Get away from me.'

She heard him mutter something under his breath as her foot connected with his shin. He said curtly in English, 'Don't be a fool, *signorina*. You called out for help. Can't you see that's what I'm trying to do? Are you badly hurt? Can you sit up?'

Wincing, Lucy allowed him to help her into a sitting position. The hands that touched her were gentle as well as strong, and a faint musky scent of masculine cologne teased her senses.

She turned her head slowly and looked at him, tensing with dismay as she realised that her saviour was none other than the man from the pavement café.

Nina's designer stud, she groaned inwardly. It would be. At close quarters, he was even more devastating.

Handsome as a Renaissance prince, and, she acknowledged as his eyes narrowed in recognition, just as distant.

'So, we meet again,' he commented without pleasure. 'What are you doing, wandering alone like this? Don't you know it isn't safe?'

'I know now.' She lifted her chin and gave him her own brand of dirty look. 'Actually I was looking for someone, and I thought things like this only happened in big cities.'

'Unfortunately, criminal elements from bigger places now sense there's a living to be made even in towns like Montiverno.' His tone was dry. 'Now, let's see if you can stand.'

She would have dearly loved to slap his patronising hand away, not to mention his sneering face, but she let him help her to her feet. She was bitterly aware that she was filthy from her contact with the ground, and that her new white cotton trousers were torn beyond repair. Every part of her seemed to be throbbing, and she knew an ignominious impulse to burst into tears.

Instead, she said, her voice wobbling slightly, 'They wanted my bag, but I wouldn't let them have it.'

'*Stupida!*' he said crushingly. 'Better to lose your bag than be killed or maimed.'

Lucy pushed her dishevelled hair out of her eyes with a shaking hand. She said, 'I've just been through one of the worst experiences of my life, and all you can do is criticise.'

'No,' he said. 'That's not all I can do. My car is nearby. I will drive you to the clinic for a check-up.'

'No.' The denial was instinctive and immediate, driven by some deep female consciousness that motorbike thieves were far from the only danger in the situation.

He was very still, his brows rising in regal hauteur. He said very quietly but with cool, relentless emphasis, 'I beg your pardon?'

To add to her other ills, Lucy felt herself blushing ab

over as the amber eyes swept over her, slowly and comprehensively.

She said hurriedly, 'I mean—thank you, but there's no need for you to bother any more. I'm fine—really. Just—a little shaken.'

'And prey, I think, to certain illusions.' He was smiling, but there was no amusement in his eyes. 'I am offering my help, *signorina*, but nothing more. I do not require sexual favours as a reward for my assistance, whatever fantasies you or your friend may enjoy,' he added bitingly.

The contempt in his face and voice stung Lucy like a flick from a whip. There was no real reason to feel so mortified, she told herself angrily. He was a stranger to her, and she was never going to see him again, so what did it matter if he thought she was tarred with the same brush as Nina?

Yet somehow, and quite ridiculously, it seemed to matter a lot.

She said stonily, 'Think what you wish, *signore*. I'm grateful for your help but not your opinion of me.'

'Then accept my aid,' he said. 'Believe that I cannot simply walk away and leave you here like this.' And, when she still hesitated, he added, 'But on the other hand, *signorina*, I do not have the entire day to devote to your interests either. So please make up your mind.'

Lucy bit her lip. 'Well—perhaps a lift back to the main square. I'm meeting my friends there.'

'Of course,' he said softly. 'No doubt there will be more male talent to be reviewed. You should take care, *signorina*. You are not in the cold Anglo-Saxon north now. To provoke a Tuscan is to play with fire.'

She gave him a frigid Anglo-Saxon look. 'Please don't worry about me, *signore*. I'm fireproof, I assure you.'

Not that she felt it. Her abiding impression was that she had been run over by a bus, but she gritted her teeth and limped along beside him to where his car was parked in an adjoining street.

It was a sports car, naturally, black, long and low, with concealed power in every menacing line. Rather like its owner, Lucy decided, trying to extract some humour from the situation and signally failing.

She accepted his assistance into the passenger seat with as much dignity as she could muster, and sat in silence, hoping she was not bleeding onto his upholstery, as he expertly wove his way through the tangle of streets and traffic, out into the bustling familiarity of the main square again. Where he halted.

He said with cool politeness, 'You are sure I may not take you to the clinic?'

'Absolutely. The damage is only superficial, and I had an anti-tetanus jab before I came away.' Lucy was aware that she was babbling, and stopped. 'You've been very...' She halted again. The only word she could think of was 'kind', so she said it, although she wasn't convinced it was appropriate.

She fumbled for the door-catch, and he leaned across her to release it. Again she was aware of that tantalising musky fragrance, and of the disturbing warmth of his body close to hers. Too warm. Too close.

She met his gaze, saw a tiny flame dancing in the amber eyes, and heard herself swallow. Deafeningly.

He said sardonically, 'So you think you're fireproof?'

He leaned forward, took Lucy's chin in his fingertips and kissed her on the mouth, slowly and very thoroughly.

Then he released her, and, with a graceful wave of his hand, indicated that she was free to go.

Burning, Lucy stumbled out of the car. Only to hear his voice following her, softly, mockingly.

'I hope your Italian stud did not disappoint you. *Arrivederci, signorina.*'

Then, silently as a panther, the car slid away, and she was left staring after it, a hand pressed to her trembling lips.

CHAPTER TWO

FOR heaven's sake, Lucy castigated herself wearily, not for the first time. You're not a child. You've been in love with a man. You've lived with him. So one kiss, even from a complete stranger, is no big deal. Pull yourself together.

She was lying on the bed in her room at the villa, staring at the ceiling. Trying to get all that had happened into some kind of perspective.

The others had been genuinely shocked and concerned when they'd returned from their boutique trip and found out what had happened to her. At first, they'd wanted to call the police, but Lucy had vetoed this. She had neither the number of the motorcycle nor any adequate description of its riders. Besides, apart from the ruin of her bag and trousers, she'd lost nothing, and her only witness had driven off into oblivion.

She'd described him solely as a passer-by. It seemed wiser not to revive Nina's interest, or lay herself open to any inconvenient questions, she'd decided, passing the tip of her tongue over her still tingling lips.

Nina had driven the Fiat back to the Villa Dante with exaggerated care, while Sandie and Fee had plied Lucy with offers of everything from grappa to a homely cup of tea.

They'd been frankly sceptical, however, when she'd told them about Tommaso. The collective feeling was that she'd gone to the wrong address.

'I mean, would a man who owns a place like this be camping out in some kind of slum?' Nina had demanded, and Lucy had to admit it seemed unlikely. Tomorrow, she'd thought, she would make proper enquiries.

19

However, there was still no sign of Maddalena, which meant Nina and the others had to prepare for their party themselves.

Lucy, however, was not expected to help. Nina had escorted her somewhat perfunctorily upstairs, asked if she wanted anything, and vanished at Lucy's polite negative.

Once alone, she'd filled the big sunken tub which took pride of place in the adjoining bathroom, and soaked herself luxuriously, letting the warm water soothe as well as cleanse.

She had superficial grazing on her knees and elbows, and there would undoubtedly be bruising to follow, but she would survive, she'd decided with a faint sigh.

But her injured feelings were not as easily mollified, she'd thought as she'd dried herself carefully and put on her lemon silk robe.

It was galling to be classified with the man-hungry Nina, but probably unavoidable under the circumstances. However, she would never have to face her tormentor again, so the only sensible course was to put the whole basically trivial incident behind her, and enjoy the rest of her holiday.

Hers was not the largest bedroom, but it had the best view across the valley, and she liked the uncluttered lines of its furnishings and the plain, heavy cream drapes. It occurred to her now that the room was almost masculine in concept. Maybe this was where Tommaso usually slept, she thought, her flesh creeping at the very idea.

Someone had brought up a pitcher of fruit juice and some paracetemol while she was in the bath. It was a genuinely kind thought, and maybe it would mark a new phase in her somewhat chequered relationship with her companions.

They were younger than her, even if it was only by a matter of a few months, perfectly aware of their own considerable attractions, and looking for a good time. And where was the real harm in all that?

You should stop being so critical and join in more, she told herself forcefully. Make the best of things, starting with tonight's party. Remember that you're single too now, instead of half of a couple.

Aided by the painkillers, she slept for a while, her dreams confused and disturbing. And, throughout them all, a man's dark figure walked on the edge of her consciousness, his face as proud and beautiful as a fallen angel's.

She awoke in the twilight with a start, her hands reaching across the empty bed for a presence that didn't exist, and lay still, waiting for the drumming of her pulses to subside.

Philip, she thought. I must be missing Philip.

She did not feel particularly rested, and she was beginning to stiffen up, too, her bruises announcing their existence. It wouldn't have taken much for her to cry off from the evening's festivities and stay in her room, she acknowledged, hauling herself gingerly off the bed and over to the big, heavily carved *guardaroba*. But then solitude had no particular appeal either. It gave her imagination too much scope, she decided wryly.

Most of the clothing she'd brought with her was casual, but at the last moment she'd thrown in a dress that was strictly after-dark gear.

She looked at it without enthusiasm. Philip had urged her to buy it, against her better judgement, during the last week they'd been together. It wasn't her style, being brief-skirted and body-hugging, with the neckline slashed, back and front, to a deep V, which did no favours at all for her slender curves. And that shade of dark red was wrong for her too, draining her own natural colour.

It seemed to have been designed for a very different woman, and having caught a brief, piercing glimpse of Philip emerging from a fashionable Knightsbridge restaurant with his new lady—a vivid brunette built on voluptuous

lines—she could guess only too well who'd he'd been thinking of when he'd picked it out.

But it was the only party wear she had, she thought as
she zipped herself into it. And maybe it would do her good
to wear it, as a tangible reminder of how little her relationship with Philip had come to mean.

She had spent days and nights since their break-up tormenting herself with self-blame. Asking how she could have
been so blind, or why she hadn't suspected in time to put
things right—win him back.

Now, as she brushed her hair into a smooth curve swinging just above her shoulders, she knew there was nothing
she could have done. And found herself questioning for the
first time whether she should even have tried.

For the truth was, she realised almost dispassionately, that
the magic had gone out of their lives long before he'd left.

In the first, euphoric flush of love, she'd ignored the fact
that their lovemaking fell short of rapture for her. That
Philip had always seemed more concerned for his own satisfaction than hers. That, invariably, she was left stranded,
aching for a fulfilment which she could only guess at, having never actually experienced it in reality. And, towards
the end, it had become perfunctory—almost a mechanical
ritual because they shared a bed.

But how was it that she could suddenly see all this so
clearly? she wondered, biting her lip in confusion.

Because today a man had kissed her—someone she would
never meet again—and in those few moments when his
mouth had possessed hers she had been shaken to the depths
of her being, her body shocked into an instant arousal she
had never known before.

In her dreams, it was not Philip she had sensed at all, but
this other man—the warmth of his breath on her cheek, the
scent of his skin, the casual strength of the arms which held

her. And in her dreams she had wanted more—much more—than his kiss alone.

She looked at herself, half-wonderingly, in the mirror, her hand going once more to her lips.

She thought, Dear God, what's happening to me? And could find no answer in her heart.

In spite of all her good resolutions, Lucy could not get into the swing of the party.

The guests had arrived, already uproarious, bringing a crate of assorted wine and a ghetto blaster blaring out heavy rock.

Fee had prepared an enormous bowl of spaghetti carbonara, which they ate in the dining room. Lucy winced as she saw Dave carelessly stub out his cigarette on the corner of the huge polished table.

'What a fabulous place,' Ben commented, leaning back in his chair. 'You were damned lucky to find anywhere in this neck of the woods. When my parents first came out here looking for a holiday place, they found everything in the district belonged to a crowd called Falcone—bankers from Florence, by all accounts. And they weren't prepared to part with one inch of land, or a single brick of property.'

'Falcone?' Lucy questioned, frowning. 'How strange. There's a carving of a bird like a falcon over the main door here. I wonder if there's a connection?'

'Lucy,' Fee said patronisingly, 'is heavily into old buildings. She notices things like that.'

Hal leaned forward. He was tall and blond, older than the others.

'Maybe she could switch to the present day and notice me instead.'

He gave a mock leer, making everyone laugh, but Lucy noticed how his eyes lingered on her cleavage, and felt uncomfortable.

Ben picked up one of the bottles on the table. 'Or we could all notice this—Chianti Roccanera—one of the Falcone local by-products.' His voice took on a reverent tone. 'Dad would kill me if he knew we'd helped ourselves to some of this.'

Nina raised her glass. 'Then let's drink a toast to Ben's father, and all the Falcones, including the one over the door,' she said lazily. 'And our landlord, Tomasso Moressi, who managed somehow to beat the system.'

When supper was finished, they rolled up the rugs in the *salotto* and danced. Lucy found herself watching the pairing-off process with detached interest. That it was not going to be to everyone's liking was more than evident.

Nina singled out Greg, with whom she'd been flirting on the plane and who was, apparently, unattached, so that was all right. But Ben's girlfriend, Sue, was frankly mutinous watching him gyrate with a laughing Fee. And Sandie was blatantly intent on winning Dave away from Clare.

Aware that Hal was heading in her direction, Lucy decided hastily that she would be better employed in clearing the remains of the meal. The dining room looked as if a bomb had hit it, she thought ruefully as she collected the dirty plates. Food had been spilled. A puddle of wine had collected on the table from an overturned bottle and dripped onto the floor. A lamp on a side-table had been knocked over and damaged, and one of the beautiful crystal goblets had been smashed.

And the kitchen was even worse. Fee seemed to have used every pan and bowl to concoct her spaghetti. Lucy sighed soundlessly, tucked a towel round her waist, and set to work.

The noise of the party seemed to be receding, and presently she heard splashing and laughter coming from outside. When she went to investigate, she found them all down at the poolside.

It was a warm, sultry night, with the sky blazing with stars. The ornamental lamps had been lit, and someone had changed the cassette for one with music of a slower, dreamier tempo.

Greg and Nina were dancing slowly, as if they were welded together. He was kissing the side of her neck, pushing down the straps of her dress as he did so.

Fee and Sandie were in the water with Ben and Dave, obviously skinny-dipping, their discarded clothing lying in untidy heaps on the tiled surround. Sue's face was frozen as she watched them, and Clare was biting her lip, close to angry tears.

There's going to be trouble, Lucy deduced resignedly. And I don't really want to be involved.

As she turned to go, she found Hal blocking her way.

'Running out on us?'

Lucy lifted her chin. 'I've had a bad day. I think I'll go to bed.'

'What a wonderful idea.' He gave her a slow, meaningful smile. 'I'll keep you company.'

She didn't return the smile. 'I think you'd do better to stay with your friends,' she said evenly. She nodded towards Sue and Clare. 'Some of them don't seem very happy.'

'They can look after themselves,' he dismissed. 'I've been watching you all evening. You're a bit of a dark horse, Lucy.' His eyes slid over her, making her feel as naked as the revellers in the pool. 'So, what's your story?'

She took his hand from her arm. 'I haven't one. And, if you don't mind, I'd like to go.'

'Oh, but I do mind.' His voice hardened slightly. 'Whatever the lads get up to tonight, tomorrow it'll be kiss and make up with Sue and Clare. I've seen it all before. I'm sticking with you. You intrigue me.'

'I'm afraid it isn't mutual.' Lucy's tone was icy. She turned away, seeking another means of retreat, but Hal grabbed her by the shoulders and swung her round to face the others.

'The lady wants to leave,' he announced. 'What do you say?'

'Oh, let her go,' called Fee. 'Winters by name, wintry by nature,' she added with a giggle. 'She's no loss.'

'No, chuck her in here.' Ben's voice was slurred. 'Serve her right for being a spoilsport.'

'But don't ruin her pretty dress,' Greg added, leering, and Nina began to laugh.

'Off, off, off,' she chanted, and the others joined in, only Sue and Clare maintaining a tight-lipped silence.

Lucy froze as she felt Hal's hands, odiously familiar, fumbling for her zip. Felt her dress beginning to slide from her shoulders.

'No.' Frantically, she kicked backwards, her sandal heel connecting smartly with his shin. He swore and his grip slackened fractionally—momentarily.

It was enough. Lucy pulled free and ran round the pool towards the sheltering darkness of the garden, desperation lending her speed, in spite of her aches and pains.

She had some crazy idea of trying to reach the car parked at the side of the house. But there was something blocking her way again. Or someone, her mind registered helplessly as she was captured and held.

Greg must have cut her off. At the very least, she was going to be stripped and thrown into the water, and every fibre of her being recoiled in revulsion from the thought.

'Let me go.' She began to struggle fiercely, punching and clawing at the imprisoning arms. 'I said, leave me be, damn you.'

'*Sta' zitto.*' The low voice was grimly familiar. 'Shut up, you little fool, and be still.'

'You?' Lucy stared up at the dark, patrician face, and he

voice cracked with relief, and another, less easily recognisable emotion, as she acknowledged, 'It's you.'

Involuntarily, she found herself pressing against him and burying her face in his chest as she drew a shuddering breath.

For a moment he let her remain where she was, then he put her away from him and walked forward into the lamplight.

All heads had turned towards him as if they were on strings. The laughing and shouting had died away as if a switch had been thrown, to be succeeded by a strangely intense silence into which his voice, quiet and cold, fell like a stone.

He said. 'I am Giulio Falcone. And this is my house. May I know what you are doing here?'

'Your house?' Nina was the first to break the spell his appearance had created. She faced him, flushed, tousled and frankly aggressive. 'What the hell are you talking about?'

'Easy,' Ben intervened sharply. 'It is him. It's Count Falcone himself.'

'I don't care who he is,' Nina flung back. 'This place belongs to Tommaso Moressi, and we're renting it from him.'

'You are mistaken, *signorina*.' Count Falcone's voice was like steel. 'The man you speak of, Moressi, is no more than the nephew of my servant, Maddalena. He owns nothing apart from what he can steal,' he added contemptuously. 'I hope you have not been unwise enough to pay him anything.'

'I'm afraid we have.' Lucy spoke, her voice hollow, her hands shaking as she put her dress to rights. 'Three weeks' rent, plus the use of a car and maid servce. Only the maid has disappeared—and so has Signor Moressi.'

'I don't doubt it.' Giulio Falcone shrugged. 'Almost certainly word of my unexpected return spread at once, and he took fright.' He shook his head, more in sorrow than in anger. 'Poor Maddalena. She has always indulged that worthless fool.'

'Poor Maddalena?' Fee echoed shrilly. 'To hell with that. What about us—our money?'

She had climbed out of the pool, and the Count's face tightened with distaste as he glanced at her.

'Be good enough to cover yourself at once, *signorina*,' he directed with icy formality. 'I regret that you have been the victim of a confidence trick, but that is hardly my problem. What I must demand is that you vacate my house immediately.' He looked around, frowning. 'Are you all staying here?'

'No.' Ben was huddling into his clothes. He looked awkward and faintly ridiculous. 'My parents have a place near Lussione.'

'Then I suggest you return there. And take your friends with you,' Giulio Falcone added bitingly.

'No,' Lucy said forcefully, her shocked negation instantly echoed by Sue and Clare.

'You bring these slags back with us and I walk out.' Sue glared at Ben.

The Count's lip curled. 'We seem to have an impasse,' he drawled. 'I suggest you settle it amongst yourselves before I am forced to call the *polizia*.' He glanced at his watch. 'Shall we say fifteen minutes?'

His mention of the police had an oddly galvanising effect. Within seconds, the poolside was clear and the erstwhile tenants of the Vila Dante were on their way upstairs to pack.

As Lucy passed the door of the *salotto*, she could hear a furious argument going on between Ben and the others. Hal detached himself from it and came to the door.

'It's all right, sweetheart.' His eyes swept over her in an appraisal that combined sensuality with malice. 'You don't have to worry about a thing. I've got my own room at Ben's place. I'll make sure you're looked after—as long as you start being friendlier.'

She said with icy clarity, 'Over my dead body,' and went up to her room, two stairs at a time.

Her heart was thudding like a sledgehammer as she began to empty the chest of drawers and the wardrobe, hardly aware of what she was doing as she tried to think—to plan. She'd have to cut her losses altogether, she told herself as she piled everything untidily into her case. Somehow she'd have to make her way to Pisa and get a flight home. Anything else was unthinkable.

She presumed she'd be able to transfer the return half of her ticket to a different flight. If not, she'd simply have to pay all over again.

I'll worry about that when I get there, she told herself as she dashed into the bathroom to collect her toiletries.

When she returned to the bedroom, she realised with another thump of the heart that she was no longer alone.

Giulio Falcone was lounging in the doorway, watching her.

'You don't have to check up on me,' she said quickly, aware that her breathing had quickened, and resenting the fact. 'I've almost finished.'

'So I see.' He was silent for a moment. 'Are you so eager to go to Lussione?'

'You know I'm not.' She pitched her toilet bag into the case and rammed the lid shut.

'No? You don't want to be with your friends?'

She bit her lip. 'They're not my friends.'

His brows lifted sceptically. 'Yet I observed an unusual level of intimacy for mere acquaintances,' he murmured.

Lucy flushed, remembering exactly what he must have seen. 'They're just some people we met on the plane,' she said. 'Nina and the others wanted to give a party—and invited them here tonight.'

'Yes,' he said with chill emphasis. 'I have seen the trail of destruction they have left—particularly in the dining room.'

'I didn't get around to that,' Lucy admitted wearily. 'But I tidied the kitchen.' She lifted her chin. 'And I'm sure we'll be happy to make good any damage.'

He laughed. 'You are being naïve, *signorina.* Both the lamp and the glass were antiques of great value. Replacement would be impossible, and the cost inestimable.'

Lucy's heart sank. 'Well, we could all chip in,' she returned bravely. 'And, of course, the police may find Tommaso Moressi and get our money back. You could have a claim on that, I suppose.'

'I think Tommaso will be a long way from here by now, with his tracks safely covered,' Giulio Falcone commented drily. 'Leaving his unfortunate aunt, as usual, to pick up the pieces,' he added cuttingly.

Lucy looked down at the floor. 'I understand now why she didn't want us here. She seemed very frightened.'

'I can imagine,' he said sardonically. 'Yet it should have been safe. I had no plans to use the villa myself until the time of the vintage. But circumstances intervened.' He shrugged. 'You are unfortunate, *signorina.* You could so easily have enjoyed your holiday uninterrupted and innocently unaware that your occupation was illegal.'

The last word seemed to hang in the air between them, raising all kinds of disturbing implications.

Lucy shivered. She said, 'I'm not sure enjoyment is the word.'

'No?' The amber eyes surveyed her reflectively. 'Yet you are dressed for an evening of pleasure.'

Lucy gritted her teeth. That damned dress, she thought.

'A bad mistake,' she said. 'Like the entire trip.' She forced a smile. 'And being mugged was really the last straw anyway. I didn't need to be conned as well.'

'How did you meet Moressi—hear about this place?' he asked curiously.

'The others used to visit a pizzeria after their Italian classes. The manager arranged it. He and Tommaso must have been in league with each other.' She was silent for a moment. 'I wasn't sure about him from that first moment in Pisa. And when I saw this house—how beautiful it was, and how old—it seemed even stranger. He didn't—fit somehow.'

'He never has.' His voice was abrupt. There was another silence, then he said, 'So, what is the alternative to Lussione?'

'Pisa,' she said determinedly. 'And the next flight home.'

'That could present problems. This is, after all, the holiday season. There will be few spare seats available—if any,' he added starkly.

Lucy shrugged defensively. 'Then I'll find somewhere to stay—go on stand-by,' she said with more confidence than she actually felt as she did a hasty mental calculation of her available funds.

'Can you affford that?' Clearly he wasn't fooled.

'I don't have a choice.' She gave him a defiant look.

'How fortunate,' he said softly, 'that I was able to read your mind so accurately.'

'What do you mean?' Lucy was suddenly very still.

'Your friends have gone. I told them you would not be accompanying them.'

Lucy stared at him, suddenly, tensely aware of how quiet the house had become.

'You mean they've left me here alone?' Her voice almost cracked. 'Without even a word?'

His smile deepened. There was something pagan in the curve of his mouth, she thought, a stir of unbidden excitement warring with the growing apprehension inside her.

He said gently, 'Not alone, *signorina*. You forget that I shall be here too. From now on you will be staying as my guest.' He paused. 'And also,' he added softly, 'as my companion.'

CHAPTER THREE

LUCY stared at him. She was suddenly aware that she was trembling. That all the warmth seemed to have drained from her body, leaving her ice-cold.

There was danger here, all the more shocking because it was totally unforeseen.

Her hands curled into fists at her sides, her nails grating across the soft palms. She tried to keep her voice level.

'Companion, *signore*? I don't think I understand.'

'It's quite simple. You will remain here, *signorina*, to make reparation for the insult which has been made to my home—my family—by you and your—acquaintances.'

'*I'll* remain?' She took a startled breath. 'But that isn't fair...'

Giulio Falcone shrugged. 'By your own admission you cannot afford proper recompense for the damage that has been done. However, there are other methods of payment.' His smile barely touched the corners of his mouth. 'I believe we can reach a settlement that would be—agreeable to us both.'

'Then you're wrong,' Lucy said furiously. Cold no longer, she was now burning with shame and anger, and an odd sense of disappointment. 'How dare you even suggest such a thing? Who the hell do you think you are—and what do you take me for?'

'I am Falcone.' He threw back his head, the dark face arrogant, brooding. 'And you are a girl who has twice trembled in my arms. Can you deny it?'

'I was upset,' she flung at him defensively. 'The first time

33

I'd nearly been robbed, and the second I was running away. I thought you realised that—and why…'

'Ah, yes.' His voice was reflective. 'But, in that case, why tempt a man by wearing a dress that begs to be taken from your body and then deny him the pleasure? Your companions, after all, showed no such reticence,' he added, his mouth curling slightly.

She said shortly, 'I'm responsible for no one's conduct but my own, and I don't play games like that.'

'Are you a virgin?'

She gasped, the colour deepening to fiery red in her face. 'You have no right to ask me that.'

'A simple ''no'' would have sufficed,' he said mockingly. 'Although—' he sent her a narrow-eyed glance '—your eyes do not have the look of a woman who has known all the satisfaction that love can bring.'

'I don't know what you're talking about,' Lucy said haughtily.

He laughed. 'I'm quite sure you don't, but it will be an exquisite pleasure to teach you some day—or some night.'

There was a caress in his voice which shivered down Lucy's spine and danced in her pulses. She felt the muscle in her throat tauten.

She managed a brief shrug of her own. 'Fortunately, shan't be around that long. As I said, I'm leaving for Pisa.'

'Ah,' the count said meditatively. 'And just how do you propose to get there?'

Lucy paused in the act of locking her case. 'Why—drive there, of course.'

'I did not realise you had brought your own vehicle.'

'Well, I haven't, but…' Her voice trailed into silence as she saw his smile deepen mockingly, and the slow negative movement of his dark head.

She said unsteadily, 'Of course, the car is yours too. should have realised.'

'Not mine,' he corrected her. 'It belongs to the *contessa*.'

She was very still for a moment, her thoughts whirling blankly. The idea that he could be married had never even crossed her mind. Not, of course, that it made the slightest difference…

She said brusquely, 'Then she has my sympathy.'

'Why?' His brows lifted enquiringly. 'Is the car so difficult to drive?'

'Certainly not,' Lucy snapped. 'I meant that I—I pity anyone who's involved with a—a Lothario like you.'

'You imagine, perhaps, that Lothario was an Italian.' Giulio Falcone shook his head again. 'You are wrong, *signorina*. He was the invention of an English dramatist. Just as you seem to be inventing me,' he added, his tone dry.

'It doesn't take a great deal of imagination,' Lucy retorted. 'Nina was right, after all. You Italian studs are all the same.'

'The looks of a dove and the tongue of a wasp,' he said silkily. 'An intriguing combination.'

'Not for much longer.' Lucy swung the case off the bed. 'Will you loan me your—*contessa's* car to drive to Pisa, please?'

'No,' he said. 'I will not.'

She lifted her chin. 'Right—then I'll walk there.'

'In that dress?' He surveyed her mockingly. 'You'd be lucky to get half a kilometre. Even if the police did not stop you first,' he added, almost casually.

'I planned to change, given some privacy,' she said. 'I don't think jeans and a shirt would make me liable to arrest.'

'No,' he said. 'But there is the matter of trespass, which you seem to have overlooked.'

Fright was building up again, making her stomach churn. Her fingers tightened almost convulsively round the handle of her case.

She said jerkily, 'You can't be serious, *signore*. I—we acted in good faith. We didn't know this was your house.'

'That is hardly a defence,' he said. 'Especially when added to the acts of vandalism committed against my possessions.'

She couldn't argue. Her knowledge of Italian law was nil. Perhaps it ws one of those countries where you were guilty until you proved yourself innocent, she thought faintly.

She tried again. 'But you can't put all the blame on me. There were others involved.'

'True,' he said softly. 'But they have gone, and you, *colombina*, are the only one left to make the recompense I require.'

'You think I'm like them—like Nina and the others.' Her voice shook. 'But I'm not—I swear to you.'

'I believe you.' He lifted a negligent shoulder. 'Otherwise I would not want you.'

The amber eyes, hooded, watchful, swept over her, lingering on her breasts, the curve of her hips, the slender line of her thighs.

The dark face was coldly, almost dispassionately absorbed. Like his namesake, the falcon—the ultimate predator—with its prey in sight, and helpless, Lucy thought wildly, her body trembling, her brain teeming with desperation.

She said, 'You have no right—no right at all to keep me here against my will.'

'I think, under the circumstances, I have any rights that I choose to assume, Lucia *mia*.'

'Don't call me that.'

Giulio Falcone frowned. 'I was told it was your name.'

'Yes, but I didn't give you permission to use it.' She stood her ground, glaring at him.

'A minor detail,' he said softly. 'At such a time.' He

paused. 'And when we are already on terms of such intimacy.'

'Because I ran to you for help?' Lucy asked scornfully. 'In that situation I'd have run to Frankenstein's monster.'

'No,' he said. 'Because you have been occupying my room. Sleeping, *mia bella*, in my bed, which presumably you chose out of all the others. Doesn't that establish some kind of bond between us?' He watched the shocked colour storm into her face and laughed. 'Don't tell me you hadn't guessed.'

'Think what you like.' Lucy gritted her teeth. 'But I'll never spend another night in it, or anywhere else under your roof.'

'I don't think that is your choice,' he said. 'Make me the restitution I require, and I promise that afterwards you will be driven to Pisa, your air fare paid, and a suite at the best hotel put at your disposal while you await your flight.'

'No deal.' Lucy made her tone brief and cutting. 'I am not for sale, *signore*.'

'And I am not buying, *signorina*. But I am prepared to— hire you for a while.'

'You disgust me.' In spite of herself, her voice trembled. 'Call the police, why don't you? Even jail would be better than another minute in your company. And I shall have my own story to tell them too,' she added bravely.

'In my bedroom—in that dress?' He sighed. 'I think appearances would be against you, Lucia.'

'Your wife might take a different view,' Lucy flashed. 'Or does she take your lousy, deceitful behaviour completely for granted?'

'It would be worth keeping you here if only to teach you to speak civilly,' Giulio Falcone said grimly. 'Anyway, you are under a misapprehension. I have no wife.' He paused. 'You are also ludicrously wrong about my motives for detaining you.'

He saw the sudden bewildered question in her eyes and smiled sardonically. 'The little comedy is over between us, *signorina*. My interest in you, alas, is more practical than romantic. I hope you are not too disappointed.'

She said between her teeth, 'Not in the slightest—if I had the least idea what you're talking about.'

'Actually, it's quite simple. I have a problem to which you could provide the solution.' He gave a slight grimace. 'Early yesterday, my sister was in a car accident. Neither she or the two children were badly hurt—cuts, bruises and shock, that's all. But the *governante*—the nanny—was not so fortunate. She broke her leg, and has to spend some time in the clinic.

'Fiammetta wishes to come here to rest and recuperate but there is no one now to look after the children, and Marco and Emilia can be more than a handful.'

He spread his hands. 'I thought, of course, that Maddalena would be here to take charge until Alison recovers. The children are accustomed to her.' He paused. 'But, of course, there is no Maddalena. Only you, Lucia.'

'Me?' Lucy swallowed, aware that relief was being overtaken by a curious sense of deflation. 'But I'm not a nanny.'

'No,' he said. 'But you are here at this moment. You have admitted you owe me a debt you cannot pay. In turn I have ruined your holiday.' The amber eyes looked into hers, and she felt her heart thud suddenly and painfully. 'Tell me truly, Lucia, do you really wish to leave Tuscany so soon when you could stay here, and be paid for doing so?'

'I couldn't possibly,' Lucy denied, trying to control her flurried breathing.

'Why not? With my sister and the children, you would be well chaperoned, if that is your concern.'

Lucy saw the amusement in his eyes, the sensuous curve of his mouth, and decided it would be safer not to explore that particular avenue.

'But I'd be totally unsuitable,' she protested instead. 'You don't know anything about me, after all.'

'You are unused to children, perhaps?'

'Well, no,' she said reluctantly. 'I have nephews.'

'Of what age?'

'Six and four,' she admitted, an involuntary smile curving her mouth. She saw him assimilate that betraying tenderness, and added hastily, 'But it's still out of the question.'

'I don't see why. Marco and Emilia are slightly older, it is true, but they have had a bad experience and they need someone who will care, as well as give them companionship.' He added softly, 'In spite of your temper, Lucia, you do not strike me as heartless.'

She said shakily, 'That's emotional blackmail.'

He shrugged. 'You say you cannot be hired, and will not be bought. What else is left to me?'

She tried again. 'But your sister may have other ideas.'

'Fiammetta, as usual, will take the line of least resistance. And this is an emergency. They will be released from the clinic tomorrow morning, and will be coming straight here. I cannot allow them to find a scene of such devastation.'

'And this is where I come in?' Lucy's tone was hollow.

'Until tomorrow, when I can mobilise help from the estate, certainly.' He gave her a measuring look. 'If this had been a genuine rental, you would have been expected to keep the house clean and tidy, after all.'

She bit her lip. 'I suppose so. But if all you want is a glorified housemaid-cum-nanny, why did you pretend—let me think…?' She halted, vexed with herself for asking.

'Because you were so ready to believe that I was just some—latter-day Casanova.' The firm lips twisted slightly. 'The temptation to confirm your worst fears became quite irresistible, believe me. But while you are in my employment and under my roof you are quite safe.' He flicked a glance towards the tumbled bed. 'Unless, of course, you insist.'

She was angrily aware that her face had warmed again. 'I don't,' she said tersely.

'Then I suggest you find yourself another room.' Both his tone and smile were pleasant, and untinged by even a modicum of regret, which, oddly enough, seemed to increase her annoyance.

She met his gaze stonily. 'So, if I agree to help out, you promise that will cancel all obligations between us?'

'More than that,' he said. 'I will ensure you suffer no financial loss as a result of Moressi's trickery.'

He paused. 'You will also take with you, I hope, some unforgettable memories of Tuscany, as well as the undying gratitude of the Falconese,' he added sardonically.

'Naturally, that would be one of my main considerations.' Her tone was sarcastic.

Giulio Falcone inclined his head gracefully. 'I knew you would see things my way.'

'Did you?' Lucy gave him an assessing look. 'Tell me, *signore*, are you related to the Medici by any chance?'

His mouth twitched. 'Only on my mother's side, *signorina*,' he returned silkily. 'Why do you ask?'

She shrugged. 'I gather they were hard men to refuse in their day. And so are you, Count Falcone.'

'Then don't refuse me.' He smiled at her, reminding her unnecessarily of the power of his attraction. 'And I don't use my title, unless I have to. Call me Giulio.'

Oh, no, she thought, the breath catching in her throat. That was an intimacy she didn't need.

Aloud, she said, 'I don't know what to say—what to do…'

'Then obey your instinct, *columbina*.'

Instinct was telling her to get out while she could. To put herself at the furthest, safest distance possible from th

man. From his smile. From the charm that seemed to reach
out to her like a caressing hand. From the sheer sexual cha-
risma that turned the blood in her veins to warm honey.
And which, she reminded herself, he seemed able to exercise at will.

Somehow, she heard herself say, 'Very well, I'll stay. But
only till you can find someone else.'

'*Grazie*, Lucia.' His smile deepened, half-mocking, but
wholly disturbing. 'And now I suggest you change out of
that dress—before I forget all my good resolutions.'

For one long moment, his eyes stripped her lazily and
quite deliberately. Then he raised his hand to his lips, blew
her an amused kiss, and walked out of the room.

Lucy watched the door close behind him, and said loudly
and clearly from the bottom of her heart, 'Bastard.'

Her first action, naturally, was to find another room. She
chose one at the furthest end of the house from his, regardless of the fact that it was also the smallest.

Quite suitable for a servant's quarters anyway, she told
herself, swinging her case onto the narrow bed.

Her pulses still seemed to be behaving oddly. She
couldn't believe how easily she'd allowed herself to be
wound up. How could she have thought, even for a moment,
that someone like Count Giulio Falcone cherished even marginal designs on her?

The trouble was that at each of their prior encounters
he'd been at some kind of disadvantage, which in turn had
stopped her thinking rationally. That was the only explanation. And it provided a kind of marginal reassurance.

She still wasn't sure why she'd agreed to stay, however,
except that there didn't seem to be much alternative. He
was a wealthy and powerful man, who could probably be
ruthless.

But it wouldn't be for long, she appeased herself. No

doubt his sister would find a replacement nanny from some domestic agency when she'd recovered from the shock of the accident. And then the whole incident would dwindle into a little adventure to be laughed over ruefully back in England. Although not with Nina and the others.

And now to get out of this damned dress.

Lucy twisted round, feeling for the zip and tugging it downwards, but nothing happened.

'Oh, come on,' she muttered under her breath. 'You can't be stuck.'

But the zip, apparently, had other ideas, and remained exactly where it was. With a sigh of frustration, Lucy decided she'd have to cut herself out.

She was searching for her nail scissors, when there was a peremptory rap on the door, and Giulio Falcone walked in.

'So this is the sanctuary you have chosen.' He glanced around. 'A little cramped, don't you think?'

'I think it's ideal,' Lucy returned with a coolness she was far from feeling.

'As you wish.' He shrugged. 'But why are you still not ready? I was going to show you where the clean linen is kept.'

'Just give me general directions,' Lucy said tersely. 'I'll find it myself.'

'Is there a problem?'

'Nothing I can't handle.' She straightened, scissors in hand.

He surveyed them enigmatically. 'If you need to defend yourself, the range of knives in the kitchen might serve you better.'

'Nothing of the kind,' Lucy said crossly. 'My zip's stuck, that's all.'

'Then allow me.' He walked over to her, and turned her so that her back was to him.

She stiffened. 'I can manage.'

'Stand still.'

His breath was warm on her exposed skin as he bent closer to examine the erring metal strip.

'A thread has been caught,' he murmured. 'I think I can free it.'

Lucy waited rigidly, trying not to flinch as his cool fingers slid under the edge of the dress and touched her back.

'Don't be so nervous,' he chided softly, laughter in his voice. 'This must be better than attacking yourself with scissors.'

Not, Lucy thought with gritted teeth, necessarily.

He was infinitely too close to her, in the exact situation she had wanted to avoid. In the wall mirror, she could see his intent dark face, his lips only a fraction away from her bare skin. She found herself remembering, starkly, the feel, the taste of his mouth on hers, and was swept by a wave of longing she could neither control nor excuse. The movement of his hand against her spine as he tried to release the trapped fabric only increased her silent torment.

She said huskily. 'Could you hurry, please?'

'I am trying to be careful. I don't want to damage the material.'

'It doesn't matter.' She moistened her dry lips with the tip of her tongue. 'I'm never going to wear it again.'

'Truly?' He shrugged. *'In tal caso…'* He took the edges of the dress's neckline in his hands and pulled at them sharply. There was a harsh, splitting sound as seams and stitching gave way, then the entire bodice slid gracefully but inexorably from Lucy's shoulders, baring her to the waist.

For a stunned second she was motionless, then, with a small wail of horror and embarrassment, she snatched at the ruined fabric, dragging it up over her breasts.

Giulio Falcone stood back, watching her struggles,

amusement dancing in his amber eyes, along with something deeper and more dangerous.

She said thickly, 'How could you? Oh, God, how dare you do such a thing?'

He shrugged. 'I merely followed your instructions. I am hardly to blame if the result did not meet your expectations.' He paused. 'Although it exceeded mine,' he added, half to himself.

'Get out of this room.' She was close to embarrassed tears. 'Get away from me. I should have known I couldn't trust you.'

'Then you'd be wrong.' His voice was stern. 'If I was the villain you imagine, you'd be in bed with me now, and we both know it, so let there be no more pretence about that.'

He paused again, his mouth twisting. 'As it is, I'm going to tell myself, *mia bella*, that you don't have skin like moonlight, or breasts like flowers waiting to be gathered by a man's hands, and go downstairs.' He added laconically, 'I'm going to make coffee. If you want some, join me.'

He sent her a brief, impersonal nod and walked out.

Lucy sank down onto the edge of the bed. In a reeling world, she was certain of only one thing. She could not risk remaining at the Villa Dante. She had to get away.

She lifted her head and looked at her reflection in the mirror. A stranger with dishevelled hair and eyes wide with confusion stared back. A stranger huddling the remnants of her dress against the pallor of her half-naked body.

'Skin like moonlight…' The remembered words sent an aching shiver through her body.

She thought, Let me get through tonight—just tonight.

And realised it sounded like a prayer.

CHAPTER FOUR

WORK, and more work, Lucy told herself with grim determination. That's the answer. Keep busy—keep out of mischief.

Not that Giulio Falcone could be described as anything so innocent as mischief, she amended stormily as she changed into the comparative demureness of jade-green leggings and a matching sweatshirt, and kicked the discarded red dress into the corner of the room. He was danger—sheer and unequivocal. And she was all kinds of a fool to let him get to her like this.

Survival was the name of the game in this situation, and she knew enough about that, even if men like the Count were an enigma to her. A mystery, she told herself tersely, that she had neither the right nor the inclination to solve.

By keeping busy—concentrating on the task in hand—she could stop herself thinking—wondering about him. And once the children arrived her time would be filled anyway, she reminded herself. Their presence would provide her with a measure of safety at least until she could make her escape.

She found all the clean bedding and towels she needed in a huge linen press at the head of the stairs. Sachets of dried herbs had been tucked amongst them, and she sniffed appreciatively as she collected her first load. However foolishly Maddalena might have behaved over her nephew, her housekeeping had been faultless, she thought wistfully.

The rooms the others had been using looked as if they'd been swept by a tornado, with unmade beds, cupboard doors winging open, and empty drawers up-ended onto the floor, along with discarded hangers.

45

Wet towels decorated the bathrooms, with trails of dusting powder, and there were smears of hair gel and moisturiser on the mirrors and tiled surfaces.

Gritting her teeth, Lucy launched herself into the task of restoring order. Most of it was cosmetic, anyway, she realised as she made the bedding into loose bundles for future laundering. Luckily, they hadn't occupied the Villa Dante long enough to create the kind of mess that had to be scoured away.

Her own room—his room, she corrected herself tersely—she left until last. She stood outside for a long moment oddly reluctant to proceed. Then, steeling herself, she pushed open the door.

The room was safely empty, and, apart from the unmade bed, tidier than the others. She felt obscurely glad of that.

The long window was open to the night, and some faint current of air made the drapes billow into the room.

She walked over to the window, intending to close it, and paused, staring up at the star-sprinkled velvet of the sky.

People said that one's fate was written in the stars, she remembered wryly. But she could see no pattern, no rhyme or reason for what had befallen her over the past twenty-four hours in those chilly, far-off specks of light.

The moon, on the other hand, looked close enough to touch, spilling silver light like a swathe of satin across the distant hillside.

'Skin like moonlight…' The words seemed to echo and re-echo in her mind. Her hand lifted slowly, and touched the curve of her breast.

For a moment, she was still, then she wrenched herself back to earth with a faint shiver, aware as never before of the silence of the encircling night. In daylight, the Villa Dante's quiet isolation had been something to prize. But in darkness it only served as an unwanted reminder of her vulnerability…

Suppressing another shiver, she pulled the window shut and secured the latch. And, as she did so, she saw reflected in the glass a shadow moving in the room behind her.

The cry of alarm choked in her throat as she swung round, the precariously balanced armful of bedding sliding to the floor, spilling sheets and pillowcases at her feet.

'You're very nervous.' Giulio Falcone was totally at ease, even faintly amused as he walked forward from the doorway.

'Can you wonder?' Lucy said crossly, her heart thudding as she bent to retrieve the linen. 'I wish you wouldn't creep up behind me like that.'

His brows lifted. 'I came upstairs in the usual manner,' he pointed out with a certain hauteur. He paused. 'You seemed lost in thought.'

'Yes.' Lucy summoned a strained smile. 'Well—I have a great deal to think about.' She tried to sound brisk. 'And now I really must get on.' She moved purposefully to the side of the bed and began to strip off the sheets.

He said, 'You may leave that.'

'Beds don't change themselves.' Oh, God, she thought. I sound like the whimsical housekeeper in some ancient TV series.

'Then let it stay as it is.' The faint smile playing about his lips deepened as he saw her straighten slowly and send him a questioning look. 'Or do you think, *mia bella*, that I would object to sleeping with the scent of your skin, your hair on my pillow?' he asked softly. 'I promise I would not.'

She was angrily aware that she'd been lured into blushing again. She said, with an assumption of calmness, 'You gave me a job to do, *signore*. This is part of it.'

'Then it must wait,' he dictated. 'The coffee is ready, and 've prepared some food for us as well.'

Lucy's eyes widened. 'You can cook?'

He said with a trace of impatience, 'I am not the effete

aristocrat you seem to think. I have learned, over the years, to be reasonably self-sufficient. I can even make my own bed,' he added drily. 'So come now and eat.'

'But we can't sit down to a meal in the middle of the night,' Lucy objected.

'Why not? If an appetite exists, it should be satisfied.' The amber eyes swept over her. 'Or don't you agree?'

Lucy bit her lip. She suspected the question had little to do with food, and that he was being deliberately provocative again, but to challenge him would undoubtedly lead her into deep waters, and probably make her look ridiculous.

So she followed him reluctantly downstairs. As they passed the open door to the dining room, she saw that it had been restored to its former shining splendour.

'Oh!' she exclaimed. 'I meant to do that next.'

'And now there is no need,' he returned. 'All the same, I hope you won't object if we eat in the kitchen.'

'I'd prefer it,' she said coolly. 'Isn't that where servants belong?' And she registered his swift frown with inner satisfaction.

But her jaw dropped when she saw the omelette he'd produced, succulent with fresh herbs, ham, tomatoes, peppers and cheese. Clearly he'd used everything in the fridge. And warmed some bread as well, she noticed weakly as she sat down. Not to mention opened a bottle of wine.

'I can't eat all this,' she protested as he put a plate in front of her. 'I'll be awake for the rest of the night...' Her voice trailed away in embarrassment as his brows lifted in overtly mocking speculation.

'You think so? Well, eat anyway. Build up your strength.' His smile touched her like silk. 'You will need it.'

The words seemed to hang in the air between them, half threat, half-promise.

Lucy stiffened. 'May I ask why?'

'To handle Marco and Emilia, of course.' He picked up his fork. 'What else, *columbina*?'

His smile seemed to mock her, and if Lucy hadn't been suddenly so ravenous she'd have thrown the plateful of eggs in his face. Instead, she decided it would be infinitely safer to pursue the impersonal topic of her future charges.

'Are they so bad?' she asked, savouring her first mouth-watering forkful.

Giulio Falcone reflected for a moment. 'Not so much bad as over-indulged,' he decided laconically. 'Sergio, their father, is the disciplinarian in the family, but his work takes him away a great deal, which unfortunately leaves the children to the tender mercies of Fiammetta.'

He sighed. 'She is, you must understand, as lazy as she is charming…and altogether too susceptible to outside influences,' he added with a slight frown.

Lucy's brows lifted. 'That's an odd thing to say about your own sister.'

'Ah.' The Count poured some wine into her glass before she could stop him. 'But then, she is not strictly my sister. She is the daughter of my father's second wife, now his widow.'

Lucy digested this along with another greedy mouthful of omelette. 'In other words, your stepsister.'

'*Sì.*' He nodded, lifting his glass. '*Salute.*'

She returned the toast uncertainly, taking only a cautious sip, conscious of the need to keep her wits about her, un-fuddled by alcohol, or anything else.

'So the *contessa* you mentioned is actually your step-mother?'

'Yes.' The word was clipped, the firm mouth suddenly harder.

No love lost there, Lucy silently deduced. Aloud, she said, 'Will she be coming here too?'

'No. She lives in Rome for most of the year, and spends

the summer mainly in Zurich and the South of France.' He added unemotionally, 'She is bored here and visits as little as possible, although I insist she attends the celebrations after the vintage. The workers on the estate expect it.'

'How could anyone hate it here?' Lucy said, half to herself. 'It's like heaven.'

Giulio Falcone shrugged a shoulder. 'The two faces of the Villa Dante.' His smile was thin-lipped. 'As the poet himself might have said—for you, Paradise, but for Claudia, Purgatory.'

'Yet the Fiat belongs to her. You said so.' Lucy frowned slightly. 'If the *contessa* comes here so rarely, why does she bother with a car?'

He shrugged again. 'As an escape route,' he said. 'Away from the tedium of the vineyards and country life to visit friends in Florence and Siena. Shopping, gossip and cards are her favourite pastimes.'

Lucy heard the edge of contempt in his voice.

She said slowly, 'We can't all like the same places—the same things…'

'This was my father's favourite retreat.' The dark face was brooding. 'Until, that is, Claudia's advent into his life, after which his visits were kept to a minimum,' he added tautly.

Lucy said haltingly, 'If your stepmother likes people—company—I can see why this wouldn't be much of a refuge.'

He looked at her sombrely. 'At your age, what do you know about needing a refuge?' he demanded.

'Perhaps more than you think,' she muttered, feeling the muscles in her throat tighten uncontrollably.

There was a brief silence, then Giulio Falcone reached across the table, tracing the pale circle on her finger where Philip's ring had been. His touch was light, but a faint tremor shivered through her nerve-endings just the same.

'What are you running from, little one? An unhappy marriage?' he asked quietly.

'No.' Lucy shook her head vigorously to disguise her instinctive reaction. 'We—we hadn't got that far—fortunately.'

'Fortunate indeed,' he murmured. The amber eyes glinted at her. 'So what went wrong?'

She shrugged. 'He met someone else.' She gave a small, painful smile. 'Someone with more to offer.'

'He told you that?'

'Not in so many words. He wasn't that cruel. But I—I drew my own conclusions.'

'And you are still sad?'

Am I? she wondered. Suddenly she wasn't sure. Philip seemed to belong to a different time—another existence. She barely recognised her own emotions any more.

Abruptly, she pulled her hand away. 'Of course. It was a—whole part of my life.'

'*Non importa,*' he said softly. 'A few weeks of Tuscan sun, *mia bella*, and that mark will soon vanish.'

Lucy tucked the offending hand away on her lap, under the edge of the table. Out of harm's way, she told herself sternly, aware of the swift hammering of her pulses.

It occurred to her that unless she was careful she could leave Tuscany not merely marked but scarred for life—the pain Philip had caused a mere pin-prick by comparison.

A few weeks, she thought, was far too long for safety. She had to get away, and soon.

She took a breath. 'To get back to the children,' she said carefully. 'Won't there be a language problem? My Italian is practically non-existent...'

'It doesn't matter.' His hand gestured dismissively. 'They are both bilingual. Much of their childhood has been spent in Britain and the States, and Sergio has insisted that they speak English as much as their mother tongue. On that score at least there will be no difficulty,' he added, half to himself.

'I see.' Marco and Emilia were clearly the children from hell, Lucy thought resignedly as she forked up the last succulent piece of omelette. She decided on another change of subject. 'Your own English is very good, *signore*,' she offered politely.

'It could improve,' he said, with a grimace. 'And it should, as so much of our bank's business is transacted in your country. Also, I have lived there for varying periods throughout my life. But not recently.' The amber eyes met hers quizzically. 'Otherwise we might have met before.'

To look away would be a sign of weakness, Lucy decided breathlessly. 'I don't think so.' She managed to keep her voice sedate. 'We move in very different worlds, after all.'

He inclined his head in acknowledgement. 'But sometimes worlds collide, Lucia. Don't you believe in the force of destiny?'

'I think I prefer to stick to practicalities.'

'So tell me about the practical side of your world. You have a job?'

'Yes. I trained in graphic design and now I work in advertising.'

'Your company?'

She told him, and his brows lifted in amused respect. 'Impressive, Lucia. But you don't think it possible that my bank or one of our associates might come to your organisation to publicise the services we offer.'

She smiled. 'I think it unlikely, *signore*. And almost certainly unnecessary.'

Giulio Falcone laughed. 'You could be right. So let me be practical again. My English has grown a little—rusty—is that the word? Perhaps you could give me some lessons.'

Lucy lifted her chin and met his teasing glance head-on. She said composedly, 'I doubt whether I could teach you thing, *signore*. Besides, I shall clearly have my hands full with Marco and Emilia.' She pushed her chair back and rose to her feet, summoning a bright, meaningless smile. 'And now I'd better get some rest. Big day tomorrow.'

Giulio Falcone courteously stood up. 'Sleep well, Lucia. But remember this.' His voice followed her as she went to the door, almost stumbling in her attempt not to hurry. 'Destiny has placed you in my world now. And there is nowhere for you to run to.'

Not, Lucy thought as she went up to her room, a thought to induce restful slumber.

She shut the door behind her with some force and leaned back against its panels, sudden tears pricking at her eyes.

She said aloud, her voice ragged, 'Damn him.'

In spite of her forebodings, Lucy went to sleep almost as soon as her head touched the pillow.

When she awoke next day, sunlight was pouring like thick warm syrup through a gap in the shutters and pooling onto the shining floor. For a moment, she was totally disorientated, then as memory returned she sat up with a jerk.

Hell, she thought frantically. I must have overslept.

She grabbed her watch from the night table, and saw with horror that it was past ten o'clock.

Hardly the right time for a working day to start, she told herself, swinging her feet to the tiled floor. She could only hope that her autocratic employer might have overslept too.

She showered swiftly, debating what in her limited wardrobe would be considered suitable for a surrogate nanny. In the end, she settled for a brief button-through denim skirt, topped by a white blouse, scoop-necked and sleeveless. She brushed her hair back severely from her face, securing it at the nape of her neck with a tortoiseshell clip, and pushed her feet into flat leather sandals.

She looked neat, she decided without enthusiasm, and relatively businesslike.

As she passed Giulio Falcone's room, she saw that the door was open and the bed, though rumpled, was unoccupied. So he'd beaten her to it after all, she thought, with a faint grimace.

She was expecting some sarcastic remark or even a silken reprimand when she arrived downstairs, but, to her surprise, there was no sign of him. The place seemed deserted, although the coffee-machine had been in use, she saw when she entered the kitchen.

She poured herself some fruit juice from the pitcher in the fridge and sipped it slowly, leaning against the frame of the back door, looking out into the courtyard which housed the garages. Giulio Falcone's car was nowhere to be seen, she realised, although the Fiat waited in its usual place.

Above Lucy's head, a flowering vine hung motionless, not a leaf or a petal stirred by so much as a passing breath of air. She put up a hand and lifted the hair away from the back of her neck with a small sigh. This, evidently, was going to be a scorchingly hot day.

The kind of day she'd come to Tuscany to enjoy, if only things had been different. If only, she thought with longing, she were a free agent again.

Free. The word shivered through her consciousness, and took hold.

She looked again at the Fiat and drew a breath. Well, why not? she argued inwardly. Her jailer had disappeared and left the prison gates open, so why stay a moment longer than she had to? Why should she carry the can for everything when Nina and co. had escaped? She'd made all the amends that were strictly necessary by getting the bedrooms ready for the new arrivals.

Last night, she'd been almost mesmerised into accepting his terms, she thought defensively. But now it was daylight and she was wide awake and ready to fight back. To escape. Because there was somewhere to run to after all.

And the noble Count Falcone could simply find someone else to look after his charming stepsister and her spoiled brats, she told herself decisively.

She said aloud, 'I'm going home—now. While I still can.'

She left her unfinished juice in the kitchen and sped back upstairs to her room, where she piled her belongings haphazardly into her case.

Then, for a long moment, she stood at the top of the stairs, heart hammering oddly, ears stretched for the least indication of his return. But there was only silence, so, resisting an impulse to tiptoe, she went downstairs and out to the car.

To her surprise, it was locked. I don't remember doing that, she thought, rummaging in her bag for the keys. In view of the villa's isolation, security hadn't seemed a major issue.

But the keys didn't seem to be there. Irritated, Lucy tipped her bag out on the bonnet of the car and sorted through the contents, only to remember with a sinking heart that Nina had driven back yesterday from Montiverno.

Oh, no, she groaned inwardly. Don't say she's taken them off with her. She thought back, trying to remember their return to the villa. She'd gone straight to her room—*his* room—and Nina had been with her. She was almost certain she could recall the other girl tossing the keys down onto the dressing table—the clatter as they skidded across its polished surface.

If that was where they'd been, there was an outside chance that they'd be there still. That Giulio Falcone hadn't noticed their presence. He'd have been too tired last night, she thought. And this morning, with luck, he'd have had other things on his mind.

At any rate, it was worth a look. She hid her case behind

a big stone trough brimming over with flowers and flew back into the house, taking the stairs two at a time.

One glance at the dressing table told her that her optimism was ill-founded. Apart from the mirror on its polished stand, the surface was totally clear.

Lucy could have screamed with frustration.

Calm down, she adjured herself. Maybe they're still here—in a drawer, perhaps.

Feverishly, she wrenched open the top drawer and scanned the contents: hairbrushes, a leather case containing cuff-links, and a selection of fine linen handkerchieves. In the next drawer down were silk socks. Which, she decided grimly, was as far as she went.

She pushed an errant lock of hair back from her forehead as she considered the situation. It was faintly possible that the keys, thrown carelessly, might have skidded all the way across the top and fallen into the gap between the dressing table and the wall.

She tried to ease out the heavy piece of furniture so that she could look behind it, but it defied her efforts. Panting, Lucy dropped to her knees, awkwardly craning her neck as she tried to peer underneath it instead.

From the doorway behind her, a familiar vioce drawled, 'Checking for dust, *mia bella*? What a paragon you are.'

Lucy jumped violently, and straightened, muffling a shriek as she banged her unwary head on a drawer's protruding handle.

Oh, God, she thought sickly. Why on earth hadn't she heard him returning? She could only be thankful that he hadn't actually caught her going through the rest of his things.

She said between gritted teeth, resisting the urge to rub the aching spot on her head, 'That's the third time you've scared me out of my wits.'

'It's the third time I've found you in my room,' Giulio

Falcone retorted silkily. 'I shall begin to think, Lucia, that you can't keep away.'

Lucy got to her feet, glaring at him. 'Then you'd be wrong,' she said crisply. A glance at her bare left wrist gave her inspiration. 'Actually, I was looking for my watch. I thought perhaps I'd left it in here.'

'I regret, no.' He came further into the room. Pale grey trousers hugged his lean hips and accentuated the length of his legs, and his coral polo shirt had been left unbuttoned at the neck. Lucy, assimilating all this, was aware of a slight flurry in her breathing.

He looked her over unsmilingly. He said. 'You were wearing your watch last night, I think.'

'Oh, was I?' She gave a little shrug. 'I couldn't be sure.'

His scrutiny of her intensified. He said, 'Did you hurt yourself just now?'

'Not at all,' she said stoutly. It was a lie. In fact, she felt as if she was going to have a lump like the dome of St. Paul's. She produced a feeble imitation of a bright smile. 'Well—I'll go and continue to search elsewhere.'

She had to pass him to reach the door. His hand closed round her arm, halting her effortlessly.

He said quietly, 'I did not intend to startle you, and for that I apologise. Among other things, I went to the vineyard to ask Franco's wife, Teresa, to cook for us on a temporary basis.' He paused, then added with a faint smile, 'I thought I would be back before you awoke.'

Lucy lifted her chin. She said coolly, 'I'm sorry to have put you to so much trouble, *signore*. It won't happen again. If you'd care to specify a time for my duties to begin, I'll make sure I'm awake and available in future.'

The smile deepened. 'Why the outrage? I am not the first man to see you in bed, after all.'

'That's not the point,' she said stonily. 'I happen to value my privacy.'

He shrugged. 'Then I must respect it.' The amber eyes met hers in unnerving confrontation. 'I promise, *columbina*, never to enter your bedroom again—without an invitation. Is that the assurance you want?'

Lucy forced herself to look away to the open door. 'It will do, I suppose.' She glanced down at his detaining hand. 'Now, may I go, please?'

'On the other hand,' he went on softly, 'you have my full permission to enter my bedroom whenever you wish, and stay—just as long as you desire.'

He strolled over to the dressing table. 'I hope you find your watch,' he added casually. 'It's so annoying to search and search, to no avail.'

Numbly, Lucy watched him produce first his own car keys then those of the Fiat from his trouser pocket. Slanting a smile at her, he tossed both bunches into the air and caught them, before dropping them unhurriedly into the top drawer. He was watching her stunned reaction, she realised, in the mirror.

He said mockingly, 'Before you continue your hunt, may I suggest an ice pack for the bump on your head, Lucia?' He paused. 'Who knows? It may also have a cooling effect on your temper.'

And his laughter followed her, even through the door she slammed behind her and down the long passage to the fragile security of her room.

CHAPTER FIVE

THE room was already like an oven, and there was nowhere to sit but on the bed, which did nothing to improve Lucy's mood.

Giulio Falcone was a snake, she raged inwardly. A devious, conniving bastard, who'd outthought and outmanoeuvred her all along the line. In fact he'd made a total fool of her, and she hated him.

Which, admittedly, was a far safer attitude than her previous naïve response to his attraction. Hard work alone wasn't a sufficient defence against the smile that curled the corners of his mouth, or the amber fire that glowed in those extraordinary eyes. She'd found that out to her cost last night.

No, she thought, she needed hate as an extra—maybe even a final line of defence, until some day, somehow, she could teach him a lesson he would never forget.

She emptied her bag onto the bed and went through its contents slowly and methodically, calculating how much she had in lira, how much in travellers' cheques. Her driving licence was in her wallet. Maybe she could—just—afford to hire a car to take her to the airport. But where could she stay if no flight was immediately available? And how long could she manage?

The questions seemed to chase each other in her brain. What a fool she'd been not to bring her credit card, she thought ruefully, yet at the time it had seemed a sensible move, a disincentive to over-spending, particularly since she was contemplating a change of flat when she returned home.

She looked through the other pockets in the wallet, just

in case she'd slipped the card in after all in a moment of aberration, but all she found were receipts, a library ticket and, tucked away and forgotten in an inside pocket, a photograph of Philip.

She took it out and looked at it. A month ago, it would have destroyed her. Now she sat and studied it almost objectively. It was one she'd taken on the flotilla holiday, the first day she'd felt well enough to venture up on deck. Philip, of course, was already bronzed, his blond hair bleached by the sun, totally accepted as one of the gang. He was leaning against the rail, smiling for the camera, his blue eyes crinkling in the way she'd always loved. But he was looking past her, not at her, focused on a different horizon. She could see that now, so clearly.

I was always swept along behind him, in his wake, she thought. Never at his side, as I should have been. As I wanted to be.

She took a breath, ripped the photograph cleanly in half, and dropped it into the waste basket.

The tap on her door brought her defensively to her feet. No need to ask who was there, of course.

She said stonily, *'Sì?'*

'My sister is here, Lucia. Will you come down with me to meet her?' As she hesitated, he added, 'However angry you are with me, please remember that the children have been badly frightened, and need you.'

Fuming, Lucy swept to the door and threw it open. She said icily, 'That is a shameless piece of manipulation, and you know it.'

He flung up a hand. *'Mi dispiace,'* he said, without a trace of penitence. 'But I have been accused of worse things. Now stop sulking, please, and come downstairs.'

He turned away, and Lucy took an impassioned step forward, only to bark her shins on her own suitcase, which had pparently deserted its refuge behind the flower trough and was now standing dejectedly outside her door.

No prizes for guessing how, she thought malevolently, glaring after his retreating figure. She pushed the case into her room and closed the door on it.

When she got to the stairs, the hall below seemed full of people and noise. There was a uniformed driver stolidly bringing in more luggage than Lucy had ever seen in her life. There was a tall blonde girl, dressed with the kind of careless elegance normally encountered only in the pages of the glossiest magazines, talking very fast and gesturing rapidly. There was a small boy with dark curly hair capering about and shouting, and a slightly older girl in tears.

She almost cannoned into the Count, who had paused halfway down the stairs and was standing as if he'd been turned to stone, staring across all this chaos to the open doorway. In which, Lucy saw with foreboding, there was yet another newcomer.

She was a much older woman, matchstick-slender and exquisitely dressed, her silver hair formally and immaculately coiffed. She was looking round her with mingled authority and disdain.

'Claudia,' Giulio Falcone said softly, and at the sound of his voice a magical silence seemed to fall on the rest of the company. '*Che sorpresa.*'

The woman in the doorway smiled. 'My dear Giulio,' she purred. 'Naturally I am here for my daughter.'

Although she spoke in Italian, Lucy had no difficulty making an accurate translation. The *contessa*, she thought, had a curious voice; it was husky, with a metallic undertone—like honey eaten off a steel spoon.

The *contessa's* eyes, vibrantly dark under heavy lids, looked past him up the stairs to Lucy herself, who had a searing impression of having been tried and found wanting. She said austerely, 'And who is this girl?'

Giulio replied in English, his tone cool and deliberately casual, 'This is Lucy Winters, my dear Claudia, who has agreed to replace Alison, and look after the children and keep house for us, until we can make other arrangements.'

The arched brows swept up. '*Dove* Maddalena?'

Giulio shrugged abruptly. 'There was trouble with Tommaso. She left—rather suddenly.'

Claudia Falcone made an exasperated sound. 'Was there no suitable local woman, rather than another English girl?'

It occurred to Lucy that she made the word *inglesa* sound like an expression of contempt.

Giulio shrugged again. 'Teresa has agreed to come and cook for us,' he said. 'But she has her own family to consider. She cannot take on other duties as well.'

'But if she was paid—' the *contessa* began, to be interrupted by the younger woman.

'Mamma, of course we want another English girl, so that the children's lessons won't be interrupted. We should be grateful to Giulio for the trouble he has taken to find a suitable replacement for our poor Alison.' She gave Lucy a cordial smile. 'How do you do, *signorina*? It is good to meet you. I am Fiammetta Rinaldi.'

'But who is this young woman, and where has she come from?' the *contessa* demanded impatiently. 'What are her credentials? Is she fit for this kind of responsibility?'

Fiammetta's tone held a touch of exasperation. 'Mamma, don't fuss so much. I am sure Giulio would engage no one whose references were not impeccable.'

Oh, no? Lucy questioned in silent irony, and found Fiammetta addressing her again.

'This has not been a good way to make your acquaintance, *signorina*—or may I call you Lucia?—but the past forty-eight hours have been—trying.' She pulled a faintly comic face.

She was indeed enchantingly pretty, Lucy acknowledged

with enormous pansy brown eyes and a frankly sexy mouth. Even the strip of sticking plaster on her forehead could not detract from her overall sparkle.

'More than merely trying,' came the *contessa's* voice, with the metallic note even more strongly in evidence. 'The accident could have been terrible—a tragedy. The life of my only grandson was placed at risk.'

Lucy saw the older child flinch, her tear-stained face hurt and fleetingly hostile, and in that moment she knew she would never like Claudia Falcone.

She said politely, 'Then your granddaughter was not in the car at the time, Contessa Falcone. That was lucky.'

Her words fell into a suddenly tense silence, broken by the little boy dancing up and down. 'Emilia was in the car,' he announced importantly. 'But she cried. She wasn't brave like me. And today she was sick.'

He gave a realistic impression of his sister's mishap and hooted with laughter. Emilia began to cry again, noisily, and her grandmother turned away, her face frozen with distaste.

Lucy, biting her tongue with an effort, decided resignedly that it was high time to intervene properly. She walked down the stairs to the Count's side, and touched his arm.

She said quietly, 'Perhaps you'd take the ladies into the *salotto*, *signore*, while I see to the children. Emilia at least will need to be washed and changed.' She looked at Fiammetta. 'Perhaps you, *signora*, know which case her clothes are in?'

Fiammetta gave the mountain of luggage a frankly hunted look. 'Unfortunately, no.' She spread her hands apologetically. 'Alison did the packing, you understand.'

And someone quite apart from the lovely Fiammetta, Lucy deduced wryly, was going to have to do the unpacking.

She said steadily, 'Well, until it's found, I'll just have to do the best I can.' She extended an encouraging hand to

Emilia, whose sobs had turned to hiccups. 'Shall we go and make you more comfortable?'

The child's face was sullen and mutinous. 'No,' she burst out. 'I want Alison.' At Lucy's approach, she swung towards her grandmother, as if to bury her face in her dress, and the *contessa* stepped swiftly backwards, her hands moving in a gesture of repugnance and negation.

Giulio moved into the breach. He said gently, but firmly, 'Alison is not here, little one, so go with Lucia.'

'I won't. I won't.' Emilia seemed on the verge of hysterics. 'You can't make me!'

'You don't think so?' He swung the child up into his arms, hugging her, making a game of it, regardless of the condition she was in, then started up the stairs with her, Lucy following.

To Lucy's surprise, he carried Emilia straight into his own room, setting the little girl down in the adjoining bathroom, ruffling her hair as he did so. 'There you are, *cara*. Everything will be better soon.'

He looked at Lucy, brows raised. 'You can manage?' It was a statement rather than a question, and she nodded.

'Thank you.' She took a breath. 'That was—kind of you. And totally unexpected, she added silently.

He shrugged. 'It had to be done.'

Lucy began to run the water into the tub. She said with a forced smile, 'You'll probably need to change as well.'

'Almost certainly,' he confirmed laconically. 'But it doesn't matter. With children these things happen.' Casually, he pulled his shirt over his head and tossed it into the adjoining linen basket, before giving Emilia a parting grin.

'Behave for Lucia, little one,' he commanded softly, and walked back into the bedroom, where he paused to select a fresh shirt from the *guardaroba*.

Lucy became suddenly, burningly aware that her gaze was following him, avidly drinking in every ripple of muscle beneath the bronzed skin. She smothered a gasp and turned away, concentrating her attention on the temperature of the bath-water, thankful that Giulio Falcone hadn't noticed.

Gawping like a sex-starved adolescent! she chastised herself mentally. For God's sake, pull yourself together, you idiot.

In spite of her uncle's admonition, Emilia was not disposed to co-operate. She was not, Lucy thought as she helped her out of her soiled clothing, a particularly prepossessing child, her current problems notwithstanding. She was thin and rather sallow, with a sullen expression and a small, pursed mouth. Unfairly, Marco seemed to have gained the lion's share in looks and grace, and Lucy suspected the little girl had been made well aware of that.

She complained that the bath-water was too hot, then too cold, and that the shampoo stung her eyes. She pushed the handspray away while her hair was being rinsed, drenching Lucy to the skin.

All in all, it was a memorable introduction to her new duties, Lucy decided grimly, struggling to lift Emilia's deliberately dead weight out of the bath. She wrapped the child in a bath-sheet, gave her hair a brisk towelling, and sat her on the bed, regardless of her protests, while she went to her own room to fetch her hairdryer.

To her surprise, she found her case standing out in the passage again. More astonishing yet, through the open door she could see a sour-looking elderly woman, dressed in black, hanging other sombre garments in the *guardaroba*.

Lucy checked. She said politely, 'Excuse me, I think there's been some mistake.'

She received a look of complete indifference in return.

She tried again. 'This is my room.'

A shrug, and a muttered, *'Non capisco,'* was the only response.

'Now that I don't believe,' Lucy said roundly.

'Is there a problem?' The *contessa's* voice came from behind her, and Lucy swung round with a slight start. Creeping up behind people must be a family trait, she thought tartly.

She said, 'I seem to have lost my room.'

'Your room?' The older woman's brows lifted. 'But this room is always occupied by my maid when I am in residence. I need to have her near me.' Her smile was wintry. 'I'm sure you understand.'

'Of course,' Lucy said pleasantly. 'I'll move into one of the others.'

The *contessa* examined a fingernail with a certain amount of care. She said, 'Unfortunately, I have guests arriving this afternoon. All the rooms in the villa are needed. But there is the *casetta* in the grounds which Maddalena used. You will be quite comfortable there.'

Lucy stared at her. She said evenly, 'I'm supposed to be here for the children. I assumed Signora Rinaldi would want me near them.'

'But of course,' the *contessa* said smoothly. 'The children will share the *casetta* with you. It is an ideal arrangement. My daughter needs a few days' complete peace and rest to recover from the shock of the accident. Although she is an excellent and most affectionate mother children of this age can be so wearing, don't you find?'

'Presumably,' Lucy said, aware that she was trembling with anger, 'your visitors will cause no disruption at all to the household.'

The *contessa's* brows lifted in hauteur. 'My niece has been visiting Florence with a friend. Naturally I wish to see her.' She paused. 'As a temporary employee, *signorina*, you could hardly expect to remain under this roof and mix on an equal footing with our guests.' Her smile was bland.

'Although, to save our good Teresa inconvenience, you will be permitted, with the children, to join us for meals.'

She gave Lucy a long look. 'One of these days, *signorina*, you and I must discuss the circumstances in which you became so readily available for this job.'

Lucy picked up her case. She said, 'I suggest you ask your stepson, *contessa*. After all, anything I had to say would only be servant's gossip.'

Head high, feeling she'd scored a minor victory, she marched back along the passage to rejoin Emilia. She extracted the hairdryer and the adaptor from her case, and began to dry Emilia's hair, a process the child endured in smouldering silence.

'Now then,' Lucy said when she finished. 'Doesn't that look pretty?'

Emilia gave her reflection a look of total indifference.

'I am not pretty. I heard Nonna say that no one would ever believe I was Mamma's daughter, and that I look like a *fanciulla abbandonata*—a child from the streets.'

Lucy sighed soundlessly. She said gently, 'I'm sure she didn't mean it.'

'Nonna means everything she says. She wants Mamma to send me away to school to nuns who will beat me when I am naughty.' There was a note of real despair in the small, sulky voice.

Lucy said robustly, 'Then you'll have to be extra good, so there's no excuse for you to go.' She reached into her case and brought out a cream-coloured T-shirt with stylised flowers in red and gold cascading across the front. 'Until your own things turn up, would you like to wear this?'

Emilia looked down her nose at it. 'Does it belong to you?'

'Yes, but I've never worn it, so you won't be contaminated,' Lucy said lightly, trying to make a joke of it. 'And it would make a very pretty nightshirt,' she added. 'You can't sleep in a damp towel.'

Emilia looked mutinous again. 'I don't want to sleep,' she denied, the heaviness in her eyes belying her defiant words.

'Remember what I just said about being extra good?' Lucy popped the T-shirt over the child's head, and after only a superficial show of reluctance Emilia consented to allow herself to be tucked under the thin coverlet.

'How long are we going to stay here?' she asked, watching Lucy replace her hairdryer in its carrying case.

'That's for your mother to decide,' Lucy returned.

The child looked woebegone. 'We were going to the sea when that car hit us. I like it there. Here, there is nothing.' She sighed. 'But Mamma will do what Nonna says. She always does when my father is not here. I hope he comes back soon.'

I'll drink to that, Lucy agreed silently.

'This is Zio Giulio's room,' Emilia went on. 'Why am I here?'

Lucy smiled at her. 'Because our rooms aren't quite ready yet. We're going to stay in our own little house in the grounds.'

Emilia sat up in bed. 'The house that was Maddalena's?' Her voice was incredulous.

Far from being a waif, at that moment she bore a strong resemblance to the *contessa*, Lucy thought ruefully, but she gave a cheerful nod.

'That very one.' She lowered her voice conspiratorially. 'And we'll have it all to ourselves.'

Emilia stared at her, clearly weighing the ignominy of being relegated to the housekeeper's accommodation against the positive advantage of being away from her grandmother.

'But why can we not stay here?' she demanded at last.

'Because there are going to be other visitors,' Lucy explained. 'One of your cousins.'

'I have only one—Angela.' Emilia's mouth twisted petulantly. 'Of course, Nonna would ask her.'

Lucy bit back a smile at the world-weary tone. 'Don't you like her?' she asked, tugging down the lid of her case.

Emilia shrugged. 'It doesn't matter whether I do or not. It's Zio Giulio who has to like her.'

The words seemed to fall into an odd stillness.

'Why?' Lucy asked at last, aware that she was concentrating with unwonted fierceness on the clasps of her suitcase.

Emilia gave a superior little giggle. 'Because she's the girl Zio Giulio is going to marry, of course.'

Lucy felt suddenly as if she was trapped inside some vast, echoing vacuum. As if all sound, colour and sensation had vanished from the world, leaving her empty and desolate.

Across some wide and stinging distance, she heard herself say, 'Are they engaged?'

The child shook her head. 'No, but I heard Mamma say to Papà that Zio Giulio was only waiting for her—' her forehead creased '—to grow up and settle down.'

Lucy looked down at her hands. There were red marks where the clasps had dug into the soft flesh.

She thought with anguish, Oh, you fool. You stupid, pathetic idiot.

Aloud, she said calmly and quietly, 'Well, it's time you settled down as well. I'm going to go and make our new home ready for us.'

With a grudging nod, Emilia slid down in the bed. Lucy went into the bathroom to tidy up, closing the door behind her. She looked at herself in the mirror, noting almost clinically her pallor, and the wide, startled, unhappy eyes.

She said softly and fiercely, 'Well, what did you think?

You knew from the start that he was only amusing himself at your expense. And now you've had it confirmed.'

She could only pray that Giulio Falcone had no idea how far she'd travelled down the road of no return to a hell of her own making.

No doubt he thought she was easy game—a woman recently rejected by another man. But if he thought she was in the market to be used—humiliated yet again—if he thought she was a pushover, then she would prove him wrong.

He might have been able to gauge her physical reaction to him, but oh, dear God, let him not have guessed the depth of her mental and emotional surrender.

She thought despairingly, Don't let me have fallen in love with him. Not that—never that.

It was in her own hands now. He must never know—she must never reveal by word or sign that he had the power to hurt her. Otherwise her time at the Villa Dante would be purgatory indeed.

And I thought I could hate him, she mocked herself bitterly. I thought I could make that my defence.

But how could things have moved so far and so fast— and with a man she hardly knew? It was ridiculous—incredible. She wasn't impulsive. She was steady and reliable, testing the ground before she moved. Her relationship with Philip had been based on secure foundations—or so she'd thought.

But what did I know? she lashed herself. A few days of that Tuscan sun Giulio had spoken of had already transmuted her, changed her into some unknown and challenging quantity.

Forty-eight hours ago, she thought slowly, she'd been unaware that Giulio Falcone even existed. Now she was enmeshed and helpless in a bitter web of jealousy and passion

She tidied the bathroom like an automaton, pushing the used towels into the linen basket, wiping out the bath with a handful of tisssue.

If she left, if she actually, physically ran away, Giulio Falcone could not follow her. His fiancée's presence would see to that.

But wherever she went, however much distance she put between them, he would be with her in spirit, the demon on her shoulder, the restless yearning that could not be appeased.

I have to stay, she told herself. I have to see him each day with this Angela, the woman he intends to marry. I have to face the certainty of it. I have to burn out this need for him before it destroys me. To treat it as the pathetic infatuation it undoubtedly is.

When she eventually returned to the bedroom, she saw without surprise that Emilia had already fallen asleep.

She stood looking down at the little girl, aware of a tug of sympathy as she saw that a single teardrop had made its way down the small, sallow face.

You poor little soul, she thought with sudden anger. I'm not the only unhappy one. Damn him. Damn all these Falconese with their beauty and their careless cruelty.

But I won't let them get away with it. I'm going to stay here—and fight, even if the real battle's going to be against myself.

And, holding her head high, Lucy went downstairs.

CHAPTER SIX

To Lucy's relief none of the family was immediately in evidence, although she could hear the murmur of voices from behind the closed doors of the *salotto*, including Marco's childish treble.

In the kitchen, she found Teresa, a big, smiling woman, already clashing pots and pans with vigour. Lucy introduced herself matter-of-factly, fended off Teresa's flood of questions with apologetic incomprehension, and removed herself with tactful speed to her new abode.

It was hardly a spacious refuge, with two bedrooms and a tiny bathroom up a flight of wooden stairs, and a combined living room and kitchen at ground level, but it would do.

It would have to, she thought with gritted teeth as she tried to decide how to allocate the sleeping accommodation. The children were still young enough to share a room, so she determined to put both the old-fashioned single beds in the larger room, and herself use the folding bed with the rather solid mattress in the small bedroom. Even the *contessa* couldn't object to that, she thought grimly.

The doorways were narrow, but, with a lot of pushing and pulling, she eventually achieved her objective.

If ever I lose my job, I can always find work as a chambermaid, she thought, pushing her hair back wearily, and wincing faintly as her fingers encountered the bump on her head. Something else to hate him for.

She'd found the linen store, and was matching sheets and pillowcases, when she heard someone enter the *casetta* with a swift, forceful stride, and then Giulio Falcone calling her name. For a moment, she experienced a cowardly urge to jump into the cupboard and hide.

Lunatic, she chastised herself caustically. You'll have to face him sooner or later.

She took three deep and calming breaths, then walked collectedly downstairs. He was standing staring around him, hands on hips, his face grim.

Lucy halted on the bottom step. I need the advantage of the extra height, she told herself. In fact, I need all the help I can get.

'Is something wrong, *signore*?' Her voice was cool.

'Everything, I would say, *signorina*,' he returned in savage mimicry of her own formality. 'I have come to apologise to you.'

Surprise jolted her. It was not what she'd expected.

'There's really no need—' she began, but he interrupted her.

'You are wrong, Lucia. There is every need.' His tone grated. Without doubt, he was very angry. 'I asked you to stay here to help Fiammetta and the children. I did not anticipate Claudia's descent on us, or that she would have invited—guests without consulting me first.' His mouth was compressed into lines of stone. 'Nor did I expect this.' He gestured contemptuously around him. 'I can only say, to excuse her, that she is a law unto herself, and has always been so.'

He took a deep breath. 'But her arrival, and its consequences, changes everything, naturally. Under the circumstances, I release you from our bargain. You are free to leave whenever you wish. I suggest the sooner the better.'

There was a silence.

It was almost funny, Lucy thought with detachment. Here she'd been, agonising over whether to go or stay, torn by decision and the pain of love. And here was Giulio giving her her marching orders without a second thought. Only she didn't feel like laughing.

She said quietly, 'And what happens to the children?'

'They have a mother and a grandmother. Between them—'

'Very little will happen. You admitted as much yourself,' Lucy said bitingly. 'To be frank, neither of them wishes to be bothered.' She lifted her chin. 'So—are you prepared to take the job on?'

He looked taken aback. 'I?'

'That's what I thought.' Lucy gave a decisive nod. 'In that case, I'm staying, *signore*, but only for the children's sake, and until you can find other help.'

He said quietly. 'That is impossible.'

'Why?' She paused, forcing herself to challenge his gaze.

'Because your presence would cause difficulties.' His tone was harsh. 'You are not aware of the identities of these—new visitors.'

'You're wrong, *signore*. I know exactly who is expected.' She actually managed a trace of cool amusement. 'And you really don't have to worry about a thing. I have no intention of being an embarrassment, if that's what you're afraid of.'

He stared at her, his whole attention sharply arrested. He said, 'You know? You have heard? But how?'

'Does it matter?' She was shaking inside, but she kept her voice even. 'It makes no difference to me, I assure you.'

'Then it should.' His eyes narrowed. 'Lucia, you don't have to pretend. Not with me.'

'There's no pretence about it.' Her nonchalant shrug took every ounce of strength she possessed. 'It was just—an interlude. I know that. Not to be taken seriously, and certainly best forgotten. That's what I plan to do. So please don't worry.'

'It seemed otherwise to me,' he said quietly. 'Forgive me.

but I had the impression that it was more—far more than just an interlude.'

Lucy bit her lip. Humiliation was twisting inside her like a knife, but she kept her voice level. 'Then you're wrong, *signore*. But at least I hope we can agree that it's over. And that it's best to act as if—as if it never happened at all.'

'Brave words,' he said. 'But how will you feel when you are confronted by reality?' He spread his hands almost helplessly. 'I don't want to see you hurt, Lucia.'

I'm hurt now, she wanted to scream at him. Can't you see I'm bleeding to death?

She straightened her shoulders. 'Please don't trouble yourself any more. You—you're really taking something quite trivial far too seriously. And I'm sorry if I've given you a false impression of my feelings—my involvement. It really wasn't intentional.'

There was a taut silence. Then he said, 'I see.' His tone was courteous but impersonal. 'Clearly my original opinion of you was the correct one.' He allowed her to digest that for a moment, then pointed to two suitcases behind him. 'I have found the children's clothes,' he added.

'*Grazie,*' she said.

'*Prego,*' he returned carelessly. His smile was brief, not reaching his eyes. 'I wish you good fortune in your newest role, *cara*. I hope you don't find it too demanding.'

'Don't worry,' she said. 'I'll remember my place.'

He was turning to leave, but swung back to face her. 'Your place?' he echoed, his voice harsh with anger. 'I'll show you your place, *mia cara*.'

The endearment sounded like an insult. Two strides brought him to her. His hands clamped on her waist, pulling her forward so that she was pinioned against him, breast to breast. Then, for one endless moment, his mouth possessed hers, roughly, almost ravenously. Shocked, Lucy felt her lips yield, part helplessly under the force of his invasion.

But even as she acknowledged her surrender it was over.

Giulio stood back, releasing her abruptly, almost contemptuously.

He said, 'And now you have something else to remember. Another item of trivia for your collection.'

He strode out of the *casetta*, and the door banged shut behind him.

Lucy's pent-up breath escaped her in a quivering sigh. Slowly, she uncurled her fingers from the palms of her hands and flexed them carefully to reduce the ache of tension. Her head was throbbing badly now, and she felt close to tears of mingled rage and disappointment.

Even before that—violation of her mouth, his whole attitude had been an insult, she thought raggedly. Clearly he was scared that she would try to make capital out of what had passed between them with his future wife.

Did he really think she was that small-minded and spiteful? Yet what else could she really expect? Giulio, in fact, was taking the more realistic stance. They were, in spite of all that had passed between them, still virtual strangers to each other.

And the fact that she seemed to have every line of his lean, arrogant body etched on some inner consciousness, that the sound of his voice made her pulses do crazy things, that the touch of his lips and hands, even in anger, made her flesh clench in yearning—this—all this was her problem, and hers alone.

Except that, to her shame, he had guessed all the emotional turmoil she had wanted to conceal, she thought bitterly. Giulio had seen through her flimsy pretence as easily as if she were transparent.

And now he was clearly concerned that this Angela might do the same. Which was why he'd tried to hustle her off in that humiliating way.

But she'll never guess from me, she vowed silently. From

here on in, Count Giulio Falcone was forbidden territory, and she would make sure their separate worlds never collided again.

Lunch, for Lucy, was a fairly tense occasion. Emilia, though reunited with her own clothes, was in a surly mood, and Marco, who'd had the undivided attention of his adoring grandmother for most of the morning, seemed bent on proving just how badly he could behave if he tried.

A beautiful child, but spoiled rotten, Lucy thought detachedly as she tried to prevent him transferring the contents of his plate to the dining-room floor.

The *contessa* kept up a constant stream of talk in her own language, her thin lips stretched in smiles, her hands gesturing restlessly. Fiammetta, clearly embarrassed, made several half-hearted attempts to switch the conversation into English, and draw Lucy into it, but these were swiftly overridden by her mother, who was at pains to ignore Lucy's presence altogether. It was an object-lesson in how to be rude, performed with the utmost charm.

And Giulio said nothing at all. He lounged in his chair at the head of the table, looking withdrawn and preoccupied, toying with the excellent escalope of veal in spinach sauce that Teresa had prepared.

Lucy, risking one swift glance at him from under her lashes, supposed that he was thinking about Angela. Counting the minutes to her arrival, no doubt. She sighed soundlessly, and helped herself to more green salad.

When the meal was over, Fiammetta said instantly that the children must rest, prompting an immediate out-cry from Emilia.

'I have used up all my sleep,' she protested. 'Marco can rest. I shall swim in the pool.'

'Not immediately after a meal, I'm afraid.' Lucy made the veto, and in return received a venomous look and a sharp kick on the shins under the table. Her smothered gasp of pain was masked by Marco's vociferous denial of his own weariness.

'Marco, *caro*.' Fiammetta put a languid hand to her head. 'Such noise.' She turned to Lucy. 'Lucia, could you do something—?'

'Of course she can,' the *contessa* broke in impatiently. 'That is what she is employed for. Take the children away, *signorina*, and amuse them.'

'There is no need.' Giulio pushed back his chair and rose. 'I am going down to the vineyard to talk to Franco. They can come with me. But only if they behave,' he added sharply as both children descended on him with whoops of joy.

'You are going out?' There was displeasure in the *contessa's* tone. 'But Angela will be arriving at any moment.'

'Then I can rely on you to make her—and her companion—welcome,' he returned coolly. 'They are, after all, your guests, my dear Claudia.' He left the room, a child hanging onto each hand, leaving behind him what Lucy supposed was a pregnant silence.

It was broken by the *contessa* with a small torrent of enraged speech, which Fiammetta interrupted with a gurgle of laughter. 'Mamma, have you not yet learned that Giulio is his own man, and that you cannot drive him? He will marry Angela when he is ready, and not before. In the meantime—' she gave a voluptuous and very wordly shrug, '—they will both amuse themselves as they wish.'

Lucy felt as if she'd swallowed a stone.

'Her upbringing should have been left to me.' Two bright spots of colour burned in the *contessa's* face. 'Then there would have been no such amusements, and the matter would have been settled long ago.'

'Perhaps.' Fiammetta shrugged again, this time with indifference, then turned to Lucy who, for a number of reasons, was trying to edge unobtrusively from the room. 'Lucia, I have found some books and toys which Alison packed for the children among my luggage. If you come to my room, I will give them to you.'

Lucy had no choice but to agree. As they went up the stairs, Fiammetta slipped an arm through hers. 'Lucia, I want you to know that I am so grateful that you are here. Also that you must not pay too much heed if Mamma is—distant. The truth is she has no great love for the English. Her younger sister, Bianca, whom she greatly loved, married an Englishman, and died in your country after giving birth to Angela. Mamma blamed Bianca's husband, the hospital—everyone, but in fact it was no one's fault. It was a tragic accident which could have happened anywhere at any time. Only Mamma has never accepted that.'

Lucy said awkwardly, 'How terrible. I'm very sorry.'

Fiammetta rolled her eyes expressvely. 'It gets worse. She wrote to my uncle, offering—no, demanding—to take the *bambina* and bring her up herself, here in Italy. When he refused—*per Dio*—what an uproar. He has never been forgiven, believe me.'

Lucy stared at her. 'You mean, having lost his wife, he was also expected to give up his baby?'

'Mamma has a mind that runs on one track,' Fiammetta admitted ruefully. 'When she married Conte Falcone, both Giulio and I were only children. She hoped very much to bear another child—another son—and when it did not happen she decided instead that Giulio and I should marry.'

She shook her head. 'What an idea. Neither of us was the least in love with the other—although Giulio is very attractive,' she added, her full lips curving in a smile that combined mischief with sensuality. 'Besides, I never knew what he was thinking, and that drove me mad. But with Sergio I always know, so it is perfect.'

Lucy was startled by the frankness of these confidences. 'Signora…' she began with reservation.

'Oh, so formal, and I cannot bear that. Alison is one of the family, and you must be too. Call me Fiammetta. You are wondering why I tell you these things?' She led Lucy into her bedroom and closed the door. 'It is not just gossip, you understand. There is something you must know, if you are to look after my children.' She paused. 'There is a big problem with Emilia.'

Tell me about it, Lucy thought ironically. She said quietly, 'I'm sorry to hear that,' and waited.

Fiammetta picked up a picture book, fiddled with it almost irritably and put it down again. 'When she was born, Mamma was pleased, naturally. Her first grandchild. But when Marco came—the longed-for boy—that was altogether different. She was crazy with joy—almost as if he were her own son. We thought, Sergio and I, that it would pass, but it has not. And Emilia sees it—and is jealous.'

She took a deep breath. 'One day, Mamma went into Marco's room and found Emilia standing by his crib with a glass in her hand. There was water everywhere—on the blanket—on his face. She said she was trying to give him a drink…' Her voice tailed away.

'Perhaps it was true,' Lucy suggested.

'Mamma did not think so. She was like a madwoman.' Fiammetta cast her eyes to heaven. 'She said that the glass could have been broken—accused Emilia of trying to harm Marco, and Emilia shouted back that we all loved Marco better than her and she hated him.'

Lucy said gently, 'A certain amount of sibling rivalry is part of childhood. My own nephews fight like crazy…'

'There were other things. When he could just walk, we found her taking him to our swimming pool—to teach him to swim, she said. Which she could barely do herself. If he had slipped…' She shuddered and put a hand to her mouth

Lucy put a hand on her arm. 'But he didn't—and it must have been a long time ago.'

'That is what Sergio says, but I cannot forget it. Mamma will not allow it.' The pansy dark eyes were suddenly filled with tears. 'Each time Marco has a fall, or hurts himself, she makes me see that it could have been because of Emilia. That she might have hit him or pushed him. And that is not all. Recently Emilia has been stealing—oh, not a great deal—a few thousand lire from my bag, or from Mamma. But it makes me so anxious.'

She spread her hands. 'Mamma thinks we should send her away—to a school that deals with disturbed children. The Mother Superior is an old schoolfriend of hers, and a trained psychologist. Instead we've reached a—compromise. I hired Alison, on the understanding that she should watch particularly for Emilia and that if there were further—incidents we would consider the treatment this school could offer.'

Lucy swallowed. 'Have you mentioned this to Giulio—I mean Count Falcone?'

'No.' Fiammetta shook her head. 'Giulio was only a young boy—fourteen years of age—when Mamma married his father. He had loved his mother very greatly, and he found it difficult to accept that any other woman could take her place. And Mamma—made mistakes, also. It would be hard now for Mamma to share this trouble with him—to admit that her granddaughter could be—sick in some way. If he was married—if he had children—the family relationship might be closer. He might understand more...'

'Well, perhaps things will be different—' Lucy's voice sounded peculiarly toneless '—when he marries—Angela.'

'Poor Mamma.' Fiammetta's sudden smile was like the sun breaking through clouds. 'She did not succeed in matching Giulio to her daughter, so now it has to be her niece.

One way or the other, he must not escape.' She giggled. 'It has become almost an obsession with her.'

'And do the happy couple have no say in the matter?'

Fiammetta shrugged. 'It will be no hardship. Angela is very beautiful, and Giulio—well, you must have seen for yourself. He is a man that any woman would want, even without his money and his power.'

She lowered her voice conspiratorially. 'I thought it would happen three years ago, when he was in London and they met constantly, but he would not commit himself, other than to say she was too young. Since then, they have both seen other people, but in the end they will take each other.'

She nodded. 'And she will make him a good wife, I think, because she can share his world, his business interests in a way I never could.' The smile spread into a grin. 'Sergio does not bother me with such things.'

Lucy was not surprised. Fiammetta had warmth and charm, but was probably not overburdened with brains, or any great depth of character. And she was certainly under the thumb of the *contessa*. She had lost count of how many times Mamma had been mentioned.

'But this time Angela has made Mamma angry,' Fiammetta went on, unconsciously reinforcing Lucy's opinion, 'by bringing her latest man-friend here. Never before has she flaunted one of her other relationships in Giulio's face like this.'

'Maybe she's trying to force the issue by making Count Falcone jealous,' Lucy suggested woodenly.

'Perhaps you are right.' Fiammetta clapped her hands. '*Bravo*, Lucia. How clever of you.' She gave an enchanting gurgle of laughter. 'And how will he retaliate, I wonder? I think the next few days are going to be very interesting—no?'

I think, Lucy decided detachedly as she returned to the

casetta with her arms full of books and games, that they're
going to be almost more than I can bear.

Over the next hour, she busied herself with putting the
children's clothes and other items away, and trying to dispel
the forlorn and spartan air of the living area with colourful
pots of flowers, brought in from the courtyard, and a bright
cloth for the table.

She was sure that it still wouldn't look anything like
home to Emilia and Marco, but at least she'd tried, she told
herself, with a brief sigh.

She had closed the shutters against the hot afternoon sun,
but the air inside the *casetta* was stifling just the same, she
thought, easing the neck of her blouse away from her damp
skin. As she had some time to herself, she might as well
cool off beside the pool.

She changed into a black bikini, covered it with a loose
silk overshirt, and stuffed her dark glasses, sun lotion and
book into a bag.

The whole villa seemed to be sleeping in the sun as she
made her way through the gardens. No bees droned in the
dense banks of lavender which surrounded the pool, and
even the crickets were silent. Not a leaf stirred as she went
softly past, the sound of her own breathing alone disturbing
the intense, burning quietness of the afternoon.

For a moment, she stood at the top of the steps, looking
down at the tranquil turquoise water, remembering the
events of the previous night—the music, the raucous laughter, her own terror—with a shiver of revulsion, allowing this
new and unaccustomed peace to enfold her like the billow-
ing silk of her wrap.

As well as the cushioned loungers and umbrellas, there
was a pile of thickly padded mattresses for sunbathing. Lucy
spread one of them under the sheltering branches of the
ancient tree which provided a modicum of shade at one end
of the pool, then discarded her shirt and slid into the water,

feeling it caress her grateful skin like cool satin. She swam one slow, easy length, then lifted herself out onto the tiled surround and sat wringing the water out of her hair.

Fiammetta's artless confidences were still revolviong in her mind, however much she might try to dismiss them, or tell herself forcefully that they were none of her concern.

Because, for good or ill, she was concerned, she acknowledged with a small aching sigh, and had been ever since that first unfortunate encounter with Giulio in Montiverno.

The mere thought of him was enough to send a tingle vibrating through her senses, however many kinds of fool that might make her.

With a snort of self-derision, she got to her feet and walked around the pool to the waiting mattress, running her hands through her damp hair as she went.

She picked up her towel and began to blot the moisture from her arms and legs, then paused, her mental antennae suddenly, oddly alert.

From somewhere above her, behind the blue wall of lavender and the thickly ranked roses, had come a faint rustle, like a passing breeze. Only the air was still. And, as Lucy listened, she heard the rattle of a dislodged pebble, as if rolling away from a careless foot.

She stiffened, scanning the barrier of flowers for tell-tale signs of movement. She called, 'Is anyone there?' But there was no answer. A total hush had descended once again.

I must have been imagining things, Lucy thought, spreading her towel on the mattress and stretching out on it, face down. She pillowed her head on her folded arms and closed her eyes, letting the silence enclose her.

She found a succession of images turning in her mind— Emilia's wan face, Fiammetta's anxious eyes, the *contessa*'s expression of haughty disdain. And, above all else, Giulio Falcone, his amber eyes sparking fire, his mouth rigid i

anger or curving in a smile. The instinctive, inherent grace
of his lean body. The masked strength of the practised, be-
guiling hands.

Lucy closed her eyes more tightly and saw tiny coloured
lights dance behind her lids. But she could not dispel his
image.

His shadow, she thought drowsily, always there in the
sunlight. On the edge of every thought and every dream.

And she knew that she was lost, irrevocably, and for all
time.

CHAPTER SEVEN

Lucy seemed to be floating on some warm current of air, her whole body totally relaxed, as she looked down at the rolling golden landscape beneath her. Her arms were wings, and she was a bird in flight, a dove, swooping earthward, then spiralling up to freedom.

But somehow she knew that her freedom was an illusion, and destined to be short-lived. Hovering above her was the shadow of a falcon, the predator whom she could never escape, twist and turn as she might.

Then she heard her name called softly through the sunlit air. Was aware of hands smoothing her feathers, stroking her into submission. Touching her with complete mastery.

Suddenly this was no dream, but sheer reality, drawing her up through the layers of sleep to swift, shocked consciousness—and to Giulio, who was kneeling over her, massaging sun lotion into her shoulders and down the length of her back, his fingers practised and very firm.

'What the hell do you think you're doing?' Lucy sat up, frantically grabbing at her bikini-top, which he had apparently unhooked.

'Preventing you from being roasted alive, I hope.' His tone was caustic. 'The sun moved while you were asleep, little fool.'

'Wouldn't waking me and telling me so have been the more obvious course?' she demanded furiously, the fact that he was correct in no way mitigating her sense of outrage.

'Perhaps,' he agreed, the amber eyes slumberously amused under their heavy lids. 'But not nearly as enjoyable, believe me.'

She bit her lip, mortified. 'And I suppose it was you playing peeping Tom earlier,' she accused. 'Not a becoming role for the master of the house.'

'What are you saying?' The dark brows drew together.

'Oh, don't pretend,' she said scornfully. 'Just how long were you lurking in the bushes, spying on me?'

'Have a care, Lucia.' His voice was silk on steel. 'There are limits, even for you. I arrived a few moments ago, intending to swim. If you had not been lying in the full glare of the sun, I would have respected your privacy and left.'

Lucy, struggling to re-hook her top, surveyed him. He was still wearing the same clothes he'd put on that morning.

'Swimming, *signore*? You don't seem to have a costume—or a towel.'

'At this time of day, Lucia,' he said softly, 'I usually have the pool entirely to myself, so I can forget about such tiresome niceties.' Watching her, his mouth curving faintly, he began to unbutton his shirt. 'You wish me to demonstrate?'

She had a potent mental image of what Giulio Falcone would look like stripped, and her mouth went dry.

'No,' she said forcefully. 'Absolutely not.' She snatched up her shirt and got to her feet. 'I—I'll leave you to it.'

He rose too, laughing, and lifting his hands in mock surrender. 'Don't run away, *columbina*. Enjoy the sun—now you are protected against it—and also your freedom, while you can.'

'Oh, heavens.' Lucy looked belatedly and wildly around her. 'The children—where are they? Are they all right?'

He gave her a curious glance. 'They are quite safe—playing with Franco's brood. Teresa will bring them back to the house when she comes to prepare dinner presently. There's no problem.'

'Are you sure Signora Rinaldi will agree?'

He frowned. 'She has never objected before,' he said. 'What is this?'

Lucy bit her lip again. 'I don't want to be accused of neglecting my duties, that's all,' she returned stiffly.

'Now, I wonder if that is the whole truth?' he said softly. 'No matter; I shall find out eventually.' He paused. 'But stay, please, anyway. I don't want to feel I have driven you away.'

Lucy stood, irresolute, acutely conscious of the expanse of honey-gold skin revealed by the scanty bikini, knowing that he was aware of it too. Knowing that he'd been touching her, running his hands over her naked back.

Giulio waited for a moment, then sighed. 'Lucia *mia*, please stop clutching that shirt as if it was a shield. It is not necessary.'

'No?' She lifted her chin. 'You have a short memory, *signore*.'

'On the contrary.' He paused again. 'If you wish me to apologise for my conduct this morning at the *casetta*, then I will. Under the circumstances, I had no right to touch— to kiss you. I admit it. But I refuse to do penance for the sun lotion,' he added. 'That was a necessity.'

She said rigidly, 'You had no right, whatever the circumstances.'

He shrugged. 'Then perhaps I was simply making good use of what precious little time is left to me,' he retorted 'I can hardly be blamed for that.'

'Except that I'm not here to be used. I'm fulfilling my side of our bargain, and nothing else.'

'Now your memory is at fault, *mia cara*,' Giulio drawled 'The bargain between us is cancelled, as I made clear. From now on, you remain at your own risk.'

She said quietly, 'So be it. But you'll understand if prefer not to take unnecessary ones by staying alone with you in an isolated place.'

His face hardened. 'First of all you accuse me of leering

at you from the bushes like some callow adolescent,' he said, 'and now I am a potential rapist, it seems.'

'I didn't say that…'

'But the implication was there,' he cut back at her. 'The implication that you cannot trust me. That I cannot be alone with you without taking something you do not wish to give.' He shook his head. 'You are wrong. I have never taken anything from any woman that has not been freely offered, and you, Lucia, will be no exception to that rule.'

She said thickly, 'Then why don't I feel safe?'

'Perhaps because you do not trust yourself.' His tone was almost grim.

She gasped, and colour flared in her face. 'How dare you?'

'Because, unlike you, I am not afraid of risks.' His shrug was negligent. 'Now, go on with your sunbathing, while I take my swim. The length of the pool should be enough space between us. Unless, of course, you wish to join me in the water?'

'Thank you,' she said, 'but I thought you realised last night that I'm not interested in that kind of—adventure.'

'And I thought you realised I was teasing you.' He pulled his shirt over his head, unzipped his grey trousers and stepped out of them to reveal brief black swimming trunks. 'Does that appease your sense of decency, *columbina*?'

It did her no favours at all, Lucy thought, the breath catching in her throat. He was magnificent—well muscled, without an ounce of surplus weight.

'It doesn't tempt me to stay.' She forced herself to speak calmly, even casually, while her heart was thumping to beat the band. She slipped on her shirt, and began to button it with clumsy fingers.

'And what is that supposed to achieve?' he demanded cynically. 'Do you think I have no memory—no imagination?'

Lucy's eyes sparked with sudden fire. 'I know you have no conscience, *signore*, otherwise you wouldn't behave like this. You couldn't.' She picked up her bag. 'Another reason why I choose not to stay here.'

'And I have no choice in this?'

'Yours is already made.' She looked him straight in the eye. 'I'm here to work, *signore*, not to provide you with— passing amusement.'

'That,' he said harshly, 'was not my intention.'

'I'm not interested in your intentions. Let's talk about responsibilities—obligations—instead. You seem to have forgotten those.

'You are wrong, Lucia.' The amber eyes travelled over her slowly, dismissing her flimsy covering, surveying her with frankly sensual reminiscence. 'I don't forget a thing. How could I?'

She swung her bag over her shoulder. Her voice sounded ragged. 'You're not being fair, *signore*.'

As she walked past him, he reached for her. His fingers closed round her wrist. Held her.

He said softly, 'What can ever be fair in this situation, Lucia, look at me, my little, sweet fool.'

The air surrounding them seemed suddenly to be quivering, shimmering with an intensity which had nothing to do with the sun's glare.

The blood in her veins was slow and heavy, the pounding of her heart a pain in her chest. She had only to turn toward him, she thought dazedly. Only to turn…

She heard, as if from nowhere, a girl's laugh, deep and throaty, rippling out, snapping the tension between them. Shattering the dream.

'Playing your usual games, Giulio, darling?' She was standing on the steps, looking down at them. She was dark and very beautiful, her frankly voluptuous body showcased by a shift dress in stinging pink, cut low over her fu breasts, and finishing well above the knee. 'And who is your latest playmate?'

Lucy's head went back, and the breath left her body in a silent gasp, as if she'd been struck and winded.

No need to guess who the newcomer was. It was—it had to be—Angela. Giulio's cousin by marriage and intended wife.

Only she was no stranger. Lucy had seen her before, and quite recently too. In London, coming out of a restaurant in Knightsbridge. With Philip.

Who was here too. Standing on the step behind her, his face frozen in disbelief and something bordering on horror.

And I know, Lucy thought, a bubble of hysteria welling up inside her, exactly how he feels.

She disengaged her hand sedately. She said, 'I'm the hired help, *signorina*. We had a slight disagreement over terms of employment, that's all.' She flashed a bright, meaningless smile around her. 'And now, if you'll excuse me…'

And she went past them, up the steps, two at a time, without looking back.

'Oh, God,' Lucy whispered to herself as she paced the living room at the *casetta*. 'This can't be happening. It can't be true.'

The shock of seeing Philip so unexpectedly had almost bowled her over. She'd always assumed that when they ran into each other again she would be devastated. But that hadn't been her reaction at all. Dismay had been her uppermost emotion, and embarrassment too. Because, without a doubt, this was one big complicated mess.

All she could concentrate on now was damage limitation. Clearly Angela had no idea that she and Philip had ever been involved. So far, so good.

Nor was there any reason for Giulio to equate her own lost love with Angela's English boyfriend, she thought. She surely hadn't given that much away in those late-night confidences.

There seemed every chance that they could both remain in blissful ignorance. Least said, soonest mended, she decided, as she would tell Philip immediately she got the chance.

As for herself, she would maintain the lowest possible profile as the children's nanny, and let things take their course. Although there was little doubt in her mind what that course would be.

There was bitterness in her throat and a pain in her heart as she thought of Angela, so beautiful, so confident, radiating sexuality. Her smile had been amused as she'd surveyed the telling little scene in front of her, her glance at Lucy totally dismissive.

As Fiammetta has suggested, she and Giulio took each other's little diversions in their stride, it seemed.

But where did this leave Philip? she wondered uncomfortably. Was he just a passing amusement too, or was his affair with Angela the real thing, at least as far as he was concerned?

And what did Angela herself feel? She'd taken Philip, but did she really want him? Set against Giulio, he had little to offer. An aptitude for adventure sports and a propensity for hard work didn't count for much against old money, power and a family tree that went back to the Renaissance. Or was Angela, as Lucy had prophesied, simply using him to spur Giulio into making a proposal?

She sighed. The way things were going, she could end up a two-time loser, she thought wretchedly.

Except, of course, that Giulio had never been hers to lose. And that was what she had to remember at all costs, if she was to keep her sanity.

It was a relief when Teresa, full of smiles, arrived with the children and the performance of getting them washed and presentabe for dinner could get under way. It stopped her from thinking. From pondering the imponderable, and coming up with no answers at all. Or none that she could bear, she amended with a pang.

'When I am a man, I shall have a vineyard,' Marco announced ebulliently.

'In the meantime concentrate on drying between your toes,' Lucy counselled. She gave Emilia a quick smile. 'And what are you going to do with your life?'

Emilia shrugged. 'I shall find a rich husband, like Zia Angela.'

'Better get a new face first.' Marco gave a crow of laughter, followed in short order by a yelp of real pain. 'She pinched me.' Accusingly he held out a chubby arm for Lucy to inspect the tell-tale fingermarks.

'If you didn't say unkind things to your sister, maybe it wouldn't happen,' she pointed out as she hung the damp towels on the rail.

'You are supposed to take my side, not hers.' The small face was outraged.

'I don't intend to take sides at all,' Lucy said cheerfully.

'Then I shall tell Mamma what she did, and she will get into trouble.'

Lucy stole a swift glance at Emilia. Her face was set and sullen, but there was apprehension in her eyes, and Lucy felt reluctant compassion for her.

She wrinkled her nose thoughtfully. 'People who tell tales are horrid.'

'But Nonna says that Emilia must be punished if she is bad to me.'

'And what happens when you are bad to her?' Lucy asked calmly.

'Nothing,' Emilia burst out. 'Because I am always blamed.'

'I have an idea,' Lucy said. 'Why don't you both try to be pleasant to each other for just one day?'

The idea was greeted without enthusiasm.

'And if we do?' said Marco. 'What will you give us?'

'I'll wait till you've done it,' Lucy said grimly, 'and then decide. Now, go downstairs and play quietly while I change.'

She had just emerged from the tiny shower cubicle when she heard a crash and a shriek from downstairs. She wrapped a towel round herself sarong-style, and dashed down. One of the plants she'd brought in earlier lay on the floor, its terracotta pot smashed, and soil and broken blooms everywhere.

'Who did this?' she demanded.

'It was Emilia. She threw it at me.'

'I did not.' Emilia was red with anger. 'He was playing with it, and I told him to stop, so he dropped it.'

'Liar,' Marco yelled.

'What is this name-calling?' an icy voice asked from the doorway, and Giulio walked in.

'One of them broke this plant,' said Lucy, crushingly conscious of her lack of attire. 'They each blame the other. No a good start to the new regime,' she added, looking fiercely from one sulky face to the other.

'Lucia said if we are nice to each other for one whol day she will give us a reward,' Marco told his uncle.

Giulio's mouth twitched. 'Bribery, *columbina*?'

'You have to start somewhere.' Flushing, she yanke hastily at her slipping towel.

Giulio looked directly at the children. 'Well, little rascal if you can do this great thing, I will reward you myself He pretended to think. 'How about a picnic?'

'*Sì, sì,*' they chorused, jumping round him like puppie all the sulks magically forgotten.

'But it is for Lucia to say if you deserve it, agreed?' H

smiled coolly at Lucy. 'Fiammetta says the children may go and talk to her while she dresses. I have come to collect them—and just at the right moment, it seems.'

'Yes.' The towel was perfectly adequate, but Lucy felt absurdly flustered under his lingering scrutiny. 'Thank you,' she added.

'*Prego.*' As the children scampered ahead into the evening sunlight, Giulio turned back suddenly from the door. The smile that curved his mouth now was intimate, and a little wry. He said softly, 'And if I am good for a day, *mia cara*, will you reward me?'

The blood burned in her face. She said quietly, 'I think I'm on safe ground, *signore*. Twenty-four hours is a long time.'

And, with as much dignity as she could muster in a bath-towel, she turned and retreated upstairs, aware that he was watching her every step of the way.

From the window she watched him cross the courtyard, her fist pressed to her mouth so tightly that her lips felt bruised.

Twenty-four hours, she thought. A very long time. Long enough to fall in love. Long enough to discover the kind of pain that could tear you apart, and leave you suffering for all eternity. Long enough to realise you wanted to die.

Only it was never that simple. You just had to go on living—and hurting.

'Hating him,' she whispered rawly, 'would have been so much easier.'

Lucy expected to find the family already assembled in the *salotto* when she eventually made her reluctant entrance, but to her surprise Philip was the only occupant.

He was standing staring moodily out of the window, holding a Campari and soda, but he turned as she came in, glaring at her.

'What's the game, Luce? What are you doing here?'

'I have a temporary job as nanny to Signora Rinaldi's children.'

'That's rubbish, and you know it. I think you came here deliberately, to embarrass me.' He shook his head, more in sorrow than in anger. 'I'm disappointed in you, Luce. I thought you had more dignity—more pride.'

'Don't flatter yourself,' Lucy advised him curtly. 'I had no idea that your girlfriend had any connection with this household. In fact, the entire family were strangers to me up until yesterday.'

'You expect me to believe that? That you've taken a holiday job skivvying for a crowd you don't even know?' He laughed rudely. 'Pull the other one.'

'I really don't care what you believe.' How strange, she thought, that it should be true. 'But it happened.' She paused. 'I got ripped off and needed some cash. They needed a nanny.' She gave him a minatory look. 'But as far as I'm concerned, Philip, you and I are strangers too. Our meeting like this is an appalling coincidence, but it doesn't have to be a disaster.'

'I suppose not,' he said crossly. 'Though it's on a par with the rest of this ghastly trip.' He sat down heavily on one of the sofas. 'It was meant to be a romantic holiday for two,' he complained. 'And then, as soon as we got to Florence, Angela suddenly turned into this culture vulture. It was a nightmare. We actually had to queue to get into the Uffizi, and, as for that guy's statue of David, there must be dozens of the damned things. Every time I turned round there was one looming over me.'

Lucy wanted badly to laugh. She said gently, 'I think most of them are copies and the original is in the Accademia.'

'Oh, well, you would know, of course.' He subjected her

) a critical look. 'I haven't seen that before.' He sounded lmost pettish.

Lucy glanced down at the floating wraparound skirt in lue, green and turquoise, which she'd teamed with a simple coop-necked white top. 'No, it's new. I bought it for this ip.'

'Hardly nanny gear,' he said sourly. 'But I suppose you now what you're doing.' He drank some of his Campari. To be honest, Luce, I wasn't expecting to stay with Angie's elatives, either. She never said a word about it in London.' Ie brightened slightly. 'But I suppose it's a good sign— /anting me to meet the family.' He lowered his voice. 'But ie aunt—the *contessa*—she's a bit of a blight.'

'I find her charming,' Lucy said mendaciously.

'There's no accounting for taste.' He favoured her with mother, longer look. 'I've got to hand it to you, Luce. 'ou're looking terrific.'

'Thank you,' she said drily.

'I mean it.' His eyes narrowed. 'As fanciable as you were /hen I met you.'

She said calmly, 'Or until you started fancying Angela nstead.'

'Oh, come on, Luce.' He gave her the boyish grin which /ould once have turned her legs to jelly. 'We had some ood times together, you must admit.'

'Did we?' She glanced at her watch. Where the hell was veryone?

'You know we did.' He put down his drink and stood up. .ucy watched these manoeuvres with disfavour.

She said, 'Whatever you're planning, Philip, forget it. .nd stop calling me Luce. I've always hated it.'

He stopped in front of her, staring down at her as if he'd ever seen her before. And maybe, she thought, he never ad, at that.

'Well, well,' he said unpleasantly. 'Aren't we suddenly

high and mighty? Could it be because you think the great Giulio Falcone is making a move on you? I wasn't blind to what was going on down at the pool when we arrived. According to Angela, he's famous for his casual flings, but his standards are usually higher.'

The smile she summoned cost Lucy a great deal. 'Thanks. I—I'll consider myself warned.'

She heard a sound behind her and turned. Giulio was standing in the doorway watching them, his face expressionless.

He said, 'Good evening. It is a poor host who keeps a guest waiting.'

'Oh, that's all right.' Philip moved back towards the sofa, distancing himself from Lucy. 'Angela said I should help myself to a drink.'

'But of course. Usually there would be someone to wait on you, but at the moment we are having servant problems.' He walked to the side-table where an array of bottles waited. 'May I offer you something, Lucia?'

'Just some fruit juice, please.'

He said mockingly, 'But how virtuous.'

He poured orange juice from a pitcher and added ice before handing it to her. It was only the tinkling of the cubes against the side of the glass that made her realise her hand was shaking.

Philip downed the remainder of his Campari. 'I think I'll go and see what's keeping Angela.'

'The eternal problem of what to wear, no doubt,' Giulio said courteously, pouring himself a whisky as Philip went towards the door.

He left a silence behind him that could have been cut with a knife.

Lucy made herself drink some of the fruit juice, forcing it down her taut throat, waiting for whatever was to come.

When at last he spoke, his voice was almost gentle. 'Keep
way from him, Lucia. He is not for you.'

Do you think I don't know that? she wanted to scream at
im. How can you be so blind? Don't you know I'd have
ied rather than have him touch me?

Instead, 'Is that a warning?' she asked, keeping her tone
eliberately light.

'No.' He shook his head. 'An order—which you will
bey.'

'Because he belongs to your cousin Angela?' she chal-
nged.

His smile was suddenly harsh, almost feral. 'Perhaps.
ntil she tires of him. She is cursed with a low boredom
reshold.'

'I imagine it's a family trait.' She drank some more of
e juice. 'And if I decide to ignore your command?'

The amber eyes met hers starkly and sombrely. He said,
hen I shall make you sorry—sorry that you ever came
ere.'

'You're too late, *signore*.' Lucy lifted her chin. 'I already
gret it more than anything in my life. So, what have I got
lose?'

The silence between them seemed to stretch into eternity.
he saw his face harden into a bronze mask. Watched him
ke one long stride towards her. And stop, as if he'd sud-
enly found himself on the brink of some abyss.

He said with remote civility, 'In that case, *signorina*, there
no more to be said.'

Then the door to the *salotto* opened and Fiammetta came
on a gale of laughing apologies, the children following
her wake.

Lucy went over to the window, staring unseeingly at the
adows falling across the garden.

She thought, So that's that. And wished with all her heart
at she could feel relief instead of this aching wilderness
desolation.

CHAPTER EIGHT

IF LUCY hadn't been feeling so raw, dinner at the Villa Dante that evening would have been almost funny.

Philip, seated by the *contessa*, found all his conversational overtures either stonily blocked or sent whistling past his ear in the verbal equivalent of a passing shot, however much charm he exerted. Before the melon and prosciutto was finished, and the next course of chicken in a wine sauce served, he had developed a hunted look.

Angela, in a cream silk sheath which would probably have cost Lucy three months' salary, and did more than justice to her seductive cleavage and long, shapely legs, was focusing all her attention on Giulio. The lowered voice, the body language which virtually excluded everyone else at the table with one turn of her shoulder, the hand toying with his cuff button, the soft, breathy giggles—all these proclaimed a long-established and unassailable intimacy.

Which Giulio's own behaviour did nothing to contradict Lucy admitted fairly and with pain. He was relaxed, the dark face amused and intent as he responded to his companion.

Lucy's forebodings, it seemed, had been perfectly justified. Philip, she addressed him silently, you haven't a prayer. So much for your romantic holiday. All this and the Uffizi too.

She concentrated her own efforts on persuading the children to sit still and eat, and lending an ear to Fiammetta's rapturous description of the apartment in New York that they would all be moving into in the autumn.

She too would move, she decided. She might even change jobs when she got back to London. Make a whole fresh start

100

Seek forgetfulness and healing in a frenzy of activity and new horizons. And pray that it worked.

Marco nudged her. 'When does the day start?' he whispered conspiratorially. 'The day when we have to be good.'

'Right this minute,' she whispered back. 'Twenty-four whole hours. So no being horrid in the night.'

His crestfallen air suggested that plans for tormenting Emilia had been well advanced. Then, with a philosophical shrug, he applied himself to his peach ice cream.

It was when coffee was served and the carafes of grappa and Vin Santo appeared on the table that everything suddenly changed.

The *contessa*, ignoring Philip, was talking to Fiammetta, waving a languid hand as she made a point, when Giulio leaned forward.

'My dear Claudia.' His voice was silky. 'I see you are wearing the Falcone ring tonight. Does this mean you are returning it at last?'

The *contessa* glanced at her hand. The ring in question, Lucy saw, was a spectacular ruby in an antique gold setting.

'*Caro* Giulio,' she purred. 'How wicked of you to raise such a subject with strangers present. We surely do not need to—wash our linen in public.'

Giulio shrugged indifferently. 'My attempts to do so privately have been fruitless. As your lawyers have told you on several occasions, the ring is an heirloom, not a piece of costume jewellery, and should have been given back to the Falcone estate after my father's death.'

'In order that the new Conte Falcone might present it to his wife?' Claudia Falcone gave a silvery laugh. 'But you have no wife, *mio caro*. Indeed, you are becoming quite famous for remaining single.'

She lifted her shoulders in an elegant shrug. 'So—the matter is in your own hands.' Her smiling glance rested obliquely on Angela. 'All you have to do is gratify the wish of my heart by announcing your engagement, and I shall willingly bestow the ring on your bride to be.'

She stretched out her hand, studying the ruby at arm's length. It glowed like blood and fire on her thin finger.

'This is a tiresome argument,' Giulio Falcone said coldly. 'My marriage plans have no bearing on the issue. The ring belongs to the estate whether or not I stay a bachelor to the end of my days.'

'And is that what you intend?' Her arched brows lifted in challenge.

'No,' he said coolly. 'I shall be married before the year is out. But that—forgive me, my dear Claudia—is no concern of yours. And the presentation of the jewel to my *fidanzata* is also a private matter, not some ritual devised and orchestrated by you.'

'What a drama.' Claudia laughed again, but a tiny muscle twitched at the side of her mouth. 'We should apologise to our guests, *caro*, for subjecting them to this boring family squabble.' She looked at Giulio, her eyes hard, her lips thin. 'I cherish the ring in memory of your dear father. I cannot believe that you could be so heartless as to deprive me of it without just cause.'

'My cause is just,' Giulio returned icily. 'And established in law.'

Claudia inclined her head regally. 'And when you decide to marry I will hand it over. Until then, it is perfectly safe with me—indeed I hardly let it out of my sight—and there is no more to be said.'

Marco was still scraping the last of his ice cream from his plate, but Emilia's eyes, Lucy saw, were like saucers.

They should not, she thought grimly, be hearing all this. And nor, she added as anguish lanced through her, should I.

She pushed back her chair. 'With your permission, signora, I will put the children to bed. It's been a long day

'Twenty-four whole hours,' Marco contributed brightly, and a laugh ran round the table, visibly dissipating the tension.

'Come to me, *carissimo*.' The *contessa* held out her arms to the child, and he ran round the table to her, to be hugged and kissed. When it was Emilia's turn, Lucy noticed with fury, her grandmother simply touched a swift, indifferent hand to the child's cheek and immediately turned away.

'I will come with you.' Fiammetta helped Lucy usher the children from the dining room. '*Dio mio*, what a scene!' she confided in an undertone as they walked through the night-scented garden, the children scampering ahead. 'The problem is, the ring has great value—it dates from the fifteenth century—and it should be kept in the bank. Mamma knows this, but always she has some excuse not to hand it back, and now Giulio has become angry, and little wonder.'

She rolled her eyes to heaven. 'And so it is war between them. I only hope Mamma does not do something foolish. She is not good with money, you understand,' she added with an expressive shrug. 'If Giulio took her to court, as he might, she could be ruined.'

'Can't you—reason with her?' Lucy suggested awkwardly.

'Over some things, but not this. She will not listen. And she provokes him constantly, as she did tonight, by flaunting it on totally unimportant occasions.' She sighed. 'Perhaps he should not have said what he did, but I cannot blame him.'

'Maybe she was trying to needle him into proposing to your cousin there and then.' Lucy spoke haltingly, the words stabbing her like knives.

'Then she does not know Giulio,' said Fiammetta dismissively. 'Although it cannot be long,' she added, after a pause. 'Did you see how they were together tonight?'

'Yes,' Lucy said dully. 'I saw.'

'And this poor Philip Winslade, who has now served his purpose…' Fiammetta gave another gusty sigh. 'If I were in his shoes, I would not stay here to be humiliated any further, would you?'

'Perhaps he loves her,' Lucy said slowly. 'Maybe he's prepared to endure anything just to be with her, even if he knows, deep down, he's wasting his time—that all the future can promise him is pain and loneliness beyond belief.'

Fiammetta shot her an amazed look. 'Why, Lucia, that came from the heart, I think.'

And it's also given far too much away, thought Lucy, seeing the inevitable questions forming on her companion's lips.

She quickened her step. 'Slow down, you two,' she called. 'It's dark, and you're going to fall and hurt yourselves.'

Any hint of possible damage to her little ones was exactly the right diversion for Fiammetta, who fussed the remainder of the way to the *casetta*.

The children's bedtime passed without trouble, although Emilia was inclined to whinge and cling to her mother. But who could blame her for that? Lucy thought wearily.

When Fiammetta had departed for the villa, and the *casetta* was quiet, Lucy went and sat down on the stone bench outside the door. After the stillness of the day, the night was full of noise and movement—the rasping of crickets, the moths swooping round the overhead lamp, the harsh cry of a bird.

And, rising above the villa, there was the moon's golden crooked smile, which seemed in Lucy's present vulnerable state to be taunting her.

She had her book on her lap, but she didn't open it. Her mind was running riot with thoughts and impressions, most of them unhappy. How could your whole life—your whole perception of who you were and what you wanted—chang so fast and so irrevocably? she asked herself, not for the first time. It wasn't sane—it wasn't rational.

Giulio Falcone had taken possession of her, heart, mind and soul. From that first encounter, she'd seen the danger—recognised what was happening to her—but been unable to resist.

Swept away helplessly, she thought, by the force of destiny. And who could tell where it would all end?

She rallied herself. Yet there'd been one positive step. She had kissed Emilia goodnight, and while the embrace hadn't been returned it hadn't been rejected either. Maybe if she could help stabilise the child, give her a sense of her own worth, then her stay in Tuscany would have some meaning—even some value.

The sound of approaching footsteps invaded her reverie, and she sat up sharply, her whole body tensing as a tall, familiar figure walked under the archway into the courtyard.

'Good evening once again, *signore*.' It took every scrap of courage she possessed to speak so nonchalantly. 'Have you come for another fight?'

'No.' His tone was dry, almost reflective. 'My battles are over for the day. I came to check on the children—and to make sure you have everything you need.' He paused. 'May I sit down?'

'Shouldn't you go back to your guests?'

'I invited Fiammetta and the children,' he said softly, 'and them alone. And as Fiammetta is playing cards, and the children, presumably, are asleep, I can now please myself.'

She moved to the far end of the bench, tucking the folds of her skirt around her. Giulio observed this manoeuvre with raised brows, then seated himself at the other end.

'You are not nervous, away from the main house?'

Not until this moment, she thought.

She said, 'I suppose you're going to tell me there are gangs of armed robbers roaming the neighbourhood.'

'No, thank God. Here we are among our own people.' He paused again. 'But down at the pool you mentioned that you thought someone was watching.'

She shrugged. 'Well, yes, but I could have been wrong.'

'Because it was not me, it follows that it must be no one?' There was an edge to his voice. '*Grazie.*'

'It might have been a cat,' she said lamely.

'*Sì,* or a wild boar, or a wolf from the hills.' His tone was exasperated.

'Or just my imagination,' she persisted. She managed a laugh. 'There's an old Chinese curse—May you live in interesting times. Well, I've lived through some fascinating ones lately. Perhaps it's made me a little paranoid.'

'I do not think you are that.' He was frowning. 'But I know you are unhappy, and it troubles me, because I am to blame.' He drew a breath. 'I never meant you to be hurt like this, Lucia, believe me.'

'Please.' All the breath in her body seemed to catch in her throat. 'I—I'd rather not discuss it.'

'But we cannot pretend that the situation does not exist.'

'You may not be able to,' she said almost savagely. 'But I can. I'm a great pretender.'

'Lucia.' He stretched a hand towards her, and she recoiled.

'No. Can't you see—don't you understand that talking about it only makes things worse? Can't you show me a little mercy at least?'

'*Dio mio,*' he whispered. 'I did not realise the wound had gone so deep.' The dark face was like stone. '*Columbina—* is there nothing I can do?'

'You said this morning that it would be better if I went.' She bunched her trembling hands into fists and hid them in the folds of her skirt. 'I—I've come to agree with you. I'll leave just as soon as you can find someone else to look after the children.'

He was silent for a moment, staring down at the rough cobbles. Then he said quietly, 'As you wish. Teresa has a cousin, training to be a teacher, who is looking for a vacation job. I will see what can be arranged.' He paused again. 'What will you do?'

'What I originally planned. Go back to England on the first available flight.' She moistened her dry lips with the tip of her tongue. 'Get on with my life.'

'How simple you make it sound.' Beneath the surface of the smooth words, something very different was bubbling. Something that could have been anger—even bitterness. 'How rational. And yet we both know it is nothing of the kind.'

Before she could guess what he was going to do, he had reached for her, the long arms drawing her roughly, inexorably towards him, lifting her so that she was lying across him, cradled on his thighs.

For a brief second, she saw his face above her in the moonlight, the suddenly harsh lines etched beside his mouth, the glitter in his eyes. The falcon, she thought dazedly, with his prey. About to swoop—to carry her off into eternal darkness.

Then his lips were on hers, fierce, searching, demanding a response which Lucy knew, in some distant, reeling corner of her mind, she should deny him. She knew she should struggle, beat him with her fists, make him let her go.

But the heat of his mouth and the scent of his skin were like some insidious drug, draining the power of resistance from her. Her head fell back helplessly against his arm as her lips parted in acceptance. Even welcome.

And when her hands lifted it was not in self-defence but to close on the whipcord strength of his shoulders and draw him down to her.

Because this was what she wanted, she thought achingly. What was the point in pretending otherwise? She could not have his love, or a share in his life, but she would take what little he could offer. A brief interlude of passion. A memory to warm her in the bleak emptiness of the future.

His mouth explored hers roughly, as if he too was driven by forces, needs he could not control. The thrust of his tongue was like burning silk, creating a sweet madness she had never known before. Awakening longings she had never realised existed.

She kissed him back, answering his fire with her own ardour, drinking him as eagerly as a flower absorbed the rain.

His hand went to her breast, outlining its rounded swell with fingers that shook slightly, before sliding with new mastery beneath the clinging top to push it upwards. To find and celebrate her warm nakedness.

For a long moment, he was still, cupping the soft weight in his palm. Then he took his mouth slowly from hers, his eyes studying her flushed face with telling awareness. As his gaze held hers, he began to move his thumb softly and rhythmically, circling—tantalising her nipple.

Lucy felt herself gasp in startled yearning. Saw him smile. Felt that smile brush her parted lips in a kiss of magical tenderness, before he feathered a caress across the delicate peak, bringing it to instant pulsating life.

He bent his dark head, his mouth seductive as it moved on her heated, tumescent flesh. The gentle tug of his lips, the faint graze of his teeth, the flick of his tongue on the hardened, sensitive bud—all these were a web of arousal enmeshing and enthralling her. As, somehow, she had always known they would be. As if she had been born for this moment alone, her body arched towards him in delight and an unspoken offering more eloquent than any words.

'*Mia bella, mia carissima.*' His voice was hushed, husky against her skin. He sounded, she thought, almost like a stranger. He lifted his head—looked at her. 'Do you know you taste of moonlight?'

Half-shyly, Lucy touched the dark, springy hair, then ran a hand down the column of his throat to the V of skin exposed by the open neck of his silk shirt. The need to touch him in her turn was overwhelming. Fingers shaking, she began to undo his shirt buttons. She spread her hands across his chest, savouring the texture of his hair-roughened skin, letting the race of his heartbeat thud against her palm.

She planted frantic little kisses over his torso, feeling the flat male nipples pucker and harden under the teasing of her lips.

He took her hands, kissed them and carried them to his body. 'This is how I want you.' The words were barely a whisper.

The breath caught in Lucy's throat as she recognised the strength and power that would soon be part of her—joined with her. She was aware of him parting the folds of her skirt, of the glide of his hand along her slender thigh, and her whole body clenched in anticipation and desire.

His mouth took hers again, but this time his kiss was subtle, sensuous, his tongue as light as a butterfly's wing as it explored the swollen softness of her lips, while with equal and unerring delicacy his long fingers began a more intimate quest.

Lucy sighed her acquiescence against his lips. Almost at once, she was caught, and drowning in a golden net of pleasure so acute that she wanted to laugh, to weep, to cry out all at the same moment.

But the scream that rang out was a very different one. It was a child's voice, shouting in fear.

The delight shattered in an instant.

'Oh, God.' Lucy tore herself, dry-mouthed, from his arms, pulling her clothing into place with frantic hands. 'Emilia! What's Marco doing to her?'

She flew into the *casetta*, taking the stairs two at a time, aware that Giulio was just behind her.

Emilia was sitting up in bed, her hands clasped over her ears, her face contorted, her mouth opening for another scream.

'Hush, darling.' Lucy knelt on the bed, drawing the child into her arms. 'What's the matter?'

She was engulfed in a flood of sobbing Italian.

But, whatever the problem, Marco could not be blamed, she noted thankfully. One glance at the other bed revealed him to be asleep and oblivious.

'She had a bad dream,' Giulio translated, sitting down on the opposite side of the bed. 'She was in a car that crashed, and she could not get out.'

'But that didn't happen, Emilia.' Gently, Lucy stroked the silky hair. 'You're here and perfectly safe.'

'Zio Giulio.' The child turned to him, still hiccuping with sobs.

'Lucia is right, *cara*.' Giulio took the damp bundle into his arms, and began to mop her face with his handkerchief. 'All is well.'

'Not Alison,' Emilia objected. 'She was hurt.'

'Yes,' he agreed. 'But even Alison will be well again soon. And to prove it I will take you to visit her. She has her leg in a big plaster cast, and she will let you draw a picture on it.'

'Really and truly?' The sobs died away as Emilia considered this new and entrancing prospect.

'Really and truly,' he confirmed, dropping a kiss on the top of her head. 'And now you must lie down and go to sleep again.'

'I want a drink,' Emilia decided fretfully. 'And for you to stay with me, Zio Giulio.'

'I'll heat some milk,' Lucy said quietly, and went downstairs.

Emilia's nightmare, she realised as she busied herself at the stove, had been her own salvation. Because she had been on the verge of giving herself, body and soul, to a man who belonged to someone else. A man who could only see her as a source of casual pleasure. And she would have been left to survive alone the pain and emotional battering of such a surrender.

Will I ever learn? she lashed herself mentally. Or am I simply stark raving mad?

But, thankfully, circumstances had restored her sanity without too much harm being done, except perhaps to her self-respect, she thought, recalling her enthralled, mindless response to Giulio's lovemaking.

She sank her teeth into her bottom lip as she poured the milk into a beaker, and carried it upstairs.

Emilia was calm enough, and even giggling a little at whatever Giulio was murmuring to her. She drank the milk without fuss, then settled back on her pillows, holding firmly onto her uncle's hand.

'And Lucia must stay too,' she decreed. 'Alison used to tell me stories. I like best the one about Cinderella.'

'So Cinderella it must be.' Giulio's eyes met Lucy's across the narrow bed. 'You know that story, *columbina*?'

I feel as if I'm living it, she thought, hurriedly looking away. Except that midnight has struck, I've changed back into my rags, and there's going to be no happy ending.

She felt absurdly self-conscious too, starkly aware of Giulio's presence, within touching distance of her. Indeed, the whole intimate scenario of the bedroom, the drowsy child, the two of them united in comforting her was almost too painful to be borne, encompassing, as it did, so many might-have-beens.

But there was still a kind of peace to be enjoyed in re-telling the age-old story of love, loss and rediscovery, she found wonderingly. She kept her voice deliberately soft and even, and long before Cinderella had fled, leaving her glass slipper on the Prince's stairway, Emilia was asleep.

'She should be all right now.' Lucy got up gingerly. 'But I'll sleep with my door open, just in case.'

Giulio rose too, detaching his hand from the small fingers with infinite care.

'I think you are wasted on the advertising industry, *mia bella*.' The amber eyes studied her ironically as she paused on her way to the door to remove Marco's thumb from his mouth. 'You seem to have a gift with children.'

'Not particularly.' Lucy went out of the room and downstairs to the kitchen, head held rigidly high, aware that he was following. 'A story and a glass of milk doesn't turn me into Mary Poppins.'

His voice reached her quietly. 'Are you so certain you wish to leave?'

'More than ever.' Her reply was curt, and she kept her back turned as she rinsed the empty glass.

He said, 'You think if you stay, then I shall try to make love to you again.' He paused. 'I shall not. My behaviour tonight was a grave mistake. As things are, I had no right to touch you.'

'At least we agree on something,' she muttered.

'I have no excuse to offer,' he went on as if she hadn't spoken. 'Except that you were very lovely.'

And very willing. He didn't actually say the words aloud, but then, Lucy thought bitterly, he didn't have to. They were there just the same, quivering in the air between them.

Her tone was biting. 'And what excuse can I make? That you're clearly an expert in seduction, that I lost touch with reality for a few moments?'

'If that is what you wish to believe.' He sounded weary. 'At any rate, there will be no repetition. Is that the assurance you seek?'

She said raggedly, 'I don't want assurances, just my freedom.' She drew a harsh breath. 'And as soon as it can be arranged.'

'Then you shall have it,' he said almost savagely. 'And I hope for your sake, *carissima*, that it does not cost you too dear.'

She heard him go out. Heard the door close behind him. Realised she had been gripping the edge of the sink so tightly that her knuckles had turned white.

Slowly, painfully she unclenched her hands.

She thought, So this is where it ends. And I should be glad. But I'm not. Oh, dear God, I'm not.

And she felt one terrible dry, aching sob force its way from the tautness in her chest and explode, at last, in the relief of tears.

CHAPTER NINE

IT WAS a wretched, interminable night which Lucy spent tossing restlessly on her hard mattress.

She felt as if she was trapped in some terrible limbo. The thought of leaving—of never seeing Giulio again—was well-nigh unbearable. And yet she dared not stay either, because she knew that if she did she would be utterly destroyed.

Nor could she come to terms with how quickly this emotional devastation had invaded her life. How could all her expectations—her values—have been turned on their heads in little more than a matter of hours? And when, by rights, she should still have been grieving for Philip, too.

I must be terminally shallow, she thought in savage self-derision. But I don't even know who I am any more—or what's happened to me.

She'd viewed love as a stable commitment growing from mutual liking and shared interests, not as a tempest force of anguish, desire and jealousy, fuelled by an uncontrollable physical attraction, sweeping into her life, wrecking all her safe preconceptions.

That's not love, she argued silently. That's lust.

And perhaps it would die as swiftly and unpredictably as it had roared into life, overwhelming her almost before she was aware.

That, anyway, was all she could pray.

But her sleepless turmoil was not solely due to her troublous thoughts. Some of it at least was down to sheer sexual frustration, although it galled her to admit it. She had been aroused almost to the brink of fulfilment, lifted to the

114

heights, and then hurled into some dark abyss of pain and longing. She had been given a hint—a promise of passion's ecstasy. Now she needed the surcease of completion, of consummation.

But it was never going to happen, she told herself, biting her lip until she tasted fresh blood.

Her hands strayed down her feverish body, retracing the path his lips and fingers had taken. Her skin burned against the rasp of the thin sheet which covered her. She was molten with her need for him. Sick with shame at the temptations which racked her.

She turned over, burying her flushed face in the thin pillow. A temporary physical release wasn't what she needed. Only in Giulio's arms could the promise of love be satisfied. And nothing less would do.

It was nearly dawn before she finally drifted into a troubled sleep, and surely only five minutes later when a feeling that she was being bounced like a ball and a shrill 'Wake up, Lucia, I am hungry' from Marco dragged her back to full consciousness again.

He was kneeling on the end of her bed, testing its resilience with a series of energetic springs.

Lucy said wearily, 'Marco, this is not a trampoline. Go and get dressed, and I'll be right with you.'

'Have we been good? Has the twenty-four hours happened yet?'

She said crisply, 'No, you still have to do exactly what you're told.'

He was struggling into shorts and a T-shirt when she went into the children's room a few minutes later. Emilia, already dressed, was sitting on her bed reading. She sent Lucy a wary but not unfriendly look.

Which, Lucy thought, was a step in the right direction—or would be, perhaps, if she was staying...

Breakfast at the villa was a buffet affair. A selection of

cold meats, cheeses, fruit, preserves and warm rolls was set out on the sideboard, with coffee and a tall frosted jug of freshly squeezed orange juice.

Lucy served the children, then helped herself to bread, cherry jam, and a pear.

She had barely sat down, when Angela arrived. She treated them all to an indifferent nod and walked to the sideboard. Without looking round, she said, 'My aunt wishes to have breakfast in her room. Will you see to her tray—er—Lucy, isn't it?'

For one dazed moment, Lucy surveyed the other girl's back, immaculately clad in white shorts and top, and wondered how it would look struck amidships by a torpedo loaded with cherry jam. Encountering a gleeful smile from Emilia, she realised that her feelings must be inscribed in capitals across her face, and hastily composed herself.

'Of course.' She paused. 'Miss—er—?'

'Brockhurst,' Angela supplied coldly as she came to the table. She gave Marco a look of distaste. 'Does he have to cram his mouth like that?'

Lucy, who'd been about to reprove Marco for the self-same thing, shrugged instead. 'I like to see a child with a healthy appetite,' she tossed over her shoulder as she left the room.

Teresa supplied a tray laid with a snowy cloth, some special china decorated with a florid gold design, and a gleaming silver coffee service, and accompanied it with shrugs, grimaces and a commiserating pat on Lucy's shoulder.

As Lucy carried the tray towards the stairs, she was halted by Giulio's voice.

'What are you doing?'

Heart thudding, Lucy turned slowly. He was standing at the open front door, a dark silhouette against the morning sun.

Fighting to control her voice, she said, 'I'm taking the *contessa's* breakfast to her room.'

'On whose instructions?' He came a few steps closer.

For the first time in their brief acquaintance, he looked less than his usual impeccable self. He needed a shave, Lucy noted with a pang, and he seemed to have thrown on the clothes he was wearing the night before.

'Aunt Claudia's, darling.' Angela appeared from the dining room. 'Please don't hang around—er—Lucy. The *contessa* doesn't appreciate tepid coffee.'

'Nor does Miss Winters appreciate being treated like a servant.' There was ice in Giulio's voice. 'Your aunt has a maid to wait on her already. Where is she?'

'Probably pressing Aunt Claudia's clothes for the day.' Angela's eyes narrowed rather unattractively. 'Anyway, *caro*, what's the big deal? It's only a breakfast tray.'

'Of course it is.' Giulio took the tray from Lucy's unresisting hands. 'And as I am going upstairs I will take it to her myself. At the same time, I can clear up any misconceptions she may have about Lucia's role in this house.'

There was a jarring note in Angela's gurgle of laughter. 'Oh, I think we've all figured that out, my sweet.' She shrugged. 'But then, who am I to object to your little—escapades? I'm not immune myself.'

Lucy, stiffening with distaste, turned and went back to the dining room and her own tepid coffee.

But not before she heard Angela's stage whisper. 'However, if you're trying to make me jealous, darling, you'll have to do better than that pallid little stick.'

Which, Lucy thought forlornly, she supposed she deserved.

Clearly, it was going to be a very hot day. Lucy spent the first part of the morning trying to beguile the children into making a get-well card for Alison, but all they did was squabble over the design, so eventually she cut her losses and took them down to the pool for a swim.

Emilia was obviously nervous of the water, but trying not to show it, and Marco, from the safety of armbands, was inclined to crow over her, so Lucy found a ball in the small cabin where the loungers and mattresses were kept, and they splashed about happily in the shallow end, playing catch and piggy in the middle. Until…

'What a hideous noise,' Angela said acidly. She was standing on the edge of the pool, with Phiip hovering behind her looking ill at ease. She was wearing a black and gold swimsuit, with a matching silk jacket, and her feet were thrust into gold wedge-heeled sandals.

The wasp look, Lucy thought uncharitably.

'I've come here to relax,' Angela went on fretfully. 'Can' you take the brats somewhere else to play?'

Lucy said quietly. 'We've only just got here, Miss Brockhurst.'

'What difference does that make?' Angela adjusted the angle of her elegant straw hat. 'I'm telling you to go. I' like some peace—and some privacy.' She flashed Philip swift smile, loaded with meaning, then gave Lucy's chain store bikini a contemptuous glance, without even changing gear.

'And I'm sure Zia Claudia doesn't allow the hired hel to use the pool at the same time as her guests, anyway,' sh added.

Controlling her anger, Lucy lifted the protesting childre out of the water and wrapped them in towels.

She said, 'I'll try to remember that.'

'I should,' Angela said curtly. 'All my friends in Englan have nannies, and you wouldn't hold down a place for fiv minutes with your attitude.' She added in an underton 'And don't give yourself airs, my dear, just because Giuli may have made a pass at you. With him it's instinctive—a reflex action—and that's all.'

Lucy fastened her sarong around her with some deliberation. In spite of her glamour and grooming, Angela, she decided with satisfaction, had heavy thighs.

'And which of us do you feel you need to convince, Miss Brockhurst?' she asked coolly, and, with a curt nod to the increasingly embarrassed Philip, marched the children away before the other girl could reply.

Both children were whingeing at full throttle by the time they reached the *casetta*, and Lucy could not blame them. She felt like whingeing herself when she saw who was waiting for them, tapping her foot in autocratic impatience.

'So here you are at last,' the *contessa* said with a snap. 'I wondered how much longer I would be kept here.'

'I'm sorry,' Lucy said woodenly. 'I didn't know you wanted to see me.'

'It is usual to present yourself to the mistress of the house for instructions each morning.' The hard eyes studied her. 'Are those intended to be working clothes?'

Lucy sighed inwardly. 'No, *contessa*, I was just going to change.'

'I am pleased to hear it.' The *contessa* paused. She herself was elegant in a mulberry dress and jacket, the Falcone ruby gleaming ostentatiously on her hand. 'I am going to lunch with some friends near Siena and I shall take Marco with me. Kindly see that he is properly and tidily dressed.'

'But Nonna—' Emilia's voice was woeful '—Zio Giulio said he would take us to see Alison in the clinic.'

'Your uncle has better things to do than attend to the wishes of a small girl,' the *contessa* said crushingly. She addressed Lucy. 'You will bring Marco to the villa as soon as he is ready. I wish to leave at once.'

Lucy said carefully, 'Only Marco?'

'You heard me, I think.' The *contessa* examined the

enamel on her nails. 'My friends possess many valuable things, and Emilia, unfortunately, cannot be trusted. She had better remain here.'

'I do not want to go anyway.' Emilia's face was stormy. Lucy, placing a soothing hand on her small shoulder, found that it was trembling. 'I hate you—hate you…' Her voice broke down in sobs.

'What an outburst.' The *contessa's* voice was like drops of cold water. 'And how dare you speak to me in such a way? Are you sure you are equipped, *signorina*, to deal with the problems of such a child?'

Lucy stood her ground, holding the weeping Emilia. 'Those of her own making, certainly,' she returned with equal ice. 'As few of them are.'

'You are insolent.'

'No, just truthful.' She put a hand on Marco's shoulder 'Go indoors, *caro*, and wait for me,' she directed gently.

'I want to stay here.' He gave an excited jump, his eyes going past her. 'Zio Giulio, come and see Lucia and Nonna having a fight.'

'What is going on here?' Giulio came striding into the courtyard, his amber eyes sweeping over them all. 'Why i Emilia crying?'

'A storm in a teacup,' the *contessa* proclaimed dismissively. 'But I have to tell you, *caro* Giulio, that Signorin Winters is not sufficiently mature to have the care of thes children. The example she sets is a poor one. I demand yo dismiss her instantly.'

'You are too late, Claudia.' Giulio's fine mouth curle slightly. 'The *signorina* seems to share your view, and o fered her resignation yesterday evening.'

'Oh?' Claudia Falcone seemed startled. 'And who wi take her place?'

'Teresa's cousin, Dorotea, as soon as she can be co

tacted.' Giulio gently turned Emilia to face him. 'What is it, little one?'

'Nonna said I was a thief.'

The *contessa* shrugged. 'I said merely that I was not prepared to take her to the Masserinis for lunch until her behaviour improves and she can be trusted.'

'Then you can have lunch with me instead, *cara*.' Giulio ran a finger down the child's tear-stained cheek. 'Go and wash and change.'

Emilia's smile was like the sun emerging from clouds, but the final glance she sent her grandmother as she went into the *casetta* was pregnant with malice. Marco trailed after her.

The *contessa* said, 'My dear Giulio, you cannot desert your guests in this way. Angela will be wondering what has become of you.'

'Then you will be able to tell her, Claudia—before you go to lunch with the Masserinis.' His meditative gaze went to his stepmother's hand. 'You are wearing the Falcone ring once again, I see.'

The *contessa* gave her tinkling laugh. 'But naturally, *caro*. Simonetta's jewellery is always so fabulous.'

His voice was too gentle. 'You think it appropriate to use a family heirloom, centuries old, to compete with that—that *arrivista*?'

Her mouth thinned. 'How dare you insult one of my friends?'

'You are mistaken. Simonetta Masserini is impossible to insult.' He paused. 'I request once more, Claudia, that you return the ring to me immediately. It is no longer your property.'

'And I repeat, dear Giulio, that I shall be happy to return it—but to your intended wife, and no other—as tradition demands.' She turned an arctic gaze on Lucy. 'Still here, *signorina*? You are supposed to be helping my grandson to change.'

'And I suggest you change too, Lucia.' There was amusement in Giulio's eyes, mingled with something deeper and more disturbing, as he looked her over. 'Firenze demands rather more formal dress, I think.'

He himself was wearing slim-fitting dark trousers and a plain white shirt, with the sheen of silk, unbuttoned at the neck, and with the sleeves turned back casually over his forearms. All traces of his earlier dishevelment had been removed, Lucy noted as she ran the tip of her tongue over her dry lips. 'You expect me to go with you?' she enquired uncertainly.

He shrugged. 'Naturally. Until your replacement arrives you will carry out your duties in the usual way. And Emilia needs a companion in the car in case she is frightened or ill again.' He glanced at his watch. 'Will fifteen minutes give you enough time?'

Lucy nodded and whisked into the *casetta*. As she went upstairs to find the children she could hear the *contessa* obviously remonstrating with Giulio in furious Italian, and his cold, clipped responses.

The children were listening too, she discovered, and ushered them firmly away from the window and closed the shutters.

'They are quarrelling about the big red ring that Nonna wears,' Marco reported as Lucy hustled both of them into the shower.

'It does not belong to her. She should not have it,' Emilia said passionately as Lucy shampooed the chlorine out of her hair. 'I have heard Papà say so to Mamma—oh, so many times.'

'It's a private argument between grown-ups, and none of our business,' Lucy said firmly. 'Now, what are you going to wear?'

Emilia for once was no problem, dressing herself importantly in a brief red skirt and white blouse before shutting herself in Lucy's bedroom with the hairdryer.

However, it was a day's work to wrestle Marco into the velvet shorts and satin shirt which Lucy reckoned the *contessa* would deem suitable attire for the occasion.

'I hate these clothes,' he grumbled. 'But I like going to lunch with Nonna's friends,' he added slyly. 'They give me presents.'

'You get altogether too much,' Lucy said severely, combing his hair sleekly back from his forehead.

When they were both dressed, she sent them downstairs with picture books, and strict instructions not to get dirty—or quarrel—while she changed.

I'm playing with fire, she told herself as she changed hurriedly into a simple pale yellow shift, tying her hair back with a scarf of the same colour. But I don't care. I don't care about anything except that I'm going to be with him again—just for a while.

It was two incredibly sedate and tidy children that Lucy was able to conduct to the villa.

Fiammetta was in the *salotto*, flicking through a magazine, which she threw aside to embrace the children and adjure them to be good.

'And Lucia,' piped Marco. 'She must be good also.'

'*Sì.*' The ghost of a smile twinkled in Fiammetta's eyes. 'And Emilia will be there to make sure of it.' She extended a hand to Giulio. 'Have a care, *mio caro*. Sometimes, I think, you go too fast.'

'You have wisdom beyond your years.' The words and the kiss he dropped on her wrist were equally light, but the glance they exchanged was loaded with amused significance.

Lucy, noting it, frowned, then promptly relegated it to the

back of her mind as the *contessa* swept in, imperiously demanding her grandson.

After Marco had been duly waved off with his grandmother, Giulio brought his own car round to the front of the house.

'Oh.' Lucy checked in surprise when she saw the sleek, low-slung saloon. 'But this isn't your car.'

'It is one of them,' he returned laconically. 'I thought it would be the most comfortable, as there are three of us.'

'I want to sit in the front,' declared Emilia.

'No, little one.' Giulio firmly strapped her into the back seat, in spite of her protests, then paused, his brows lifting as Lucy got in beside her.

'What is this?'

She said quietly, 'I think I should be with her—in case as you say, there's a problem.'

His mouth twisted. 'Are you sure you are not considering some problem of your own?'

'Quite sure.' Lucy gave him a straight look. 'I'm not the one having nightmares.'

There was a brief silence, then he said, 'Forgive me Lucia. I should not have needed such a reminder.' He smiled at Emilia. 'You see, *cara*. You can pretend to be a great lady—a princess with your own *conducente*, and your lady in-waiting beside you.'

'And where is my prince?' Emilia pouted a little.

'I think you may have to be patient for a while. But he will come one day, never doubt it.' Giulio swung himself lithely behind the wheel and started the engine.

'So, the day is ours,' he added, over his shoulder. '*Avanti* Where shall we go, *principessa*?'

'To Firenze, Zio Giulio; you said so.'

'Ah, yes, but perhaps I've forgotten the way. You will have to give me directions, or we could end up in Rome

And you will have to speak loudly, because I'm old and growing deaf.'

Emilia giggled delightedly and sat up, peering out of the window, waiting eagerly for the first road sign.

There were sometimes muddles over which way was right and which left, and once the approach of a lorry rendered the child mute and visibly frightened, but, helped along by Lucy's soft-voiced interventions and encouragement, the game lasted cheerfully all the way to Florence.

'Thank you,' Lucy murmured to him as they left the car. He had parked in the middle of a vast square, dotted with bronze copies of Michelangelo's most famous statues, including the towering *David*. 'That was very kind of you.'

'And you think cruelty is more natural to me, perhaps?'

She was taken aback. 'Why—no.'

'*Grazie.*' He sounded faintly amused. 'Maybe I just wanted to avoid another reprimand,' he added silkily.

'Oh.' Feeling suddenly awkward, Lucy looked around at the rows of tourist buses disgorging their clients, at the vendors' stalls selling postcards and ceramics, and the inevitable ice-cream sellers. 'What is this place?'

'The Piazzale Michelangelo. The one place that everyone who comes to Firenze must visit, if they see nothing else. Look.' Threading a way between the pavement artists and watercolour sellers, he led her and Emilia to the balustraded wall.

Below them, bisected by the languid Arno, lay Florence, all pale stone and gleaming terracotta, her towers and domes gilded by the sunshine like some glorious medieval painting. And beyond, in the distance, rose the Tuscan hills, misted in shades of grey, blue and purple.

'It's almost too lovely,' Lucy whispered.

'*Sì.*' His voice was gentle, almost reflective. 'Lovelier than any dream.'

Lucy turned her head and found that he was watching

her, his eyes fixed on her face. Instinctive colour flared in her cheeks, and she hurriedly transferred her attention back to the view.

'Whenever I have been away, this is always the first place I return to,' he went on, after a pause.

'Is that the Ponte Vecchio?' She craned her neck, feigning intense interest, trying to disguise her swift, burning awareness of his physical proximity, of his arm almost brushing hers on the stone of the balustrade, the hint of the expensive cologne she would always associate with him, and, more intimately, the unique male scent of his skin, warm and alive and tantalising her senses.

'Yes. It was the one bridge over the Arno left standing after the war. My father always said no one would ever know why the Germans spared it. As it is, many of the goldsmiths there have been able to hang up their signs without interruption since the time of Cosimo de' Medici.'

'Your ancestor,' Lucy said, straight-faced.

He laughed. 'One of them, perhaps.' He paused. 'You wish to buy something on the Ponte Vecchio—some trinket to remind you of Firenze?'

'I think I'll have to stick with rather cheaper souvenirs,' she said ruefully, and straightened, looking for Emilia, who had become bored, and wandered off to look at one of the exhibitions of paintings a few yards away. 'But I'll never forget this view as long as I live,' she added, conscious that she sounded like a polite schoolgirl. 'Thank you for showing it to me.'

He shrugged. 'Maybe this is my day for acts of kindness.' He straightened too, looking down at her, the amber eyes veiled by the sweep of his lashes. 'Yet I know very well I have not always been kind in my dealings with you, Lucia. And probably, in the end, I will have to be cruel—in order to be kind.'

His hand descended on her shoulder, swinging her suddenly and urgently towards him, and for one heart-stopping instant she felt the swift, bruising pressure of his mouth on hers, the shock of his body moulded frankly and demandingly against hers.

Then, with equal speed, before any of their fellow sightseers could register what was happening, she was free again, standing in the sunlight, a hand raised to her startled, throbbing lips, watching him walk away from her. Knowing that, one day soon, she would have to watch him walk away for ever.

And that, she thought numbly, would be the ultimate cruelty. But who could say she hadn't been warned?

CHAPTER TEN

BY THE time she caught up with Giulio and Emilia at the car, Lucy had steadied her hectic breathing, and managed to meet his sardonic gaze with a measure of composure.

'The little one is demanding ice cream,' he said. 'Perhaps we should have lunch before anything else. Do you agree?'

Without waiting for her reluctant nod, he swept them back into the car, and drove down into the city, eventually leaving the car in a quiet side-street off the Piazza della Signoria.

'Now we walk,' he ordained. He took Emilia's hand 'We'll take the tourist trail for Lucia.'

He led the way briskly across the piazza, Emilia bouncing beside him.

'You recognise this?' he tossed over his shoulder.

Lucy was about to respond with a tart 'How could I?' when she realised that her surroundings were oddly familiar She stared at the huge statues from Greek mythology, the commanding figure of yet another bronze *David*, the foun tain, and the wide flight of stone steps leading up to a arched colonnade.

She laughed suddenly. 'Of course. *A Room with a View* The scene where the young man was stabbed.' She halted 'Have you seen it too?' she asked with surprise.

'In London, the year it came out.' Giulio paused too. ' made me homesick.'

'And it convinced me I had to come here at all costs.'

'At all costs?' he repeated thoughtfully. 'Are you sur you have not already paid too highly for your journey?'

She said in a low voice, 'I'm not sure of anything any more.'

Giulio nodded, his face expressionless, and strode purposefully on.

Lucy found herself traversing a busy market, with crowded stalls selling table linen, souvenirs and Florence's famed leather goods. She wanted to linger, but Emilia seized her hand.

'Lucia, come and see Il Porcellino.'

Lucy found herself confronted by a bronze statue of a wild boar, his snout incredibly smooth and shining in contrast to the rest of him.

Giulio leaned down and spoke in her ear, his warm breath fanning her cheek. 'The legend says if you stroke his snout, *columbina*, you will come back to Firenze.'

Clearly it had been the ambition of a lot of people, Lucy thought drily, but it was hardly a safe one in her particular circumstances. Nevertheless, she lifted a reluctant hand and ran it over the gleaming metal, urged on by Emilia, who then demanded some coins from her uncle to drop from the boar's mouth into the grating below.

'That is good luck too,' she beamed.

'Good luck for the children's home which benefits from the money,' Giulio added.

'May I have some more money?' the child wheedled.

Giulio ruffled her hair. 'Later, little one. When we've eaten, I will bring you back.'

They ended up at a small restaurant in one of the narrow streets leading away from the Duomo, with pavement tables shaded by a dark green awning. A small, tubby man who was clearly the proprietor came bustling out to meet them, his face wreathed in smiles. He shook hands with Giulio, hugged Emilia ebulliently, with a promise that when she had eaten she would see the new litter of kittens in the courtyard at the rear, then turned a look of melting admiration on Lucy.

'*Bella donna,*' he breathed, disregarding Giulio's more laconic introduction. '*Bella donna.*'

They were shown almost reverently to the best table, and wine, mineral water and warm bread appeared instantly.

'Giovanni serves some of the best food in Firenze, and we're having the specialities of the house,' Giulio told her as a dish of *crostini* was brought—toasted bread spread thickly with rich, garlicky liver pâté. And this was followed by steaming platefuls of a stew made from thick chunks of sausage, haricot beans, sage and tomatoes. It smelled ambrosial, and tasted even better, as Lucy, who had planned to have a simple salad, soon discovered. She ate every mouthful. And afterwards there was tiramisu, thick and creamy and wickedly alcoholic.

'Food for the gods, eh?' Giulio smiled at her across the table, and forgetting she'd decided to be cool and distant she smiled back.

'You must come here often to be treated so well.'

He shrugged. 'I live and work here, after all.' He poured some more wine into her glass. 'So, are you glad to be visiting Firenze?'

Lucy nodded. 'Naturally, I'd planned to come here.' She bit her lip. 'But I was overtaken by events.'

'As I was myself,' he reminded her silkily. 'But one visit is not enough. You must see more of my city before you leave.' He saw her lips curve involuntarily, and his brow lifted. 'Why do you smile?'

She shrugged. 'I live and work in London, but I'd never refer to it as *my* city.'

'Here in Tuscany, our sense of belonging runs very deep. For centuries men have fought and died for these same cities, whether as defenders or aggressors.' He drank some wine. 'And we Florentines like to win, sometimes at any cost.'

She looked at the careless strength of him, the firm lines of his mouth and chin, and could believe it.

She hurried into speech. 'The poet Dante was a Florentine, wasn't he?'

'*Sì*, and so was Beatrice, the girl he loved all his life. But Dante could not be content with poetry. He involved himself in politics, and was driven out of the city to Ravenna. There is a story in our family that he was given shelter in our home on his way into exile, which is why the present house bears his name even today.' He smiled at her. 'I like to think it is true.'

'Did he ever return to Florence?'

Giulio's face was suddenly sombre. 'No; he had too many enemies for that. But now, each year, on the anniversary of his death, the city sends oil to light the lamps on his tomb, so peace has been made with him at last.'

'I'm glad,' Lucy said softly. 'That's a nice story. Even if it does mean he never saw his Beatrice again.'

'Legend has it he only saw her once anyway,' Giulio said drily. 'As a young girl on her way to school. But she became his ideal, even though they both married other people.'

'That is silly.' Emilia, scraping the last vestige of ice cream from her dish, intervened. 'People who are in love should marry each other, don't you think, Zio Giulio?'

Giulio stroked her hair. 'It is not always possible, *cara*. Besides, although Dante loved Beatrice, she may not have returned his love. So perhaps it was better that he carried his passion in his heart only, and married for reasons of policy and sense.'

'I have finished all my food,' Emilia announced. 'May I go now and see the kittens?'

'Yes. I will join you when I have drunk my coffee.' He sent Lucy a faint smile, halting her instinctive protest. 'Relax, *columbina*. She will come to no harm. Enjoy some peace while you can.' He paused. 'Is it good to escape?'

'It's hardly that.' She tried to speak lightly. 'More a temporary reprieve.'

'And one which we all deserve.' The dark face was brooding, coldly introspective. 'Even Angela has the chance to be alone with her *amante*,' he added, with bite.

The sudden silence between them seemed to lengthen into pain.

Lucy found herself wondering if he had told her the story of Dante's hopeless love for Beatrice deliberately, as a warning of how quicky and how fatally love could strike. One glimpse and the young Alighieri had been lost for ever, without kisses or the promise of passion to fire his ardour either, she remembered.

And maybe Giulio wished to remind her too that she also could hope for nothing but heartache and endless yearning. And that hope itself was futile. Because Giulio's future was already mapped out for him for 'reasons of policy and sense'.

But I knew that already, she thought wearily. And it's far too late for any warning.

Before she could stop herself, she said huskily, 'Don' you—care about—that? About Angela's affair?'

'Yes.' His voice was grim. 'I find that this time I care very much.'

She swallowed. 'You—you could always put a stop to it,' she ventured.

You could ask Angela to marry you, she cried out to him in her heart. That would end her relationship with Philip i a flash, because she's only using him to make you jealous Because she's greedy and ambitious, and he can't offer her what you can.

'I could,' he said. 'But it would solve nothing. Wha would be the point?'

Past the tightness in her throat, she said, 'When you—love someone…'

'Ah, love.' His voice was soft—mocking. 'That little dangerous word that can cover such a multitude of sins.' He leaned forward, his amber eyes lambent, intent. 'How far should one go for love, I wonder, Lucia?'

She looked down at the table, tracing meaningless patterns with a fingertip on the white cloth. 'For the real thing, to the ends of the earth—to infinity,' she answered quietly.

'But is it right to love, and to go on loving someone when they have shown you plainly that they do not return that love? When they have hurt you quite deliberately—and very deeply too.' There was anger there, just below the surface, and anguish. Lucy heard them and winced.

'Maybe we can't control our emotions so easily,' she suggested with difficulty. 'Perhaps real love—the kind that lasts—doesn't allow any choice.'

'I hope,' he said grimly, 'that you are wrong.' He pushed his chair back and rose to his feet. 'And now I had better take Emilia to feed Il Porcellino again.'

'Not your usual lunchtime pursuit?' She was glad to change the subject, lighten the atmosphere.

'No.' He glanced at his watch. 'Normally at this time I would go back to my apartment for a brief *riposo*. A rest, *columbina*, in the cool and shade.' The amber eyes were hooded. 'Does the idea appeal to you?'

Her mouth felt dry. 'I suppose it's usual—in this kind of heat…'

'Quite usual.' A faint smile played round the corners of his mouth. 'And most enjoyable.' His voice sank huskily to a whisper as he leaned towards her across the table. 'Would you come with me, Lucia *mia*? Would you lie on my bed, in my arms, when the shutters are closed, and watch the sun make patterns on the ceiling?'

She was lost, whirling in the complex of emotions

aroused by his words, in an agony of longing, of desire, that clenched her entire body, In that moment, she knew she would go anywhere—become anything he asked.

Then Emilia's shrill voice broke in impatiently, shattering the spell. Drawing her back from the brink of the abyss. 'Zio Giulio, Il Porcellino is waiting for us.'

Giulio sighed, briefly and harshly, then turned away, smiling at the child. 'And it would never do to make a wild boar impatient, of course. So, let us go.'

Lucy watched him walk away. She supposed she should be thankful that she'd not been required to answer. That Emilia had been there as an unwitting chaperon. Otherwise she could have put herself in Giulio Falcone's power for ever.

She shook herself mentally, glancing around her at the other tables, watching almost wistfully the people wandering past, many of them couples, their footsteps slow in the heavy midday heat.

The ever vigilant Giovanni, spotting her restlessness, appeared at her side. 'More coffee, *bella signorina*?'

She smiled and thanked him, told him haltingly how good the meal had been, and watched his delighted reaction.

'You tell Conte Falcone that next time he bring you for dinner I cook special meal. There will be candles, music. He nodded vigorously. 'Very romantic.'

Lunch, Lucy thought ruefully as she sipped his hot, aromatic brew, had been quite perilous enough.

'*Ciao*, sweetheart. Have you escaped, or are you just out on parole?'

The drawled words brought her head round in shock. So this, she realised with irritation, was why she'd thought she was being watched. Hal, in brief shorts and with a shirt tied casually at the midriff, was standing beside her. The smile he gave her was frankly pro-prietorial. 'Mind if I join you?'

'Actually, yes.' Lucy reached for her bag. 'I was just leaving.'

'You keep telling me that,' he complained. 'You're not very friendly, are you?'

She shrugged. 'Perhaps I don't appreciate your brand of friendship.'

He laughed. 'You like it better Italian style?' He sat down. 'Nina was bug-eyed with jealousy that the handsome Count chose you out of all of them, but I told her you had hidden depths.' He paused. 'She hoped, when he showed up at Lussione, that he might have had a change of heart—or partner—but all he wanted was to ask a lot of questions about your background. She was spitting nails about it.'

Lucy frowned. 'Lussione?'

'Yes, he arrived yesterday morning just after breakfast, doing his magnifico act. Ben's parents were terribly impressed.' He laughed. 'I hope he was pleased with the reference Nina gave you. I wouldn't have been.'

Lucy could imagine. No wonder he thought she was such easy game, she thought bitterly.

She moistened her lips with the tip of her tongue. 'How are the others?' she asked quickly.

'The in-fighting has been spectacular. You never know who's with who, or for how long. I stay clear of it all.' He put out a hand and ran it down her bare arm. 'Having lost out on the one I wanted.'

His touch seemed to have left a trail of slime on her skin. Lucy wrenched her chair away to a safe distance as Giovanni materialised again.

'You wish to order, *signore?*'

'No, just exchange the time of day with the *signorina.*'

Giovanni stood his ground, his usually merry face unsmiling suddenly. 'This is my restaurant, *signore.* People come here to order food, and nothing else.'

'What the falcon has, he holds,' Hal remarked mockingly.

'Well, I can take a hint.' His smile lingered on Lucy's frozen face. 'If things don't work out with the Count—and rumour has it he loves them and leaves them in pretty short order—then you know where to find me.'

He bent towards her, and Lucy, sensing his intention, turned her head swiftly, so that his insolent kiss landed nearer her ear instead of on her mouth.

And she saw, over his shoulder, Giulio standing a few yards away, his face a bronze mask of hauteur.

'Ciao, baby.' Hal wore his triumph like a badge as he sauntered away.

'Your friend from the villa,' Giulio commented icily as he joined her.

'You both share a curious view of friendship.' Lucy was still shaking with temper.

'Is that all we share?' The question was so swift, so harsh, it was almost like a blow in the face.

Lucy felt the blood rush into her cheeks. She said sharply. 'Just what the hell are you implying? I wasn't aware there was anything to share.'

'Then you have a short memory, *mia bella*.' Giulio tossed the package he was carrying onto the table, nearly overturning a glass, and signalled imperiously to Giovanni for the bill.

'And so have you, apparently.' She glared at him. 'You can't imagine—even for a moment—that I wanted *that*.'

'I don't need imagination. I know what I saw.' His tone was harsh. 'For a woman who claims to be deeply, even painfully in love, Lucia, you bestow your kisses with astonishing ease.'

For a moment she stared at him, stunned, mute with outrage. How dared he level such an accusation, when he himself had quite cynically tried to seduce her? When the woman he planned to marry was conducting an affair under his own roof? Not only was he totally amoral, she decided in bitter disillusion, but an expert in double standards to boot. And how could she have allowed herself to forget that, even for a moment?

Mentally squaring her shoulders, she went recklesssly on the offensive. 'Think what you like, *signore*,' she flung at him. 'Believe whatever you were told at Lussione. I gather you went there to check up on me.'

His eyes narrowed. 'Among other things.'

'And decided I had just sufficient moral fibre to look after the children?' She glared at him. 'You, of course, being a fit judge in such matters.'

'I am the head of my family, Lucia.' He looked past her, and she saw his profile, sculpted in bronze, as proud and remote as a hawk's. 'And I will go to any lengths necessary to protect its well-being and reputation.'

She achieved a small, contemptuous laugh. 'Occupying the high ground, *signore*? You surprise me.'

'And you, *cara*, have never ceased to amaze me.' His voice had slowed to a drawl as he turned back to face her, the amber eyes like smouldering flames. 'I presume you have now decided that Lussione is the ideal place to find consolation for your wounded heart?'

The silken cruelty of the words was like a knife turning in her heart.

She said tonelessly, 'Why not? After all, I have to go somewhere when Dorotea takes over.' She paused. 'Have you any idea when that might be?'

'No,' he said icily. 'But believe me, *signorina*, you will be the first to know.'

She bit her lip. 'And while we're on the subject, did you forget Emilia, or simply abandon her somewhere?'

His mouth thinned. 'She is there.' He indicated a pavement stall. 'Choosing flowers for her mother.' He indicated the package on the table in its black and silver wrapping. 'As I, like a fool, chose this for you.'

Lucy's chair scraped across the pavement as she got to her feet. She said raggedly, 'A kiss-off present, Count Falcone? Something to remember you by, instead of a session of love in the afternoon?' She shook her head. 'If you're expecting me to curtsy, and whisper, *Grazie*, then you're doomed to disappointment. I want nothing from you—not now, not ever.'

'Have the goodness to lower your voice,' he advised coolly. 'We are attracting attention.'

A swift glance around told her that they were indeed the fascinated cynosure of all eyes in the vicinity.

Biting her lip, Lucy rallied. 'Don't tell me they're not used to it, *signore*. Most people here seem to conduct ordinary conversations at the tops of their voices.'

'But not usually with me.' His voice was satin edged with steel. 'Now we had better leave before Giovanni has a heart attack.' He paused. 'I presume you have seen enough of Firenze for one day?'

'More than enough,' Lucy flung back at him, and retreated to join Emilia at the flower stall.

'They are all so lovely,' she breathed. 'Would Mamma like these yellow flowers, do you think, or perhaps the tall pink ones?'

'Why not a mixed bunch?' Lucy suggested over-brightly, furiously aware that Giovanni was no longer looking nervous, but was rocking with laughter at something Giulio had said to him. A remark at her expense, no doubt, she thought smouldering.

The flowers were paid for and wrapped elegantly in gilt-edged paper. Emlia insisted on carrying them back to the car, chattering nineteen to the dozen as she clung to her uncle's hand.

She continued to talk throughout the journey home, happily oblivious to the icy silence that prevailed elsewhere in the car.

When they reached the villa, Emilia wanted to rush in and present her flowers to her mother, but Giulio was firm. 'Mamma will be resting, and so should you, little one. Go with Lucia, and Teresa will put your flowers in water until later.'

Emilia pouted, but turned away with Lucy. As Giulio mounted the steps to the main door, it opened and Angela appeared. She was smiling and holding out both hands to him.

'Darling.' Her voice dripped reproach. 'Why didn't you tell me you were going to Firenze? I'd have gone with you. I simply must do some shopping at Ferragamo, and Pucci.'

'Next time, *cara*.' Giulio took her hands, raising first one then the other to his lips. He added something else in a laughing undertone, which Lucy, thankfully, was by that time too far away to hear, her head held high, her facial muscles feeling as if they'd been paralysed.

You still have a job to do, she told herself. Do it.

Once in the shaded bedroom at the *casetta*, Emilia made no further protest, and Lucy, moving softly round the room, picking up and folding her discarded clothes, could see she was fighting sleep. And not prepared to give in without a struggle, either.

'Tell me a story,' she demanded, drowsy but imperious.

Lucy sat down on the edge of her bed. 'What story shall it be?'

'Cinderella.'

'Again?' Lucy queried teasingly.

'Yes, because Cinderella becomes a *principessa*, as Zio Giulio says I shall.' There was a small silence. Then she said, 'Do you hope a prince will marry you, Lucia?'

'Most of the princes in England have other commitments,' Lucy said drily. 'I'd be content with a good man who loved me.'

'Zio Giulio is a good man. And today I saw him kiss you. Will you marry him now?'

Lucy gathered her suddenly reeling wits. 'People sometimes kiss each other for all kinds of reasons, Emilia. It doesn't necessarily mean they want to spend their lives together. Often, they're going to marry someone completely different.' She saw a sudden image of Angela, smiling triumphantly, complacently, and cleared her throat. 'Now—once upon a time…'

Emilia was asleep long before the story ended. Lucy went quietly down the stairs. She would sit in the corner of the courtyard under the pergola and do some sketching, she told herself. And she would not allow herself to think, or wonder. Or to hope. Especially not to hope.

The first thing she saw was the package in its black and silver wrapping, lying in the middle of the living-room table, a note slipped under the ribbon tie.

He must move as quietly as a cat, Lucy thought. Because she'd not had the least inkling of his presence downstairs.

Lucy unfolded the slip of paper and looked at the words marching decisively across the page. 'Regard this, please, as a gift without strings,' she read. 'Or even as compensation. And believe that I want nothing in return.'

Impelled by curiosity, and something less easy to define, Lucy tore off the wrapping paper and opened the box inside. She unfolded the layers of tissue and, hands shaking, drew out a handbag. On lines of classic simplicity, it was made of the softest, most exquisite leather, and the clasp was gold. For a moment, she stood quietly, looking down at it, running a hand over it, savouring the luxurious texture, the expensive scent of the leather. Then she undid the clasp.

Inside, she found a plain white card. Across it was written 'Giulio' and nothing else.

Aware of the thundering of her heart, Lucy lifted the card

swiftly and gently to her lips, then slipped it back into one of the pockets in the rich silken lining.

A remembrance of him, she thought, that would remain with her, bitter-sweet, for the rest of her life.

CHAPTER ELEVEN

IT WAS a very long afternoon. Despite all Lucy's gritted-teeth determination, her beloved drawing and painting failed to provide their usual anodyne effect. Whatever sketch she attempted, the image of Giulio's tall figure intruded somewhere, her fingers, it seemed, powerless to exclude him.

She had, of course, to thank him for the bag. The realisation hung over her like a cloud. Somehow she had to find words that would accept the gift in the spirit with which it had been given.

Whatever that was, she reminded herself ironically. She'd read his note a dozen times, but she was still none the wiser.

It was almost a relief when Marco returned, fretful with over-excitement, clutching the latest and most expensive model car with remote control. Emilia had just woken from her nap, and, seeing the sullen lines of her mouth as Marco exuberantly demonstrated his toy, Lucy diplomatically suggested that the car should be put away, and that both children do some painting instead.

They entered wholeheartedly into the project, and preventing them covering each other and the surrounding area in her precious watercolours kept Lucy fully occupied until it was time to order them indoors to change for dinner.

As they walked up to the villa, her mind seemed emptied of everything but the prospect of seeing Giulio—facing him again. She found herself silently rehearsing over and over again the polite, formal words of thanks which seemed safest. But the first person she encountered in the hall was Philip, his face like thunder.

'I'd like to know what the hell's going on,' he said savagely. 'I've just learned from that aunt of hers that Angela's going out for the evening with the Count. She's never said a damned word to me about it.'

'I'm sorry,' Lucy said levelly, directing the children to run on ahead of her to the *salotto* as she suppressed the involuntary pang his words had induced. 'But they're both free agents.' She bit her lip. 'After all, you and Angela aren't engaged, are you?'

'No,' he admitted sulkily. 'But we had an understanding—or so I thought, anyway. Now I'm not sure of anything. She's been a different girl since we arrived in Italy.'

I doubt it, Lucy thought drily. I think she's always been like this, and that now she's just not bothering to pretend any more.

'I don't know what to do for the best,' he went on fretfully. 'I've a good mind to clear out myself. Cut my losses and go back to England. What do you think?'

Lucy gave him a look of total disbelief. 'I think the decision has to be yours, Philip. I'm hardly the best person to advise you.'

'You're a woman,' he said impatiently. 'Would it bring her to her senses if I walked out on her?'

It certainly brought me to mine, Lucy thought wryly, but not in the way you mean.

She said quietly, 'I think that when you love someone you should stand your ground and fight for them, whatever pain it may cause you. I don't believe in giving up—in running away.'

'*Bravo*, Lucia.' A familiar voice, tinged with mockery, broke in as Giulio walked down the stairs towards them. His smile was taut as he surveyed her. 'I wonder if your courage will get the reward it deserves?'

The careful little speech—grateful without being grovelling, she'd assured herself—was immediately erased from her mind. For a fleeting instant, she allowed herself one devouring glance, absorbing the elegance of the light summer suit, sitting easily across his broad shoulders and unashamedly defining the narrow male hips and long legs. His shirt was pale cream, and the silk tie bold with colour.

Dressed to kill, she thought. And she should be glad she wasn't the intended victim. Should be—but wasn't...

She felt her lips twist crookedly, achingly. 'I wouldn't think so for a moment, Count Falcone,' she returned composedly. 'Now I must go and find the children.'

She had just reached the *salotto* when she heard Emilia's voice rising in a torrent of angry words to a scream.

'Oh, God.' Lucy flung open the door in time to see Emilia, tears pouring down her face, launch herself at the *contessa*, beating at her with her fists.

She started forward, but Giulio was there before her, striding ahead to seize the hysterical child and pull her away, holding her with firm hands.

'What is the meaning of this?' His voice was harsh. 'What happened?'

'My flowers.' Emilia's voice was thick with sobs. 'The flowers I bought for Mamma—*she* has thrown them away. I hate her—I hate her...'

'Hush, darling.' Lucy intervened swiftly, going down on one knee and putting a sheltering arm around the child's heaving shoulders. She gave the *contessa* a level look. 'I'm sure there must be some mistake. Your grandmother wouldn't deliberately destroy your mother's present.'

Claudia Falcone's painted mouth was set like a snare. She shrugged. 'I found this tasteless jumble of flowers in a bowl on that table. They were clearly dying so I disposed of them.'

'They weren't dying—they weren't...' Emilia lifted a tear-stained face from Lucy's shoulder. 'You're lying. You're wicked—a witch.'

'*Basta!* Enough.' Her uncle's voice silenced her. He turned to the *contessa*. 'You did this thing? Why?'

She sighed elaborately. 'I cannot bear to be in a room with wilting flowers—it is a foible of mine and—' a metallic note had crept into her voice '—surely a minor matter compared with the outburst of wild and violent temper to which I have been subjected. As you saw for yourself, *caro* Giulio, Emilia is clearly beyond control—maybe even unbalanced. Perhaps Fiammetta will believe me now when I say the child needs strict and disciplined supervision.'

She took a step forward, and Lucy felt Emilia shrink towards her.

'This nomadic life, following their parents from one city to another, is not the kind of stable existence that children need. How many times have I said it? And after this latest episode Fiammetta must and shall agree with me.'

Giulio was frowning, his expression withdrawn. 'Something will certainly have to be done,' he said, after a pause, his amber eyes resting expressionlessly on Emilia.

'You can't mean that.' The words seemed to burst from Lucy as the child flinched in her embrace. She looked up at Giulio in passionate appeal. 'Emilia shouldn't have behaved like that, but she was hurt and upset. And provoked,' she added hotly. 'Treating the flowers she chose for her mother like unwanted garbage was cruel—and heartless.'

There was a taut silence, then the *contessa* said, 'So Signorina Winters is now the arbiter of conduct in this house.' Her laugh jarred. 'We need not ask ourselves who has been encouraging Emilia to behave like some child from the gutter. The child attacks me violently, and the young woman to whom she has unwisely been entrusted makes excuses for her.'

Giulio's face was stern. He said quietly, 'Take the children back to the *casetta*, Lucia. I will ask Teresa to serve your meal there.'

Lucy scrambled to her feet, Emilia's hand trembling in hers. She said, '*Signore*—Giulio—please may I speak to you alone?'

He seemed to look through her. 'I regret that I have no time at present, *signorina*. We will speak tomorrow.'

'Then I'd like a private word with Signora Rinaldi.' Lucy stood her ground.

'Fiammetta is suffering from a severe headache. She will be dining in her room and does not wish to be disturbed.' He spoke with faint impatience, as if his mind was elsewhere. 'Now do as I ask, Lucia, *per favore*.'

As if on cue, Angela appeared in the doorway. '*Caro*.' Her voice dripped reproach. 'I'm waiting. We're wasting a beautiful evening.'

Her hair gleamed like black silk, and the vivid pink dress showed off her tan to perfection.

Lucy, with detachment, imagined her bald and with several front teeth missing as she shepherded her charges, one still sobbing, the other protesting hotly, to the door, and safely out of the room.

But not before she heard Giulio say, 'Forgive me, *mia cara*. I promise the remaining hours will be devoted solely to you.'

Not to mention the rest of his life, Lucy thought wearily as they all trudged silently back to the *casetta*. But if he was determined to tie himself to such a spoiled, manipulative bitch there was nothing more to be said. And for the sake of the Falcone bank she could only hope he had better judgement in financial matters then he did in his choice of wife.

'Why are you crying?' Marco demanded.

'I'm not,' Lucy denied, blinking hard.

'Zio Giulio will not take us on the picnic now,' he opined gloomily. 'And I have been good. It is just Emilia.'

Lucy sighed. 'That's unkind and unjust,' she said sternly.

'How would you like it if your grandmother threw away a present you'd bought?'

'She would not,' he said, unanswerably.

So sure of his position as the favoured child, Lucy thought sadly, unlike the sniffing waif walking at her other side.

She managed to persuade Emilia to eat some of the delicious food which Teresa, full of sighs and commiserating looks, brought down to them, and then diverted both children with games of picture snap and snakes and ladders until bedtime. She'd expected problems with Emilia, but the little girl was asleep almost as soon as her head touched the pillow.

Lucy herself felt restless and on edge. She washed up the supper things and piled them onto a tray, ready to return to the villa, then tidied away her paints, pencils and sketch blocks.

She played solitaire for a while, but found herself deadlocked after only a few moves in each game. How like life itself, she thought with irony as she shuffled the cards together and thrust them back into the pack.

She tried to read, but the story failed to hold her attention.

Almost as a last resort, she went to bed, but her attempts to sleep were futile. She found herself tossing restlessly on her pillow, her mind awake and all too alert, her imagination filled with images of Giulio and Angela, dining together on some moon-drenched terrace high in the hills, their voices hushed and intimate, his hand assured as it reached for hers across the table...their fingers clasped closely in promise...

'Oh, to hell with it,' Lucy said angrily, sitting up and pushing away the encircling sheet. 'Midnight or not, I'm going to wash my hair.'

In the past it had always worked as a kind of panacea. Now, standing under the cascading water, allowing her fingers to massage away the tension in her scalp, Lucy felt soothed and refreshed almost in spite of herself.

Changed into a clear white cotton nightshirt, she glanced in at the children to make sure they hadn't been disturbed, before going quietly downstairs in her bare feet. She put water on to boil for coffee, then unlatched the front door and wandered outside, wincing a little at the chill of the cobbles.

After the heat of the day, the night air felt still and strangely heavy, and, glancing up, she saw the moon, hazy and unsubstantial behind a mask of vapour.

A clouded moon, she thought, grimacing, as she unwound the towel she was wearing turban-fashion and began to rub vigorously at her damp hair. Storms ahead.

She paused, stiffening suddenly, as every instinct warned her that she wasn't alone. That one of the shadows in the corner of the courtyard was real and substantial, turning into the figure of a man, and coming towards her.

For a desperate instant, she asked herself what she was doing outside and defenceless. She opened her mouth to scream, and found that no sound would come.

Above the swift pounding of her heart, the roaring in her ears, his voice reached her, quietly and unmistakably. 'Lucia.'

'Giulio—oh, God.' Almost sick with relief, she slumped back onto the bench, her fist pressed to her lips. 'It's only you.'

'I must apologise.' He sat on the bench beside her, maintaining a careful distance between them. 'I seem always to be frightening you.'

And angering me, she thought. And bewildering me. And filling my heart with such ridiculous, overwhelming joy and delight that I don't know whether to laugh or cry. As in right now.

Aloud, she said sedately, 'Isn't it a little late for social calls?'

'It was not my intention to disturb you.' She could hear a slight undercurrent of anger in his voice, which instinct told her was not aimed at her but at himself. 'It did not occur to me that you would still be awake at such an hour. I—I could not sleep, and came out for a walk—to clear my head.'

'With me, it's hair-washing.' Lucy ran her fingers through the tangled, still damp strands, tossing them back over her shoulders, realising too late, when she heard him draw a quick, harsh breath and curtly turn his head away, that the action had clearly outlined her breasts under the thin cotton shirt, reminding her quite unequivocally that she was naked beneath it.

She said hurriedly, trying to conceal her dismay and embarrassment, 'I—I hope you had a pleasant evening.'

'It was all that I could have hoped for.' His silky tone gave little away. 'But I did not come here to discuss my social life.'

Lucy swallowed. 'No—you said you'd talk to me tomorrow—which it now is, I suppose.'

'But hardly the interview I had in mind.' He met her gaze again, a faint smile playing round his mouth, making her wish more than ever that she'd put on a robe—something that buttoned from throat to ankles.

'But we're here, all the same, and we may as well get it over with.' Lucy drew a quick breath, fighting for composure. 'If you wish me to apologise to the *contessa*, *signore*, I can't. I think her treatment of Emilia is a disgrace, and I always will.'

'Fortunately, it will soon no longer be your concern.'

She bit her lip. 'No—but you can't believe it would be good for her to be sent away to some ghastly school?'

'Whatever I think, the final decision must be left to Fiammetta and Sergio.'

'Over whom you naturally have no influence.' Lucy's tone was crisp.

'Not as much as Claudia has over Fiammetta.' Giulio pushed the hair back from his forehead in a weary, irritable gesture. 'And Emilia does not aid her own cause by clashing with her grandmother—whatever the provocation,' he added swiftly as Lucy's lips parted indignantly.

'If you really wish to help the child,' he went on, 'then keep her away from Claudia—make sure there are no more confrontations—between any of you. My stepmother makes a vindictive enemy.'

'I think I'd managed to work that out for myself.' Lucy's voice was subdued. 'I suppose leaping to Emilia's defence was about the worst thing I could have done.'

'Without a doubt.' He gave a quick, sharp sigh. 'When I asked you to look after the children, I had no idea there would be all these difficulties—these added complications.'

'Or you'd have thought twice about it,' she said quietly.

'Yes.' He sounded as if he'd been goaded into the admission. 'But at the time, Lucia, it seemed the only possible way. How could I have known that it would all go so terribly wrong?'

She said haltingly, 'You mustn't blame yourself—really. After all, everything's working out for the best...'

He drew a harsh breath. 'You can truly believe that?' he demanded. 'In spite of everything?'

'I have to believe it.' Lucy got to her feet. 'I don't have a choice.' She turned determinedly towards the door of the *casetta*. 'Goodnight, *signore*.'

'Wait.' His voice halted her. 'I want to tell myself,' he said savagely, 'that you will be happy.'

One day, she thought, when I've managed to cut you out of my heart, and erase you from my mind, I shall manage a measure of content. But never more than that. Because I can never be happy without you. I feel as if I've been shown paradise, then told I'll always live in outer darkness. But at least I've had that one glimpse. So many people can't even comfort themselves with that.

She smiled at him, lifting her chin. 'I'll be fine. And now you really must go. It's so late…'

'Yes,' he said. 'Too late for us both.'

She took a step backwards into the lamplit room, and he followed, as, somehow, she had known he would from the beginning of some distant time.

He closed the door behind him and leaned back against it, his hands spread against the timbers, as if he was keeping in touch with some last remnant of sanity and dared not let go.

His eyes met hers. Held them. He said very quietly, 'I want to see you, Lucia. Just this once—will you show yourself to me? So that I have it to remember—when you are gone?'

For a long moment, she looked back at him, letting the torment in his amber gaze, the shaken yearning in his voice blind and deafen her to the dictates of reason.

She was trembling inside, but her hands were steady as she began slowly and deliberately to undo the twelve tiny buttons which fastened her shirt. When the last one had been dealt with, she shrugged the garment from her shoulders, letting it pool at her feet. She stood naked in the lamplight, an offering of rose and pearl, dazzled by the flame in his eyes.

He was totally still as he looked at her, only the convulsive movement of a muscle in his taut throat betraying his tension.

She said his name once, softly, pleadingly.

And saw him shake his head, a slow, reluctant movement as if he was in pain.

He said softly, 'I cannot come to you, *mia cara*. I cannot kiss you or touch you because I dare not. Because if I did I would take you, and we both know that is not possible. Not now. Not ever.

'All I can promise is that I shall never forget this moment. That I shall always be thankful I can carry this picture of you in my soul.'

He turned and went from her.

For a while, she remained where she was, then, shivering slightly, she bent stiffly to retrieve her shirt from the floor and wrap it protectively round her body.

'And I shall remember too,' she whispered into the silence. 'I shall remember the sound of the door closing behind you—finally and for ever.'

CHAPTER TWELVE

LUCY was woken from a restless sleep by an unusual sound—the persistent splashing of water. For a moment, she thought she might have left the shower running the previous night, but, as she scrambled out of bed to check, the cool grey light permeating the room through the shutters told a different story.

The clouded moon had fulfilled its gloomy promise, and a curtain of rain was sweeping the hills, hiding the landscape behind a dank, impenetrable curtain.

The change in the weather had made the children peevish and uncooperative, she soon discovered, when she went in to get them washed and dressed.

'No picnic today,' grumbled Marco.

They were halfway to the villa, under the shelter of an ancient black umbrella which she'd found slumped like a dead crow in the corner of the living room, before Lucy had time to worry about coming face to face with Giulio again in what was literally the cold light of day.

The remembrance of their parting last night was an agony to her. She had offered herself, and been rejected, not because she was undesirable—the burning look in his eyes, very taut line of his body had told her differently—but for purely practical reasons.

His course in life was set. He was going to marry Angela, and Lucy was an inconvenient diversion, nothing more.

At least he had never tried to deceive her about his intentions, she thought, with an inward grimace. She didn't have to bear the humiliation of being used and discarded in a casual holiday affair—which was what she might have been offered if Angela had not suddenly arrived at the villa.

On the face of it, Angela might not seem the ideal wife, but at least Giulio had no illusions about her. She was from his background, approved by his family, and clearly they were both able to shrug off each other's pre-marital peccadilloes. It would be a pragmatic marriage, and who could say it would not work better than a relationship born of a sudden conflagration of passion?

But there was to be no immediate confrontation between them. As Lucy was bracing herself to shepherd the children into the dining room, Fiammetta appeared wanly in the door of the *salotto*, indicating that she wanted a private word.

'I hear there has been a problem with Emilia,' she said unhappily, closing the door behind them.

'Emilia had a problem, certainly,' Lucy returned evenly. 'The present she bought you in Firenze was destroyed. She was very upset.'

'And my mother is—oh, so angry.' Fiammetta sighed. 'She says that Emilia is out of control—on the path to delinquency.'

Lucy bit her lip. 'I'm sure that's an exaggeration.'

'Well, I do not know what to believe.' Fiammetta's tone had become pettish. 'Sometimes I think Mamma is right and Emilia does need the discipline of a strict school.' She sighed again. 'If only Sergio were here. He would know what to do.'

Amen to that, thought Lucy. Aloud she said persuasively, 'Then why not postpone any decision until his return? I'm sure the *contessa* couldn't object to that.' And, seeing that Fiammetta did not look entirely convinced, she went on, 'In the meantime, I'll try and keep Emilia apart from your mother.' She paused. 'She and Marco like to play with Teresa's children down at the vineyard, so we'll spend more time there.'

'*Cara* Lucia.' Fiammetta gave her a weak smile. 'What should I do without you? Especially now that Giulio has gone back to Firenze.'

Lucy was on her way to the door, but that stopped her in her tracks. 'Gone?' Her voice sounded wooden. 'I didn't realise…'

'Very early this morning,' Fiammetta confirmed. She sighed. 'He is such a comfort to me that I sometimes forget he has his work—his own life.'

Lucy had herself firmly under control. She said, 'But surely he'll come back in the evenings?'

Fiammetta shook her head. 'He does not usually spend time here during this season,' she explained. 'He came only for me—because there was a crisis. Now he probably will not return until September—for the vintage.'

'I—see.' Lucy swallowed. 'I thought that as Angela—Miss Brockhurst—was here he might make an exception to the rule.'

'I think Angela will be joining him in Firenze.' Fiammetta paused. 'Which leaves us with the problem of her guest. So embarrassing.' Her glance was suddenly speculative. 'It has seemed to us that he takes an interest in you, Lucia.'

Lucy forced an answering smile. 'Most unlikely.' Oh, dear God, if you only knew, she thought.

'But why not?' Fiammetta spread her hands. 'He is young and quite attractive.'

And it would provide a neat solution to the current difficulty, Lucy silently supplied.

She said pleasantly, 'I'm not looking for romance, *signora*. I'm a relief nanny, that's all.' She paused. 'Is there any word of Dorotea—when she can take up her duties?'

Fiammetta sighed again. 'It seems she is taking a vacation and cannot be contacted immediately. So vexing, when you too, Lucia, must wish to get on with your life. After all, you cannot always have been a nanny.' The pansy eyes were suddenly shrewd, and Lucy felt faint colour steal into her face.

She said, 'I shall just have to be patient for a little while longer. Now, I'd better go and see to the children.'

'You will have the house to yourself today.' Fiammetta examined the immaculate enamel on her nails. 'I am going to the clinic for a check-up, and Mamma accompanies me.' She glanced towards the window. 'I am sorry the weather is poor. What will you do?'

'I expect I can keep them amused,' Lucy said with spurious brightness, and went off to the dining room.

The children were in their seats, bickering loudly, while at the other end of the table, Angela and Philip were engaged in a low-voiced but clearly furious altercation.

As Lucy hesitated in the doorway, Angela jumped to her feet and pushed past her rudely, muttering something in which 'like living in a zoo' were the only discernible words.

Philip rose also, watching her go. He gave Lucy a grim smile. 'Welcome to another lousy day in paradise.'

Lucy felt a flicker of compassion for him as she hushed the children and helped herself to some ham and cheese. If he really cared for Angela, he must be feeling totally gutted, she thought as she sat down.

She said quietly, 'I suppose you'll be going home.'

He shook his head, sliding into the seat next to her. 'Wrong. This is my holiday, and I'm going to enjoy it.' He gave Lucy a sideways look and his voice lowered intimately. 'I thought I'd drive over to Lucca. Fancy coming with me?'

'Thank you,' Lucy said evenly, 'but it wouldn't really appeal to the children, and Emilia's not a very good traveller anyway.'

'I didn't suggest taking them. Hand them back to their mother and give yourself a break. Let's face it, Luce, we'r both about as popular as a boil on the nose. And you don't owe these people a thing.'

'I gave my word,' she said shortly. 'I'm not going to break it.'

Philip shrugged. 'Please yourself.' To her relief, he pushed back his chair and rose to his feet. He smiled down at her, exercising his own brand of boyish charm. 'I can wait.'

Then don't stand still, Lucy thought as he left the room. Because moss might grow on you.

In spite of her inner turmoil, Lucy found the day passing much more quickly and pleasantly than she could have hoped. And having the house to themselves was a bonus.

They had another painting session, then the children made a batch of small sweet almond cakes under Teresa's indulgent supervision. And the proceedings were rounded off by a prolonged and noisy game of hide-and-seek.

Marco was always easily found, giving himself away by shrill giggles of excitement, but Emilia was a far more difficult quarry, thought Lucy as she left Marco in the *salotto* happily playing with his new car while she resumed the quest for his sister.

She had just reached the top of the stairs when she saw Emilia coming along the gallery towards her, carrying something carefully in her hand.

'Lucia—see.' Her voice was censorious. 'Nonna has left Zio Giulio's beautiful ring on her dressing table. A robber might have stolen it. I shall give it to him when he comes so he can keep it safe.'

Lucy gave the crimson fire of the ruby an appalled look. 'What were you doing in your grandmother's room?'

'Hiding,' Emilia said simply. 'But you did not find me, so I won.'

Lucy groaned inwardly. Why the hell hadn't she declared

the *contessa's* room strictly out of bounds? she berated herself. Without knowing it, Emilia had supplied her grandmother with all the ammunition she needed.

She said gently, 'I think the best thing would be to put the ring back at once.'

'No.' Emilia clutched it firmly. 'I shall give it to Zio Giulio.'

'He's in Firenze.'

'Then I shall take care of it for him until he comes.' Emilia's expression was mulish. 'He does not want Nonna to have it anyway.'

'That,' Lucy said grimly, 'is not our concern. And your uncle will not be coming back—at least not for the foreseeable future,' she added.

'What is that?' Emilia frowned.

'A very long time.' Lucy held out her hand. 'No arguments, Emilia. I'm going to put that ring back where you found it. Your grandmother would be very angry if she knew what you'd done, or that you'd been in her room at all.'

'I do not care. I hate her.'

Lucy bit her lip. 'But she would also be very cross with me for allowing you to do it, and she would send me away. Is that what you want?'

Emilia considered her doubtfully. 'Would she truly do this thing?'

'Undoubtedly,' Lucy said briskly. 'Now give me the ring and we'll pretend this never happened.'

The *contessa's* room was untidy, with clothes spilling out of the wardrobe and draped over the bed. The sour-faced maid was in no hurry to get on with her work, thought Lucy as she picked her way through the various pairs of shoes littering the carpet.

The ring glowed in her hand like a living flame. The temptation to slide it onto her finger, to see for one brief instant how it would look—how it would feel to be the chosen bride of the Falcone—was almost overwhelming. But that kind of dreaming was dangerous, so all Lucy did was deposit the ring among the general clutter of jars and bottles on the dressing table.

The air smelt cloyingly of Claudia Falcone's perfume. Lucy half expected to turn and find the *contessa* standing at her shoulder.

Feeling horridly like an intruder, she emerged, closing the door behind her, and hearing the sound echo along the gallery.

Another secret, she thought unhappily as she went downstairs, to add to all the others that must never be spoken.

It was very still, and very hot. Lucy, perched on a large rock on the hill above the vineyard, tested the wash on her painting, then began carefully to block in the jumble of faded terracotta roofs below her.

In the past week, the vineyard had become a sanctuary for herself as well as the children. Since Giulio's departure, the *contessa* had not bothered to disguise her animosity. Conversation at mealtimes was now conducted exclusively in Italian, and usually *sotto voce*, thus excluding Lucy on both counts. And Fiammetta's embarrassed efforts to remedy the situation had proved totally ineffectual.

Angela, who spent every day in Florence, though not, as far as Lucy was aware, any of her nights—at least, not yet, she qualified painfully—wore an air of glinting triumph that was almost tangible.

And, worst of all, Philip had quite openly transferred his attentions to Lucy, taking the adjoining seat at the dining table, making excuses to come down to the *casetta*, turning up at the pool when she was swimming with the children.

He was all smiles, confidential murmurs and admiring looks, apparently undeterred by oblique hints, studied indifference, even downright hostility, all of which Lucy had tried in turn.

With Fiammetta's well-meaning encouragement, he was constantly inviting Lucy to go sightseeing with him, or to drive out to dinner in the evening, and if he'd been anyone else, she acknowledged with a sigh, she might have been tempted, just for the chance of escaping the Villa Dante for a few hours.

As it was, she persevered with her stony rejections of his advances. And, as he hadn't seemed to have found his way to the vineyard, that was where she opted to pass her time.

Franco and Teresa's comfortable house, teeming with children and animals, fragrant with cooking smells, had become a second home for her, the language barrier easily overcome with Marco and Emilia's eager assistance as translators.

Teresa was the soul of discretion, but Lucy had noticed how her merry eyes clouded when the *contessa's* name was mentioned. It was clear that she cooked at the villa for the sake of Count Giulio, the beloved *padrone*, and no one else.

Lucy was fascinated by the day-to-day workings of the vineyard, laboriously explained by Franco. The big modern *cantina* with the vast concrete vats where the grapes were stored after picking, before being transferred to stainless steel casks, was impressive, but she preferred the old *cantina* with its ancient oak casks and the dry, musty air redolent of generations of vintages.

Walking between the terraces of vines which lined the valley, feeling the rough ground under her feet, the sun on her back, made her feel closer to Giulio in some indefinable way, even if she knew in her heart it was only wishful thinking, and that, in reality, she was only setting herself up for more heartbreak.

Because he was far away in Florence, a remote figure in a dark suit, conducting formal meetings, enshrined in a gli

tering cage of high finance which she could barely compre-
hend. Occupying a different world from her own, just as he
always had. And always would. And she'd been all kinds
of a fool to indulge in the dangerous dream that their worlds
could somehow touch.

She was suddenly aware of movement behind her, the
scrape of a shoe on the rough incline, a shadow falling
across the painting clipped onto her easel. For one sickening
instant, she thought that Philip had finally managed to trace
her to her refuge, and froze.

'Lucia.' Her name was spoken quietly by the last voice
in the world she was expecting to hear. Her hand jerked,
sending a trail of terracotta droplets across her picture.

He swore softly, dropping to one knee beside her, his
frowning gaze assessing the damage. 'I did not mean to
startle you.' He sounded shaken. 'But I did not expect to
find you here either.'

'I come here most days.' Lucy forced control on her quiv-
ring senses.

'Alone?' His frown deepened.

'Usually I bring the children.' Her tone was stilted. 'But
today they've gone to the clinic with Fiammetta to visit
Alison. So I thought I'd catch up on some painting while I
had the chance.'

'And I have ruined it.' He sighed briefly and harshly. He
got to his feet, dusting the knees of his trousers. 'I am sorry,
Lucia. You have real talent.'

'Thank you.' She hesitated. 'I didn't know—I mean—no
one said you were returning today…'

He shrugged. 'No one knew. It was an impulse on my
part. I had some free time, so I thought I would take the
children on the picnic I promised.'

'Oh.' Lucy caught her breath. 'I thought you'd forgotten
about that.'

Giulio shook his head. 'You will find, *columbina*, that I

forget very little.' His voice was reflective, his gaze lingering openly on the deep unbuttoned V at the neck of her shirt, and the length of slim brown leg revealed by her brief shorts.

Aware that her colour had risen, Lucy said hurriedly, 'They'll be so disappointed.'

'I think they will,' he agreed. 'Especially as it is unlikely I shall have another opportunity.'

He must mean his engagement to Angela was announced, Lucy supposed unhappily. The other girl had never concealed her indifference to the children, and certainly wasn't the type to enjoy the rough and tumble of al fresco eating in some field.

She said quietly, 'What a shame.'

He shrugged again. 'So much for impulses,' he drawled There was a pause. 'So, who is at the villa?'

'No one. Your stepmother and Miss Brockhurst have gone shopping, I think. But they'll all be back for dinner.'

'But I, alas, shall not. I have to return to Firenze.' He paused. 'You did not choose to accompany Fiammetta?'

'She asked me. But I thought she might like to be alone with the children for once. That it would be good for all of them.'

'And so you came to paint alone.' There was an odd note in his voice. 'A picture which I have ruined.'

'Maybe not.' She considered the painting, head on one side. 'Perhaps I can turn the spatters into birds or butterflies It might even be an improvement.'

'You are very forgiving—and also an optimist,' he said drily. 'But leave your improvements until later.' His hand was under her arm suddenly, lifting her to her feet. 'Now you have a picnic to eat.' Sensing her hesitation, he added 'You cannot leave me with a hamper of food and no one to share it with, Lucia.'

She should resist and she knew it. She should shun this exquisite forbidden pleasure, so unexpectedly offered.

A few hours alone with him, she thought yearningly. Their first shared meal alone since that night at the villa when he'd cooked her an omelette. Her heart soared and sang, and she knew she would not refuse him. That she could not.

She said sedately, 'Very well.'

CHAPTER THIRTEEN

APART from the whisper of the engine, it was silent in the car. The breeze from the open window lifted tendrils of Lucy's hair away from her face, and soothed her heated skin.

She could still hardly believe she was doing this.

She'd assumed Giulio intended to stage the picnic in a secluded corner of the villa's grounds. Instead, she was seated beside him, being driven down some unfamiliar narrow road which appeared to be leading nowhere.

'Patience.' There was a note of laughter in his voice, indicating that he'd sensed her inner restiveness and was amused by it.

'I feel I should have left a message at the villa.' Lucy bit her lip. 'If Fiammetta comes back early with the children she'll wonder where I am.'

'Is she your only concern?'

'Not entirely.' Lucy could visualise the *contessa's* reaction if she ever discovered that the temporary nanny was cavorting round the countryside with her stepson.

She heard Giulio sigh almost impatiently. 'Do you wish you had not come with me?'

'No.' Her mouth felt suddenly dry. Her hands were gripped tightly together in her lap. 'It's very kind of you.'

'The kindness, as ever, is yours, Lucia.' He sounded suddenly remote, and her swift, sideways glance revealed that he was frowning again. Perhaps, she thought, he was having second thoughts about the expedition.

She tried to think of some way to bring Angela and his commitment to her subtly into the conversation—to assure

him that he did not have to worry. That she had no intention
of reading too much into this unexpected treat. But she knew
it was impossible.

Best to keep quiet and enjoy herself for as long as it
lasted, she thought. A memory to store away and cherish
during the bleak times ahead.

She came out of her reverie with a start as Giulio swung
the car off the road and parked it in the shelter of a tree.

'Now we walk.' He took a picnic basket from the boot
of the car, handing Lucy a rug. He led the way through a
timbered gate and down a track winding its way through a
grove of ancient olive trees, their leaves shining silver in
the sun. Somewhere ahead of her, Lucy could see the glimmer of water, and hear a faint, muted roar.

When they emerged from the trees, she stopped, her lips
parting in a gasp of pure pleasure. They were on the bank
of a small river, its waters cascading over a series of steep
rocks before emptying almost vertically into a deep pool.

'Do you like it?' Giulio was smiling at her.

'It's wonderful.' She cast a worried look around her. 'But
should we be here? It looks like someone's private land.'

'It is.' His face was straight, but the note of amusement
danced in his voice again.

'Of course.' Lucy sighed. 'I'm an idiot. It's part of your
estate. Do you own the whole of Tuscany by any chance?'

'Only in my dreams,' he returned drily. 'In reality, my
property is quite small compared to others.'

And I, Lucy reminded herself ruefully, own a one-
bedroomed flat with a window box. Way down on the relative scale of property values.

She did not want to contemplate the chasm of wealth or
the centuries of history which divided them, so she busied
herself with spreading the rug and unpacking the food from
the basket. It was a varied selection, ranging from quail's
eggs, a whole boned chicken stuffed with pâté and ham,

salads in rich and subtle dressings and tiny savoury pastries to more homely slices of pizza, intended, Lucy guessed for the children. For dessert, there were peaches and grapes, and there was a bottle of dry, sparkling wine which Giulio cooled in the river.

She said shyly, deeply aware of his nearness beside her, 'You've been to a great deal of trouble.'

'More than you know, Lucia.' He was cutting deft slices from the chicken and putting them on her plate. 'You see, I did not come back solely to see the children but to bring some good news.'

She thought, He's going to tell me that he's marrying Angela very soon. And how can I bear it?

With a calm born of despair, she said, 'Good news, *signore*? That sounds exciting.'

'It will solve certain problems,' he said. 'But, all the same, you may not approve.'

The chicken was wonderful, but she might as well have been chewing sawdust.

She said carefully, 'It's really none of my business.'

'You are wrong, Lucia. It concerns you very closely.' He paused. 'Maddalena is coming back.' He observed her stunned expression, his mouth twisting. 'You were not expecting that, I think.'

'Well—no.' None of her tortuous imaginings had come up with that one, she thought, swallowing. 'How—how did you find her?'

'She found me. She came to the bank in a terrible state, distressed and crying, begging me to forgive her—to help her. It seems Moressi has been arrested for some other fraud and is now in jail.' He spread his hands. 'She has worked for our family for a long time. She is not a criminal herself—just fatally weak where her nephew is concerned.' He paused. 'Although now she has learned, with great sadness, that she can be weak no longer.'

Lucy ate some salad. 'And of course she'll want to come back to the *casetta*.' She spoke her thought aloud. 'I'll need to move out.'

'Yes.' She was aware of his searching gaze, but took care not to meet it. 'So, you are free, Lucia. Free to go home at last—to get on with your life. Does that please you?'

'Well, naturally.' She put down her plate and fork. Her mouth was dry, her heart hammering. 'It—it's marvellous news. Although I shall miss Emilia and Marco, of course.'

She hesitated. 'What about the children? Will Maddelena be able to look after them as well as the house?'

'I think so. When she is not terrified out of her wits about Tommaso and what he will do next, she is very capable.' He paused. 'Anyway, it will not be for very long.'

Lucy said woodenly, 'Then it's all worked out perfectly.' She wanted to cry and howl, to beat the earth with her fists, and scream her misery at the uncaring sun.

But, more dangerously, at the same time she wanted to reach across the small space between them and touch his hand, feel the crispness of his dark hair under her fingers just once more, encounter the lean strength of his body under her questing hands.

Free to go, she thought with irony. What freedom will I ever know again?

'All for the best, indeed.' His tone was expressionless. 'And you, Lucia. What will you do?'

She shrugged. 'Get the next available flight back to Britain, naturally.' Her voice sounded light and rather brittle.

'Of course.' There was a silence. 'As I told you originally, Lucia, I shall meet all your expenses in this matter. But are you so keen to rush away? Would you not like to continue your vacation—to explore my Tuscany? You have seen and done so little…'

She thought, I've changed my life. I've discovered what

love should be. I've broken my heart. What more could there possibly be?

Anguish gripped her by the throat, but she managed to speak normally. 'It's a kind thought, *signore*, but I have to go back—pick up the threads. And the sooner the better.'

He said quietly, 'You touched *il Porcellino*. So one day you will have to return to Firenze.'

She forced her stiff lips into a smile. 'I don't believe in superstition.' Or in fairy tales. Or in happy ever after, she added silently. She drank some wine, feeling it run down her throat like ice. 'And, anyway, this is the perfect place— the perfect way to say goodbye.' She held up her glass in mimicry of a toast. '*Salute*.'

Something flickered in the amber eyes as he lifted his glass in response.

'You are glad to be leaving?'

'Well…' Lucy studied minutely the bubbles in her wine '…all good things must come to an end.'

'You consider that your time here has been a good thing?'

'I think I've done a reasonable job.'

'That,' he said, 'is not what I asked.'

She said in a low voice, 'It hasn't always been easy.'

'No,' he said, and anger burned in his voice. 'It has been *il purgatorio*—the tortures of the damned.'

Lucy bent her head. 'I'm sorry.'

'Why do you apologise when I alone am to blame? The entire situation was of my making.'

She said painfully, not looking at him, 'Not—all of it.'

'No.' The fine mouth twisted. 'You are right, of course. The wanting was—mutual, I think, and for that we must share the guilt.'

Her voice was husky. 'We—we shouldn't talk about guilt. Not on a day like this—when everything's so beautiful.'

'And you,' he said, 'the most beautiful of all. Ah, Lucia…'

She had not dared reach for him, but his fingers closed round hers instead, drawing her towards him with an insistence, a mastery that withstood any thought of denial. Words of negation—of self-preservation—drummed in her head, but she had no time to utter them. No time, nor any real inclination, she realised with her last coherent thought as she went into Giulio's arms.

His other hand possessively cradled her head as he bent from the dazzle of sunlight to kiss her mouth.

Her response was instant, incandescent, her lips trembling apart in welcome and surrender. Mouths locked, they drank from each other in the sweet delirium of their kiss.

Lucy was hardly aware of the actual moment when his weight bore her backwards down onto the rug. She already felt part of him, her entire being brought to vibrant life by the warmth of his body against hers.

The rush of the nearby water was echoed by the singing of her blood, by the moist heat of longing in her loins.

He kissed the line of her throat, his lips lingering erotically on the sensitive area below her ear. When he finally reached the delicate hollow at the base, he buried his face there for a moment, raggedly breathing in the scent of her skin.

His hands were shaking as they loosened the buttons on her shirt and drew it apart. The amber eyes were lambent, almost golden as he looked down at her.

He whispered, 'There has not been a moment of any day—of any night—when I have not thought of you—remembered you—wanted you—like this. Ah, *mia bella—mia carissima…*'

His mouth was reverent, almost worshipful as it moved on her skin. His palms cupped the roundness of her naked breasts, while his thumbs brushed her nipples with gentle sensuality, making her whole body twist beneath him in quivering delight.

When he took first one aroused, rosy peak and then the other into his mouth, an involuntary moan of pleasure tore from Lucy's throat. Her hips lifted towards him in mute entreaty, begging him to remove the last barrier. Longing for the ecstasy of his caress at the secret core of her womanhood, for the triumph of his maleness to be enclosed in her deep liquid flame.

She wanted to pleasure him—to satisfy him in undreamed-of ways. To be his woman, his lover, throughout some passionate eternity, and to die the little death of all lovers in his arms.

And felt him, instead, suddenly and unbelievably, draw back from her. Heard his voice, like a stranger's say, 'This is madness.'

'Giulio?' She knelt upright, her hands clinging to the front of his shirt, feeling the hurry of his heartbeat under her palm. 'What's wrong?'

His laugh was mirthless. 'Almost everything, I would say, *columbina*—wouldn't you?'

'You said you wanted me.' Pride no longer mattered, she realised numbly.

'Yes,' he said quietly. 'I want you—so badly that I was ready to forget honour—every other obligation—so that I might lose myself in you for a while. And I lose my own soul in consequence,' he added with sombre bitterness.

The golden radiance of the sun was shattering, fragmenting into shimmering droplets which stung her eyes and burned like acid on her skin. She shivered, forcing back the tears. Drawing the rags of her courage around her.

'Forgive me, Lucia.' He took her small, clenched fists and carried them to his lips. 'I should have stayed in Firenze. He threw back his head and looked up at the sky, the muscles taut in his throat, his voice suddenly harsh. 'I should have known I could not trust myself.'

There was a silence, then he looked at her again, still

kneeling rigidly in front of him, and his face and tone softened. 'Try not to hate me. Try to understand why I must be strong for us both, even now—at the moment of no return.'

'There's no such thing.' Somehow Lucy clambered to her feet, her fingers clumsy as she forced her shirt buttons back through their holes. 'There's always a way back.'

Unless you love someone as I love you—beyond pride, or honour, or even reason. Unless you're prepared to sacrifice them all for the beloved—as I would have done for you.

The unspoken words beat at her brain and scalded her heart. Anything, she thought with pain. I would have done anything...

She lifted her chin. 'Will you take me back to the villa, please? I—I want to pack.' And she saw him bend his head in silent acquiescence.

The return journey seemed endless. Giulio stared ahead of him, his face like a bronze mask, in a silence Lucy did not dare to break, even if she could have found the words to do so.

To her relief, he drove straight round to the *casetta*. As soon as the car stopped, she scrambled out, desperate to get away, to be alone when her self-control snapped.

But Giulio came after her, stopping her in the doorway, turning her to face him, his hands like iron on her shoulders. He said huskily, 'Don't hate me, *mia cara*, or I shall not be able to bear it. This is for the best. We must both believe that.'

'Yes.' Her smile felt as if it had been nailed there. 'All for the best.' She took a step backwards, away from him, holding out a determined hand. 'Goodbye, *signore*.'

'*Al diavolo!*' He almost spat the words. 'To hell with it. That is no way to part, Lucia. It must be like this.' And regardless of her stifled protest, he took her in his arms, and kissed her slowly and deeply on the mouth.

'*Addio.*' He held her for a moment, and she felt him trace the sign of the cross on her forehead. He said very quietly, 'Remember always—as I shall.'

Then he turned and walked away. Lucy stood very still, staring after him, listening to the subdued growl of the car engine as it powered into life, watching as he drove swiftly away, under the arch, leaving a faint haze of exhaust fumes in his wake, which would soon disappear also.

And she knew that she had never felt so alone in her life.

CHAPTER FOURTEEN

LUCY was halfway through her packing when she heard someone knocking at the door. When she went down, she was surprised to find the *contessa's* sour-faced maid waiting on the doorstep.

I must stop calling her that. Her name's Agnese, she thought guiltily, and tried a welcoming smile which was not reciprocated. In fact, the older woman looked grimmer than ever as she explained, in a few terse words of Italian, that Signora Rinaldi and the children had returned, and Lucy was wanted at the villa.

More goodbyes to be said, she acknowledged with an inward sigh and a polite word of thanks.

She found Fiammetta in the *salotto*, with Marco, who was playing with his car. Emilia, however, was nowhere to be seen.

Fiammetta was transformed, her face alight. 'Lucia—such wonderful news. Giulio was here, waiting for us, when we returned.'

'Yes, I know.' Lucy forced a smile. 'He—he told me, too—about Maddelena.'

'Maddalena?' Fiammetta echoed scornfully. 'Maddalena is nothing to this.' She raised rapturously clasped hands. 'Sergio is coming back. Giulio says he will be here tomorrow.'

'That's marvellous,' Lucy said, and meant it for all kinds of reasons. 'I'm really happy for you.'

'Oh, I cannot wait to see him. In the morning, I shall go to the beauty salon in Siena. And buy something new to wear.' Fiammetta plunged into a world of fabrics, colours and designers.

When she paused for breath, Lucy said mildly, 'I'll take the children down to the *casetta* to change for dinner. Is Emilia playing outside?'

'I left her in my room. She wished to dress up in some of my clothes.' Fiammetta's pretty brow creased. 'Blue, do you think, or perhaps a really deep yellow…?'

Lucy sighed, and went upstairs. She found Emilia parading up and down in a pink dress which trailed everywhere, a handbag dangling from her wrist.

'I am a *principessa*,' she announced.

Lucy dropped a curtsy. 'Then it's time Your Highness changed for tonight's state banquet.'

Emilia allowed herself one pout, but submitted with rare docility to being divested of the pink creation and taken back to the *casetta*.

Both children were in good spirits, sky-high over the news about their father. And Emilia was clearly relieved that Alison was making good progress, and soon to be discharged from the clinic.

'I miss her.' A small hand was slipped into Lucy's. 'Not that I do not like you, Lucia.'

'Yes.' Marco gave her a quick hug, too. 'Shall we ask Papà if you can come to the sea with us, Lucia?'

'That's sweet of you.' Lucy smiled at him. 'But I have to go back to England now. Maddalena's taking my place, you see.'

'Since I woke up this morning, everything has changed.' Emilia sounded slightly uncertain about this swift passage of events.

'That's life,' Lucy confirmed drily.

She would have to finish her packing in the morning, she decided, glancing at the half-full suitcase on her bed as she changed into a simple black shift which she'd selected from the garments still hanging in the wardrobe. Only one more meal to endure, she reminded herself, trying to cheer herself up—to alleviate the aching hollowness inside her which had nothing to do with hunger.

The walk up to the villa was lively enough, with a child attached to each hand, chattering nineteen to the dozen. But as soon as they entered the hall Lucy knew something was wrong.

Teresa was standing in the doorway to the kitchen, her face blank with dismay, while from the *salotto* the *contessa's* shrill voice could be heard ranting fortissimo, interspersed with Fiammetta's softer tones.

'*Cosa succede?*' Lucy asked. 'What's happening?'

Teresa lifted her shoulders in a shrug that mingled incomprehension with incredulity and vanished back into the kitchen.

Lucy found she was bracing herself as she pushed open the *salotto* door. Her instinct had not misled her.

'Ah.' Claudia Falcone turned like a tigress sighting her prey. 'The so-good, so-trusted Signorina Winters. Perhaps she can explain this mystery.'

'Mamma,' Fiammetta protested instantly. 'You have no right…'

'I have any right I choose. We know nothing of this girl, who appeared from nowhere so conveniently in this house. She has no references—no recommendation from anyone we know.'

'From Giulio,' Fiammetta ventured unhappily.

The *contessa* made a sweeping gesture of dismissal. 'That is another acquaintance which has never been explained to my satisfaction. Who knows what they have been to each other—or what this—this *puttana* may have read into it?'

Lucy's Italian might still be sketchy, but she knew what she'd just been called, and outraged colour stormed into her face.

She said in a choked voice, 'How dare you…?'

'Oh, do not play the innocent, *signorina*. Do you think we are all blind—that we have not seen the way you gaze at my stepson…?'

There was a small, stifled sound, and Lucy saw that tears were running down Emilia's cheeks.

'*Cara.*' She went down on one knee beside the child, as Marco too burst into noisy sobs.

'Mamma!' This time Fiammetta's voice held a note of steel. 'That is enough.' She went to the door and called to Teresa, who appeared with discreet promptness and whisked both children away.

'Lucia, we have a problem. Something bad has happened, and we are all a little upset. The ruby—the Falcone ring—has vanished from my mother's bedroom. We have searched everywhere but found no trace of it.' She paused in obvious distress. 'You understand we must ask, difficult though it is, if you have seen it.'

There was a brief, loaded silence, then Fiammetta went on almost desperately, 'You see, Lucia, you were here alone today. Both Angela and Philip left for the day while my mother was still in her room, and neither of them has returned yet.' There was another pause. 'Perhaps you saw someone—a stranger—who could have entered the villa—'.

'Fiammetta, you are a fool,' the *contessa* broke in impatiently. 'There was no *stranger*.' She spat the word. 'The girl already pries where she has no business. Agnese saw her coming out of my room a week ago. And today Giulio tells her that Maddalena is returning, and that her time here is at an end, so she decides she will award herself a bonus for her dubious services. No more discussion—let us call the police.'

Lucy stared at her. She said slowly, 'You think I stole the Falcone ring? You must be mad.'

'No. It is you that is mad—crazy because my stepson is

to be married and no longer wants you. And you think to take revenge by taking the family ring—the symbol of his engagement to my niece.'

Lucy turned to Fiammetta. 'Signora Rinaldi, surely you don't think…?'

'I do not know what to think.' Fiammetta's face was as miserable as sin. 'But we have searched here, and now Mamma insists we must look in the *casetta*. You do not object, I hope.'

'Of course not—' Lucy began, and halted, beset by a sudden feeling of trepidation. Emilia, she thought slowly, remembering the sudden, unexpected outburst of tears. Emilia playing upstairs alone—being a *principessa*. Surely—*surely* after Lucy's warning she hadn't taken the ring again. She couldn't have done. Or could she…?

'Signorina Winters seems to be having second thoughts.' The *contessa's* voice sounded almost triumphant.

'No,' Lucy denied swiftly. 'I'm quite prepared to have my things searched.'

As long as it ends there, she thought. As long as they don't go into the children's rooms. If Emilia has taken it, I'll get it back and return it somehow. Make them think they didn't search thoroughly enough.

'And will you also explain why you were in my room the other day?'

Lucy paused. 'I was playing hide-and-seek with the children.'

'Ah.' The *contessa's* smile was thin. 'And today, once more, we will—seek what you have hidden.'

'Mamma.' Fiammetta sounded desperate. 'You must not say these things. The ring may simply be lost…'

'Nonsense,' the *contessa* said with contempt. 'It has been stolen, and by this girl—this *sciattona*. We will search the *casetta* now.'

'May I ask a question?' Lucy kept her voice even. 'How

did you know Count Falcone has spoken to me—about leaving?'

'Agnese saw you together—at the *casetta*.' Claudia Falcone's tone held jeering malice. 'Since you have been here, *signorina*, she has maintained a watchful eye—on my instructions.'

Lucy remembered that last passionate kiss, and felt as if she'd been dipped in slime.

She said quietly, 'I see.'

But at least I wasn't just being paranoid when I thought someone was spying on me, she thought wearily, recalling her unease that day beside the pool.

Agnese was waiting to accompany them back to the *casetta*. So the *contessa* wasn't going to soil her hands with the actual search, Lucy realised angrily, encountering her sly, knowing look.

She turned to Fiammetta. 'Is this really necessary?'

'My mother wishes it, Lucia—I am sorry…'

'Not half as sorry as I am,' Lucy said grimly, and set off.

Claudia Falcone didn't waste a second in the living room. Agnese following, she went straight up to Lucy's bedroom. She pointed to the open case on the bed. 'Look there.'

As if in a dream, Lucy watched Agnese pick up her yellow dress and shake out the folds. A small tissue-wrapped bundle fell to the floor, and the *contessa* pounced on it with a cry of triumph. The Falcone ring gleamed like blood in her hand.

The dress I wore to Firenze, Lucy thought numbly. Odd that Emilia should have chosen that one as a hiding place. But at least she had the sense not to conceal it in her own things.

'Not even a clever thief, *signorina*.' Claudia Falcone replaced the ring gloatingly on her finger, and looked at Fiammetta. 'Now we will call the police.'

'No.' Fiammetta sounded more firm than Lucy had ever

heard her. 'I will not permit it. You have the ring, Mamma, so be content. Lucia is leaving tomorrow, and Giulio—believe me—would not wish a scandal.' There was pain in the glance she directed at Lucy, and reproach. 'You have some explanation, Lucia?'

Yes, thought Lucy, but not one I can ever make. Emilia's only a child. She doesn't understand that her actions can have consequences—and this would be a hard way to teach her. In fact, it would probably be disastrous. And what real purpose would it serve—as I'm going anyway? As I'll never have to see any of these people again.

Lifting her chin, she said quietly, 'I cannot account, *signora*, for the ring being in my case. I can only say I did not put it there.'

'Then there is no more to be said.' Fiammetta's sigh rose from the soles of her elegant shoes. 'I will arrange for a meal to be served to you here this evening, and tomorrow Franco will drive you to Montiverno, where you can catch a bus to Pisa. You will understand that I do not wish you to have any further contact with my children. They can sleep at the villa tonight.'

After the shocks and insults of the past half-hour, it was strange how that hurt the most...

Moving like an automaton, Lucy completed her packing. From what Fiammetta had said, it was evident that she was going to be dumped, and left to make her own way home as best she could. She counted her money, then counted it again, doing rapid sums in her head and deriving no comfort from her calculations. If she couldn't change the return portion of her air ticket to an earlier flight, she would be in real trouble.

When an unhappy Teresa brought her supper tray, she steeled herself to give her a note for Philip.

The evening dragged endlessly past, and she was just on

the point of giving him up altogether and going to bed when he appeared reluctantly at the door.

'You've got a damned cheek, sending for me,' was his greeting. 'They'll probably think we're in it together.'

Lucy gasped. 'You can't possibly believe I stole the ring.'

'Well, someone did,' he returned unarguably. 'Although Angela thinks it was an act of spite rather than a theft, because you wanted Giulio Falcone for yourself.'

'I'm sure it's the twisted way she would think,' Lucy said icily. 'But her opinions don't interest me. The thing is—' she took a deep breath '—I need to borrow some money to get me back to Britain.'

'And you want me to give it to you? When you've done your best to freeze me out for the past week?'

'A temporary loan, that's all.' Lucy swallowed. 'Philip, believe me, I wouldn't ask if I wasn't desperate. And I'll repay you as soon as I get back.'

'Or you could repay me now—in kind.' His tone was calculating. 'What do you say, Luce? A roll in the sack for old times' sake?'

His hand on her shoulder, and then sliding down insinuatingly towards her breast, made her realise, with shock, that he wasn't joking.

She stepped backwards. She said between her teeth, 'On second thoughts, I'd rather walk home.'

'Fine.' His voice was savage. 'You're just not very lucky, are you, Luce? Two men in your life, and you've lost them both to Angela. No wonder she's laughing all over her face.'

The carafe of wine was still on her untouched supper tray. Lucy said crisply, 'Then let's give her another giggle,' and threw it at him.

For a moment, he stood frozen, the ruby liquid dripping off his nose and chin, soaking into his expensive silk shirt. Then he said, 'Bitch!' with venomous clarity, and walked out with as much dignity as he could muster.

*   *   *

Franco arrived apologetically at the door almost as soon as it was daylight. It was clear that the family could not wait to get her off the premises, Lucy thought, biting her lip, as her luggage was loaded into the car. It was an awkward, embarrassing journey, and she was glad when they reached Montiverno.

She was surprised to find her hand shaken warmly in parting. *'Ti credo, signorina,'* Franco told her. 'I believe you, and Teresa also.'

There were tears in her eyes as he drove away. And she could have cried all over again when she worked out how long she was going to wait for the bus to Pisa. Partly because she was starving and partly to fill the time she bought herself a cup of coffee and a brioche at the café near the bus stop, then settled herself on a bench to wait.

She tried to read, but couldn't concentrate. Her head was whirling with disconnected thoughts, most of them unhappy. She hated leaving Tuscany under a cloud, even though it was no fault of hers. The knowledge that Angela and the *contessa* were gloating over her downfall was agonising, and so was the loss of Fiammetta's good opinion. Above all, however, two people dominated her reverie: Emilia, her small face pinched and wan, and Giulio.

Nausea twisted in her stomach as she tried to imagine what he would be told—what he would think. How she would inevitably be condemned unheard.

Yet he was the only one who would understand what Emilia had done—and why. The only one who would keep the information to himself, and forgive the child. As well as give the help she so badly needed.

She heard the hiss of brakes, and saw a bus pulling up at the stop, its destination board showing 'Firenze'.

Lucy got to her feet, aware of a trembling in the pit of her stomach. I have to tell him, she thought. For Emilia's sake, he has to know, so that he can protect her. Or it will happen all over again, and his stepmother will have her put in some ghastly institution, where she'll be marked for life.

It was a quick and straightforward journey, but Lucy was chafing with impatience just the same by the time they arrived in Florence. The bus stopped near the train station, so Lucy checked her case and bags into the left-luggage facility, then called into the nearby tourist office for directions to the Falcone bank.

It was a relatively new building in an anonymous street off the Piazza della Repubblica, and Lucy found herself having to negotiate stringent security precautions at its imposing glass entrance.

Her insistence that she needed a personal interview with Count Giulio Falcone was received politely but sceptically. Eventually, she was confronted by a middle-aged secretary who explained with remote civility that Count Falcone was not available.

Lucy's hands twisted together. 'Then if you could just give him a message…'

'I am sorry, *signorina*. He will not be here for the rest of the day. He was called away earlier on urgent family business.'

And that, Lucy thought wretchedly, could mean anything.

Well, I tried, she thought, trying to comfort herself as she made her way back to the station, only to find that she had just missed a connection to Pisa, and had an hour to wait.

But what real hurry was there anyway? she asked herself. She walked slowly out of the station and back into the city. Giulio's city. Wanting to see it through his eyes. Wishing she could know it as he did. Retracing the steps of the route she had followed during their brief time there together. It was, after all, her last chance.

In the little street near the Duomo, Giovanni's restaurant was already bustling, getting ready for the day. Lucy wished she could have eaten there, but the need to conserve her money in case of problems at the airport seemed more important, she conceded with a sigh, before turning into the long street leading down to the Piazza della Signoria.

In the adjoining Mercato Nuovo, Il Porcellino, the bronze wild boar, sat grinning amiably.

I did return, Lucy told him under her breath, but not in the way I wanted. And I won't be coming back. She lifted a hand and stroked the gleaming snout in final farewell.

Pisa lay baked in mid-afternoon sun when Lucy finally arrived at Galileo Galilei airport. She loaded her bags onto a trolley, and set off for the terminal building, mentally rehearsing what she'd have to say.

As the doors slid apart to admit her, he was the first—the only one—she saw.

He was standing directly in front of her, hands on hips, his face tired and serious, the golden gleam of laughter and life gone from his amber eyes. It occurred to her as she hesitated, the chatter of voices, the buzz of movement fading into obscurity, that she would give a year of her life to see him smile again.

He stepped forward and put a hand on the trolley, halting its progress. 'So,' he said quietly. 'You are here at last.'

Lucy's heart performed a peculiar kind of somersault. She said huskily, 'Are you having me arrested? Or just making sure I leave the country?'

'Neither of those things, Lucia. You should know better than that.'

She wasn't sure of anything any more. But one thing she had to make clear.

She threw back her head. 'Giulio—I swear to you I didn't do it—I didn't take the ring.' She paused. 'But I'm afraid I know who did.'

'I do too,' he said, the weary lines beside his mouth deepening. 'And I am more sorry than I can say.'

She wanted to take his head in her hands and kiss away the strain and unhappiness. She said, 'Don't be too hard on her—please. She's unhappy and confused—and I think she was doing it for you.'

'You can say that?' he asked harshly. 'If she'd had her way you would have been in a police cell by now.'

Lucy shivered. 'She doesn't think things through. I'm sure she never intended…'

'You are wrong, Lucia. She wished to destroy you. Sergio and I have had to listen to it all—to every poisonous, twisted thought she has ever had.' He drew a harsh breath. 'It was—vile.'

Lucy moved sharply in negation. 'Darling—don't. She's only a child. She doesn't realise…'

'A child?' His brows lifted. 'I doubt that Claudia was ever a child.'

'*Claudia?*' Lucy almost screamed the name. 'But she didn't steal the ring.'

'*Sì.*' Giulio bent his head. 'She gave it to her witch of a maid to put among your things. Surely you must have known?'

She said numbly. 'No. I—I thought it was Emilia.'

'Emilia?' Giulio echoed. 'But what possible reason…?'

Lucy stared up at him. 'She'd heard you arguing with your stepmother about it and wanted to help. She took it once before—so that she could return it to you. I knew what Contessa Falcone would make of it if she found out, so I put it back. Only Agnese saw me, it seems.'

'So that was it,' Giulio said grimly. 'She has been spying on you from the beginning, and saw me kiss you yesterday. When she reported back to Claudia, they hatched this plot to get rid of you, hoping that you would be back in England in disgrace before I heard of it.'

'It's unbelievable.'

'Not if you know Claudia.' Giulio sighed, then glanced

around, regaining authority as he registered the curious glances being directed at them.

'We cannot stay here,' he said. 'We'll take your luggage to the car, and find somewhere to talk in private.'

Lucy hung back, her face troubled. 'I've got to see about my ticket. I—I have to leave—to go back. I just needed you to know that I wasn't a thief.'

'*Idiota.*' His voice was very tender. 'Little fool. Little dove. Did you really think I would let you go?'

'You can't keep me here,' Lucy protested as he began to steer the trolley out of the terminal building. 'You have no right—not when you're going to marry Angela.'

'Let us be clear.' He didn't even pause. 'I am not marrying Angela now, or at any future time. I do not love Angela, and I never have. As she and Claudia are now finally aware,' he added with chill emphasis.

'You don't want her?' Lucy's voice shook.

He said gently, 'I love you, Lucia, and as soon as we have some privacy I shall ask you to be my wife. But not, I think, standing in the middle of a car park.'

Lucy, rendered unexpectedly dumb, followed him meekly to the car.

'So, here we are,' he said as he slid into the driver's seat beside her. 'Back where it all began.' He reached into the inside pocket of his jacket and brought out the Falcone ring. 'Give me your hand, *carissima.*'

She obeyed, and he put the glowing ruby on her finger.

'Now,' he said softly. 'Now, my love, my wife, do you believe me?' And he kissed her deeply and tenderly, and then with a mounting passion that sent her head and her heart reeling.

When she was allowed to speak, Lucy said breathlessly, 'But you sent me away. You said it would be dishonourable for you to—touch me. That you had other commitments—obligations.'

'Not I, *mia bella*, you, or so I thought. I believed you were still in love with your worthless Philip. I found his photograph torn up in your room that first day at the villa, and recognised him as the new man in Angela's life.'

'But how could you? You'd never met him, surely?'

Giulio shrugged. 'Angela is going to be a rich woman,' he said drily. 'Her father is naturally cautious about any man she dates—has private enquiries made about his background. And I see the information as a security precaution, because of the connection between our families. I was not impressed with what I read,' he added levelly.

He paused. 'When I went to Lussione and questioned your friends, they confirmed that Philip had left you for another woman, and that you were devastated—heartbroken. The last thing I bargained for was Angela's arrival with this Philip.

'I could think of nothing but how hurt you were going to be, and of how much I wanted to protect you from that hurt. That was when I knew I felt more for you than a passing attraction. When I knew I had fallen in love with you the first moment that you trembled in my arms.'

The beginnings of a smile curved Lucy's mouth. 'I think that's when it began for me too—*caro* Giulio.'

He lifted the hand that wore his ring to his lips. 'What fools we have been. The time we have wasted.' He sighed. 'But, you see, I'd made up my mind that if Philip—' he pronounced the name with disdain '—was the man you truly wanted I would not stand in your way, however much I wanted you for myself.'

His mouth hardened. 'It wasn't such a problem. I know Angela only too well—know how easily she can be diverted. So I—quite cynically, I confess—provided the appropriate diversion.'

'But how could you have thought I still wanted Philip?'

he colour rose in Lucy's face. 'When you saw how I—
acted to you—responded to you.'

He stroked her flushed cheek with a gentle hand. 'Sex is
great deceiver, Lucia. I tried so hard to tell myself you
elonged to someone else. That I had no right to confuse
ou—to seduce you away from your real love.'

He shook his head. 'I tried desperately, too, to hold back
rom you—and each time I failed I despised myself more.
hat's why I went to Firenze. Because I could no longer
ust myself to be near you.'

'But I never gave Philip any encouragement,' Lucy pro-
sted. 'In fact I realised almost as soon as he went that our
elationship had been going nowhere, and that he'd done us
oth a favour by pulling out. I admit it was a shock when
e first left, but my pride was hurt far more than my heart.'

'But the girl—Nina—was so sure. She said you were a
ne-man woman. That you'd been close to a breakdown
ver him.'

Lucy bit her lip. 'Nina and I work for the same company
ut we've never been close friends, and I've never confided
1 her. I think she had her own agenda in this.'

Giulio groaned. 'I should have asked you what your feel-
1gs were—but I did not dare.'

Lucy touched the crimson fire of the Falcone ring with a
entle hand. 'Presumably something happened to change
our mind?'

'Ah, yes.' The familiar gleam of laughter had returned to
1e amber eyes. 'Fiammetta told me something about him
eing drenched in wine last night. That did not seem like a
oken of love, *columbina*. Coupled with the fact that he had
llowed you to leave alone, his eagerness to dissociate him-
elf from the supposed theft—and certain ill-judged remarks
bout your frigidity,' he added with something like a snarl.
le has Sergio to thank that I did not break his jaw. But

when I left he and Angela were engaged in mutual recrim-
inations, so I suppose that is punishment enough.'

Her mouth trembled into a smile. 'Almost certainly.' She
paused. 'But how did you find out about Claudia?'

'We have Sergio to thank. He arrived at the villa early
this morning, just after your departure, and found the place
in uproar. It did not take him long to realise that Emilia was
troubled. She'd overheard part of a conversation between
Agnese and Claudia, and although she did not completely
understand it she told Sergio enough to make him suspicious. He thought it best to send for me, and between us we
got the truth from Agnese, and eventually Claudia herself,'
he explained grimly.

'I ordered her to pack her things and leave immediately.
But not before I had told her that all her plotting had failed
and that I would never willingly see her again. Then I left
poor Sergio to sort out the mess and came to Pisa to find
you. I've been here most of the day.'

Lucy sighed. 'And I was in Firenze looking for you. I
couldn't bear to leave without seeing you again.'

'Oh, you would have seen me again,' he told her softly.
'Even if you had gone with Philip, I would have followed—
tried to make you change your mind. You see, *cara*, I canno
live without you.'

'Nor I without you.' Lucy looked at him from under he
lashes, suddenly shy. 'But it's all happened so fast…'

'It was the same with my mother and father,' he sai
gently, his mouth curving in tender reminiscence. 'On
look—one smile—and they were lost.' He smoothed
strand of Lucy's hair back from her forehead. 'Now, *co
umbina*, do you believe in the force of destiny?'

'I think I must,' she said softly.

Giulio nodded. 'By the time we get back to the vill
everyone will have gone. Sergio is taking his own famil
away, so you will meet him later—when Fiammetta is le

distraught,' he added with a small grimace. 'So you and I, *mia bella*, will have some time to ourselves at last to make plans for our marriage.'

He paused. 'But now you have something to tell me, I think.'

'Have I?' Lucy frowned. 'We seem to have covered everything.'

'Not quite.' The amber gaze was steadfast, intent on her face, brilliant with tenderness and need. 'You have never yet, Lucia *mia*, told me that you love me.'

Lucy put her arms round his neck and drew him towards her.

'I think,' she whispered as her lips touched his, 'that I shall spend the rest of my life doing exactly that, *mi amore*.'

Born in London, **Sophie Weston** is a traveller by nature who started writing when she was five. She wrote her first romance recovering from illness, thinking her travelling was over. She was wrong, but she enjoyed it so much that she has carried on. These days she lives in the heart of the city with two demanding cats and a cherry tree – and travels the world looking for settings for her stories.

THE LATIN AFFAIR
by
Sophie Weston

PROLOGUE

'YOU'RE a fraud, Nicky.'

Andrew Bolton thrust himself away from her and stood up.

In the half-dark of her sitting room, Nicky Piper clutched her elderly dressing gown round her. Andrew had arrived at midnight, bearing flowers and champagne. High on the success of a new contract and several hours celebrating it, he had woken her up, danced her sexily round her sitting room and then, laughing, carried her to the sofa.

Where they'd both come face to face with a truth they had been avoiding for months.

'Face it, Nicky. You don't want me.' The honesty was brutal. 'In your heart of hearts, you never have.'

Nicky ran her fingers through her loosened hair. In the light reflected from the street lamp outside her window stray fronds gleamed like diamonds. Even with all the gold leached out of it, the soft, curly mass was spectacular. Andrew eyed it broodingly.

'Oh, boy, did I want you,' he said, almost to himself. 'Gorgeous blonde. Legs to your eyebrows. Figure like a paradise houri.'

Nicky said nothing but her jaw ached with tension. Although she said nothing Andrew picked up on it at once. The look he sent her was wry.

'I know. I know. I'm not supposed to mention it.' His sigh sounded as if it was wrenched out of him. 'You're a lovely girl, Nicky. Why don't you want anyone to notice? Even when they're making love to you?'

Nicky shaded her eyes. This was truth indeed.

'I—tried.'

Andrew swung round on her. 'That's the point,' he said, suddenly fierce. 'You're not supposed to have to *try*.'

Nicky knew he was right. She hugged her knees to her chest, feeling guilty. She had so wanted to be in love with him. Until tonight she would have said she was. But all he had to do was to come to her when she was not expecting him and the façade cracked to pieces.

And suddenly there was the real Nicky—tense as a drum and armed to the teeth against invasion. And that was Andrew's problem—for all their shared laughter, when he took her by surprise, Nicky turned and saw an invader.

She said, half to herself, 'I didn't realise.'

He sat down on the bamboo chair under the window and looked at her. In the sodium light from the street lamp his expression was sombre.

'Someone has given you a real pasting, hasn't he?'

'No,' said Nicky, horrified.

It couldn't still hurt. It *couldn't*. Not after all these years. She had been a child then. Now she was a woman, independent and in control of her life. She couldn't still be in the power of something so *stupid*.

She knelt down in front of his chair and looked up into his face. 'Andrew, I'm so sorry.'

He touched her cheek, quite without his usual passion, his eyes searching her shadowed face.

'Have you ever been in love, Nicky?'

Nicky shrugged evasively. 'I don't know what you mean by love.'

'I mean,' said Andrew drily, 'has there ever been a man you wanted to make love with? Without pretending.'

And, fast as a lightning strike, Nicky thought, *He knows about Steve.* Her whole body juddered with the shock of it. And in that moment she gave herself away.

'I see,' said Andrew at length.

Nicky pulled herself together. She stood up.

'One adolescent crush,' she said drily. She was glad to

hear she sounded more like herself at last. 'Very adolescent and very short-lived.'

Andrew watched her. 'Returned?'

Nicky gave an unamused laugh. 'He despised me,' she said flatly. 'Very understandable. Looking back, I despise myself.' Her voice rasped.

Andrew was taken aback. 'Isn't that a bit extreme? For a teenage mistake?'

Nicky had told herself the same thing a million times. It made no difference. Every time she thought about Steve and what she had so nearly done with him, she wanted to hide.

'I made a fool of myself,' she said between her teeth. 'It's got nothing to do with you and me.'

'Hasn't it?'

He got up and touched her shoulder. Nicky's shoulders went rigid. His hand fell.

'You see?' said Andrew tiredly. 'It's got everything to do with you and me. And any other man who tries to get near you.'

'Don't say that,' protested Nicky involuntarily.

He said in a low voice, 'Nicky, I love you to bits but this is getting us nowhere.'

'But—'

'No!' he said forcefully. 'I don't want a girlfriend who braces herself every time I touch her.'

'I don't!'

He turned her round to face him. For a long moment, he looked searchingly into her eyes. Even in the half-dark his expression said as clearly as words that he could still hear what she could. High on his triumph, Andrew had been too excited to give her *time*, thought Nicky. And in that fatal instant when he had carried her to the sofa all the ancient horrors had crowded in. She did not know which of them had been more shocked by her animal cry of rejection.

Now, as she remembered, Nicky's hands flew to her burning cheeks.

Andrew said quietly, 'I deserve better than that, Nicky.'

There was a long, agonised pause. Nicky's hands fell.

'I know,' she said almost inaudibly.

'And, frankly, so do you.'

He looked round for his jacket. It was where he had thrown it, on the floor. The bottle of champagne he had brought lay on its side, half crushing the bright chrysanthemums he had found at the late-night store. Nicky blinked back sudden tears.

'I'm sorry.'

Andrew had behaved well but he was still smarting. 'So am I.'

He went to the door, then turned and kissed her cheek, quickly, with a new and awkward formality. Nicky leaned against him, burying her face in his chest so she did not have to see the pain in his eyes. He touched her hair fleetingly.

'If you want my advice, you'll find the guy. Get him out of your system. Or you'll never be free.'

He went.

Nicky put the chain on the door and leaned her back against it. She was too shaken for tears.

She had thought she loved Andrew. Well—she was too shaken for dishonesty as well—she had thought that Andrew would take her as close to love as she was ever likely to get. She had thought it would be enough. It had never occurred to her that she was cheating Andrew.

'Now what?' said Nicky aloud.

She had no idea of the answer.

CHAPTER ONE

IN THE morning, of course, things looked different. They always did, thought Nicky. There was a job to do, her brother to meet for lunch, the last sunshine of autumn to savour. The small things, as always, would carry her through.

'I will survive,' Nicky told her mirror.

The gorgeous reflection stared back, only partially convinced.

Why on earth do I look like this? she thought. Andrew was right when he said she was a fraud. Even in her sober business suit she looked the original party blonde. What was more, she always had. Nicky winced at the thought.

Of course, there had been changes over the years. When she was sixteen her skin had been golden with a Caribbean tan; her untamed hair used to be a sun-streaked lion's mane. These days she was city-pale and her daffodil hair shone. But, in spite of her best efforts, it was never quite immaculate. Soft tendrils always escaped to lie enticingly against her long neck. Add to that a kissable mouth and wide, long-lashed blue-grey eyes and it was not surprising that men looked at her and thought they had found their dream babe. Nicky bared her teeth at her reflection.

'Some babe,' she said bitterly.

She was still brooding when she got to work.

'Hey, what did I do?' said Martin de Vries in mock alarm.

Nicky jumped, conscience stricken. Martin was the boss of Springdown Kitchens and she was late for work. Now she'd compounded her sins by glaring at him. She shook her head ruefully.

'Nothing. It's just one of those Monday mornings, that's all.'

9

Martin nodded briskly. 'That's a relief. I need to get off to the exhibition hall soon.' But he hesitated. 'Are you sure you're all right?'

Damn, thought Nicky. Martin was an old friend of the family. Of course he could see right through the last twenty years to the six-year-old with scabby knees and pigtails. It gave him an unfair advantage.

She summoned up a bright smile. 'I'm fine.'

Martin knew how to interpret that. He had daughters of his own. He nodded. 'Boyfriend trouble,' he diagnosed.

Nicky winced theatrically. 'You sound like my mother.'

'No, I don't. I sound like a caring employer.'

'My next job is going to be with a hard-hearted tycoon who doesn't know a thing about his employees. And cares less,' Nicky muttered.

Martin ignored that. 'What's happened, Nick? Did he do something unforgivable, like want to marry you?'

Nicky smacked her conscience back in its box and glared at him for real.

'That's my business. Get down to the Lifestyle Fair and sell some kitchens,' she retorted.

Martin was torn. He was fond of Nicky. On the other hand he ran a vulnerable small business and the fair was the show-case of the year.

'As long as it isn't a crisis,' he said, patently anxious to be reassured.

Nicky gave a small huff of fury. But then genuine affection took over.

'No crisis,' she said more gently. 'Just something that's been building up a long time. All under control.'

'OK,' said Martin, relieved. He went.

Squaring up to the work on her desk, Nicky found that he had left her plenty to do. It was a relief. It took her mind off the uncomfortable truths Andrew had exposed last night.

Besides, she knew that what she was doing was worth-while. Martin was an inspired salesman, whereas Nicky liked practical organisation. She had her head down over the speifications of a small hotel kitchen when a cup appeared in front of her.

'Coffee,' said Caroline Leith, Martin's newest and most sophisticated assistant. 'You're going to need it.'

Nicky looked up. 'What's happened?'

'Martin refused to take any phone calls before he left.'

Nicky's heart sank. That meant clients who would already be annoyed when she called them back.

'Who?'

Caroline consulted her notebook. 'Two from Mr Tremain's secretary. One from Weber Hotels. Three from Mrs Van Linden. All of them only wanted to talk to Martin.' She grinned. 'Mrs Van Linden positively refused to talk to you under any circumstances. What happened? You told her what you thought of her horrible kitchen? Or she's seen how you look?'

Nicky raised her eyes to heaven. 'What's wrong with how I look?' she said dangerously.

'Nothing as long as you aren't a trophy wife worried about the competition.'

Nicky frowned. Caroline chuckled, unabashed.

'What do you expect, with a figure like yours?' she said frankly. 'It may be unfashionable to have all those curves but it sure as hell presses all the right male buttons.'

Nicky tensed. That was more or less exactly what Andrew had said last night. To say nothing of a man called Steve under a Caribbean moon... But the phone rang and broke that particular unwelcome train of thought.

Caroline answered it, listened, then put her hand over the receiver. 'SOS. Sally's in trouble. Sounds like she's going to cry.'

Nicky frowned blackly. Sally was the ideal receptionist, unfailingly sunny even with the most difficult clients. Anyone who reduced her to tears needed to be put in their place without delay. She held out an imperative hand.

'It's Tremain,' Caroline warned.

It gave Nicky pause for a moment. 'Who?'

'Tremain. Martin knows him personally. From the yacht club.'

Nicky scanned her memory. Nothing. She said so. 'But he's not going to bully Sally.'

'Kid-gloves time,' advised Caroline, surrendering the phone.

Nicky knew the warning tone was justified. She squared her shoulders and tried to remember the bit in her management course about dealing with difficult clients.

'I'm sorry to keep you waiting—' she began, uncharacteristically soothing.

'Then don't.' It was impatient and very male. At once she knew why Sally had not been able to calm him down. Mr Tremain did not want to be calmed down. Mr Tremain wanted blood.

And, true to form, it made Nicky want to fight right back. She curbed her combative instinct but it was a close-run thing.

'How can I—'

He did not let her finish. 'Where's de Vries?'

'—help you?' Sweet reason was not paying off. Well, then, she would give him a taste of her real reaction to a man who interrupted her twice. 'What can I do for you?' she finished, the frost showing.

Caroline did not go. Instead she propped herself up against a drawer of files and waited, prepared to be amused.

Mr Tremain was not impressed by Nicky's chilly formality. 'You can get me de Vries,' he said grimly. 'Now.'

'I'm afraid that's not poss—'

'*Now.*'

Nicky could feel her fuse shortening. Caroline grinned. Nicky frowned her down and raised her voice. 'If you would just let me finish—'

'I haven't got time to waste talking to lieutenants.' Even allowing for the distortion of the telephone, the dismissive tone was an insult. Nicky's fuse suddenly became very short indeed. And her frost dissolved into simple temper.

'Then try listening,' she flashed. 'Martin de Vries is not here. I can ask him to call you when he gets back or you can talk to me now. Your choice. Frankly I don't care which—but make up your mind. I haven't got time to waste either.'

Across the office, Caroline raised her eyebrows. Oh, *hell*, thought Nicky, remembering the management course too late.

But at least her outburst seemed to give Tremain pause.

He said slowly, 'Work closely with de Vries, do you?'

Nicky was all dignity. 'Of course.'

'So you're fully briefed on everything that's gone wrong with the blasted kitchen he sold me?'

'Well, I would have to look at the file…'

'And of *course* you're empowered to agree on compensation?' he went on sweetly.

Nicky knew quite well what he was doing. Silently she ground her teeth.

'I would have to consult Mr de Vries,' she conceded stiffly.

'Quite.' His tone was suddenly a lot less sweet. 'So let's stop playing games. We both know de Vries is ducking and weaving. Cut the feeble excuses, dig him out of wherever he's hiding and put him on the line *now*.'

If Nicky did not like being dismissed, she positively hated being patronised.

She yelled, 'I do not play games. I do not tell lies. And Martin isn't here.'

And banged the phone down.

Caroline gave her a slow, mocking hand-clap. 'That showed him.'

Nicky was steaming. 'So it should. Bully,' she threw at the phone, as if the man were there in person.

'Esteban Tremain must be shivering in his shoes,' murmured Caroline.

'Quite right too,' Nicky announced, militant. 'He shouldn't have tried to bully Sally. And he shouldn't have talked to me like that. I haven't got the time to take a lot of rubbish from people who don't listen. It's too close to lunchtime.'

She glanced at her watch as she spoke. She had a date with her brother and Ben had been known to leave a restaurant if people kept him waiting.

'Tell that to Martin when you explain how you handled his biggest problem client,' Caroline said with feeling.

Nicky stared. 'Biggest problem client? What are you talking about?'

'You mean you don't *know* who Esteban Tremain is?'

'Never met the man in my life,' said Nicky, adding darkly, 'And, on present showing, I'll be quite happy if that's the way it stays.'

'Stately home?' prompted Caroline. 'Cornwall? Try, gorgeous.'

'Oh, please!'

'You can't have forgotten him. A Savile Row suit with muscles. When he came in to the showroom every woman in the place wandered by for a look.'

Nicky shook her head. 'None of us is that sex-starved,' she protested, trying not to laugh. 'What is he? A film star?'

Caroline said in a practical tone, 'No. Just tall, dark and smouldering with sex appeal. And threatening to sue Martin for every penny he's got.'

'*What?*'

She cocked a mocking eyebrow. 'Come on, Nicky. The kitchen at Hallam Hall must have cost us more grief than any other contract this year.'

'Hallam Hall!' gasped Nicky, enlightened at last.

Now she knew exactly who Esteban Tremain was. And how much he could cost Springdown Kitchens if he put his mind to it.

'Oh, my Lord,' she said. 'Get the file into my office *now*.'

Caroline ran.

Esteban Tremain looked at the suddenly buzzing telephone with disbelief. Nobody cut him off. *Nobody*. He began to punch buttons savagely.

The door opened. 'Er—' said his secretary.

One glance was enough to tell her that he was in a temper. She did not think much of Francesca Moran's chances of getting in to see him when he looked like that.

Esteban glared at her across the telephone.

'What?'

'Miss Moran,' said Anne fast. Her tone was strictly neutral. 'She's been shopping. She wondered if you would like to take her to lunch.'

Esteban breathed hard.

Anne held her breath. When she'd come to work for him three years ago there had been plenty of people to warn her that Esteban would be impossible. He was a heart-breaker; he was a workaholic; he had a fiendish temper. She had learned that it was all true. Only he did not take any of it out on his secretary. Normally…

With an angry exclamation, he threw the telephone from him and flung out of his chair. Anne quietly restored the telephone to its cradle and waited.

Esteban strode up to the floor-length window. He thrust his hands into his pockets and glared out at the rain-lashed lawns. A muscle worked in his cheek.

Esteban wrestled with his temper. None of this was Anne's fault, he reminded himself. He gave an explosive sigh and swung back to the room.

'My regrets to Francesca,' he said rapidly, not sounding regretful at all. 'Anything else?'

Anne, the perfect secretary, did not protest. She just said carefully, 'I'll go along and tell her you're too busy to see her, shall I?'

There was a small, sizzling pause.

'She's here?'

'I'm afraid so.'

'But I told her last time—' He remembered again that it was not Anne's fault and stopped. *'Damn.'*

Esteban thought, then took one of his famous lightning decisions. 'OK. You'd better wheel her in for a bit. But not long.'

He reached for his jacket.

Esteban never received visitors in his shirt sleeves, Anne thought. Not even a lady he regularly spent the night with. Though she was not sure that Francesca Moran was in that category these days, in spite of the gossip or, indeed, the hints that Miss Moran herself let fall so heavily.

'I'll just clear a space,' murmured Anne, again the perfect secretary, advancing on a tower of papers.

Esteban looked around his room in faint surprise. Apart from the papers that covered his desk, there were two large books open on the floor beside him and piles of more papers that needed his attention on every one of his comfortable chairs. He looked amused suddenly.

'Don't bother.'

'But she's got to have somewhere to sit.'

'Why? It will only encourage her,' said Esteban wickedly.

He flicked his lapels straight. Looking up, he gave her a conspiratorial grin.

'Buzz me in five, max. Right?'

'Right,' said Anne.

Francesca Moran, she thought with satisfaction, would be back in the rainy garden a lot sooner than she expected. Anne did not like Francesca.

It would have been impossible to tell from Esteban's manner whether he liked her or not. He kissed her on both exquisitely made up cheeks in welcome. But he adroitly avoided her move to deepen the embrace and retired behind the bulwark of his desk. Francesca accepted the rebuff as gracefully as if she had not recognised it. She took up a perch on the arm of an ancient leather chair and gave him a sweet smile.

'We need to talk,' she said caressingly.

Esteban raised his eyebrows. 'Oh?'

Francesca's myopic grey eyes made her look vague and fragile. It was misleading.

'Yes. I was thinking all the time I was in Cornwall. It's

stupid for us to be like this. We ought to let bygones be bygones and pool our resources.'

Esteban's poker face was famous. But for a moment he could not contain his astonishment. At once, he controlled his expression. But one corner of his mouth twitched.

'Are you proposing to me, Francesca?' he asked politely.

She was not disconcerted. She batted her eyelashes and gave him a smile of calculated charm.

'Well, you're not going to propose to me, are you?'

Esteban was surprised into laughing aloud. 'You're right there,' he agreed, watching her with fascination.

Francesca shrugged. 'So it's up to me,' she said with no sign of rancour. 'You need a wife. It would be ideal.'

'I'm afraid I don't, you know,' said Esteban. He was gentle but quite firm.

But Francesca, as he had learned in Gibraltar last year, did not recognise firmness when it meant someone not doing what she wanted.

'It would be perfect,' she said, unheeding. 'The time is right for both of us.'

Esteban leaned back in his chair and surveyed her in disbelief. She smiled back, not discouraged. He decided to try another tack.

'What makes you think I need a wife?' he drawled.

She gestured round the untidy room. 'You're in a complete mess. You need someone to run the practical side of your life so that you can get on with your career.'

'That's what Anne does,' he objected.

'Don't be ridiculous, darling. That's not what I meant and you know it.'

'Then explain,' he said blandly.

Francesca refused to be annoyed. 'You're being silly,' she said in an indulgent tone. 'What about your private life? Where would you have been if I hadn't gone down to Hallam Hall and sorted out those workmen?'

'Ah. I wondered when that would come up,' said Esteban with satisfaction.

Francesca frowned. 'You would have been lost without me,' she said, her tone sharpening. 'You were out of the country and those cowboys were getting away with murder.'

'And I was grateful for your help but—'

Francesca regained her good humour. 'I bet you haven't even talked to the kitchen people yet.'

Esteban looked at the telephone. His expression darkened. He was not going to admit to Francesca that the woman had hung up on him. Why did women always have to play *games*?

'I've got it in hand,' he said brusquely.

Francesca got up and came over to him. A faint hint of expensive scent wafted as she settled herself on the corner of the desk beside him. She crossed one leg over the other and smiled down into his eyes.

'Don't you see, darling? Marry me and you would never have to deal with kitchen designers again.'

Her high-heeled shoe tapped at his thigh to emphasise her point.

'An alluring prospect,' said Esteban drily.

He pushed his chair back, removing his immaculate suit out of range.

'And you need a hostess,' Francesca went on, her smile unwavering. 'Someone to organise the dinner parties, make sure you meet the right people.'

He almost shuddered.

'I don't think so.'

'Of course you do.'

She would have gone on but Esteban put an end to it. He stood up and looked down at her, all vestige of amusement gone.

'I thought I had been clear, Francesca. If you misunderstood me, I'm sorry. But the truth is that my stepfather needs a housekeeper. You said you wanted a job. A job is all that's on offer.'

'But—'

'If you remember,' Esteban said drily, 'I said at the time

I thought you would find Hallam very isolated. But you wanted to give it a shot.'

Francesca's mouth thinned. For a moment the pretty face looked almost ugly.

'Are you saying you used me?'

Esteban stiffened imperceptibly. 'Excuse me?'

There were people—witnesses for the prosecution, say, or opposing counsel—who would have run a mile when he spoke in that soft tone. Francesca did not read the danger signals. She tossed her head.

'Of course I adore Patrick,' she said unconvincingly. 'I was very willing to *help*—'

Esteban said quietly, 'You wanted a job.'

Francesca did not like that. 'You know quite well what I wanted,' she said sharply.

It was a moment of total self-betrayal. There was a nasty silence. Francesca bit her lip.

Esteban said heavily, 'I seem to have been very stupid. I thought you knew that all that was over. I told you so last year.'

'Darling, just because of a silly article in a magazine—'

He stopped her with an upraised hand. 'It was not about the article. I don't care what some tinpot journalist writes about me.'

'Well, then—'

'But I care that someone I trusted talked to a tinpot journalist,' Esteban went on softly. 'About stuff I told you in confidence.'

There was another nasty silence. Francesca watched him, frustrated.

At last she burst out, 'It's such a stupid *waste*. I could really help your career. Daddy's contacts—a bit of networking—'

'And what about love?' he said wryly.

'Love?' Francesca sounded as blank as if he had broken into a foreign language. 'Grow up, darling.'

'You think love's an irrelevance?'

'Oh, come on. We're talking real life here.'

Esteban gave an unexpected laugh. 'We are indeed. And we seem to have different views on it.'

'Are you saying you're looking for love?' Francesca sounded disbelieving. 'You?'

'I don't think you need to look for it,' Esteban said coolly. 'In my experience it tends to sock you in the eye.'

Francesca snorted. 'Your experience? So now you're the last of the great romantics?'

Esteban gave that his measured consideration. 'No,' he said at last. 'I wouldn't call myself a romantic.'

'Thank God for that, at least,' Francesca muttered.

'On the other hand, I'm not fool enough to marry anyone I'm not in love with.'

Francesca pulled herself together. She moved close to him, though she did not quite dare to touch him again. She gave him a winning smile.

'But if both parties agree—'

He bent towards her so fast she took a step backwards in simple shock. At once she could have kicked herself. He had not come so close to her voluntarily for over a year.

But it was too late. Esteban had seen her alarm. He gave her a mocking smile.

'Agree to change my nature? How?'

Francesca recovered fast. 'But you've just said you aren't romantic,' she reminded him.

'No, but I am passionate and possessive and I have a nasty temper,' Esteban told her evenly. 'Believe me, you wouldn't like being married to me.'

'No woman would,' snapped Francesca, unexpectedly shaken.

He raised his eyebrows. 'I'm glad we agree on the matter.' He sounded amused.

The telephone rang. He reached behind him, not looking, and swept it up to his ear. 'Hi, Annie. Now? Yes, of course.' He put the phone down. 'Sorry, Francesca. Busy morning. Goodbye.'

Francesca was looking poleaxed. His court opponents would have recognised the feeling. Esteban gave her an enigmatic smile and held the door open for her. She did not move.

'You're not going to treat me like this. I'm no little boat chick,' she jeered.

Esteban went very still. Francesca knew she had made a bad mistake. That was one of the few confidences she had not spilled out to the handsome young journalist in the quayside café last year.

She nervously touched her hair but said defiantly, 'It just slipped out. You told me about it yourself, after all. I couldn't help it. You upset me so much I forgot I wasn't supposed to mention it.' A thought occurred to her. She lowered her lashes. 'If you go on being nasty to me, it might happen again—and who knows who could be listening?'

Esteban's watchfulness dissolved into unholy appreciation.

'Threats?' he said, his eyebrows flying up. 'Very attractive. Just the stuff to get me to marry you. You're really one on your own, Francesca.'

There was nothing she could say. Once again Esteban Tremain had taken her well thought out strategy and turned it on its head. Francesca was determined but she was not an idiot. She recognised defeat, at least for the moment.

'I'll go.' She gathered up her handbag and elegant serape but was not leaving without the last word. 'Call me when you've got your head together. You need me.'

'I don't think so,' Esteban said quietly.

'Oh, but you do.' She had gone back to her caressing manner. She gave him a sweet smile. 'You just don't know how much yet. But you will.'

She left.

Immediately Esteban banished her from his mind. He flung himself back into his chair and reached for the Hallam file again. He picked up the telephone, his voice coming alive with the anticipation of battle.

'Annie, get me that kitchen place again, will you? And this time I want to talk to de Vries in person.'

But when Anne put the call through it was the lieutenant again.

'Hello?' She did her best to sound composed but Esteban was used to reading the smallest nuance in his opponents' voices and he recognised nerves. It was a lovely voice, Esteban noted, warm with an underlying hint of laughter. Currently, of course, the laughter was almost extinguished. *Good*, he thought.

'What is your name?' he demanded softly.

He did not have to say anything else. The tone alone intimidated opponents. Esteban knew it and used it effectively in court. If it could silence Francesca Moran, a judge's daughter, it would make this obstructive girl crumble.

But, to his astonishment, it did not. There was a little pause, in which he could almost hear her pull herself together.

Then, 'Piper,' she said coolly. 'Nicola Piper.' She spelled it for him.

It disconcerted him. Esteban was not used to hostile witnesses spelling out their names and then asking kindly if he had got it all down. Where had she got that kind of confidence? Did he know her? Surely he would not have forgotten that golden sunshine voice?

'Have we met?' he asked slowly.

Nicky had remembered his visit as soon as Caroline had mentioned Hallam Hall. She had just come in from dealing with another client. And she had noticed him all right: a tall, dark man in the doorway of Martin's office, watching her with lazy appreciation.

'You could say that. In passing,' she said frostily.

That startled him too. And intrigued him. 'Where did we pass?'

'At the office. We weren't introduced.'

There was a thoughtful pause.

'You're the blonde,' Esteban said on a long note of discovery.

He remembered now. She had shot in from somewhere, silk skirts flying, laughing. Her briefcase had bulged with papers and she'd been clutching it under one arm with decreasing effectiveness. He would have gone to rescue it, but Martin had detained him with some remark and one of her colleagues had got there first.

This picture was still vivid, though. Summer evening sun had lit her hair to gold. It had clearly started the day confined in a neat bow at her nape but by now it was springing free into wild curls about her shoulders. And her figure— Esteban found his mouth curving in appreciation at the memory. She had a figure to rival one of Patrick's Renaissance goddesses at Hallam, lounging in naked voluptuousness among their sunlit olive groves. Add to that perfect legs, creamy skin— and, when she'd caught his eyes on her—a glare like a stiletto.

'I remember,' he said.

Alone in her office, Nicky winced. It was not the first time a man had called her a 'blonde' in that tone of voice. Or looked at her in blatant appreciation, as she now remembered all too clearly. It still stabbed where she was most vulnerable. Particularly this morning.

She hid her hurt under icy distance. 'The *name*,' she said with emphasis, 'is Piper.'

'Is it, indeed?'

Nicky could hear his amusement. She set her teeth and tried to remember that he was a customer.

He went on, 'Well, Piper, you can tell Martin de Vries that I paid for a working kitchen and that's what I expect to get.'

Nicky was bewildered. In spite of what Caroline had said, the file had been clear. Admittedly, there had been complaint after complaint but they all seemed to have been dealt with. Moreover, the complainant was not Mr Tremain. The name on the telephoned demands was a Ms Francesca Moran.

In response, machinery had been tested and tested again, cabinets resited, floor tiling replaced. A month ago, Tremain had threatened legal action. But as far as Nicky could see all the disputed work on the Cornish mansion had been completed ten days before.

'Do you have another complaint?' she said warily.

'Complaint!' His derisive bark of laughter made her eardrums ring.

Nicky held the phone away from her head until he had finished.

'Would you like to be more specific?' she suggested sweetly, when she thought he might be able to hear her again.

'Gladly.' He launched into a list.

Nicky listened in gathering disbelief.

'Don't be ridiculous,' she said when he finished. 'That would mean every single appliance had gone wrong.'

'Precisely,' said Esteban Tremain.

In her astonishment Nicky forgot she had decided she loathed the man.

'But they can't have done. They've been checked. And they're *new*.'

'I certainly paid for new machines,' he agreed suavely.

Nicky took a moment to assimilate that. 'Are you suggesting—?'

He interrupted again. 'My dear girl, I am suggesting nothing.'

Of course, he was a lawyer, Nicky remembered with dislike. He knew exactly how to hint without actually accusing her or Springdown Kitchens of anything precise enough to be actionable.

Her voice shaking with fury, she said, 'I object to the implication.'

'Implication?' His voice was smooth as cream. 'What implication was that?'

'Springdown Kitchens honour their contracts,' Nicky said hotly. 'If we charge you for new appliances, you get new appliances. You're accusing us of installing substandard machines—'

'Stop right there.' It sliced across her tumbling speech like an ice axe. 'I'm not accusing anyone of anything. Yet.'

Just that single word brought Nicky to a halt. She looked at her hand, gripping the telephone convulsively, and saw that she was shaking. Justified indignation, she assured herself.

But it did not feel like justified indignation. It felt as if she was a schoolgirl in a tantrum, not a serious professional dealing with an awkward client. Nicky breathed deeply.

She said, 'You'd better take this up with Mr de Vries.'

'As you may recall,' Esteban Tremain said blandly, 'that was exactly what I wanted to do in the first place.'

Nicky could not take any more. 'I'll tell him to call you as soon as I can catch him,' she said curtly.

And flung the phone down before she screamed.

This time he did not call back.

It had made her late, of course. She had promised Ben she would be there at twelve-fifteen at the latest, before the little bistro filled up with the lunchtime trade. Ben hated to be crowded. Just as he hated to wait. Impatience ran in the family.

Nicky gathered up her coat and bag with clumsy fingers. Caroline, having seen the phone call and its effect, wandered in.

'Tremain again, I take it. That man thinks he only has to crook his little finger.' She raised an eyebrow. 'What are you going to do?'

'Have lunch,' said Nicky, scribbling furiously on Martin's notepad, just in case he came back during the lunch break.

Caroline was intrigued. 'A date?'

Nicky tore off the note she had penned and stuck it over the top of Martin's phone where he could not miss it, no matter how hard he tried. She looked up.

'What price respect for personal privacy?' she asked resignedly.

'Never heard of it,' Caroline said with a grin. Nicky bared her teeth and dived past her.

'What will I do if Martin calls?' Caroline yelled after her.

'Tell him everything,' Nicky called back. 'It's all in the note. Tell him I'll deal with it if he wants. But not before lunch.'

She flung herself at the showroom door. Caroline followed her, grinning.

'And what if the frustrated client turns up in person?'

A wicked light invaded Nicky's eyes.

'Tell Mr Tremain he'll have to wait. I'm lunching with a man who won't.'

CHAPTER TWO

HER brother was waiting outside the bistro, lost in thought. Nicky broke into a run, calling his name. Ben looked up. He surged towards her, cleaving his way through the lunchtime crowd, and flung his arms wide.

It was an old joke. But Nicky felt oddly weepy as she ran full-tilt into them. Ben swung her off her feet with a rebel yell. Even on a rainy autumn street, dense with lunchtime crowds, heads turned; people smiled. He was so handsome, so full of life. He threw her into the air, looking up at her with a devilish grin.

'Put me down,' gasped Nicky. She was breathless, between laughter and unaccountable tears.

Ben only noticed the laughter. He returned her to the pavement and held her at arm's length, surveying her appreciatively.

'You look great,' he said. 'Even if you're late.'

'I know. I know,' she said placatingly. 'Sorry, I hit a natural disaster. Let's eat.'

The waiter showed them to the small corner table for which Nicky had managed to wrest a reservation out of the management. He brought them water and menus and a carafe of wine while Nicky regaled Ben with the account of her battles with the difficult client.

It entertained him hugely.

'Don't know about a natural disaster. It sounds to me as if you've met your match,' he said when she finished.

Nicky bridled. 'Oh, no, I haven't. He just—took me by surprise, that's all.'

'It's the only way,' murmured Ben teasingly.

Nicky sent him a look that would have crushed him if he had been anyone but her brother. He laughed.

'It's good for you,' he said hardily. 'You've been getting downright bossy.'

Nicky laughed. They both knew what he meant.

Ben was twenty-eight to her twenty-six but sometimes she felt as if he was still a teenager. He had been in London for three years, living a rollercoaster life. One day he was living in the lap of luxury with an old mate and earning a fortune. The next, he was standing on Nicky's doorstep at three in the morning without even the wherewithal to pay the taxi that had brought him.

Nicky always paid the cab, gave him a bed for the night and a loan to tide him over. It never took long. Normally Ben was on his way up again within a week.

He repaid her scrupulously and, as often as not, took her somewhere wildly expensive to celebrate the revival of his fortunes. And then she would not see him again until there was something else to celebrate or he was back at the bottom of the ride again. In fact Nicky had been wondering ever since he rang which it was this time.

But she knew him too well to ask a direct question. Instead, she let him pour wine for them both.

'You know, sometimes I feel like a changeling,' she said suddenly.

'You?' Ben paused, the carafe poised over his glass. He looked across at her in unfeigned surprise. 'But you're the only sensible one in the family.'

'Quite.'

'You mean the parents are rogues and vagabonds and I'm a financial disaster,' he interpreted.

Nicky shook her head.

'No. I mean you're relaxed. Free. You don't have to plan everything.'

Ben shrugged. 'So you're a planner. Somebody has to be.' He chuckled suddenly. 'The parents didn't do so well without you running the itinerary, did they?'

Nicky was startled into a little crow of laughter. When she'd moved to England eight years ago, her parents had announced that now, at last, they were going to sail round the world. But between one thing and another they had not quite set out yet.

Ben leaned across and patted her hand.

'So don't knock yourself just because you have some common sense.' His expression darkened. 'I wish to God I'd been as sensible.'

Nicky was concerned. 'Problems? Can I—?'

But he shook his head decisively. 'No. I can't keep touching you every time I'm short. Anyway, I've got something to keep me going while I sort myself out.'

Nicky did not argue. She knew his pride. So she just said, 'What do you think you'll do?'

He pulled a face. 'Winter's coming. I'm tempted to go south, see if I can get some sailing. There's bound to be a gin palace looking for a crew somewhere.'

Nicky could not repress her sudden shudder. Ben raised an eyebrow enquiringly.

'You mean a boat like the *Calico Jane*?'

Ben grinned. 'Hardly. Showiest boat in the Caribbean. Too many electronics for me. What made you think of her?'

She shrugged, regretting her unwary question.

But the name had awakened a forgotten mystery and Ben was not going to let it go.

'Was she the one, then? When you went moonlighting?' He laughed reminiscently. 'God, Mum was furious.'

'It was a long time ago,' Nicky said repressively.

The summer she was sixteen. It could have been yesterday.

Ben was intrigued. 'What did happen? I never knew.'

Nicky shrugged again, not answering. She found that Ben was looking at her in sudden speculation.

'You know, back then you were a babe to die for.'

That was more or less what they had said on board *Calico Jane*. Nicky could feel the colour leave her face. Fortunately, Ben was too taken up with his sudden memories to notice.

'My friends were always on at me to bring you to parties.' He grinned, remembering. 'It used to drive me mad.' He looked at her, shaking his head sorrowfully. 'Who would have thought you'd turn into a wage slave? You were born to be a party girl.'

In spite of herself, Nicky choked. 'I have a living to earn,' she pointed out drily.

Ben put his head on one side and smiled the charming smile that had girlfriends falling over themselves to share his bed and do his laundry. 'You can earn a living and still have some fun, you know.'

'I do. It's just that your idea of fun and mine is different.'

Ben flung up his hands.

'I give in. You will live and die a businesswoman. And the wildest day of your week will be the girls' night out.'

Since Ben had met all her friends and, indeed, made a spirited attempt to lure at least one of them into his sex and laundry net, Nicky did not take this slight too seriously.

'I want wild, I'll call my brother,' she said tartly.

And that, for some reason, silenced Ben.

Their food came. Slowly they eased back into their normal easy gossip about family and friends and her despised job.

'What's Martin going to say when he finds you've savaged one of his customers this morning?' Ben teased.

Nicky pulled a face. 'Any savaging that took place was in the other direction. You should have heard the way that man called me a "blonde".'

Ben laughed aloud. 'But you are a blonde. And gorgeous with it.'

'Not in the way he meant it,' said Nicky, ungrateful for the compliment. 'He made it sound as if all blondes are empty-headed nymphomaniacs.'

Ben waved his fork at her. 'And too ready to go to war. All you needed to do was sweet-talk him a little. The man would be eating out of your hand by now.'

'What a horrible thought,' Nicky retorted. 'Esteban Tremain is not the sort of man you sweet-talk lightly.'

The effect on Ben was electric. He sat bolt upright, his eyes narrowing. 'What?'

Nicky was faintly surprised. She amplified, 'If I have to butter up some man, at least let it be someone I can like.'

Ben ignored that. '*Who* did you say?'

'Esteban Tremain,' said Nicky, puzzled. 'Do you know him?'

That commanding voice had nothing in common with her erratic brother. She could not imagine how they could have met.

'I've heard of him,' said Ben, suddenly grim.

'And you don't like what you've heard,' Nicky interpreted.

It did not surprise her. Ben was easygoing to a fault but he would not take kindly to Tremain's habit of ordering everyone around. He was like his sister in that, at least.

'I've never met the man,' he said curtly. 'But—' He broke off, looking disturbed.

Nicky was intrigued. Not much worried her casual brother.

'But—?' she prompted.

He still hesitated, clearly torn.

At last he said, 'He's an ugly customer, from what I've heard. Steer clear of him.' He sounded serious.

Nicky was touched. She reached across the table and covered the back of his hand reassuringly.

'Don't worry. He's Martin's client. Martin can deal with him.' But she could not resist adding naughtily, 'So cancel the advice on sweet-talking him, then?'

Ben's frown disappeared in a great shout of laughter.

'Sharp,' he said when he could speak. 'Very sharp.'

The beep of Nicky's mobile phone interrupted them. She pulled it out of her capacious bag and flicked the switch.

'Hello?'

It was Caroline. 'Told you,' she said smugly. 'He's *here*. He virtually went through the broom cupboard looking for Martin.'

Nicky sniffed. 'Well, at least now he knows I was telling

the truth about Martin being out of the office. Did you call him? When will he be back?'

'Not this evening,' said Caroline with gloomy satisfaction. 'Better get back here before Tremain starts throwing things.'

Nicky looked at Ben apologetically. He nodded.

'Duty calls, eh? Fine. I'll walk you back.'

He did. And then, to her surprise, he slid one arm possessively round her waist and strolled into the showroom beside her.

Caroline came towards them. 'He's in Martin's office.'

Nicky looked across the showroom. A tall figure was pacing behind Martin's glass walls. As she looked, he stopped, turned, went still... Their eyes locked.

Nicky felt her heart give an odd lurch. It was like catching sight of someone she recognised; someone very important. Hardly knowing what she did, she removed herself from Ben's encircling arm. She did not take her eyes off that still figure.

Behind her Ben said, 'So that's Esteban Tremain.' He sounded as if he was committing him to memory.

The man left Martin's office and came swiftly across to her. His eyes never left her face. Nicky thought, *He knows me too.* She felt as if the earth's crust was suddenly gaping, leaving Ben and Caroline on the far side of the gulf, and Nicky and Esteban Tremain alone.

She blinked. Ben muttered something. She hardly heard him. Esteban Tremain paid no attention to anyone but Nicky. She shuddered under the intensity of those dark eyes.

I am not afraid, Nicky told herself.

Esteban Tremain said, 'So we meet at last, Nicola Piper.'

It broke the spell. She shook her head and the world came back into its proper focus.

At her shoulder, Ben said warningly, 'Nick?'

Esteban transferred his dark gaze. His eyes narrowed. He sized Ben up in silence.

They were a total contrast. In his well-cut suit, dark brows knit in frowning concentration, Esteban Tremain gave an impression of overwhelming power, only just contained. Ben meanwhile lounged against a pillar like a Greek god, all streaked blond hair and tanned forearms. Esteban Tremain stiffened.

Sheer panic found Nicky's tongue for her. 'Mr Tremain,' she said breathlessly. She held out her hand to him with more friendliness than she would have believed possible an hour ago.

He ignored her hand.

'I wouldn't want to interrupt your social life,' he said with awful courtesy.

Nicky frowned. She turned back to her brother.

'See you soon, Ben,' she said meaningfully.

'What?'

Nicky resisted the urge to tread heavily on his foot.

'I will be in touch,' she said between her teeth. She backed him to the door and opened it pointedly. 'Goodbye.'

Ben went reluctantly, with a long look over his shoulder at Esteban Tremain. It was almost menacing and totally out of character.

But Nicky had no time to think about that. Squaring her shoulders, she turned to deal with the most difficult client of her career to date.

Esteban Tremain did not acknowledge Ben's departure. But his displeasure was dissolving, she saw. It was replaced by sheer interest. He looked her up and down.

'So I was right,' he said softly. And smiled. Not kindly.

Nicky watched the curve of the sensual mouth and felt a hollow open up in the pit of her stomach. She moistened suddenly dry lips. He was looking at her the way she imagined Victorian naturalists looked at a new species of penguin, she thought. Delighted, amused—and quite unconcerned about the feelings of the penguin.

How could a man make you want to run and hide from him just by looking at you?

Nicky cleared her throat. 'Right about what?'

'Blonde,' Esteban said.

And smiled right into her eyes.

It caught her on the raw. But Nicky was not going to let him see that. She gave what was meant to be a light laugh. Then wished she hadn't, as the dark gaze transferred, pleasurably, to her breasts.

Nicky resisted the desire to hold the lapels of her jacket tight up to her throat. She pulled herself together with an effort.

'I can't deny it,' she said lightly.

She realised that they were attracting an interested audience. Once again Esteban Tremain had proved an irresistible draw to every girl in the place. They had all found jobs which brought them into the main showroom and were now busily engaged in them, ears flapping. Sally was gaping unashamedly.

Hurriedly Nicky said, 'Why don't we go into Martin's office?'

Esteban Tremain took in the audience with one comprehensive glance. He looked amused.

'By all means, if it makes you feel safer.'

Nicky set her teeth and reminded herself that her management course had taught her how to deal with all sorts of difficult clients, even sexy and amused ones. She led the way, trying to ignore the fact that it felt as if every eye in the showroom was burning between her shoulder blades. She decided she loathed Esteban Tremain heartily.

He followed close on her heels. Too close. As she stood aside to let him precede her, she breathed in his cologne. A shocking wave of something like memory hit her. The sea, she thought. He smells of the sea.

She swallowed and shut the door of Martin's glass case of an office with a bang that made the walls tremble.

Esteban Tremain frowned. He looked intrigued and annoyed in equal measure. But there was a simmering attraction there as well.

Out of nowhere the thought came: He's going to touch me.

And, for no reason, the memory of Andrew's words last

night came back to her, disastrous in their clarity. 'You'll
never be free.'

Nicky had a moment of pure unreasoning panic. He saw
it. Startled awareness leaped into Esteban's eyes. He seemed
on the point of stepping towards her and her breath stopped
in her throat.

Then steep eyelids hid his expression. He shoved his hands
hard in his pockets. And Nicky's famous common sense
kicked in.

She said rapidly, 'I'm afraid I haven't had the chance to
talk to Mr de Vries yet. You can't expect—'

He said abruptly, almost as if the subject now bored him,
'None of those damned machines work. Sort it.'

Nicky clenched her hands. In her previous dealings with
dissatisfied clients she was used to complaints about builders
who did not work fast enough or colour schemes that their
originators were now regretting. This sort of complaint about
the appliances was a new one. She had not understood it
when she'd read the file and she did not understand it now.
Until she talked to Martin she did not know what to do about
it.

Frowning, she said, 'Did you read the instructions properly?'

Esteban Tremain looked at her for an incredulous moment.
Nicky realised she had made a mistake. She added hurriedly,
'I mean *all* the appliances going wrong. The statistical
chances of that must be off the graph. Surely you can see
that.'

He gave her a sweet, poisonous smile.

'Oh, I do. I can only conclude that it is not chance.'

Nicky was so bewildered by that, she did not even take
offence at his tone.

'No one else has had a problem. Martin uses only the very
best suppliers,' she said, thinking aloud. 'And even if one
supplier has suddenly lost the plot on quality control we
didn't get everything in your kitchen from just one company.

There were too many machines.' She looked up. 'You're sure every one of them was bad?'

Esteban Tremain looked down his nose. It was a thin, aquiline nose and it made her think of a particularly dictatorial Roman Emperor.

'I have not test-driven every waste-disposal unit and coffee-grinder, if that's what you mean.'

Nicky began to feel a little better.

'Well, which have you test-driven?' she demanded. That did not come out quite as she intended either. It sounded downright truculent.

His eyebrows, she noted irrelevantly, were very dark and fine. Just at the moment they were locked together across the bridge of his nose in a mighty frown. A Roman Emperor in a mood to condemn a gladiator.

'I am informed,' he said with precision, 'that neither the dishwasher nor the fridge/freezer are in working order. As a result my companion did not have the opportunity to test the oven to its fullest. However, her observation and my own lead us both to the conclusion that the oven is not working either.'

Nicky was not going to admit it but she was impressed. She also noted that Esteban Tremain delegated investigations of the fridge and the dishwasher to a female companion. She suspected that he shared Ben's ideas about the relationship between women, laundry and sex. Though Mr Tremain would undoubtedly present it in a more sophisticated manner. She did her best not to glower at him.

'Well, that is of course very serious.' She riffled through Martin's desk drawer for a notepad. 'Let me make a note—'

Esteban Tremain strolled forward.

'No more notes.'

He sounded quite pleasant. But, looking up, Nicky realised that he was a lot closer than she wanted him to be. And that he was in a cold rage. It must have been that rage which made her heart lurch, then start pounding so hard she was sure he must hear it.

He said gently, 'I didn't take the time out to come here so you could take more notes. This kitchen has taken four months longer than de Vries estimated. Hasn't it?'

The question somehow demanded an answer. Nicky could not help but nod. She knew from her reading of the file that he was right.

She could feel sweat breaking out along her spine. It was not fear. It was not, God help her, attraction. But it had some of the symptoms of both. She breathed carefully, praying that he would not notice.

'So what do you want?' she asked.

Esteban Tremain smiled dangerously and Nicky hung on to her pleasant expression, but it was an effort.

'I want action,' he said softly.

There was a sharp silence which Nicky did not entirely understand.

Struggling for normality, she said in a placating tone, 'So do we all. But there has to be some planning—'

True to form, Esteban Tremain did not waste time listening to her.

'I don't just mean as a general principle, some time in the future,' he explained, still in that chillingly friendly tone. 'I mean here and now. Today.'

He sounded cool and amused and as if he did not care one way or the other. Which was odd, considering the trouble he had caused. And her own instinctive feeling that he was so angry he could barely contain himself.

It took real courage to say drily, 'I don't do magic.'

For a moment his eyes flickered. Then he gave her a charming smile. It really was chilling.

'Then I won't ask for magic,' he said softly. 'Just my kitchen working like it's supposed to. Now, I suggest you personally get into your car and go—and—put—it—right.'

She was not deceived by the gentle tone.

'I can't do that at a moment's notice,' she protested.

Esteban Tremain looked her up and down. Slowly. It was a

deliberate put-down and they both knew it. Nicky felt the shamed heat rise in her cheeks. She *hated* him.

Her chin came up and she glared back at him, right into those dark, dark eyes. It amused him. One eyebrow rose enquiringly.

'Do you mend machinery by remote control, then?' he asked pleasantly.

Horribly conscious of her blazing cheeks, Nicky said curtly, 'Don't be ridiculous.'

'Then I suggest you do as I ask. And sooner rather than later. My secretary will sort out the arrangements.'

He paused, waiting. But Nicky was speechless. With a faint triumphant smile, Esteban Tremain walked out of the office.

On a surge of fury she had never felt before, Nicky picked up the Waterford ornament and threw it. Hard. It did not break but it brought in the watchers hot foot.

'What did he *say*?' demanded Sally, half shocked, half thrilled.

'What are you going to do?' asked the more practical Caroline, returning the small glass sculpture to Martin's desk.

'Is it damaged?' asked Nicky. Restored to herself, she was a little conscience-stricken.

'It bounced,' Caroline reassured her cheerfully. 'Tremain really got you wound up, didn't he? Tea, that's what you need.'

And while Sally went to get it Caroline produced a photocopied sheet from behind her back.

'Read this,' she said with relish.

It was a copy of a gossip column piece, dated nearly a year earlier. Headed 'Heart Throb Wins Again', it described a yacht race in the Mediterranean. Nicky read it aloud.

'Brilliant bachelor barrister Esteban Tremain's winning streak continues. After recent notable victories in court, he and his crew on *Glen Tandy* have won the Sapphire Cup. Famously elusive, these days the Latin Lover, as the Law

Courts call him, is spending time with very good friend Francesca, the popular daughter of Lord Moran. Friends say that Esteban does not tolerate criticism but he will have to smarten up his client list if he is going to tie the knot with a judge's daughter.'

Nicky looked up. 'What does that mean?'

'It means he's made mincemeat of better adversaries than you. Let Martin deal with him.'

'Do you know him, then?' said Nicky suspiciously.

Caroline had been brought in by Martin when the business had begun to expand and she was older than the others by several years. As a result, she had become the office guru. She did not disappoint now.

'Friends in common,' she said airily. 'He is some sort of Latin American by birth but he was quite young when his mother remarried so he was brought up in England and took his stepfather's name. He's as tough as they come. Always has to be in control.'

Nicky thought of those unfathomable eyes, so dark, so guarded. She shivered.

'I can believe it.'

'Don't try and handle this one yourself,' Caroline advised shrewdly. 'It's Martin's baby. Make him come back and deal with it.'

Nicky tried. It got her nowhere. Oh, Martin came back from the exhibition hall, all right. But by the time Nicky got in to see him he had already returned Esteban's calls and his expression was sober.

'Do what the man wants, Nick,' Martin said, before she had managed more than a couple of sentences.

Nicky stared.

'Have you listened to a word I've said?' she demanded.

'All of them.' Martin had had a hard day and it showed. He pushed a weary hand through untidy grey hair. 'You don't like Tremain and you think I should run him off the territory. Well, tough. For one thing, I haven't got the time. For another—we agreed when I took you on that that was your job. You do the trouble-shooting.'

'Not this sort of trouble-shooting.'

'Any sort of trouble-shooting,' Martin said firmly.

'You said yourself, I'm no good with clients,' Nicky pointed out.

This was true. On at least one occasion, Nicky had been so forthright that the client in question had banged out of the showroom, slamming the door so hard behind her that its handsome glass insets had cracked. Martin had laughed. But he had also said, 'It's safer to keep you away from the paying customers, isn't it?' Watching him woo back the offended client afterwards, Nicky could only agree.

Now she decided to remind him. 'Remember Mrs Lazenby?'

Martin remained infuriatingly unmoved.

'Jennifer Lazenby is a woman with too much time on her hands and not enough brain cells to know what to do with it. Add to that a millionaire husband and the fact that she is a trophy wife with ten years on the clock, and you've got someone who doesn't want anything to do with a younger woman. Especially not a blonde with attitude.' He paused before adding deliberately, 'Not to mention a figure that stops traffic.'

Nicky winced, just as he had expected. Just as she always did when anyone mentioned her looks. Martin pushed home his advantage.

'Compared with Mrs Lazenby, Esteban is a pussy cat.'

Nicky gave him an incredulous look. He laughed.

'Well, OK, maybe not a pussy cat. But he's not stupid and he's not jealous of you. And he has got a genuine problem.' He added in a wheedling tone, 'Just your sort of problem, in fact.'

Nicky could hardly deny that.

'And he wants you to deal with it personally.'

Nicky grimaced.

'You and no one else. You obviously impressed him.'

'I made him spitting mad,' corrected Nicky.

'Well, that makes two of you, doesn't it?'

Before she could answer, Martin leaned forward and studied her earnestly.

'Look, Nick, you know how I'm placed, with the exhibition and everything. I can't afford the time to go haring off to Cornwall. I'm sorry Esteban Tremain rubs your fur up the wrong way but you've just got to be professional about it.'

Nicky's jaw jutted dangerously. 'Or?' she said in a soft voice.

Martin closed his eyes. 'Nick, don't be difficult—'

'Will you give me the sack if I refuse to go?'

His eyes flew open. 'Of course not.'

'Then I refuse,' she said triumphantly.

Martin did not laugh. 'I won't need to give you the sack,' he said grimly. 'If Tremain doesn't pay his account by the end of the month the bank will probably foreclose. Then we're all out of a job.'

Nicky sat down hard. 'What?'

'I've let it get out of hand,' Martin admitted.

He stood up and thrust his hands into his pockets. He began to prowl round the room.

'My accountant tells me I've spent too much time marketing and not enough collecting the debts. To be honest, we probably shouldn't have taken a stand at the exhibition. But by the time I realised how bad things were it was too late to cancel without paying up. So I thought, What the hell?'

Nicky shut her eyes. It was all too horribly familiar. It was what her father had said all through her hand-to-mouth childhood. She had never thought to hear it from steady, sensible Martin, even though he was a long-standing friend of her ramshackle family.

'You're more like my father than I thought,' she said involuntarily.

Martin had the grace to look ashamed. But he did not back down.

Nicky watched him. She felt numb. 'I knew there was something wrong. But I had no idea it was this bad.'

'It wasn't. It's all gone wrong in the last six weeks. To be honest, I was relying on Tremain settling his account to keep going until I can put in a bill to Hambeldons.' He looked at her helplessly.

Nicky knew that look. It was just how her mother used to look when they landed on the next Caribbean island without money or stores and her father began declaring loudly that nothing would induce him to take another tourist out fishing. And Nicky knew she would do just the same now as she had then.

She swallowed. She could feel the volcano heaving under her feet, she thought.

'All right,' she said with deep reluctance. 'Leave it to me.'

Martin cheered up at once. The others were unsurprised by Nicky's decision when she was heard to telephone Esteban's secretary for route instructions and a key. They were even envious.

'He looks lonely,' sighed Sally.

'Lonely!' muttered Nicky, scornful.

'He has never met a woman to thaw his heart,' Sally went on, oblivious. She spent a lot of her time reading the stories in the magazines where Springdown Kitchens advertised. 'Don't you agree, Nicky?'

Nicky was cynical. 'I should think he's found several and returned them all to store,' she said unwisely.

Caroline laughed. 'You are so right,' she agreed. 'The shelf life of an Esteban Tremain squeeze is about six months they say.' She added wickedly, 'That should give you a fun Christmas, Nicky.'

'He won't be there,' Nicky said hurriedly. 'I double-checked with his secretary. She says he's in London all week. As long as I'm away before Friday night, I don't have to see Esteban Tremain at all.'

It was a long drive. Normally Nicky liked driving but on this occasion it gave her too much time to think. Alone in the car

with a ribbon of motorway unfolding in front of her and
recipes for a bonfire-night party on the radio, her mind
slipped treacherously sideways.

Why did Esteban Tremain have this effect on her? She
knew nothing about the man, after all. Just that slightly spiky
article, a couple of personal encounters—that slow, dispas-
sionate assessment—the note in his voice when he'd called
her a blonde. And he smelled like the sea.

She could not suppress her involuntary shiver of awareness
as she remembered that. There was something about him that
set all her warning antennae on full alert.

Impatiently she leaned forward and twiddled the radio dial
until she found some music with a cheerful beat. She moved
her shoulders to it, trying to relax. Trying to remember how
to relax. Trying to remember that some people actually
wanted to be blonde.

She flicked her hand through her hair. For once, knowing
she was going to be alone, she had left it loose.

'Why don't you dye your hair, if you hate it so much?'
one of her friends had said impatiently, when she was complaining about the blonde image.

Well, you could dye out the golden fairness, Nicky thought
now. There was not much you could do about an hourglass
figure and long, slim legs, unless you wanted to diet yourself
into ill health. Her dislike of her looks had not yet taken her
that far.

So she contented herself with wearing dark long-line jack-
ets that disguised her remarkable figure and pulling her hair
back into severe styles. Even so, it did not always work. She
had learned to dread that speculative stare, as a man suddenly
discovered her looks under the businesslike surface. It was
too horribly reminiscent…

The car had speeded up as the memories approached.
Nicky shook herself and made herself slow down.

These days she had almost forgotten that crippling sense
of wanting to run until she disappeared into the horizon. Al-

most. Until someone like Esteban Tremain called her a blonde in *that* tone of voice.

Again Andrew's words came back to her. 'Find the guy. Get him out of your system. Or you'll never be free.'

It was getting dark. Nicky shivered. The memories of the dark were worst of all.

She left the motorway at the next exit. She found a small inn and a fire and company. For a while the memories receded.

But in the end she had to leave the friendly landlord and his wife and go up to the pretty chintz hung bedroom alone. After getting ready for bed Nicky went to the window and looked out. In this country village you could see the stars. They were more brilliant than they were in London but even so they did not compare with the jewelled coverlet of the Caribbean.

Nicky closed her eyes in anguish. No, she was not going to banish the memory tonight. She knew what that meant. No sleep until she faced it.

She sank into an armchair and tipped her head back. She let memory do its work…

CHAPTER THREE

IT WAS one of the worst times on the ramshackle Piper boat.

Oh, they were always short of money, of course, but Margaret Piper usually kept a small secret store for emergencies. This time, when she went to it, there was nothing there. Leon had found it and spent the contents. He did not even know where it had gone. Money, as he said charmingly when she challenged him, just trickled through his fingers. Money, he added, was not important.

It was one of the few times Nicky remembered seeing her mother angry with him. Not only angry but hopeless.

'I was saving that to buy Nicky a birthday present,' she heard her mother shout. 'She's sixteen next month and she hasn't even got a *skirt*.'

There was not enough money to pay the mooring fee in the small island harbour, of course. They had to drop anchor off an isolated beach, out of town, and forage for food and water. Margaret tore her arm on an acacia bush and began to cry. When Leon put his arm round her, she twitched him away, turning her shoulder so that Ben and Nicky should not see her tears.

Ben did not. But Nicky, maturing fast and increasingly aware of the strains that their itinerant life imposed on her mother, saw all too clearly. It was then that she decided to go to town.

She ignored the scratches on her bare brown legs. She ignored the fact that her old shorts and shirt had shrunk as well as faded in the wash. If, as her very own Nemesis later accused, she looked like a voluptuous Cleopatra in urchin's clothing, Nicky did not know it. All she knew was that she

must do something to take that look of despair off her
mother's face. Anything.

There would be work at one of the cafés on the main drag
or the marina, Nicky thought. She had grown experienced in
the finding of casual work on the islands. Even if they did
not pay her until the end of the week—which was all too
likely—she should be able to beg some food from them at
the end of the evening.

Well, she got the food all right. And a lot more than she
had bargained for. Or than she was equipped to deal with.

There was no work at any of the cafés. But a harassed
woman laden with gaping grocery bags stopped her as she
came out of the Golden Lobster.

'You looking for a job, kid?'

Nicky nodded.

'I'm cooking for a party on the *Calico Jane*. I could do
with another pair of hands. Just for tonight. Fifty dollars in
your hand.'

To Nicky it was a fortune. More than that, it was a lifeline.
But she was clear-headed enough to remember that casual
labour didn't have guaranteed hours. By the time she got off
work tonight the shops could all be shut.

'Fifty dollars and the left-overs,' she said firmly.

The woman laughed. 'No way. This lot are on vintage
champagne. You're not waltzing off with two-hundred-dollar
bottles of wine.'

Nicky lifted her chin. 'No alcohol. Food. I want bread and
salad and meat. Oh, and some milk.'

Her prospective employer stared. Then she shrugged, to
the imminent danger of her grocery purchases.

'If that's what you want. Now take this damned bag and
let's get going.'

Nicky did.

The *Calico Jane* was in the luxury class. Anyone who
chartered her had to be well off. Nicky was used to that.
There were plenty of the seriously rich who moored yachts

on one Caribbean island or another. She and Ben had crewed for several of them.

But she had never seen anything like the party that greeted her as she climbed aboard *Calico Jane* in Ruth Demarco's wake. From their vintage champagne to their caviare snacks, they were behaving as if they had money to burn. They were also surprisingly young.

'More money than brains,' said Ruth briefly, retrieving three empty champagne bottles as she led the way to the galley.

'Who on earth are they?' asked Nicky, her head full of wild rumours about the Hollywood brat pack.

'New York money brokers, mainly. The guy who chartered the boat is OK but he's having dinner with some serious sailors tonight, so it's just the flotsam.' Ruth was clearly not impressed. 'Pushing the good life to the limit. Watch out for Piers. He's got more arms than an octopus.'

Nicky found out the truth of that.

It was much later. The party was over. Ruth was bagging up the last of the trash. She sent Nicky on deck to collect any remaining plates and glasses before she sent her home. The left-overs were already packed into a grocery sack and waiting for her on the countertop.

It was three in the morning and Nicky's eyes were closing. Which must have been why she did not see Piers Lane until it was too late. There were plenty of lights on deck. She should have seen him. But when he reached out and took her by the wrist Nicky nearly leaped out of her skin.

'Hey, babe.' It was not easy to slur on two words but Piers managed it. He leered up at her foggily.

Nicky stumbled. She had thought all three of the men sprawled on deck were asleep or too drunk to move. But there was a strength in Piers Lane's grip which told her exactly how wrong she had been.

She took rapid stock. The other bodies were stirring too, beginning to look interested and not very kind.

Suppressing alarm, she said in a neutral voice, 'Is there something you want, sir?'

Piers grinned and told her exactly what he wanted. In the light of her parents' philosophical commitment to freedom, Nicky was used to taking care of herself, young though she was. She reviewed the situation rapidly and decided to play down the drama.

'Maybe another time,' she said with a meaningless smile. 'I've got to clear up now.'

She pulled at his restraining hand. For a moment, his grip relaxed and she thought she would get away with it. Then one of the other revellers said something mocking in a slurred voice. Nicky did not catch the words but Piers's head reared up as if his manhood had been insulted.

He pulled at her wrist. Nicky lost her balance. And that, of course, was when the strain on the elderly buttons of her shirt became too great. Two of them shot across the deck, leaving the garment gaping. It revealed a bra that no self-respecting girl would have been seen dead in: yellow from much washing and three sizes too small.

There was an astonished silence. Piers stared at her rounded breasts under their inadequate covering. His eyes popped. Then all three of the men began to crow with glee.

'All *right*,' Piers said enthusiastically.

He pulled her down on top of him. Nicky was not experienced enough to curb her alarm in a situation like this. She let out a yell for Ruth that must have been heard all round the marina. She also kicked him hard.

She was wearing battered deck shoes, hardly younger than her blouse, so she did not make much impact. But she startled him enough to make him loosen his grip on her wrist. She twisted away, falling to her knees in her urgency to get away from him.

That was when the others decided to join in. They both jumped up. One of them hauled her to her feet but, instead of letting her go, he pushed her back against the side of the boat and knelt down in front of her, pretending to take a photograph with an imaginary camera.

'Nice!' he said, grinning.

In an anguish of embarrassment, Nicky hated them all.

Piers struggled to his feet and lurched towards her, brushing the pretend photographer out of the way, announcing, 'I saw her first.'

'Stop this,' said Nicky.

They did not hear her. Behind them she caught sight of Ruth's head appearing at the top of the companionway. The woman gave the little tableau one horrified look and darted away over the side.

Nicky had no time to call her because Piers and his friends were circling, like pre-school children round the class outsider. They were laughing drunkenly. It was as if they were playing a game and had not noticed that she did not want to join in.

She was afraid. But she was also furious. She backed up against the side of the boat and yelled hard enough to make them blink. And pause.

Her cry for help was answered.

There was a sound of running feet, an angry exclamation, then a thud which shook the deck as an athletic body vaulted lightly on to the boat.

Nicky's tormentors were confused. They turned to see what was happening. Seizing her chance, Nicky ducked and made a bolt for freedom.

She cannoned straight into a muscular body travelling just as fast in the opposite direction. Nicky reeled. Strong hands shot out to steady her but it was too late. She fell at his feet in an inelegant sprawl.

'What the *hell* is going on?' There was a force of anger in the cool voice that made the decks thrum.

'Steve?' Piers was blearily pleased to see the newcomer. He had clearly not picked up the wild anger that Nicky heard. 'Now for some fun, *mi amigo*.'

'What is this?' Even the surface of his voice was not so cool now.

Piers picked up the anger this time. He blinked, injured.

'Party time, *compadre*.'

'You call this is a *party*?' The irony was savage.

They shuffled, sobering. The pretend photographer began to back away. Only Piers threw his arms wide and gave a shout of drunken laughter.

Nicky was getting her breath back. She looked up at Steve through the curtain of her tumbled hair. Unlike the others in their bright Hawaiian shirts, he wore the minimum—brief shorts, bare chest, bare feet. He was also wearing glasses with reactive lenses. In the light of the bright lanterns on deck, they had darkened to an opaque cinder colour, making it look as if the eye sockets were empty. He looked muscular, competent and—as the eyes behind the reflecting visor brushed Nicky's semi-clad body for an electric moment—furious. Nicky's heart gave an unaccountable jolt.

'Where did she—' Steve nodded at Nicky's prone form without bothering to look at her again '—come from?'

Nicky went cold. Suddenly she was acutely aware of her sprawled length of tanned leg, torn clothes, and bare shoulder where the disreputable shirt had twisted half off her as she fell.

It was crazy! By *not* looking at her the man called Steve was making her more self-conscious than the other idiots had done when they'd leered.

She writhed inwardly, hating herself. Hating them. But then her pride kicked in and she jumped to her feet.

'Ruth took me on to help out for the evening.'

She suddenly realised that Ruth was there, hovering at a distance behind Steve. She must have gone to fetch him, Nicky realised. That made her feel worse, knowing that he had been summoned to defend her. And he had: and then he could not bear to look at her. Paradoxically, it fanned her temper to white heat.

'Waitressing and washing up was what I signed on for,'

she snarled. 'Not—' she directed a glance at Piers with loathing '—wrestling.'

Steve still did not look at her. His mouth tightened.

'It sounds like you should have asked,' he told Piers curtly.

Piers looked hurt. 'It was just a bit of fun.'

Nicky looked at him incredulously. 'Not for me it wasn't.'

Both Piers and Steve ignored her.

Steve, whoever he was, said wearily, 'Don't you get enough of that at home?'

Piers grinned. 'Can't get enough of it anywhere, old buddy. Why the disapproval? *Señoritas* fall over themselves for that Latin charm. You've had your share.'

'Not of unwilling adolescents,' snapped Steve, goaded.

'Adolescents?' Piers looked blank.

Steve looked at Nicky—briefly but at least he was acknowledging that she was there and had a voice. 'How old are you?' he demanded grimly.

'Nearly sixteen.'

He looked round the group scornfully.

It startled them. Even Piers looked uneasy.

Steve pressed the point home.

'See? She isn't just dressed like your fantasy of a schoolgirl. She *is* a schoolgirl.'

Piers was taken aback. It made him truculent. 'A bloody well-developed schoolgirl,' he muttered.

Nicky flinched and crossed her arms across her breasts. And found that she had forgotten how wide her shirt was gaping. She grabbed it closed, feeling the colour flood up. Not just into her face—her whole body felt as if it was burning with humiliation. She shook her hair forward, knowing that her eyes were filling with tears and there was not a thing she could do about it.

And that, of course, was the moment that Steve turned his attention full on her at last. Nicky could have screamed. She could not even dash the tears away, with both hands hauling her ruined shirt closed.

He watched her for a tense moment. Then he ripped off his glasses and said abruptly, 'Where do you live?'

Nicky swallowed a large lump in her throat. 'On a boat.'

'Here? In the marina?'

The lump was too big to swallow twice. Nicky shook her head.

His voice gentled, though he still looked as if he could barely contain his anger. 'In town?'

She shook her head again. He was obscurely different from the others. Older somehow. Certainly tougher. They were a little afraid of him, she thought. It came to her that she ought to be afraid of him too. And she wasn't.

The thought was so astounding that she stopped hiding behind her hair and stared full at him. His eyes narrowed.

'You mean it's a drive to get you home.'

His reluctance was palpable. Nicky flushed even harder. Pride came to her aid. Her chin rose.

'You don't have to do that,' she said in a cool little voice. 'I walked into town. I can walk back.'

'Not alone, you don't,' Steve told her.

He put his glasses on and pushed them up his nose with one forefinger. It was quite final.

Nicky was genuinely outraged. 'You can't stop me.'

In the act of turning away, he paused.

'You,' he said evenly, 'don't get a vote. You may look like Cleopatra on one of her more voluptuous days, but it's the urchin's clothing that tells the true story, isn't it? You've just admitted it.'

Nicky was lost. 'What do you mean?'

'Fifteen-year-olds do what they're told,' he told her. 'Come on.' He turned back to the gangway, motioning her to follow him with an abrupt gesture. 'Let's get going.'

Ruth met them at the top of the companionway. She pushed Nicky's grocery bag at her.

'Steve will take care of you,' she said loudly, and touched Nicky's shoulder in silent encouragement.

Steve flashed her an ironic look over his shoulder.

'All right, Ruth. Point taken.'

Gee, thanks, thought Nicky, confused and annoyed. She stamped after him bad-temperedly.

Steve looked down at her. 'Now what's wrong?'

'I wasn't doing so badly at taking care of myself,' she muttered. 'In spite of the Neanderthal kindergarten back there.'

He gave a snort of surprised laughter. But he said, 'Just as well Ruth came to get me, though.'

She hunched her shoulders sulkily and followed without another word.

The marina was modern and well lit. Disastrously well lit. About to help Nicky into the Jeep, Steve unthinkingly took the grocery sack from her. Before she could catch them, the edges of her shirt blew wide in the night breeze. Which left him staring straight down onto her inadequately covered breasts. Floodlit.

She forgot her sulks. 'Oh, no!' she shouted, scarlet-faced.

He froze. The light-sensitive glasses hid his eyes but his mouth looked as if it was etched in stone. Nicky made a small sound of total despair and shut her eyes.

'I guess I'm going to have to find you something to wear,' he said ruefully. 'Or neither of us is going to be able to concentrate.'

Nicky set her teeth and did not answer. He went to the back of the Jeep and began to rummage. She opened her eyes cautiously. The marina was deserted. Heavily rhythmic music blared intermittently down the breeze from one of the beach cafés beyond. But there was no one to be seen on the boats or the brightly lit waterfront. Just Nicky and the man she ought to think of as her rescuer—and was rapidly coming to hate.

She hauled the shirt round her so hard she heard one of the seams rip. Great. That cut her wardrobe of wearable shirts down to two.

Steve straightened and came back to her. He held out a

rag that smelled noticeably of gasoline. Nicky took it reluctantly.

'Put it on.'

She hesitated.

He was impatient. 'It's not Chanel but it will keep the cold out.' And, as she still hesitated, he added deliberately, 'You're not getting into the Jeep until you do.'

Nicky pulled it on without a word.

He opened the passenger door for her but he did not help her to climb up. She tied the corners of the flapping shirt at her waist and then hauled herself up into the Jeep. She did not look at him. Once up, she sat as far away from the driver's seat as she could manage.

He got in and drove out of the marina, handling the Jeep with the careless ease of long practice. Nicky watched his hands on the wheel. They were long-fingered and powerful. She saw a man who was so used to being in control of the machinery of his life that he did not even think about it. She shuddered a little and drew even further into her corner.

Except for a curt request for directions, Steve did not speak at all. Nicky was equally silent. They met nothing on the road. Once away from the marina, there were no lights at all, just the black funnel of the road in their headlights, and the murmuring shadow of the sea to their right. Nicky turned her head towards it and tried not to think about the silent man beside her.

It was not easy. She had only to turn her head the slightest and she could see those confident hands. For some reason, they filled her with a strange excitement. In fact the man called Steve made her feel uncertain in a way she had never experienced before.

It was quite different from the black panic she had felt on the boat. It was half discomfort, half anticipation. Like the evening breeze on sun blasted skin, it was a shock and a pleasure at the same time. It kept her on the edge of her seat.

Above all, she realised, she wanted him to stop the Jeep. She wanted—no, she *needed*—him to take those sure hands

off the steering wheel and touch her. It seemed all wrong that
he had not touched her already. He had rescued her, protected
her, delivered her home—well, nearly—and yet he stayed at
a stranger's distance.

Well, he is a stranger, Nicky told herself.

She took herself to task. She was shaky, jittery, not herself.
The events of the evening had taken a toll of her common
sense. Just because he had long, beautiful hands and had
saved her from an awkward situation that was no reason to
feel they were no longer strangers.

But she was so distracted by her wayward thoughts that
she almost missed the turning.

'Here,' she said, so sharply that he had to brake hard before swinging the Jeep onto the beach track.

The lurch sent her sideways. Their shoulders touched.
Nicky felt her body stop, as if suddenly all its systems had
gone on hold, waiting for new instructions. Then her insides
seemed to start shivering, as if she had been drenched in ice.

Steve did not appear to notice anything. He took the Jeep
down through the bushes until the beach opened out ahead.
He stopped and cut the lights. In front of them the dark sea
stretched and rolled like a lazy animal. The sky was frosted
with stars. Nicky held her breath.

'Here?'

Was it her imagination or did his voice sound strained?

'The boat is moored further up.'

'Oh.' He did not move. Then he said, 'Have you got a
torch?'

Yes, definitely strained.

'No.'

'There's one in the back. I'll get it and walk you down
the beach.'

But still he did not move. Nicky detected reluctance. She
was consumed with humiliation.

'There's no need. It's bright enough to see.'

'Don't be prickly. I'd prefer to walk you home.'

Nicky shrugged. But she could not resist another sideways

look at those powerful hands. She found he was gripping the wheel as if it were a life belt. It astonished her.

'Are you all right?' she said involuntarily.

She saw his throat move as he swallowed. She wished, passionately, that she could see his eyes. But it was dark. Anyway, the mirrored lenses stayed firmly in place.

'I'm fine. Come on. Let's get you home.'

He got the torch—a square box of a thing that lit up the beach like the car's headlights. He also pulled on some deck shoes. Nicky, who knew that sea urchins could lurk in the powdery sand, approved this forethought. It showed that his air of competence was not all window-dressing.

He hefted her grocery sack onto one hip and hooked the light onto his belt. Then he motioned her to lead the way.

She could feel his eyes on her as she plodded through the sand. She slipped several times. He never put out a hand to help her, though once she thought he was on the point of it and curbed his instinct.

So she was not wrong, Nicky thought wretchedly. He was not touching her quite deliberately. What a nuisance he must think her. What a clumsy, useless nuisance. The back of her neck felt hot with embarrassment.

At last she stopped.

'Here.'

He came close beside her and turned, raking the sea with the flashlight. The beam caught the lines of the *Pompilia*. Steve drew in a breath as if the sight surprised him.

'So there really is a boat,' he said, confirming it.

'Of course.' Nicky was bewildered. 'What did you think?'

The glasses turned towards her briefly. 'Frankly, I thought you were probably sleeping rough. On the beach.'

Nicky gasped. 'But that's against the law.'

'So?'

She rounded on him. 'What do you think I am?' she cried hotly.

There was an odd silence. She could hear the blood pounding in her ears. But the sounds of the night, the sea and the busy cicadas, were suddenly muted. Nicky thought suddenly, I wish I hadn't said that.

Then Steve said, very evenly, 'You wouldn't want to know.'

Nicky froze. She wanted to move way, pelt for the water and swim out to the *Pompilia* and never see him again. She wanted not to move a muscle until he touched her. Her mouth parted. The moment stretched out for ever. She wanted him to take her in his arms...

Shocked, she thought, Have I gone *crazy*?

The picture in her mind was so vivid—and so utterly beyond her experience—that she flinched away from it, physically. Steve felt the movement and put out a hand to save her at last. But it was too late. He was closer than she realised and she stumbled against him.

He gave a grunt of shock and dropped the groceries. Worse, the flashlight shot off his belt. It landed squashily in the sand and the light went out.

The stars were suddenly a lot closer. He was breathing hard as if she had really hurt him.

'Oh, I'm sorry,' Nicky cried, horrified.

'It's all right.' It sounded as if he was saying it between his teeth. He must be furious with her.

'I didn't mean to—'

'It's all *right*.'

She dropped to her knees, reaching for the groceries, the flashlight, apologising feverishly. Only then she scraped her hand along the leaf of a hidden clump of sea clover and recoiled, with a sharp exclamation.

'Ouch.'

'What is it?' he said in quick concern.

He took a hasty step forward and stumbled over her foot. It brought him down on one knee. Which meant they were both kneeling in the sand. Very close and both of them off balance.

He put out a hand to steady himself. It brushed her bare

flesh where she had knotted the shirt at her waist above her shorts. Steve went very still.

Slowly Nicky turned her head. His body was so close that she had to blink in order not to sway against him. The sense of his body's heat and strength overwhelmed her. She could see the dark shape of his head; his shoulders against the sky; hear his breathing. Hear when, just for an electric moment, it stopped.

She leaned forward and kissed him quickly, clumsily.

He started breathing again, dragging the air from the very bottom of his lungs in harsh gasps.

'Don't—' It sounded strangled.

But Nicky was beyond thought, shaking with need. This was new. It was dangerous. She knew it but she did not care. She just wanted Steve to take charge again and lead her into the new place that she dimly realised she had been making towards since she'd first seen him this evening.

He knows it too, she thought, listening to his harsh breathing. He knew it before I did.

She wound her arms round his neck and pressed trembling lips to the base of his throat. He felt like rock.

'I tried.' It sounded as if it was torn out of him.

Then, as if he could not help himself, he slammed an arm round her and hauled her against him. Their bodies fused along their whole length. Suddenly Nicky knew, beyond question, exactly how aroused he was. Her indrawn breath was half shock, half wonder.

Steve's palm was warm at the naked skin of her waist. He tipped her gently down on to the sand. She went, with a sigh of deliverance. It all felt inevitable, somehow.

After that, it happened in slow motion, Nicky thought afterwards. He seemed bent on learning her body, touch by exquisite touch. She felt her clothes pushed aside; the roughness of his unshaven cheek against her tender breast, his breath on her skin. This was utterly new to her. But she felt no fear. Only a deep, wondering delight. Shyly she ran her hand down his beautiful naked spine.

And then his touch was no longer a slow revelation but urgent, urgent...

As she remembered, Nicky's nails dug into her palms. This was the point when she used to exclaim aloud, jump up, walk away, do anything to block out what happened next. But these days she knew better. Maturity came from taking responsibility for your mistakes. And accepting the consequences.

And she had been responsible. There was no doubt about that. Carried away on a tide of feeling, she had twined round him like a vine. Met his every demand eagerly. Made demands of her own that, inexperienced as she was, she had never dreamed of before.

Until, twisting to get rid of their last scraps of clothing, Steve had given a yelp of pain.

'What?' Nicky was dazed. 'What did I do?'

'Nothing.' He pulled away from her, nursing his foot as he rocked with pain. 'I stubbed my toe.'

She gave a soft laugh, nuzzling his shoulder. 'Shall I kiss t better?'

'No.'

He stopped rocking. Nicky said his name voicelessly, her ips moving against the warm skin of his shoulder. But he lid not take her in his arms again. Instead he drew back so harply that she fell forward and had to put out hands into he powdery sand to save herself. He looked down at her rouching form. Against the starry sky, she saw him shake is head slowly.

'What am I doing?' It was a ragged whisper. He was not alking to her.

Nicky sat up and pushed the flying hair off her face. 'We,' he whispered. She reached up to him. 'We are doing.'

He caught her wrists, pushing her away so hard that she ell back, flat in the sand. He bent over her, holding her arms aptive behind her head.

'All right, I admit it. You're dynamite. But I—will—not.'
He sounded as if he was in pain.

Nicky did not understand. She wrapped a leg round him,
murmuring. She felt him shudder deeply.

He drew a long breath. 'I can control this. I *can* control
this.'

And even then she did not understand.

'Steve,' she whispered longingly. It was the first time she
had dared to use his name.

And the last. He flung himself away from her as if she had
spat poison.

'I must be out of my mind.'

Nicky did not move. Although he had released her hands
she just lay as he had left her, staring. She felt as if she had
been turned to stone. Her voice would not work.

'This is as far as I go.' His voice was ragged.

Even in the darkness, she could see that Steve's chest was
rising and falling as if he had run a hard race. He leaped to
his feet. Nicky had no doubt at all that he meant every word.
Bewildered, she sat up.

He took three rapid steps away and stumbled over one of
Ruth's foil-wrapped packets of food. He picked it up, astonished, turning it over in his hands as if he thought it was a
bomb.

Nicky said in self-defence—as if it mattered, *now*—'Ruth
said I could take home what was left after the party.' She
sounded defensive, even sullen. And—to her fury—*young*.

Steve looked at the packet again. He slapped it down on
to the sand beside her. There was distaste in every line of
him.

'There. Take your pickings and—'

Another thought occurred to him. He paused.

Then he said in tones of despair, 'Were you paid this evening?'

Nicky had forgotten about payment. Now, constrained and
wretched, she shook her head.

She thought he said, 'Oh, God.'

He rummaged in his pocket and brought out a fold of notes. Without counting them, he thrust the wad down at her. Nicky pushed it away.

He drew in several lungfuls of air. Then, carefully not touching her, he said in a gentler tone, 'Can you afford to refuse?'

Nicky put her hands over her face.

He gave an exasperated sigh and dropped the money on the sand beside her.

'Look, this evening— You shouldn't— Oh, *hell*.'

Nicky struggled to her feet. She bent and picked up the money, stuffing it into the grocery sack along with such packets of food as she could find. In the darkness her hands unexpectedly found a cylindrical object, hard—was it glass? A jar, of some sort? Enlightenment dawned. The coffee? He must have stubbed his toe on the jar of instant coffee Ruth had given her.

Nicky could not help herself. It was hysteria, of course. She began to laugh. For a terrible moment she thought she would never be able to stop.

Steve stopped dead. She saw him turn his head. The black shadow watched her, oddly menacing in its gathering stillness.

Eventually he said, 'So at least I've given you a good laugh.'

Nicky's laughter died abruptly as he took three steps forward. Nicky gave ground.

Under the jewelled sky he looked as tall as a tree. A powerful arm shot out. No dragging her against his aroused body this time. He held her at arm's length, his teeth a flash of white in a mirthless smile.

'I should have let Piers get on with it, shouldn't I?' he flung at her. 'It was a really successful production: schoolgirl meets dirty dog. I suppose you were both enjoying it. I should never have interfered.'

Nicky did not understand. She was shaking. 'N-n-no—'

'That was what you really wanted, wasn't it? No woman dresses like that unless she intends a man to strip her.'

He pulled her against him at last. Anger made him clumsy. The kiss was an assault. No semblance of seduction now.

The urgency was still there but even Nicky, inexperienced and humiliated, could recognise rage. She struggled but he was too strong for her. He held her, devoured her, until her resistance broke and she stood passive in his arms.

When he let her go she was sobbing inwardly. But some remnant of pride would not let him know.

She said harshly, 'If you don't go now I shall scream.'

'Very dramatic.' He sounded furious. 'Who would come?'

Suddenly her lip was trembling, her voice thick. 'M-my parents.'

'Your parents?' He was thunderstruck. 'You mean—' His hands on her shoulders gripped like a vice. 'You really are fifteen after all.'

'S-sixteen the week after next.'

Through the hands on her shoulders she felt his whole body flinch.

'Oh, my God,' he said quietly.

Nicky threw the glass jar at him. She was trembling. It was an anger as great as his own, she assured herself.

He caught the jar one-handed and put it down in the sand with exaggerated care. It felt like an insult.

'Go away,' she shouted.

As if on cue a light appeared on the deck of the boat. Then another.

'Looks like your fine protective parents are lining up,' Steve said cynically. 'Better late than never, I guess. Tell them they're lucky it wasn't too late.'

He turned on his heel.

'I hate you,' Nicky shouted after him.

But he kept on walking.

When her parents came to get her she was alone on the beach. Leon was inclined to be amused that his cautious daughter had given her parents cause for concern at last.

Margaret was not. One look at Nicky's face in the torchlight and she told Leon to shut up. It was so unusual that he did.

Nicky let them take her back to the *Pompilia* as if she were in a dream. But when she went to bed she could not sleep. She curled up in a tight, tight ball, closed her eyes hard and willed herself to forget everything: his savage contempt, that kiss, everything that, heaven help her, she had *wanted*. It did not work.

In the morning she was hollow-eyed enough to disturb even her father. Her mother, who by then had found the roll of notes in the grocery sack, was white with concern.

'Oh, Nicky, what have you done?'

Nicky flinched away and would not tell.

'We must leave this horrible island,' Margaret told Leon with unheard-of resolution.

He was so surprised that he did not argue. Only they needed to get supplies, didn't they? So before they left the island completely he sailed the boat round the coast.

When they got to town they found that it was market day. There was a general air of carnival about the quayside. Tourists were moving through the crowd, snapping their fingers to the beat of the bands and laughing. And the first person Nicky saw was Piers.

He was looking very sorry for himself. Last night's excesses had clearly taken their toll. Resisting the rhythm, he was walking slowly with the careful air of a man who was not quite sure whether he was going to be sick or not. He did not take his eyes off the cobbled road. If Nicky had not stopped dead, so that Margaret bumped into her, Piers would probably not even have noticed her.

But she did. Margaret, behind Nicky, did not see the look of horror on her face. But Piers did. He flushed; then looked angry.

He turned and called over his shoulder, 'Hey, Steve, the blonde totty is back.'

Nicky could not move.

'Darling, do get a move on. We haven't got all day,' said Margaret, oblivious.

Then, strolling among the vendors of red snapper and butter squash and sugar apples, appeared the man of her nightmares. This morning he was wearing crisp khaki shorts and an olive shirt. He still hadn't taken off those beastly dark-lensed glasses, Nicky saw, hating them and him.

He stopped beside Piers; looked across the quay; saw her. Nicky made a strangled sound. Steve went very still.

The air was full of cheerful talk. There was the inevitable bouncy beat of the local band, playing just ten steps away along the quay. Behind both, the sea slapped steadily against the dock. The traders had taken up places under bright umbrellas, their wares equally fluorescent. It was one great big street party. Nicky was the only person not lazy and happy.

She thought she would hate carnivals for the rest of her life.

Steve's eyes were hidden, of course. But as far as Nicky could see his expression did not change when he saw her. After the briefest pause, he nodded, unsmiling.

Margaret realised something was wrong. She stopped fussing with her shopping list.

'Darling, do you know those men?' she asked under her breath.

Nicky could not speak. She shook her head, not taking her eyes off Steve's unresponsive face. He hesitated; then, after a quick look at Margaret, he came over to them.

'Good morning. No ill effects from your late night?' he asked lightly.

Nicky stood as still as stone. Margaret's eyes sharpened suspiciously.

'So it was you my daughter was with last night.'

Steve said hastily, 'She was with all of us. We had a party on board. She helped out in the galley.' He gave her a kind indifferent smile. 'Very well. We were grateful.'

Nicky said nothing. She would remember those blanke eyes for the rest of her life.

'Oh,' said Margaret, her worry dissipating.

Nicky had helped out on plenty of boats and never come to harm. And, while Margaret didn't like the look of the other boy, people who had hangovers could not be expected to be at their best. Steve, whoever he was, was clearly mature and responsible. Too mature and responsible to do to Nicky what she had been more than half afraid of this morning.

She gave him a wide, relieved smile. 'I'm glad—'

Which was the moment at which Piers took a hand.

'Going to come and play again tonight, sweetheart?'

Steve silenced him with a savage expletive. Piers grinned.

'Hell, don't be a killjoy. I really dig that trick with the buttons—' And he flapped his shirt in a pantomime gesture, horribly explicit.

There was a terrible moment when nobody said anything. It was like waiting for the headland you were standing on to crumble, Nicky thought. Her heart beat with agonising hammer blows. Her eyes turned to Steve, helplessly.

'I said, shut *up*,' he flung at Piers furiously.

It was too late. Nicky did not wait for any more. She knew her mother was staring. She could not bear it. Pushing past them blindly, she took off into the covered market, running as if the whole world were after her.

She had to go back in the end, of course. Shamefaced, she slipped back on to the boat, half hoping, half fearing that Margaret would demand an explanation. But Margaret had talked to Steve and drawn her own conclusions. Now she was struggling with remorse.

'Darling, I just hadn't realised how you were growing up. I'm so sorry. I should never have let it come to this. We are going to buy you some new clothes the moment we get to Kingston.'

'New *clothes*?'

Nicky could hardly believe her ears. Her life was shattered and her mother was worried about her wardrobe? Margaret looked uncomfortable.

'You really have outgrown everything. *We* know that's

why your clothes are a bit skimpy. But other people—well, men—can get the wrong idea.'

Nicky whitened.

'It's not your fault,' Margaret said hastily. 'But, my point is, it's not theirs either. You do look—'

'A blonde totty,' said Nicky, tightly.

Margaret laughed. 'Well, a bit, darling.'

'I won't ever again.'

And she had not.

Ten years later, Nicky found she was pulling her dressing gown round her so hard that her fingers were white with the effort. Deliberately she relaxed her clenched hands. She was holding her breath as if bracing herself against an expected pain.

But it was not painful any more, she assured herself. At least, it shouldn't be. She had dealt with it, put it behind her. No matter what Andrew said, she could handle it. She had got up and gone to work the next day, got her life back on track, picked herself up ready to go on again. Hadn't she?

She let out a slow, ragged breath.

Well, yes, she had. Until Martin had told her to do what Esteban Tremain wanted.

Why?

Nicky had no answer for that. Maybe it was the hint of masculine coercion. Or maybe— She did not know.

She did not take the dressing gown off when she got into bed. She told herself it was because the room was cold. It was not true. It was because she wanted the protection of heavy cloth huddled round her. As if she could take its defences into her dreams with her, Nicky thought wryly. After she had let the memories surface again, she knew exactly the sort of dream she was likely to have.

She was right. Only this time there was another man stalking through the terrible carnival. In the dream Nicky followed him along the quay. Only then the sea wall ran out and he turned to face her. It was Esteban Tremain.

CHAPTER FOUR

IT WAS late. He should have been working. Esteban looked at the papers spread out over his big desk and recognised that his concentration was shot to hell.

He stood up and moved restlessly to the window. He was gazing down on to an exclusive London private quay. But other images danced in front of his eyes so that he did not know what it was that was really disturbing him.

Francesca, of course, was appalling. He had never been in love with her but he had liked her. And when he'd found she had spilled his private life to a journalist her disloyalty had shocked him. Not that, in the end, the journalist had printed all that much. But when she'd threatened to talk about the girl from the boat he'd believed her.

A pulse started to beat in Esteban's temple. He touched irritable fingers to it.

Why did it still matter so much? By now, the girl would have forgotten, anyway. She certainly would not be the brave, vulnerable, fighting creature that had awakened something in him ten years ago. Something that Francesca and a dozen others had never managed to touch since.

Esteban looked out of the window and saw not the lights from the building reflected in the oily water, but a pale, furious face, surrounded by a mass of gold curls; lips that trembled in spite of her fierce words; legs that somehow seemed too long for her, like a young colt…

'Hold it right there,' he said to himself. Just as he had said ten years ago.

In spite of her spirited defence on the boat she had been so unsure, so *young*. Too young. Too young for the feelings she'd aroused in him. Too young, when she'd kissed him on the beach, to know how dangerous her innocent sensuality was. And far, far too young to understand the adult anger when he'd lashed out at her.

Esteban closed his eyes against that memory. It made no difference. He still saw her shocked face, that morning on the quay. As if she could not believe that anyone could be as heedlessly cruel as he had been the previous night; as if she hated him.

He'd deserved it, he thought dispassionately. In fact it had probably been a good thing for her that she had hated him. It would have helped her get over it. That was why, in the end, he had given up trying to find her, although he probably could have done if he had stuck at it.

He had thought it best to let the whole incident slip into the past. Only—it wouldn't stay there. 'Do something wicked and it stays with you,' Esteban told himself bitterly. The only reason Francesca knew about the girl was because he had told her one day when his conscience was pricking him and she seemed sympathetic.

He shook his head. Why was he thinking about things that happened so long ago? He had urgent problems sitting there on his desk. He needed to find a way to sort out his stepfather's precarious finances.

His expression darkened. There was a simple answer to Patrick's difficulties: sell some paintings. But every time Esteban suggested it Patrick just blanked out. So far Esteban had managed to subsidise Hallam. But he was already working all hours, taking every case that was offered him, and Hallam's expenses went on growing. In fact he wondered now whether the new kitchen had been a waste of money, if Patrick was going to have to sell the Hall after all.

Unexpectedly, Esteban's mouth quirked. If he had not bought the new kitchen, he would not have crossed swords with Nicola Piper. Now, that had to be worth it. In her way she had the same passionate belief in herself as his urchin Cleopatra.

He left the window and went back to his papers.

By three in the morning, his eyes were gritty with tiredness and Patrick's finances seemed, if anything, in greater turmoil than ever. Really, Esteban ought to see him; make him understand that there was no alternative to selling one of the paintings.

'Fat chance,' said Esteban aloud.

He stood up, flexing his cramped neck. What I want, he thought, is fresh air. Or, even better, a run.

He ran along the silent quay, his feet pounding in regular rhythm. In the summer the small dockside had been full of tubs of bright flowers. Now the plants were straggling and withered, waving in the strong wind off the river. There was rain in the air.

Esteban finished his circuit and hesitated for a moment outside his luxurious apartment block. He looked up. There was no way you could see the stars through the sodium lights and the blanket of London vapours. He was filled with a great longing for the sea and the cool, sharp air of Cornwall.

Well, why not? He wasn't in court for the next few days and he had no meetings he couldn't postpone. If he took his laptop computer and his modem, he could work in Hallam just as well as here. And if he talked to Patrick over several days perhaps he could convince him at last.

He yawned hugely. There was something in the back of his mind that felt like a reason not to go but he could not remember what it was. He shrugged. He would deal with the future of Hallam once and for all. It was time.

The morning chased the ghosts away. In fact Nicky began to enjoy herself, driving down country lanes in the late October sunshine with a bouncy dance tune filling the car's interior. Even when she thought she was lost, she only laughed and resolved to ask at the next village pub.

'If there is a pub between here and the end of the world,' she said aloud as the road got narrower and narrower.

By now the car doors were being scratched on both sides by autumnal blackberry bushes, their spines exposed as leaves and fruit withered. The road surface was deeply rutted, too. It felt as if no one had been down this road for months.

'Or maybe I should turn back now to the last village,' she said blithely. 'At this rate I'll be able to write the definitive Lost Guide to Cornwall.'

Only then she saw the sign. It was small and so old that she could barely make out the words. What was more it looked as if, even when it was new, it had been scrawled on a piece of bark by an amateur. The lane it indicated was no more than a rough track. But it did, indubitably, say Hallam Hall.

'Go with the flow,' said Nicky bravely.

She did. The car bounced so badly on this track that her head twice bumped the roof. Well, that would account for the damaged appliances, she thought. Shaken to pieces before they even arrived. The unkempt bushes nearly met, so that it looked as if the car was cutting its way through jungle.

'What a dump,' Nicky said.

She turned up the music, snapping her fingers to the beat defiantly. And then she saw the sea.

Nicky gasped. It was as brilliant as a tilting mirror in the October sun. She had a brief, disconcerting vision of driving straight out into the gleaming air. Then, when she had hardly got her breath back, the path dropped abruptly downhill and she saw the house.

'Oh, wonderful,' she said. 'It's not a house. It's a blasted castle. There's probably wet rot, dry rot and enough damp to short every single machine Springdown put in.'

Her diagnosis was reinforced when she stepped into a dark, panelled hall. The smell of damp and old polish smote her. Nicky made a face.

She pulled out her mobile phone and reported in.

Sally answered. 'Find it all right?'

'No problem. Hallam Hall is the only thing that stops you driving right off the cliff.'

'Is it wonderful?' Sally sounded envious.

'Bit creepy, so far. It smells like a church.'

'Ghosts?'

Nicky looked round the tapestry-hung stone walls. The sunlight did not penetrate this far.

'Dozens, I should think.'

'Will you be afraid to be there on your own?'

Nicky laughed. 'If I'm not afraid of angry plumbers, I'm not going to be seen off by any Blackbeard the Pirate Spook.'

'Oooh, you are brave. How bad does it look?'

'Haven't started yet. Have you heard any more from the client?'

Nicky could hear Sally riffling through pages of messages on her desk. 'His secretary rang to say if there is anything more you want to call her. The cleaning lady has gone to Madeira for two weeks but she should have left everything ready for you.'

Nicky shivered. 'That doesn't seem to run to putting on the central heating. Oh, well, I suppose I'll find the controls somewhere.'

'Of course you will.' Sally thought Nicky could cope with anything. 'Is it very cold?'

Nicky peered out of the leaded window. The sea was grey, the wind whipping the waves into foam.

'Yes.'

Sally moaned sympathetically. 'And you're really sure you don't mind being there on your own?'

To her private disgust, Nicky knew that she would have been a lot of happier if Martin had been at Hallam Hall too. Or even Ben. Then she had a thought and grinned.

'It beats being here with the client,' she said with feeling.

She rang off and set about unpacking the car. Then she tracked down the heating controls to a cloakroom cupboard. She turned them on. An asthmatic boiler wheezed into action without noticeable effect.

It will take for ever to heat a house this size, thought the experienced Nicky with gloom. And as for hot water! She could only pray that there was an immersion heater somewhere. She began to explore the cold house.

And was astounded. The place might look like a fortress

from the outside, but inside it was pure Mediterranean paradise.

There were paintings of riotous gods and peasants in every
room. On walls where there were no paintings, sculptures
were set against *trompe-l'oeil* alcoves. Painted terraces were
half hidden by swathes of real velvet. The whole of one wall
in the high-ceilinged dining room was an olive grove, with
nymphs in wafting draperies dancing through a lemon-tinged
twilight.

In fact, thought Nicky grimly, she had never seen so many
nymphs in all her life. Some played among trees, some
dreamed by fountains, some languished on flower-strewn
banks and looked frankly wanton. They were every shape
and size, from tall, graceful girls with hair as loose as their
draperies to the plumply luscious whose elaborate garments
looked as if they had been specifically designed to fall off at
the touch of a godlike hand. It all added up to a rich mixture
of sun, sex and classical landscape.

Great, thought Nicky. Just what I need.

She hunched her shoulders and turned her back firmly on
the laughing nymphs.

'Immersion heater,' she said. 'Work. Get moving.'

She stood up and began to make her way systematically
round the kitchen. To her huge relief she found an immersion
heater quite quickly. The next hurdle was to see whether it
was working.

'Well, the pilot light is on,' said Nicky, trying to encourage
herself.

She set out her work plan, her files, the instruction books
for the appliances and the box of provisions she had brought
down with her. She set out the food and looked at her sched-
ule. First check the main fuses. Well, that was easily done.

Nicky went back to the control cupboard. Yes, there it was
clearly labelled 'power points, ground floor east wing'. The
circuit breaker was still in place. She knew enough about
electricity to check, just to be sure. But it did not take long

to establish that the reason that the machines were not working had to lie somewhere else.

'Probably mice,' muttered Nicky as a castle-sized draft whipped round her ankles.

She went back to the kitchen and plugged in the small travelling kettle she always brought with her. She was going to need coffee.

While she was waiting for it to boil, she took critical stock. This was one of Martin's rustic kitchens, all mellow cherry wood and brass handles. It was—as far as she could see—perfectly finished. But, until Nicky had arrived and set out the tools of her trade and messed it up, it could have been in the showroom. There were absolutely no signs of an individual occupant.

If Esteban Tremain had a lady in residence, she had not left her mark on the kitchen. Nicky grimaced at the thought. Probably not surprising. No doubt she was perfectly groomed, with cool, elegant manners, and research-laboratory standards of hygiene. Not, Nicky thought wryly, someone who lost her temper at the drop of a hat and blushed when he looked at her.

'Not that it matters. Whoever he chooses is welcome to him,' Nicky said with feeling.

She worked her way through a cycle of preparing and cooking a full meal. Springdown had found it was the best way to test everything. By the time the light was failing she had established that the freezer did not work. Nor did the shining new Aga, the microwave, the kettle, the waste disposal unit or the coffee-grinder.

Judging by the delicious smells which emerged after Nicky put the pheasant casserole in to cook, however, the small gas stove had life of a sort, though neither the automatic ignition nor the timer worked. Nicky noted it carefully and sipped coffee. Suddenly the kitchen was warm, with the sort of smells a kitchen should have, and Hallam felt a friendlier place.

The preparation of an apple pie and a chocolate cake had

left her with throbbing wrists, though, because she had established that the electric mixer was not working either. Nicky had had to cream butter and sugar and crumb flour and fat all by hand. As a result, her hands were caked, she had smears of flour on her face and her autumn-gold sweater looked like army camouflage under its additions of butter and chocolate.

'Bath,' said Nicky with resolution.

She had found only one bed made up, presumably for her use. The bathroom next door had another immersion heater.

'Thank God,' she said devoutly, switching it on.

Her reflection in the bathroom mirror told her only too clearly how badly she stood in need of a bath.

'You're a messy cook,' Nicky told her image.

She was feeling more cheerful by the second. The house was getting warmer, more human, as she put her stamp on the place.

She checked the pheasant and looked at the clock. The bath water should be hot by now. Outside it was fully dark. If she were really Hallam Hall's hostess, this would be the time when she would go and have a bath and get ready for her guests. But then if she were really Hallam Hall's hostess she would be the cool and elegant lady she imagined.

Nicky gave an involuntary shiver, all her cheerfulness shrivelling as the thought touched her. It was like borrowing somebody else's life. But she needed a bath and Esteban Tremain was safely far away in London.

So as soon as the water was hot she climbed into a bath with claw feet and limescale deposits under the taps that would have made a geologist swoon with envy. There was no soap or bath preparations. Not even towels.

'Just as well I brought my own,' murmured Nicky.

But the immersion heater was efficient and the water was blessedly hot. She sprinkled a few drops of her precious Roman bath oil into the water and lay back in the scented steam. Slowly, slowly, she felt the tensions of the drive and the strange house float away. Even the unwanted memories slipped back into the past where they belonged.

Scented steam clouded all the bathroom's Victorian mirrors. It hung in the air like aromatic fog. Nicky breathed in luxuriously. She relaxed, dreaming…

And suddenly came bolt upright, water spraying everywhere. *What if the fault was electrical after all?* Not at the mains but in the individual plugs? Why hadn't she checked at least one plug earlier?

Nicky shook her head to clear it. The mirrors were still clouded but the fog had dispersed. What was worse, she found the water had cooled. She leaped out of the tepid bath, shivering.

Hurriedly she pulled on her elderly dressing gown and thrust her feet into flip-flops. Neither was enough protection in this freezing cold pile but at least the kitchen would be warm. She ignored the cold as she dashed along the corridor. The inadequate lighting made every dark corner spooky but Nicky was too excited by her idea to notice.

Her dressing gown swung wide as she scampered down the grand staircase. Impatiently she knotted the sash. The smell wafting up from the kitchen was rich. She had better just check on the casserole before starting to look for the screwdriver.

In the kitchen she grabbed a tea-towel. She had brought several too, and just as well. In the absence of an oven glove one of them would have to serve. She opened the gleaming oven door and a warm, appetising smell rolled out. Well, at least the gas stove had not collapsed while she was in the bath.

She was easing the casserole out of the oven when the kitchen door banged open. Concentrating, she did not really notice.

Not, at least, until a voice said blankly, 'What the *hell*…?'

Only the greatest self-possession stopped Nicky from whipping round. As it was her hands tightened so hard on the casserole that she burnt herself through the imperfect insulation of the cloth. She banged the casserole down and shook her singed fingers as she turned to face him.

It was, of course, Esteban Tremain.

Nicky's heart lurched. She felt her colour rise.

'You!' she exclaimed, glaring.

Esteban blinked. He looked as if he had been miles away and had suddenly been brought back to the present with a jolt. Not, Nicky thought, a very welcome jolt. There was an unnerving silence.

Then he said, 'Nicola Piper,' on a low note of discovery.

A look of unholy appreciation dawned. Exactly the sort of look that made Nicky's hackles rise. 'What are you doing here?'

'You took the words right out of my mouth,' he drawled.

Nicky's blush deepened. She ignored it.

'You knew I was here,' she said hotly. 'Your secretary arranged it. And,' she added accusingly, 'she said you were fixed in London.'

His eyebrows twitched together.

'I was,' he said briefly. 'I changed my mind. I have business down here. Should I apologise for being in my own house?'

Nicky shifted in annoyance. It brought imminent danger to her hastily knotted sash. She felt the thing begin to slip untied and clamped the lapels of the dressing gown across her breast, flustered.

Esteban Tremain looked amused. That enraged Nicky even more. But there was nothing she could do about it. She felt rather breathless.

He let his eyes rest on the exposed vee at the top of her dressing gown. It suddenly felt incredibly bare. Involuntarily Nicky shuddered. It infuriated her. His expression grew frankly speculative.

'You seem to have made yourself comfortable.'

That was the final straw.

'I am not comfortable,' Nicky yelled.

There was a tense pause.

Then he asked, 'Do you expect me to apologise for that too?'

Nicky took hold of her temper. It was an effort. But she was an adult, she was a professional and she was here representing Springdown. Or so she reminded herself.

'I can do without apologies. I do expect reasonable courtesy,' she said levelly.

A faint look of annoyance crossed the handsome face. 'And how have I been discourteous?'

In the way you look at me. No, she couldn't say that. It sounded too prim for words, even though it was true. And it should not have been true, thought Nicky rebelliously.

She was not fifteen any more. These days she could handle male salaciousness. Nine times out of ten it was purely for show. The moment you challenged them they backed down. And on the tenth—well, she could handle that too if she had to. Her chin rose.

'You implied that I was here for my own amusement,' she said with dignity.

One eyebrow shot up. 'Are you saying that you're here for mine?'

Her eyes flashed. 'Of course not.'

'Well, then—'

Nicky took an impetuous step forward.

'You keep complaining about your blasted kitchen,' she reminded him. 'You wanted it all sorted out immediately. If not yesterday. You even insisted it was me that did it, God help me. Well, here I am. But don't think you can sneer at me. I won't stand for it.'

He blinked. 'I can see that.'

Nicky narrowed her eyes suspiciously. He was not laughing—well, not openly. She checked on the security of her dressing gown anyway.

'I shall do what I came for,' she said loftily. 'And then I shall leave.'

But it didn't seem that was what he had in mind at all.

'We will need to talk about that.'

Nicky would have liked to sweep out. But she had a pheasant casserole that was beginning to smell faintly of caramel. It clearly needed attention.

So she turned her shoulder and busied herself with the dish. She ignored him loftily. But she was well aware that Esteban Tremain did not take his eyes off her. It sent a prickle of constant awareness up and down her spine. Nicky did not like it.

Sexual tension, she told herself. Nothing personal and nothing that won't go away if you don't feed it. Not surprising in the circumstances. Just don't acknowledge it and it will evaporate.

Nicky had had a lot of practice at ignoring sexual tension and she knew what she was talking about. But this was a first in her experience. She was very conscious of her nakedness under the old velvet; the damp hair that was falling out of its pins to send drips down her nape along her bare spine; his eyes on both...

She did her best to ignore him and concentrated on tasting: the pheasant needed mustard, thyme, more wine...

Esteban clearly did not like being ignored. He strolled over, standing so close that he might as well have been touching her. Nicky could feel an electric response all along her flesh. Unobtrusively, she took hold of the front of the dressing gown again, ensuring it stayed in place. It left her with only one hand to season and stir the food but it made her feel safer.

Esteban was not looking at her, however. He had picked up the wine and was inspecting the bottle critically.

'You never got this from my cellar.'

Nicky was indignant at this slur on her professional ethics.

'Of course not. I brought everything with me.'

'Impressive.' He put the bottle down. 'Who is he?'

Nicky was tasting the dark gravy.

'Who?' she said absently.

His voice was light but there was an undertone of anger when he said, 'The guy all this is for.'

Nicky froze. Then, very slowly, she put down the ladle, and turned to face him.

'I—beg—your—pardon?'

'It's quite a package. Gourmet dinner. Good wine.' His twitched his nose and gave her a sexy, slanting smile. But his eyes were not smiling. 'Scented bath,' he finished softly.

Nicky increased the grip on her dressing gown until her hand shook with tension. The look she sent him held acute dislike.

'So?'

'So—it all adds up to a lover.' There was an edge to the casual voice. 'Lucky man.'

Nicky's head went back as if he had hit her. It was all too horribly reminiscent of that scene on the *Calico Jane*. Why, *why* had she chosen this week of all times to rerun that particular bit of memory?

Esteban did not seem to notice her reaction. He was smiling. It was not a nice smile. 'Is he upstairs now? Or are you still waiting for him to get here?'

His tone was tolerant but Nicky had the fleeting impression of fierce anger. It was swept away in anger of her own, as great as any she could remember.

Shaking with it, she said dulcetly, 'Why would it matter to you?'

His eyes narrowed. Quite suddenly he stopped even pretending to be amused. 'It's my house.'

'Very territorial,' she mocked.

He took a step forward. It brought him close. Too close. Nicky found she was arching backwards over the countertop to get away from him.

'And it's my time,' he said. 'I assume I will be getting a bill for this service?'

She stayed mocking but it was an effort. 'Not at all. With the compliments of the management—'

She broke off. For a moment the mask flicked aside and Esteban Tremain looked absolutely murderous. Nicky pulled herself together. This was no way to placate a dissatisfied client. She dropped the mockery. 'There will be no bill.'

Their eyes locked. To her fury, Nicky felt herself still straining away from him. It was pure instinct.

And then the unthinkable happened. The tense arc of her body finally put too great a strain on the knotted tie at her waist. Suddenly aware, Nicky tried to grab it. Too late. The dressing gown fell open and then, before she was aware, slid off shoulders still slippery from her oiled bath.

'Oh, *no*,' she cried.

Esteban's eyes flared wide. There was an instant's disbelieving silence.

'Spectacular.' There was an odd note in his voice, as if he was not as unmoved as he wanted to be.

Nicky decided she hated him. For a paralysed moment she could not move. That steady gaze seemed almost to have stopped time. It was like a touch. Like a caress. Like a memory from ten years ago.

And then his eyes lifted and gazed straight into hers. Nicky felt the ground fall away. She made a small panicky sound. At once his eyelids dropped, masking his expression. It was as if a current had been switched off. Nicky swallowed. She felt as if she had been let off something she dreaded. With clumsy fingers, she hauled the dressing gown back up her arms and clutched it across her breasts, hard.

Fortunately the countertop had stopped it sliding all the way to the floor. So at least she did not have to humiliate herself by scrabbling at his feet to gather it up. But that was not much of a consolation. Not when Esteban's eyes lingered with blatant appreciation on the shadowed cleft between her breasts which the clutched garment still revealed.

Nicky said bitterly, 'You could at least *pretend* to be a gentleman.'

His eyes glinted. 'And what does that mean? Pass you a saucepan to hide your modesty?'

Nicky redoubled her grip on the gown. She glared. 'You could stop—staring.'

Esteban propped himself against the kitchen table and folded his arms.

'I could,' he agreed cordially. 'Give me one good reason why I should.'

'It's not kind,' she flashed.

He pretended to give it serious consideration. Then he shook his head.

'Not good enough. I've never claimed to be kind.'

'I can believe it,' Nicky muttered.

'Well, then.' He shrugged.

Nicky met his eyes with a shock. The current was on again. Her face, her whole body felt hot. Hurriedly, she levered herself away from the countertop.

'I am going to get dressed,' she announced.

His smile flickered into life again. 'Shame,' he murmured.

Nicky recognised deliberate provocation. She ignored it.

'I shall get dressed,' she repeated. 'Then I shall finish cooking the supper.'

Esteban was all politeness. 'And who gets to eat it?'

Nicky looked at him with dislike. 'You. Tonight if you like. Or I can put it in the game larder for tomorrow. The deep freeze isn't working.' Her idea suddenly returned. 'Except that—'

He interrupted. Back on form, thought Nicky sourly.

'You mean you cooked a meal and no one was supposed to eat it?' He sounded incredulous.

Nicky shrugged. Carefully.

'I'm putting the machines through their paces. What happens to the resulting meal is immaterial.'

'Isn't that rather a waste?'

'Maybe. But it's more ethical than what you had in mind,' she said with satisfaction.

His eyes narrowed. 'And what exactly do you think I had in mind?'

'I don't think,' Nicky pointed out. 'I know. You accused me of inviting a boyfriend to join me here.'

If she had hoped to discompose him, she was disappointed.

'The word I used,' he said deliberately, 'was lover.'

Nicky flushed to the roots of her hair. Embarrassment warred with indignation. Indignation won. But only just.

'I haven't forgotten,' she said grimly.

Esteban was watching her. He looked intrigued suddenly. 'And?'

'I resent the professional slur,' Nicky said with precision. 'Which is the same whether you thought I was entertaining a simple friend or the Emperor Nero.'

He let out a surprised crack of laughter. One wicked eyebrow went up.

'No lovers?' he asked outrageously.

Nicky was literally speechless.

'You're between candidates?' he pressed.

Oh, he was a barrister all right. Nicky felt as if she was on a witness stand, being grilled. She glared.

It had no effect on Esteban at all. Of course, he must be used to his victims glaring at him in impotent fury.

'Or one of the new Puritans?' he pursued ruthlessly.

'No,' Nicky choked.

'No, I thought not,' he agreed. 'It would be a terrible waste. Besides, I saw you with a man who was definitely no Puritan.'

Nicky remembered the way he had sized up Ben in the showroom. 'I wouldn't want to interrupt your social life,' he had said, sneering. But she was not explaining her brother to him, or anything else for that matter. In fact Nicky was not going to say any more to Esteban Tremain than she absolutely had to.

She said sweetly—and untruthfully—'Of course, I'm sorry to disappoint you. But before you get any more exotic ideas let me point out that this is what I always do when I'm testing a kitchen.'

Esteban clearly thought he had won that particular exchange. He smiled like a satisfied tiger.

'And you bring your own dressing gown to do it.' He looked her up and down eloquently.

Nicky gave him a glacial smile. 'I bring everything. The dressing gown in the kitchen is, I admit, a mistake.'

'Not at all. I look on it as a bonus.'

She gritted her teeth and refused to blush.

'Thank you. How flattering,' said Nicky, not meaning a word of it.

'I never flatter.'

He moved towards her. Nicky stood her ground, her eyes warning him.

She said curtly, 'I had a thought in the bath. So I came down to check the fuses in the plugs on the machines. But as you're so smart you'll already have done that before complaining, right?'

'So you're an electrician as well.'

Esteban looked at her with admiration. Nicky was quite certain it was mocking. She wanted to scream. She wanted to hit him. She wanted to dance with temper. 'Fine,' she said, finally losing it. 'You find the screwdriver. You do it.'

She stalked past him without another look.

The bath water was cold, of course. She pulled on her grubby clothes rapidly, muttering to herself. How on earth could she have been so stupid as to let Esteban Tremain see how he was getting to her?

It had to be because she had let herself think about what happened all those years ago. She could not imagine why she had done so. It must have been seeing Ben that had brought it all back. It was nonsense to think it could have anything to do with Esteban Tremain, no matter how autocratic his manner. It was not his autocratic manner that she remembered about Steve.

In spite of the central heating, the room was getting chilly as the dark closed in. Nicky went back to her bedroom and rummaged in her overnight case for a loose wool jacket. She dragged it on and turned back to the chest of drawers, seeking her image in the spotted mirror that stood on top of it.

She was fluffing out her drying hair absently when her eye fell on the photographs. There were several: a studio portrait of a beautiful woman with wistful eyes in an oval silver frame; a tall military-looking man in formal clothes at a wedding; a posed group of men, clearly a team of some kind; several informal pictures of people, dogs, children, boats...

Boats. And one particular picture.

Nicky stopped fluffing her hair and picked it up. She could hardly believe her eyes.

It looked like a holiday snap. It showed three people on the deck of a catamaran. They were holding up champagne flutes in a toast and laughing. One was a spectacularly beautiful woman. The two men were in shorts, shirtless, their bodies gleaming with health. All three were wearing sunglasses as they looked into the camera.

Nicky looked at the taller man and felt a flicker of panic. I don't believe this, she thought. And then, But of course I do. Only I'm not ready for it.

Slowly, reluctantly, she turned the leather picture frame over. It was there on the back, in neat script. '*Glen Tandy III*, Gibraltar. Francesca Moran. Fernando Arauho. Esteban Tremain.'

She turned it back. She had thought she would never forget that face.

Well, her conscious mind had not recognised him without those alienating tinted glasses. But something had. Something visceral had been plucking at her ever since she'd heard his voice on the phone. Why else were all these hateful memories stalking her? Usually she suppressed them without difficulty.

Nicky looked again at the photograph in her hand.

The taller man, laughing on the deck of his boat, was Esteban Tremain. That was what it said on the back of the snap. And anyway she could see it, in the set of the shoulders and the arrogant tilt of the head.

But he was also a man called Steve. And he had ruined her life.

CHAPTER FIVE

Nicky sat down hard on the side of the four-poster bed. She felt cold with shock. For ten years the man had haunted her. And when she saw him again she did not even *recognise* him? She could not believe it.

But then she thought about it.

That was not true, was it? Or not the whole truth. She had recognised him all right. At some deep, unconscious level she had *known*. From the first day, when he had looked at her across the showroom, a part of her had known. Even in the distance that dark figure had set a chord of memory thrumming.

Why else had she kept so far away from the Hallam Hall contract? Oh, of course you could say it was chance, that she was doing other things for other clients. But the truth was that she had not even asked a question or glanced at a plan until he'd rung. Then, and only then, she had picked up the file. Was there a single other Springdown client about whom she knew so little? Had taken care to know so little about, Nicky admitted now.

'Oh, God.' The strangled sound was wrenched out of her.

How could it have happened? You would have thought it was impossible. A crazy coincidence across the distance of ten years and a quarter of the world. Nicky did not believe in coincidence.

Just for a moment, her heart lifted. Maybe it was not true after all. She had been remembering too much in the last few days. Maybe she was just applying it to an innocent stranger. Maybe she was mistaken. Maybe…

She turned back to the picture.

She was not mistaken. She wished with all her heart that she was. But he was Steve, all right.

There was no escaping it. Those blanked eyes were the last piece in the jigsaw puzzle. Now she saw clearly what her senses, more alert than her mind, had been picking up all along.

God help me, I even knew his smell, Nicky thought.

She passed a shaking hand over her face. What was she going to do? Go downstairs and talk to him as if nothing had changed?

No, she thought. She could not do it. She still remembered that scene on the boat in every wince-making detail, and she could recall every word he had ever said to her.

As for that harsh kiss on the beach—well, if she was honest, had it not spoiled her for every kiss since? Andrew Bolton was only the latest in a long, long line of men who did not know what they had said or done to turn Nicky to ice. And the worst of it was that it was not their fault.

Every time a man took her in his arms, she had to fight to remind herself that he was not Steve and he did not despise her. When they touched her in passion all she could think of was another night and the stars and an angry man walking away from her. And she froze.

Nicky drew an unsteady breath. She put the photo frame down very carefully. It seemed important to restore it to the exact spot. She felt very cold and slightly light-headed.

She remembered a little too clearly the men she had dated in the last ten years. It was not a comfortable memory. Oh, she had not told them she froze when they touched her. Of course she had not. She was a modern woman. She knew how to smile and flirt and kiss. She just did it all with a little metronome ticking in her head, marking the seconds until the man lost interest. And, when he did, she made sure she was the first to walk away.

Nicky looked at the photograph and thought, I have never kissed a man without thinking of him.

She shut her eyes.

'I can't bear it,' she said aloud.

Unexpectedly, the sound of her own voice steadied her. She opened her eyes. What on earth was she going to do?

Her instinct was to run. As far and as fast as her little car would take her. But she only had to think about that for a second to realise she could not. Or not without getting into a whole maze of explanations she could bear even less: to Caroline and the other assistants at Springdown, to Martin de Vries and, not least, to Esteban Tremain himself.

At the thought, Nicky shuddered convulsively. So far the only good thing about the whole mess was that Esteban Tremain did not have the slightest idea who she was. He had probably forgotten the whole incident as soon as it happened, of course. After all, a teenage beach bunny wasn't going to have much impact on a man as sophisticated as he was, even ten years ago. In the interim he had metamorphosed from Steve to Esteban and acquired a worldliness that hit you between the eyes. So he certainly would not remember her now.

She found she was pressing her hands together so hard that her wrists shook. In the mirror it looked as if she was praying. Nicky gave a shaky laugh and loosened her grip.

Of course he would not remember her now. Thank God. And it was up to her to make sure that it stayed that way. She could go down and act as if nothing had happened. She *could*.

She would be as sweet as pie to him. She would busy herself so totally with his damned kitchen that he would think of her as just another piece of equipment. Until she could get away, she would be so neutral, she would just disappear into the background. No confrontations, no arguments. She would agree with his every suggestion. She would challenge nothing.

It should not be too difficult. A man like Esteban Tremain was not going to take too much notice of a humble kitchen advisor, was he? She tried hard not to remember that he had already taken notice of her to the tune of three first-class rows and a toe-curling appreciation of her exposed flesh.

Taking her courage in both hands, Nicky went downstairs. Esteban was still in the kitchen. He had discarded his jacket for a dark sweater. He must have rumpled his hair as he'd pulled it on. To Nicky's dismay, his slight air of dishevelment made him look a lot more like the man she remembered on the beach. She swallowed hard.

I must not think of him as Steve, she thought. *I must not.*

He had found a bottle of champagne and two glasses. He must have just opened it. The bottle stood on the kitchen table with a faint plume of smoke escaping from its neck.

'What's this?' said Nicky, distracted.

He looked up from the task and gave her an unexpectedly charming smile. Nicky blinked.

Careful, she thought.

'Peace offering,' he said lightly.

He poured, tilting the glasses professionally so the pale liquid did not foam over the top. He put the bottle down and surveyed the pale gold flutes with satisfaction before he strolled over. He held out a glass to her.

Nicky did not take it.

'Where did you get that?' she demanded. She was suspicious of the charm and shaken by her own reaction to it. 'I didn't bring any champagne. And there was nothing in the fridge.'

'We have a cellar.'

He took her hand and curled her fingers round the cold glass. Nicky shuddered. *How* she remembered that touch.

Esteban gave her an enigmatic look.

'Yes, I agree,' he said provocatively.

Nicky nearly dropped her glass. Was he reading her mind? *'What?'*

His eyes laughed at her. 'The champagne,' he explained. 'Just cold enough.'

But he ran one long finger lightly across her knuckles where her hand was closed convulsively round the stem of the wine glass. The touch left Nicky breathless—and in no doubt that he was reading her like a book. *Help,* she thought.

Esteban turned back to the table and retrieved his own glass. He raised it to her.

'Your very good health,' he said softly.

In spite of all her resolutions, Nicky did not find she could toast him back.

'Why champagne?'

She knew she sounded sulky and could not help it. His dark brows twitched together as if she had hit a nerve suddenly.

'That voice,' he said.

Nicky was wary. 'What?'

'You have a memorable voice. The trouble is, I can't remember where I've heard it.'

Panic flared in Nicky, as sudden and violent as a forest fire. She fought it down. But not quickly enough.

'What did I say?' he demanded.

Oh, yes, he was certainly reading her like the simplest book in his library.

'N-nothing.'

He scanned her face. 'Have we met before?'

This was terrible. Nicky knit her brows, pretending to think.

'I don't remember any Esteban Tremain.' It helped that it was the literal truth.

She could see he was not convinced. Alarm fluttered in her throat. She curbed it. Smile, goddammit. *Smile,* she told herself.

It was clearly not very successful.

'Don't look like that,' he said. 'I'm not going to jump on you.'

Nicky bristled at the superior tone. The obvious retort leapt to her lips: 'That makes a change'. Just in time she stopped herself, folding her lips together tightly. It was a close-run thing, though.

And not before Esteban had seen her reaction. His smile died and his eyes grew keen.

'*Now* what have I said?'

Nicky shook her head, taking a sip of champagne. Esteban sent her a shrewd look.

'You're as jumpy as a flea on a hot plate. Is that my fault? I know we got off on the wrong foot—' he began. Nicky could not help herself. She gave a snort of laughter. How right he was and how little he knew it.

Esteban was disconcerted. 'I'm sorry?'

'I didn't say anything,' Nicky assured him hurriedly. The shock of discovery was beginning to wear off. She gave him a sweet smile. 'You were talking about the wrong foot?'

He looked at her narrowly for a moment. Then gave a slight shrug.

'The first time we spoke. I was already in a temper,' he admitted.

It was the last thing Nicky had expected.

'You mean when you shouted down the phone at me?'

Esteban had the grace to look uncomfortable.

'I was furious about something else entirely. When I couldn't get hold of de Vries it was just the last straw.'

'So you took it out on me,' she agreed pleasantly.

Esteban stopped being apologetic. He looked irritated. 'It was a perfectly legitimate complaint.'

'You were very nasty.'

He made an impatient noise. 'Well, now I'm trying to make amends.' He raised his glass to her.

Nicky did not drink in response. 'Try harder.'

'That's not going to be easy if you won't meet me half-way,' he pointed out. 'Come on, drink your champagne and let's start again.'

For a moment she was speechless. He'd ruined her life and he wanted her to wave it aside and *start again*?

But of course he did not know he had ruined her life. Unless she decided to tell him, that was. And Nicky thought that she would rather die.

'To our better acquaintance,' he was saying.

Nicky blenched.

'To our better understanding,' she temporised.

He was too quick to miss the way she had changed his toast. His brows rose.

'Nicola Piper, you're an unforgiving woman,' he said softly. 'I can see I shall have to do something about that.'

She managed not to wince. 'I wouldn't advise it.' It was light enough but there was no disguising the fact that she meant it.

Esteban looked at her speculatively. 'You don't think I can change your mind?'

She shook her head. 'I'm a pretty hopeless case on the unforgiving front.'

'But don't you know that's my profession?' he said softly. 'I specialise in reversing hopeless cases.'

She said more sharply than she intended, 'I don't know anything about you at all.'

And don't want to, said her tone. To her annoyance, Esteban Tremain laughed as if he had won his first point. His eyes danced. His charm was as heady as wine—and he knew it. Careful, Nicky said to herself.

'What an excellent place to start.' He stood up and made her a bow. 'Let me introduce—Esteban Felipe Tremain, age thirty-eight, marital status unattached, qualifications numerous, hobbies sailing and baiting harmless kitchen planners.'

He held out his hand. His dark eyes were so warm, you could almost believe that the charm was for real, she thought. Careful, Nicky.

'Pleased to meet you—what do I call you? Nicola? Nick?'

'Nicky,' she agreed reluctantly. She could not think of any way to deny him her name but it felt like another small surrender to that lethal charm.

Even more reluctantly, she took his hand.

'Truce,' she offered, trying not to remember the last time they had touched.

He pursed his mouth. 'Oh, I think I want a lot more than a truce.'

Nicky was sure she was being baited again. There was only one way to deal with that. Fight fire with fire.

'You're getting a lot more,' she told him dulcetly.

His eyebrows rose. She retrieved her hand with some difficulty.

'You're getting dinner,' she concluded.

He gave a choke of surprised laughter. 'Good point.' Nicky felt a small glow of triumph. She put her champagne glass down and removed herself from that disturbing closeness. She had the ideal excuse, busying herself with the food.

Over her shoulder she said, 'When would you like to eat?'

Esteban laughed lazily. 'What luxury. I usually microwave a pizza.'

Nicky looked wryly at the dead microwave. 'Not here, you don't.'

As soon as she said it, she could have kicked herself. What a chance for him to start complaining about Springdown again! But he did not.

Instead he picked up the bottle and replenished her glass.

'I was talking about my own place in London. My stepfather hates fast food. When we planned the kitchen, we slipped in the microwave when he wasn't looking.'

Nicky was intrigued in spite of herself. 'Your stepfather? But I thought this was your house.'

He shrugged. 'Technically it is. He made it over to me some years ago. But it's his home; he was born here. I only get down here every couple of months. He lives here.'

Nicky looked eloquently round the characterless kitchen.

'Not so as you'd notice.'

Briefly his expression was sombre. 'He's been away.'

Absently he topped up his own glass. Nicky thought he would take the wine to his room and unpack but he did not. Instead he settled himself at the kitchen table as if he belonged there. As, she supposed with a slight shock, he did.

He looked round approvingly.

'The kitchen looks better.'

'You mean with some food in it?' Nicky said tartly.

He nodded slowly. 'I suppose I do. And light and som—

good smells as well, of course. It's been a long time.' He looked bleak suddenly.

Nicky felt an unwelcome twinge of sympathy. Where was the 'very good friend' the article talked about? If she was the woman Esteban had mentioned trying out the appliances, why hadn't she made the kitchen her own?

She said with constraint, 'I am sorry, Mr Tremain. I didn't mean to pry.'

He came back to the present with a grimace. 'You weren't prying and my name is Esteban.'

Nicky did not say anything. She did not need to. Her silence said for her how totally she rejected the idea of calling this man by his Christian name.

Esteban considered her thoughtfully.

'You really don't like me, do you?'

Nicky shifted uncomfortably. 'Are you surprised?' she hedged.

It was not the answer he wanted. 'Well, that's honest, I suppose.' He surveyed her for an unsmiling moment. Then he said abruptly, 'Why do I make you nervous?'

Nicky's heart lurched sickeningly. The last time he had looked at her like that was on a boat in the Caribbean and—

'You don't!' she said loudly.

Esteban's eyes narrowed in an arrested expression. 'Oh, that voice,' he muttered. '*Where* have we met before?'

To her consternation, he leaned forward across the table and took her by the wrist.

The floor surged under Nicky's feet like the deck of a boat. *Stop it,* her mind yelled, panic-stricken. She wrenched herself away.

'Don't *touch* me.'

This time she had really startled him. For a moment she read blank amazement in the dark eyes. And not just amazement, either. Attraction, sizzling and irrefutable. When he looked at her like that, Nicky shot back over the years in the

blink of an eyelid. She was a trembling teenager again, surrendering to a magnetic pull she did not understand.

Not again, thought Nicky, her mouth suddenly dry. *Never
again.*

She fought for control. 'I'm here to sort out your kitchen,'
she said crisply. 'Not play games with you.'

'Who's playing?'

Her every instinct was to retreat. By a supreme effort of
will she managed not to. Instead she took a step towards him
and slapped her hand down on the table between them. It
made the glass and bottle ring.

'Stop right there,' she said with quiet force. 'You know
perfectly well you've been baiting me since the moment you
arrived.'

And before in London, she thought, though she was not
going to say it. She heard again, 'You're the blonde.'

'You push me around.' She was almost shouting. 'You
won't tell me anything—not about who uses the kitchen, not
about anything. You— Oh what's the use?'

There was silence. Nicky was sure he could hear her heart
thundering. She put a hand to her throat to quieten the pulse
that drummed there.

Esteban watched the gesture through narrowed eyes.

'I think this is about more than inadequate briefing,' he
said at last.

'No,' said Nicky, her voice shaking.

It was exactly the same unheeded protest she had made on
the beach all those years ago. Even Nicky could hear the tell
tale tremor. She shut her eyes. How long before Esteban real
ised that the last time he'd heard her voice she had been
shouting 'I hate you'? How long before she said it again?

He said conversationally, 'Are you always this dramatic?'

Nicky opened her eyes. He was looking annoyed. But no
angry; not embarrassed and guilty; not like a man who'
realised a disreputable incident from his past had risen t
haunt him.

She took her hand from her throat. Disaster averted. This time anyway.

'I don't like being messed about,' she said with truth.

'Evidently.'

He seemed to take a decision. He gave a quick shrug.

'OK, you can have the full run-down. It's no big deal. My stepfather was getting too old to run the estate but he wanted to keep it in the family. Since my mother died, I'm all the family he's got. I took over the administrative side of things and he carried on living here. I took control of the land. He ran the house. At least that was the theory—'

He broke off, lapsing into a brown study. Nicky thought of the smell as she'd unlocked the front door. It had not smelled like a house that was lived in. She said so.

'What?' He looked up. 'Oh. Shrewd of you. No, it isn't. It's been empty for the best part of a year. Except when I can get down here. Which isn't as often as I should.'

'So why the kitchen?'

He was puzzled. 'What?'

'Nobody lives here full time,' she pointed out. 'You're happy with microwaved pizza. Why the glossy-mag kitchen?'

'Oh, that.' He sounded bored. 'My stepfather has always wanted to come back. He's been ill, you see. The doctors said it would probably be good for him to come home but he couldn't live on his own. The district nurse would visit but he needed a full-time housekeeper if he was going to live here again. The person I—' he hesitated '—had in mind said the existing kitchen was a death trap. So my stepfather stayed in his nursing home and the builders came in to the Hall.'

'And then even the new kitchen didn't work,' Nicky said. She felt an unwelcome compunction. She did not like it. She did not want to start feeling sympathetic towards Esteban Tremain.

'And the potential housekeeper walked out. With a few choice words about false pretences.'

Nicky began to see why he had lost his temper with Springdown.

'Have you found a replacement?'

'I haven't even looked yet.' Esteban sounded weary suddenly. 'I thought it was sorted. Now I'll have to see my stepfather before I go to New Zealand.'

'You're going away?'

Esteban looked up and all weariness fell away.

'Just for a job. I'll be back in two weeks.'

He gave her the sudden, wicked smile she was beginning to recognise. It made her stomach turn over. She was beginning to recognise that too.

'Why, Nicky! You sound almost as if you'd miss me,' he said softly.

Nicky stiffened. He laughed.

Careful, she thought.

'You're so easy to tease,' he said with satisfaction. 'Very rewarding.'

At least he wasn't asking questions she didn't want to answer, Nicky told herself. That was what she wanted, wasn't it? But his easy superiority set her teeth on edge.

He stood up and stretched.

'Since the water and the heating are on and supper is in the oven, I think I'm going to indulge myself. Pretend I'm Mr Average come home from a hard day at the office.'

Nicky tensed. She knew he was teasing again but she could not help herself.

She said acidly, 'Don't get carried away.'

Esteban grinned. 'Don't worry. I only meant I'll unpack my briefcase. Make a few phone calls. Take a shower.' His eyes gleamed. 'Come down and finish the rest of the champagne with you.'

Nicky stayed cool. 'I look forward to it,' she said untruthfully. She did not like the sound of it at all. She just hoped she could handle it.

'So do I.' He gave her a long, speculative look. 'We have so much to talk about.'

She liked the sound of that even less.

'H-have we?'

'Two life histories. To say nothing of kitchen appliances,' he said blandly.

And, with an enigmatic smile, he strolled out of the kitchen.

CHAPTER SIX

DINNER turned out to be less than the ordeal of intimacy which Nicky feared. Esteban was preoccupied. Oh, he was polite, even complimentary about the food, but she had the feeling that he was far away, turning over a problem in his mind that he was not willing to share with anyone.

So it must have been sheer perversity that prompted her to say, 'Problems?'

He shrugged. 'Nothing new.'

The meal was over. Esteban was sitting at the kitchen table, idly shaving slivers off the Cheddar cheese she had brought, frowning. At her question, he'd looked up abruptly as if he had forgotten anyone else was there.

His eyes met hers. Nicky almost jumped at the impact. It shocked her. She could keep telling herself the attraction was all in the past but the moment she looked into those dark, dark eyes it was *there*.

Esteban was beginning to sense it too, she could tell. Now his eyes narrowed on her hair as if the golden strands could tell him something. Nicky put up a defensive hand and found she had lost the clip which kept it in a neat queue at the back of her neck. Hurriedly she bundled it into a knot and rummaged in her pocket for an elastic band.

'Don't do that.' Esteban seemed as if he could not keep his eyes off her hair. He leaned forward and prised it gently out of its loose knot. 'Leave it free.'

She caught it and held it into the back of her neck.

'I prefer—' Her voice scraped. She cleared her throat and started again. 'I prefer to keep it tied back. It's more professional.'

'But work is finished for the day.'

But keeping a professional distance wasn't, Nicky thought grimly. Though she was not going to say that to Esteban Tremain. Going by his behaviour this evening, he would only take it as a challenge.

'There's still the washing-up. And that machine wasn't working either.' She stood up and started to gather plates. 'Unless you did check the fuses?'

He made an impatient gesture. 'I'm willing to buy one duff fuse. Not—' he looked round the kitchen, counting '—a dozen or more.'

'I thought the same myself,' Nicky admitted. 'Still, there's an outside chance, I suppose. Maybe the installers had a bad batch of fuses. I ought to check before I call in the mechanics.'

Esteban shrugged, supremely uninterested.

'If you want. But I warn you, I'm going to light the fire in the study. When it's lit I want you to stop working and come and have coffee with me.'

Nicky did not like the sound of that. She did not want to spend the rest of the evening in front of a blazing fire with Esteban Tremain. There was something horribly intimate about open fires.

So she made a noncommittal noise and finished clearing the table.

'As long as that's understood,' he said. It was soft but quite, quite determined.

Nicky gave a little inward shiver and did not look at him. 'Understood.'

He went.

Nicky switched off the current to the kitchen power points. Then she collected her all-purpose screwdriver from her bag and dived under the countertop to remove the plug from the electric socket.

Five minutes later she was sitting cross-legged in the middle of the kitchen floor, surrounded by three dismembered plugs. She looked at them in disbelief. The screwdriver fell from her hand with a clatter. She did not notice.

'This is *crazy*,' she said aloud.

Esteban came back into the kitchen, dusting off his hands.

'A fine healthy blaze—' he began.

And stopped at the sight of Nicky sitting on the floor. One look at her frozen face and he crossed to her in quick concern.

'What is it?'

Mutely she held out a plug to him. He took a cursory glance and shrugged, puzzled.

'So?'

Nicky realised that she was very scared. It was such a *malicious* thing for someone to do. Unbalanced.

She swallowed. 'The fuse wasn't faulty. The wire had been mutilated. And there wasn't a fuse in the plug at all. Or this.' She picked up the flex to the kettle with its stripped plug. 'Or this.' A state-of-the-art steam iron. 'I'll bet all these machines are the same. That's why the gas on the stove worked but the electric controls didn't.'

He turned the plug over in his hand. 'Odd.' He picked up the mangled flex and frowned. 'I think Springdown needs to take a serious look at its quality control. Still, easy enough to put right now you've found the hitch.'

Nicky felt very cold.

'You don't understand,' she said. 'It's not a hitch. It's deliberate.'

'*What?*' He stared at her.

She shook her head, still not quite believing it herself. No *wanting* to believe it.

'I didn't check the fuses because, like you, I thought they couldn't *all* have gone. And anyway Springdown give the installers worksheets. The last thing they do is fuse the plug connect the machine and check the wiring is OK. It's a whole section on the form.' She waved a hand at her file, now on the cherry-wood dresser. 'Every single one of the forms ha been filled out showing the electric plug in working order.'

He was unimpressed. 'Workmen have been known to fal

sify worksheets. And if it's the last job they'd have been in a hurry.'

'Different workmen,' said Nicky. 'Different days. Different suppliers.' She gestured round the kitchen. 'There isn't a fuse in any machine I've looked at. Someone must have taken them out.'

Esteban stared. 'Taken them out? That's stupid.'

Nicky shivered. 'It's such an easy way to disable a machine. When I was working in advertising, we used to do it all the time when we had children on photo shoots.'

Esteban said categorically, 'No one would have done such a stupid thing deliberately.'

She touched the damaged flex. 'That sort of damage can't happen by chance. It has to be vandalism.'

'But what's the point?'

Nicky looked at the half plug in her hand. 'That's what makes it so nasty. Pointless and mean.'

Esteban took the plug out of her hand and put it on the countertop.

'Don't you understand?' Her voice rose. 'Someone set out to disable your kitchen.'

His reaction was not what she expected. He did not rage or scoff. Instead he hunkered down in front of her and turned her chin gently towards him.

'It has really upset you,' he said on a note of discovery.

Nicky shook her head. But there was not much point in denying it when the truth was written all over her face.

Esteban stroked her cheek with an oddly comforting finger.

'This is no big deal, Nicky. Probably just a mistake by some half-trained assistant who isn't very bright.'

'You don't have to be bright to know that a plug needs a fuse,' she flashed.

He tucked a swathe of golden hair behind her ear absently.

'Even if you're right and it was deliberate, so what? It's scarcely life-threatening. Just a prank.'

It did not feel like a prank to Nicky. 'It's so—spiteful. And underhand.'

Esteban was unmoved by the thought. He swung down on to the floor beside her and put an arm round her shoulders.

'Sure. But it's only a temporary inconvenience. I contacted Springdown. Springdown got you down here. You'll put fuses in the plugs. End of problem.'

'Except that whoever did this is still out there.'

His arm fell from her shoulders. His voice cooled noticeably. 'There's no need for melodrama.'

Nicky turned her head. His eyes were very close. They were expressionless. Don't ask any more, they said.

She said involuntarily, 'Have you got any enemies?'

He looked at her with an unnerving lack of expression for a minute. Then he smiled, a crooked slant of the sensual mouth that got nowhere near his eyes.

'Sure. Who hasn't?'

'Enemies who would want to hurt you?'

'I've got a better class of enemies than people who would waste their time messing about with dishwashers.'

Nicky remembered rather suddenly that he was superior, dictatorial and altogether hateful. She pushed away from him and stood up.

'I think I've just been put in my place,' she remarked.

She turned away.

Esteban came lightly to his feet.

'Nicky?'

He turned her back to face him. His touch was quite gentle but somehow it brooked no resistance. Something inside Nicky went very still. He searched her face.

'What is it about you?' he said, almost to himself.

Her mind whirled. But she stood unmoving under his hands. Like a trapped animal whose only chance of escape is playing dead, she thought.

Esteban shook his head as if to clear it.

'Put it this way.' He sounded strained. 'Most of the people who wish me ill are international criminals I have failed to keep out of jail. Bomb under the car, maybe. Fuse out of the dishwasher—no way.'

His hands were warm. Even under the old sweater she could feel the heat of his fingers against her shoulders. She felt as if she was drowning in warm, silky water. Nicky struggled to concentrate.

'Bomb under the car?'

Was it his pulse or hers she could hear? It slammed through her, slow and sweet and almost deafening.

Esteban's eyes were uncomfortably acute.

'Joke.'

Nicky swallowed and the thunder of the pulse subsided. She removed herself carefully from his grip.

'A very bad one.' It was clipped because her every instinct was to gasp for air and she did not want him to see it.

He shrugged. 'Just putting the thing in context. No one's going to sabotage a kitchen, for heaven's sake.'

'It depends what you think is important,' Nicky pointed out. Her breathing, thank God, was coming back under control. 'Annoyed any good cooks lately?'

'No, of course not. I—' He broke off abruptly.

Nicky took the other half of the plug away from him and turned away. It was better when she was not looking at him. Then the terrible vulnerabilities of her teenage self retreated into the past where they belonged.

The modern, professional Nicky said briskly, 'I've only got a couple of fuses in my bag. I'll wire up the dishwasher tonight so we can use it. I'll get some more fuses and do the rest in the morning. Then you'll have a fully functioning kitchen and I can go back to London and get on with my life.'

He was frowning. 'What?'

She repeated it, patiently. Esteban did not seem very interested.

'Oh, yes. Of course,' he said absently. 'Look—why don't you make us some coffee? I've got a couple of calls to make.'

He walked out without another word.

Nicky breathed more easily. But she found that her hands were shaking as she made the coffee. Was that her fear of possible saboteurs? Or of Esteban? Or—it was not a welcome thought—of herself?

It took her time to find the library. In the end it was only the sound of his voice which led her to it, down a flagged passage where the tapestries wafted in the old house's draughts. She was shivering by the time she pushed open the door. Not entirely from the cold.

As he had promised, the fire was blazing. A huge log lay across a vast fire basket, glowing red-hot, while flames danced up through logs and fir cones around it. It drew Nicky like a magnet.

The heavy velvet curtains were still open. In the blackness beyond the long windows, Nicky thought she could make out the shifting shadow of the sea. That was where Esteban was standing, one foot on a window seat, his back to the room. He was talking rapidly into a telephone. He did not hear her come in.

'—completely stupid,' he was saying icily.

Nicky stopped dead. She had heard that tone before. When he'd taken her to pieces in the showroom. On a beach when he'd said, 'That was what you really wanted, wasn't it?' She shivered. She felt sorry for whoever was on the receiving end this time.

Esteban did not notice her. She had the impression he was very angry.

'I did not ask you to do me any favours,' he said in a level voice. 'It was a job, pure and simple. If you didn't want it all you had to do was say so. Not play childish tricks.'

The other person clearly burst into speech. Esteban waited

'I don't believe you,' he said finally.

He cut the connection and slammed his mobile phone shut

'You're a real charmer on the phone, aren't you?' Nicky remarked drily.

He swung round, startled.

She raised her eyebrows. 'I gather you've thought of some one who might have sabotaged your kitchen after all.'

She looked round for somewhere to put down the mugs o

coffee that was not an antique. There was nowhere. She compromised by putting them on the edge of the hearth.

She held out her hands to the blaze.

He came over to the pool of light and warmth in front of the fire.

'It's nothing to worry about. Just someone being silly.'

Was he trying to reassure her? It hadn't sounded silly. She shivered.

'Was it a disgruntled cook?'

He kicked a log into blazing life.

'In a way.'

'Still not a very high-class enemy?'

He looked at her broodingly for a moment.

'Let's say I haven't been very clever about my dealings with that particular person.'

'Really?' There was an edge to Nicky's voice. 'Not very clever? Or not very kind?'

Esteban winced. He sank down on to an ancient sofa at right angles to the fire.

'Probably both,' he admitted after a pause. He leaned forward, changing the subject decisively. 'You found the coffee, then?'

Nicky took the hint and passed the mug up to him.

'I brought it with me. Like everything else. Including the kettle.'

'How efficient.' He took the mug. 'Thank you. Is that normal or just because you were coming out to the wilds of rural Cornwall?'

'Standard procedure,' Nicky assured him.

It was a relief to talk about something that did not stir up her unmanageable memory. For the first time she could hear herself sounding almost friendly.

'You daren't use anything in a client's kitchen. It might be the very special vintage mustard they searched half of France for. Then you can go and put a couple of tablespoons of it in the stew. End of good relationship.'

He pushed away the tiredness to allow himself to be entertained. 'It sounds terrifying. Do you enjoy it?'

Nicky sipped her own coffee. 'It's only a small part of my job. Not the best bit, I admit.'

He cocked an eyebrow. 'Don't like cooking?'

'Cooking's fine. I don't like—' Too late, she stopped.

Esteban laughed softly. 'Don't like dealing with clients, eh?'

'It is not,' Nicky admitted, 'my strongest point.'

'Why not?'

'I—er—don't seem to have the rapport,' Nicky said carefully.

'You surprise me. They can't all be as unreasonable as I am,' he murmured provocatively.

Nicky was not rising to that one. 'Most of our clients are women who are going to spend more time in their kitchens than I have ever done in my life. Martin understands them. His wife is a chef. Their family life is centred on the kitchen. So he can imagine what the client needs. I can't, really.'

Esteban leaned forward. 'So where is your family life centred?'

'I live alone,' she said unexpansively.

His eyes flickered, registering the information. But he was much too subtle to pursue it.

'OK. So where was your family life centred when you were a child?'

Nicky hesitated. Then realised it would not betray her if she told him the truth.

'On a boat,' she said briefly.

Hundreds of children lived on boats, after all.

'Ah,' he said, as if he had been given the answer to a question he had not asked.

Nicky's eyes flew to his face in alarm. He saw it. His eyebrows went up.

'So that's how you know Martin de Vries,' he explained slowly. 'What did you think I meant?'

She did not answer.

He went on idly, 'In fact I met him through a yacht club myself. Maybe that's where we've met before.'

'*No!*' It was a strangled sound, frankly appalled.

'Why are you so jumpy?' Esteban leaned forward and took her chin in his hand, turning it towards him to scan her face in the firelight. 'Are you hiding a guilty secret?' It was lightly said but his face was serious.

Nicky jumped to her feet.

She said at random, 'I didn't know you and Martin were old friends.'

He did not move. But Nicky could feel him watching her measuringly.

Then he said slowly, 'We're not. My stepfather chose him to do the kitchen. De Vries built a catamaran for him years ago. Frankly it was a relief that Dad was taking an interest in anything. I just accepted it.'

So for the time being he was willing to let her off the hook. She had a nasty suspicion it would not last.

She said rapidly to deflect him, 'I'm confused. Is it you or your stepfather who makes the decisions here?'

He hesitated. Then shrugged.

'Oh, what the hell? It's no secret. Not round here anyway. If you go buying fuses in the village, you'll find out soon enough. The decisions are mine.'

Somehow Nicky was not surprised.

'My stepfather is a wonderful man but he never quite caught up with modern economics.' He sounded rueful. 'In his day, money just flowed in without him having to do any vulgar calculations. These days I do the sums. And I pay the bills.'

'That must be difficult for him,' said Nicky with instinctive sympathy.

Esteban looked surprised. 'Yes. Yes, it is. Though I would have thought— No, never mind.'

'Thought what?' Nicky demanded, bristling, though she did not quite know at what.

'Well, you don't look as if you've ever had to count the pennies yourself.'

'Then my looks belie me,' Nicky said sharply. 'I've counted the pennies. And worse.'

Esteban was taken aback. 'Worse?'

'My father was hopeless with money too.' Nicky was remembering too clearly. Unconsciously, her hands balled into fists. 'We used to take tourists out scuba diving. Some of the kind ones used to leave exaggerated tips. We were so poor, people on other boats used to give us their casts-offs—sails, equipment, even clothes sometimes. My father used to swear and my mother used to cry but the truth was we couldn't get by without them. I can understand your stepfather, believe me.'

Esteban studied her. In the leaping firelight his eyes were deeply shadowed

'Yes,' he said at last. 'Yes, I can see that you would.'

Damn, thought Nicky. Why did I tell him that? But it was too late. The only thing she could do now was rush on before he could question her.

'Having to be grateful all the time destroys you.'

Esteban glared at that, distracted as she had somehow known he would be.

'My stepfather does not have to be grateful,' he snapped.

'I bet that's not how he sees it.'

'My father rescued my mother from an impossible marriage and took me with her,' Esteban said flatly. 'Any gratitude goes in the other direction.'

Then, quite suddenly, his anger evaporated. He laughed as if it was torn out of him.

'I see why you don't like dealing with clients. Do you always jump up and down on their sorest spots?'

So she had successfully steered him away from the danger zone again. Feeling reprieved, Nicky came back to the fire and sank on to the edge of a leather chair.

'The others say that I either tell the paying customers to make up their minds or yell at them to get out of my way.

Suddenly she was full of mischief. 'But you're my first invasion of privacy, I promise.'

Esteban's expression stilled. 'You should do that more often.'

'What, dig into clients' private lives?'

'Smile.' He leaned forward and touched one corner of her mouth. 'It looks good on you. Like a girl coming out to play after too long.'

Nicky felt as if the floor had given way under her. From relief she went to black panic. She thought, He knows.

Then, No, he doesn't know; of course he doesn't. It doesn't matter to him who I am or where I come from, he thinks he can do whatever he likes with me—just as he did ten years ago. This is a game to him, just as I said it was. He has not changed a bit. She shut her eyes.

He said softly, 'You must know you're a very sexy woman. A hundred times more so when you smile.'

Nicky tensed until her jaw ached. She knew this scene. She had played it so often, most recently with Andrew Bolton. They spoke in that soft, intimate tone, they teased, they touched... They *looked*. A familiar slow dread began to build.

She said harshly, 'I suppose you think that's a compliment.'

There was a small silence. Then Esteban said slowly, 'Well, I didn't think it was something to be ashamed of.'

Nicky's eyes flew open.

Frowning, he said, 'What's wrong?'

She shook her head, unable to answer.

Still in that tone of quiet reason, he said, 'All I did was say you are attractive. What's wrong with that?'

Nicky felt like a wild animal being lured out of hiding by soft words she could not trust. Oh, no, she could not afford to trust Esteban Tremain, of all men.

She swallowed. 'What makes you think I want to be attractive?' she said past the constriction in her throat.

He stroked one finger along the line of her tense jaw. The

movement was very gentle, very slow. It was hardly a touch at all. And totally intimate. Nicky thought, *Not again.*

'Don't you?' he murmured.

'No,' she said, so fiercely she felt tears well up in her eyes.

She wanted to push his hand away. But she did not trust herself to touch him. Instead she jerked her head back.

The stroking finger paused, then moved again, rhythmically, hypnotically. She had to do something to break the spell. She *had* to.

'What a waste.' He sounded as if he had less than half his mind on what he was saying.

She looked him squarely in the eye, her face a mask of irony. 'Oh, please. Not that old line.'

It angered him. His hand stilled against her cheek. 'What a contrary creature you are.'

Nicky jumped to her feet. Beyond the fire, the book-lined shelves struck chill. But anything was better than sitting in that deceptive pool of light letting him mesmerise her.

She said pleasantly, 'And what a patronising rat you are.'

His dark brows twitched together sharply as if she had struck him. 'Rat? Why on earth…?'

But at least he sounded as if all his attention was back on what he was saying, not on some magic trap which she was not supposed to notice until it was too late. It was a relief.

'Think about it,' Nicky advised crisply from her safe haven in the shadows. 'Think about everything you've said to me since you arrived this evening.'

He stood up and came round the sofa. Not such a safe haven after all.

'What do you mean?' he demanded.

Nicky retreated a couple of steps.

'I was supposed to turn into the little woman and cook for you, while you dealt with your big important business deals, wasn't I?' she said breathlessly. If she stoked her anger at his behaviour this evening, she could suppress the older, darker memories. 'What did you call it? An evening as Mr Average?'

'I was wrong,' he said positively.

She backed. He followed. Nicky went on retreating, skirting a heavy oak table, bumping into a worn tapestry chair and nearly oversetting a set of library steps. Eventually there was only the long window at her back, with its skin-tingling draughts and the surge and thud of the sea beyond. And in front of her…

'Where are you going to run now?' Esteban challenged her provocatively.

Nicky gulped. 'I'm not running.'

One eyebrow rose. 'Aren't you?'

'No, of course not. But I should go and clear up…'

'Running,' he taunted softly.

Nicky's chin came up. He did not remember what she remembered after all. 'Why should I do that?' she retorted, challenging in her turn.

'Because you suspect I'm interested in you,' he said calmly. 'And you don't know how to handle it.'

Nicky stared at him blankly. He suddenly seemed very tall and much too close. His mouth smiled faintly. But the dark eyes were not amused.

'You're mad,' she said, shaken.

'Not at all. Though I'm surprised you're so unsure of yourself.'

That fired her up. 'I am not unsure of myself,' said Nicky between her teeth.

He ignored it. 'And of course you're right.' It was a purr. 'I am interested.'

Her indignation dwindled abruptly. His eyes travelled over her like a caress.

'The point is, are you?'

The silence shuddered with possibilities. Nicky's lips parted. Then she found she had nothing to say. She could only search his face, trying to read him.

A bit of her mind went scrabbling round on a hamster wheel that repeated frantically, Get out of this. Get out of this. Get out of this *now*. But another bit—a frighteningly calm bit—said, You've waited ten years for this. Go for it.

Nicky swallowed loudly.

The smooth voice roughened. 'Let's see, shall we?'

He reached for her.

It was not at all like ten years ago. For one thing he was— as he said he aimed to be—in total control. For another, Nicky was not fifteen and clumsy with the first anguish of sexual hunger.

To her surprise, his mouth was soft, questioning. Control, yes. But he explored without pressure as if he savoured every sensation. She had the feeling he registered every tiny quiver of response as her lips parted and, with a little sigh, she abandoned herself to the moment.

Her eyelids fluttered closed. She was floating. She heard herself give a muted sigh, half delight, half despair.

Esteban heard it too. His arms tightened bruisingly. Nicky surrendered. In his hands she felt impossibly slight, as if her body was a flimsy thing he could mould to his will. She drew a little breath of pure pleasure.

Suddenly urgent, his mouth ravaged hers. Oh, he was in control all right. Under his mastery her muscles turned to water and her bones became as flimsy as thistledown. For heady moments Nicky revelled in it.

Out of nowhere realisation struck her: *this was what it was like before*. It shocked her back to reason. She broke the kiss and leaned away from him, hands flat against his chest.

Esteban looked down at her as if he hardly recognised her. They were both panting.

'Nicky—' She hardly recognised the ragged voice.

What was more, she hardly recognised herself. Her blood was singing. For the first time since that night on the beach, she was not bracing herself to pretend that she was physically moved when she wasn't.

I can deal with this, thought Nicky in a flash of enlightenment. She could hardly believe it. *It's all right. I'm cured.* Off her guard with relief, she gave him a brilliant smile.

Esteban's eyes flared.

And that was when Nicky realised the danger she was in. Another of those searing kisses and she would be surrendering to his every last whim. Maybe even giving him the key to the memory he had not yet unlocked.

Shocked, she whipped out of his arms.

'No!'

His arms let her go. But his eyes, dark and intent, didn't. 'No? Why not?'

She could not tell him the truth. She searched desperately and found something that was halfway true.

'I don't want you experimenting with me.'

His eyes assessed her. She could almost see the acute brain working.

'I don't think you know what you want,' he said at last.

Nicky made a great business of looking at her watch.

'Well, I'm very tired.' She managed a huge and almost convincing yawn. 'I'll be asleep as soon as my head hits the pillow.'

His expression was shuttered. 'You don't have to draw me a diagram. Which room was made up for you?'

She described it.

'Ah,' he said.

For a moment, an unholy smile just touched the corners of his mouth. All Nicky's suspicions awoke again.

'What? What is it?'

He shook his head. 'Nothing. Just—'

But before he could finish what he was going to say the telephone on the windowsill rang. In pure reflex she reached for it at the same time as Esteban. Their hands collided.

There was an arc of energy. It shocked them both. Esteban's arm recoiled as if it burnt. His breath rasped, loud as a drumroll. Their eyes met. Nicky vibrated.

But she was the one with the telephone receiver in her hand. Shaken, she said, 'Hello?' in a voice so high and strained that she hardly recognised it.

Esteban watched, frowning.

There was as silence on the other end. Then a brittle voice said, 'I think I must have the wrong number. Who is that, please?'

Nicky checked the face of the old telephone and gave the number.

There was another pause. Then the voice queried, 'Hallam Hall?'

'Yes.' Too late Nicky realised that the voice was female and was obviously expecting to talk to Esteban. She said, her words falling over themselves in her confusion, 'Do you want to speak to Mr Tremain? He's right here. I'm sorry—'

But she was speaking to a buzzing line. The connection had been cut.

She looked across at Esteban. 'She's hung up. I'm sorry. That wasn't very bright of me.'

He did not seem as if he could be bothered to question her about it. 'No harm done.'

'But—she hung up.'

Esteban was impatient. 'Which means it can't have been very important. Now—we were talking about your room. Will you be warm enough?'

Nicky did not trust this sudden metamorphosis into a concerned host.

'I'll be fine,' she said firmly. 'In fact, I think I'll go to bed now. I've had a long drive today.' And she gave another huge yawn.

If she thought he would argue, she was disappointed.

'I'll say goodnight, then.'

He was waiting for her to go so he could call the woman who had hung up.

'Goodnight,' Nicky said distantly.

She went quickly through the corridors, not looking at the paintings. The dancing nymphs seemed to laugh after her as she hurried past them. It made her feel oddly bleak.

She hurried through a scrappy wash in the chilly bathroom and jumped into the four-poster bed. There were plenty of blankets. But the creaks and the draughts did not make it easy to go to sleep.

Nicky read as late as she could. When her eyelids were threatening to close of their own volition, she shut the book and turned off the light. But she could not relax, even though she was so tired.

She had never expected to confront Steve again, Nicky realised. He was a figure out of myth, haunting her yet distant. She had thought he was out of reach for ever. If she was honest, she had wanted him out of reach.

Now she was faced with the fact that he was a man, not a mythical monster. Not a kind man, maybe, but living flesh and blood. What was worse, the old pull was still there. In fact, it was stronger than ever.

'But so am I,' said Nicky aloud.

The problem was that Esteban was stronger too. More sophisticated, more controlled and all too acutely aware of the sexual tension between them. He might have forgotten that meeting on the beach ten years ago but he knew what had been happening tonight all right.

Nicky stared into the darkness and recognised an unwelcome truth.

If she was not very careful, it would all go the same way again.

CHAPTER SEVEN

SHE dreamed of cypress groves and a wild dance in which, for some reason, she was taking part covered in flour and not much else. The other girls laughed and did not seem to notice. But she was painfully conscious of her state of undress. Especially as she knew they were all waiting for the Lord of the Wood.

She had to get away before he looked and found her. She had to…

Nicky jackknifed into wakefulness, the dream still running. For all it was so silly it felt as if it carried a message of danger.

'Nicky?' She knew that soft voice.

Her sense of danger increased. For a crazy moment she lay there in the darkness, her heart thundering.

'Nicky.' Louder this time.

What had he said in the library? 'I am interested… The point is, are you?'

She thought, He's going to make me face my feelings. All my feelings. I'm not ready for this.

Her mouth dry, she hauled herself up on to her elbow, groping for the unfamiliar bedside light. But before she could find it the light snapped on. Nicky blinked.

Esteban was standing not in the doorway, as she had expected, but by the dressing table. The top drawer was open. And he was still fully dressed.

She cleared her throat. 'What are you doing?'

He pulled out a black box of some kind and slammed the drawer shut, turning to her.

'Just remembered something I wanted.'

Nicky huddled the heavy blankets up to her chin.

'What?' she said suspiciously.

'A torch.'

Nicky was blank. 'What do you want a torch for? And what's it doing in my room, anyway?'

Esteban hesitated. 'Sometimes the power goes off in old houses. It's always a good idea to have a torch at hand. And—er—it's my room, actually.'

Nicky was so shocked that she did not notice the evasiveness of the rest.

'*Your* room?' she echoed, disbelieving.

'Yes.'

Nicky forgot to clutch the blankets. Her hands twisted in agitation.

'But it was the only one made up. I thought it was for me.'

'Don't worry about it. You're very welcome.'

Nicky ignored that. 'You should have said,' she muttered.

She was torn between guilt and embarrassment at her suspicions. Even though he did not know what she had thought, she could feel the heat in her cheeks. She looked anywhere but at him.

'Why? Would you have offered to share?' His voice was amused. But there was a thread in it that had nothing at all to do with amusement.

And it demanded an answer.

Nicky lifted her head and met his eyes. There was a moment when the whole world seemed to hold its breath.

Then he said something—she thought it was her name—and cast the torch away as he strode forward. Dazed, Nicky let herself be swept up into his arms. She did not make even a token protest.

His hands were like fire. Through the creased cotton she wore, her traitorous body pressed wantonly against him. She was starkly aware of sheer male power. And even more starkly aware of her response to it.

Shocked and exhilarated, she opened her mouth to the invasion of his tongue. As hungry as he, she kicked away the tangled covers and reared against him. She was trembling with need.

Somewhere at the back of her mind, Nicky thought, *This is exactly the same as last time*. She did not care.

Esteban fell on to the bed, hauling her on top of him in a bone-crushing embrace. Nicky gave a small moan, half pain, half longing. Her breasts were hot and hard under the old nightdress. She writhed, hobbled by the twisted stuff. Esteban muttered in frustration. Nicky felt his breath hot in her mouth, his hands fierce.

And then the old cotton tore like paper.

Esteban lifted his mouth and flung her down among the tumbled covers. At once he began to slide down her body, his mouth hungry. Nicky screwed her eyes tight shut. The sensations were close to agony. But she thought she would die if he stopped.

'Say you want me.' His voice was muffled against her trembling flesh.

Nicky blenched. Her eyes flew open. This was facing her feelings with a vengeance. Could she do it?

Esteban felt her recoil. He looked up, his eyes black with desire. And dawning dismay.

'Don't you?' He sounded appalled.

Nicky swallowed.

'I—'

But she couldn't.

Esteban threw himself off the bed as if she had shot him. 'I think I'd better go.'

Nicky pressed her lips together so tightly they hurt. Her throat felt like sandpaper. She swallowed.

'I'm sorry,' she said in a voice she did not recognise.

'So am I,' he said curtly. 'Put it down to a difficult day. For both of us.'

'I should never—'

But he interrupted, his voice level. 'Nor should I. But there's no harm done.'

Oh, yes, there is, thought Nicky. Her every sensitised

nerve quivered, exactly as it had ten years ago. As it never had since. That revelation shocked her into wild alarm.

'Heaven help me.' Her voice spiralled upwards, on the edge of panic.

Esteban winced. Engrossed in her own self-betrayal, Nicky did not see it.

He said harshly, 'It's no big deal. Mistakes happen all the time.'

Nicky looked at him blankly. He made a quick, instinctive movement towards her. And curbed it as quickly. His dark face was quite unreadable.

'You'll find it will look different in the morning.'

And he picked up his torch and walked out.

For once things did not look better in the morning.

Nicky had spent a restless night, torn between listening to the slam of the sea on the rocks below and the disturbing dreams of half sleep. In the end, she gave up trying to sleep and got up as early as she decently could.

There was no sign of Esteban. Which was half a relief, half frustrating. Nicky shook her shoulders and refused to think about where he might be.

Instead she applied herself to the problems of the kitchen. She might not be able to replace all the fuses until the shops opened but at least she could find out which appliances needed them. Then she could be on her way back to London and out of Esteban's force field—and all it revealed of her own bewildering weakness.

She made herself a large mug of strong coffee and concentrated. If she kept her mind on her work, she reasoned, she would not have to think about last night. And if she could avoid thinking about it until she got back to the safety of her flat, then she had a sporting chance of looking Esteban in the eye before she left.

Work helped a bit. It took her a couple of hours to go round the kitchen thoroughly, pulling out units and wriggling behind machines. But in the end she was pretty sure she had the measure of the problem.

Not all the fuses had been removed. Sometimes the wiring had just been disconnected so there was no longer a circuit through the plug. Usually the wiring had been mutilated. Nicky had no doubt that the kitchen equipment had been sabotaged. By somebody who had plenty of time and was not afraid of being challenged if found in the kitchen. Somebody, she was pretty certain, whom Esteban Tremain knew.

She put in a call to Martin, reporting in. She knew he would be in the office early before he went to the exhibition hall.

'Hi. How's it going?' he said breezily. 'The girls have been worried about you. They thought you were going home this morning.'

'I was,' said Nicky. 'Something turned up.'

'Like what?' Martin asked, amused. It was an office joke that nothing diverted Nicky from her chosen path once she had made up her mind.

She took a deep breath. 'Our respected client.' Her tone of cynical unconcern was masterly. No one would guess she had been going mad in his arms last night.

'Esteban? That must have been a party and a half.'

Nicky shut her eyes, thanking heaven that Martin could not see her anguish.

'Offered my choice of companions for the evening, he would not be a hot favourite,' she said with careful irony.

And Martin suspected nothing.

She reported on the evening, editing heavily. Martin did not like the implications of any of it. His instructions were curt and businesslike.

'Put things right and get out pronto.'

Nicky was surprised at his tone. So surprised that she forgot that Martin was telling her to do exactly what she had already decided on.

'I don't think I'm in any danger, Martin. As Esteban said, it was just a silly trick.'

'Too silly. Whoever did it is not rational. And Hallam Hall is just too damned isolated.'

Perversely, Nicky objected. 'But I'm not alone. The client is here.'

Martin knew Hallam. 'My guess is that Esteban Tremain is working at the other end of the house. The Beast of Bodmin could come and tear you to bits in the kitchen and he wouldn't even hear the screams.'

Nicky shivered. There was a beast tearing her to bits, all right. Memory had a whole new set of claws after the way she had behaved last night.

'I'm not joking, Nicky. Do the business and get out.'

She knew it was the only sensible thing to do.

So she decided to take the car off to the nearest small town she could find on the map. She left a note for Esteban in the middle of the kitchen table.

She felt self-conscious, propping it up against her file. Something else that felt too intimate. But it was only practical to let him know that she had gone out.

Hell, she did not even know what to call him. She started the note four times: 'Mr Tremain... Dear Mr Tremain... Esteban... Dear Esteban...' None of them looked right.

In the end she did not head it at all, just scribbled it out as if she were in great hurry. 'Gone to get the fuses. Will bring back some bread and milk.' She signed it with the time she left and her initial. Nothing anyone could call personal there. She hoped Esteban would recognise it and behave accordingly.

The little market town was just about waking up when Nicky got there. A small ironmonger's proved to have the required fuses and replacement cable but the man serving her was not willing to surrender them until he knew where she had come from. Having extracted the information, he gave her a comprehensive run-down on Hallam Hall, its owner, Colonel Tremain, and how lucky he was to have a stepson like Mr Esteban.

'I'm sure,' said Nicky, acutely uncomfortable. She held out her hand for her change.

'He works hard, Mr Esteban,' said the shop man, not handing it over. 'You'd think he wouldn't need to bother—his real dad being a millionaire and all.'

He paused invitingly. But Nicky was almost dancing with discomfort.

'I wouldn't know,' she said curtly. 'I just work there. Good morning.'

She seized her change and ran.

The baker's shop was no different—though she learned there that Mr Esteban was a very fair employer, even though everyone had been worried when he'd taken over running the farm from the Colonel—and the woman in the small general provisions store virtually barred Nicky's exit while she told her every daring exploit that Mr Esteban had been up to since he'd first arrived at Hallam at the age of eleven.

Nicky felt as if everyone in the single street was watching her as she made her way back to the car. It was all she could do not to run the last few yards. She did run into the kitchen when she finally got back to the Hall.

'Phew,' she said, pulling off a headscarf and shaking out her damp blonde hair.

Esteban Tremain was at the kitchen table reading a newspaper and drinking coffee. Nicky stopped dead when she saw him. It was like walking into a waterfall. At once every idea roared out of her, leaving only the memory of last night's turbulence. And dread.

Esteban looked up. His expression was unreadable. Nicky's mouth dried.

Was he going to reproach her? Demand an explanation? Touch her? Wild images shot across her brain. She stood, frozen, in the middle of the kitchen floor.

He lowered the paper slowly.

'How are you?'

Nicky swallowed. 'Soaked,' she said, taking refuge in briskness.

He studied her searchingly. 'That's all?'

She turned away, tossing her shopping on to the dresser.

'Well, I feel I've just run the gauntlet.'

'Local people are always very interested in what happens at Hallam.' He was still watching her.

As if he expected her to burst into flames or start throwing things, she thought. She forced a laugh.

'Interested! I think I've had your life story.'

He folded up the newspaper and stood up. 'Nicky—'

She rushed into speech, not looking at him.

'I'll replace all these fuses. Then make sure that everything's working.' She was gabbling. 'After that I'll be on my way.'

He stood very still. 'Is that what you want?'

She risked a glance at him then.

'I think it would be sensible.'

Esteban looked at her gravely.

'Are you always sensible?'

Nicky was full of self-mockery. 'Usually.'

Except with him.

'Then maybe it's time for a change,' Esteban suggested softly.

He was not touching her. He was not anywhere near her. But the energy beating out of him forced her to look at him. Nicky found she was actually tilting backwards in a physical effort to resist.

'Don't you think we have things to talk about?'

Panic flared, swift as a forest fire. Did he suspect they had met before? Had he, too, started to remember a night on a Caribbean beach?

'*No*,' said Nicky forcefully.

Oh, no, it would not be sensible to stay. It would be crazy.

Nicky broke that mesmeric eye contact and said woodenly, 'No, I'd rather get back. I have a lot of work to do.'

There was a long silence. Nicky turned her head away. She could feel his eyes on her profile, but he did not ask any dangerous questions. And he did not try to persuade her.

'Shame,' he said at last.

She thought, He doesn't really care.

Which, she assured herself, was exactly what she wanted. Wasn't it?

Esteban turned away, picking up his car keys. 'Will you be all right if I leave you to get on with it, then? I have to see my stepfather.'

'I'll be fine.'

On his way out of the door, he paused. 'Will you be here when I get back?' He could not have sounded less interested.

'If you get back before I've finished the kitchen,' she said pleasantly.

'I see.'

She thought he would leave then but he did not. Instead he surveyed the keys for a moment, then looked across at her very directly.

'What has sent you into retreat, Nicky? Village gossip?'

Nicky gave a false little laugh. 'I don't know what you're talking about.'

'No?' He patently did not believe her. 'Have it your own way.' He shrugged, turning away. 'I'll be back in a couple of hours. If you leave before I get back, lock up but don't bother about the burglar alarm.'

He left. Nicky felt bereft. She flung herself at the machines.

Putting the fuses back and then restoring the kitchen to its former state took longer than Nicky had expected. In the end she found she would need to touch up some of the paintwork and even replace a couple of tiles. A quick call to the local installers told her where the spare materials had been left. She rooted them out from the cupboard off the pantry and made the repairs.

All the time, she worked with an ear alert for the sound of Esteban's Jaguar. It did not come. At last she could not convince herself that there was anything more for her to do. She packed up her files, stuffed her few clothes back into her overnight bag and loaded both into her car.

She left a brief, neutral note for Esteban on Springdown headed paper. Then locked the mighty wooden door and climbed into the car. There was a strong wind off the sea which made the car rock. But it was not that which made her shiver convulsively as she settled behind the wheel.

She would have given almost anything not to be setting off, Nicky realised. The drive was long. The autumn day was already starting to darken. The wind shook the car. And she would probably never see Esteban Tremain again.

'Stop it,' Nicky said aloud to herself. 'You did not succumb to his charm and he still doesn't know you've met before. You've got away with your tail feathers. Be grateful. And drive.'

The car started easily, drove for about sixty seconds and then rolled gently to a halt as if it had run out of petrol. Nicky checked the fuel gauge. No, it was more than half full. She tried the ignition again. The engine flickered into life and died.

She got out. The car had got her out of the lee of the Hall and the wind made her stagger. Nicky set her teeth and had a look under the bonnet. Everything looked normal. But then how would I know if it wasn't normal? Nicky thought in self-disgust. She felt inadequate and it infuriated her.

'Blonde,' she said aloud furiously.

She could have cried. Or pushed the thing into the sea. Instead she contented herself with kicking a tyre viciously. Then she trudged back to the Hall.

Esteban was still not back. Nicky tried to tell herself that it was a relief. This way she might be able to contact someone to tow the car away and take her to the station before he returned. So she would not have to see him again. Which was what she wanted. Wasn't it?

She found a telephone directory in the study. It was easy to identify the nearest garage. The man who answered was frustratingly unhelpful until she mentioned that she was staying at Hallam Hall.

'Tell Mr Esteban I'll be out as soon as I can,' he said,

ringing off before Nicky could point out that the car in question was hers.

And then she heard the sound of a powerful car's wheels on the gravel. Slowly, she put down the phone.

It had to be Esteban. Her heart leapt.

Nicky shook her head. This was no good. She squared her shoulders, did some deep breathing, and went to the kitchen.

He was standing at the kitchen table, head bent, reading the paper in his hand. Nicky realised that it was her note. She cleared her throat.

Esteban looked up. She saw that his brows were knotted in a fierce frown. He regarded her blackly for a few unspeaking moments, almost as if he did not believe it.

'I thought you'd gone.'

'I had.' For some reason her voice was thready. She moistened her lips.

The black frown did not lighten but a little flame lit in the depths of those dark eyes.

'What made you change your mind?'

'I—'

He did not move a muscle but she felt as if he had come towards her. As if he was reaching for her.

'Decided to have a go at not being sensible after all?' he suggested softly.

For a crazy moment Nicky was tempted to say yes. To take the two steps that would take her to him and see what happened. *Be sensible,* she told herself.

'My car,' she managed.

'Ah. Of course.' His frown disappeared. So did the little flame. 'I should have expected it. We are haunted by mechanical disasters. What's wrong?'

'It stopped.'

'Well, that's pretty final,' he agreed.

He gave her a lazy smile. Nicky knew it should have charmed her to bits. Instead it was oddly chilling.

'It won't start. I don't know why. The petrol is all right. I need a mechanic.'

'Did you leave your lights on?'

Nicky had had a hard day and she was coming close to the end of her endurance as far as this man was concerned.

'Oh, isn't that just typical?' she flashed. 'Is that what blondes do? Run their batteries down because they're too fluffy-headed to remember to turn their lights off?'

Esteban shrugged. 'Anyone can forget they've got their lights on. Especially on grey days like these.'

'Well, I didn't.' Nicky was still fulminating. 'You think I'm a complete bimbo, don't you?'

Esteban shook his head. 'Whenever did I say that?'

Put on the spot, of course, Nicky could not remember. Except—

'You called me a *blonde*!' She did a savage imitation of his dismissive tone on the telephone.

He stared at her incredulously.

'Is that what this is all about?'

Nicky stared at him with hot eyes. 'All what?'

'This morning. When you wouldn't talk.'

'I talked—'

'Last night,' he went on as if she had not spoken. 'When we nearly made love.' He paused, then added deliberately, 'Should have made love.'

It was the last thing Nicky expected.

'You're out of your mind,' she said when she could speak.

He considered that dispassionately. 'You could be right. I thought that the moment I walked out on you last night.'

The old feelings of vulnerability washed over her like a tidal wave, drowning every other sensation. She felt adrift; helpless. For a moment she hated him.

Esteban saw it. His eyes widened. He looked shocked.

'What *is* it?'

Nicky whipped round and almost ran to the sink. She ran her hands under the tap, lathering them recklessly with washing-up liquid.

'I got grease all over me.' She was talking at random, breathless. Esteban came up behind her.

'I never meant to upset you.'

He brushed the drifting hairs off her neck, where they had fallen out of the knot she had skewered on top of her head. Nicky froze.

'Of course you're blonde.' His voice was husky. 'Blonde and beautiful.'

'Don't.' It was hardly more than a breath.

She could feel his eyes on her.

'Don't what? Tell you you're beautiful? Or kiss your neck?'

Nicky stood like a statue. She felt his breath against the exposed skin of her neck. Or she thought she did. She quivered. A thought came: I've been waiting for this for ten years.

He brushed the nape of her neck with his fingertips. Nicky let out a strangled breath.

'Well,' he said in an odd voice.

She did not turn round.

'If you touch me again,' she said harshly to Martin's finely crafted plate racks, 'I shall call a cab to Exeter and go now. I don't care about leaving the car. I can get the train or stay in a hotel or—' Her voice became suspended.

He turned her round to face him. His arms were strong. There was nowhere to go.

'This is nonsense,' Esteban said harshly.

And kissed her.

Against her will, against every consideration of common sense and her own decision, Nicky kissed him back. Her kiss held all the fire of anger, all the desperation of last night's self-betrayal. When they fell apart they were both panting.

He stared at her as if he had never seen her before. Or rather, as if he had suddenly realised that she was somebody quite other than the person he had thought.

He's remembered! thought Nicky, horrified.

'Don't look like that!' he shouted.

She jumped.

'I'm sorry,' he said in a more moderate tone. 'But you

keep looking at me as if you think I'll hurt you. I don't like it.'

'Then don't give me cause,' retorted Nicky.

She pushed past him. The kiss had shaken her more than anything that had gone before.

He gave a laugh that was half a groan. '*What* cause? And don't give me any nonsense about calling you a blonde. You must have got used to the idea after all these years.'

Oh, God, he *had* remembered. Nicky felt sick.

'What years? What do you mean?' she said sharply.

'Even if you don't believe your mirror,' he said judicially, 'your lovers must have told you how beautiful you are.'

The mockery was unexpected, and so cruel that Nicky could have screamed. Then she saw the look in his eyes. Unbelieving, she realised he was perfectly serious. Oh, boy, am I out of my depth, she thought.

But all she said was, 'N-no.'

He did not touch her. But the way he looked at her was a potent caress.

'Then let me be the first,' he said softly.

There was a deafening silence. Out of my depth and drowning, Nicky thought.

They just stood looking at each other, not moving. It might have been an hour; it might have been a few seconds. Nicky felt the steady floor shift under her as if it were preparing for an earthquake. She put an uncertain hand behind her and grasped the countertop.

'From the first time I saw you,' Esteban said at last.

Nicky could have wept. 'You don't even remember the first time you saw me,' she said bitterly.

'Oh, but I do. Across a floor full of fridges.' He gave a soft laugh. 'Hardly romantic. You'd come in from the street and your hair was all blown about.'

He touched the hair at her temples gently. She was so stunned she did not retreat.

'All gold, like the summer.'

Nicky felt his hands loosening the pins that held her knot

in place. She did not resist. The pins clattered on to the flag-stones. Her hair slid down over his fingers. To her amaze-ment, it felt voluptuous as velvet as it flowed over his skin. She shook it out deliberately, so that it caressed his fingers. Heard his little indrawn gasp of pleasure. Leaned into him…

This time the kiss was long and slow. Half a question, half a promise of passion. The passion was unmistakable, thought Nicky, who had avoided passion for years. Until last night. She was deeply shaken by her certainty. Especially as she was almost sure Esteban shared it.

His eyes were intense. 'At least now you know I wasn't making fun of you.'

Nicky shook her head, dazed and trembling. No, he was not making fun of her. He was starting to make love to her again. His sort of love, not hers. But she did not think she could resist.

She said as she had said last night, 'Oh, heaven help me.' She hardly knew she was speaking aloud.

Esteban shook her slightly. 'Stop fighting it,' he mur-mured. 'You know you need this as much as I do.'

And the trouble was, she *did*. She did not know which was worse—the way she despised herself or the sexy confidence in Esteban's eyes.

He slid a hand round the back of her waist under the grubby shirt and ran a mischievous finger down her spine. Nicky could not suppress the bolt of sensation which shot through her. His eyes gleamed with triumph.

'We'll call the garage tomorrow,' he said roughly, prepar-ing to swing her up into his arms.

At that moment Nicky did, literally, hate him. Nobody should be that sure of another human being.

She pushed him away and strengthened her wavering back-bone. 'Too late. I've already called. They said they'd be here as soon as possible.'

Esteban groaned.

But when the man arrived Esteban was courtesy itself. He

made him coffee before taking him out to the beached car. To small effect.

The dungareed St George took one look at Nicky's car and shook his head. In spite of Esteban's objections, he insisted on escorting her back to the car for diagnosis. Esteban slipped an oversized waxed jacket over Nicky's clothes and accompanied them, one arm protectively round her.

'You won't get that started,' said the garage man with gloomy relish.

Nicky was suspicious. Had Esteban slipped him a bribe to claim her car was beyond repair tonight?

'How can you tell?' she demanded. 'You haven't even looked inside the engine.'

The man traced the edge of the fuel cap with his finger. 'See that?'

Nicky leaned closer. It looked as if there was some sort of gritty discharge from it. She touched it. The crystals felt sticky.

'What is it?'

'Sugar.'

Esteban, who had been watching with detached interest, suddenly lost his detachment. He leaned forward.

'What? Joe, that has to be nonsense.'

The man stood back. 'See for yourself.'

Esteban did, frowning.

'But how could sugar have got into the petrol?' Nicky said, puzzled. 'And why?'

'Gums up the pipes,' said Joe laconically. 'Sugar doesn't dissolve in oil, you see. Just forms into a mass and stops the petrol flowing. Bet you thought you'd run out.'

'But how can it have got into the tank?'

'Only one way. Someone put it there.'

Esteban said, 'But that means someone deliberately—'

'Sabotage,' said Nicky shakily. 'Again.' She felt a cold which had nothing to do with the wind buffeting them off the sea.

Esteban looked down at her in quick concern. 'Well, vandalism, certainly. Can you do anything about it, Joe?'

'Needs to be stripped down. I'll take it back and see what I can do.'

Esteban took the keys from Nicky's nerveless hand and passed them across.

'Do that. Let us know how it looks. Put it on the Hall's account.'

Nicky came out of her shocked reverie. 'I can pay for it. I've got my credit card.'

Esteban put his arm round her again. The gale made them both stagger and whipped her hair across her mouth. He brushed it gently behind her ear.

'We'll talk about it later. Let Joe see what's wrong first.' He hugged her comfortingly. 'Go back. You're frozen.'

She turned to him instinctively. His body was warm. His strength seemed to revive and sustain her. Nicky felt herself steadied.

'Yes,' she said thankfully.

He gave her a little push. 'Go and get warm. I'll just help Joe hitch up your car.'

'My case—'

'I'll bring it in,' he assured her. 'Go on.'

She went.

After about ten minutes Esteban followed. He took one look at her white face and came over to her.

'Don't look so worried.'

'What was it you were saying about your enemies?' Nicky said. 'Is sugar in the petrol tank their sort of form?'

His eyes did not quite meet hers. 'Much too childish.'

She huddled her arms round herself, although the kitchen was warm as toast.

'But effective.'

'Only in the short run.'

He reached out but Nicky drew away. A thought had occurred to her and she needed an answer.

'Is that what you were doing in my room last night?'

His eyes narrowed. 'What?'

She was seeing him standing at the dressing table, still fully dressed. He had not come bent on seduction, had he? She had just jumped to that conclusion. And then let her long-repressed hunger take over.

'You really were looking for a torch, weren't you?'

Esteban watched her. 'I told you I was.'

And she had just brushed it side. Nicky's whole body burned with shame. She tried to ignore it.

'What happened?' Her voice was harsh. 'Did you hear an intruder?'

He seemed to debate with himself. Then he shrugged.

'I wasn't sure. I thought I'd take a look. Only then—' his voice warmed to sexy amusement '—something came up that seemed more urgent.'

He slanted a look at her. It said as clearly as words that he enjoyed the memory. It invited her to share his pleasure. Nicky winced.

'And did you find anything? I mean—' she swallowed painfully '—afterwards.'

The amusement died out of his face. 'Nothing definite.'

'Have you told the police?'

'Until now there was nothing to tell.'

She looked round the kitchen, at all the machines she had spent the day rewiring.

'Wasn't there?' she said heavily.

His jaw tightened. 'Nothing I couldn't handle.'

Nicky shivered, not answering.

His voice gentled. 'Look, Nicky, I know this feels bad. But I'm almost sure you were right when you said it was all my own fault. So I'll deal with it.'

'Great,' muttered Nicky. 'Like you'll beam in a new engine for my car?'

'I can't do that,' Esteban admitted, his mouth wry. 'But I can take care of everything else.' His eyes compelled her to look at him. 'Believe me,' he said with great deliberation, 'I will take care of you.'

All Nicky's memories attacked. Miserably undecided, she wrung her hands.

'Trust me,' he said strongly.

What choice did she have? For tonight, at least, she was stuck. In the end she admitted it, at least to herself.

'All right,' she said reluctantly.

Esteban's mouth turned down as if he had bitten on something sour.

'I'll make you forget all this,' he vowed.

Nicky thought of all she had to forget. More than he knew. 'You can try.'

From his alert glance, she knew he'd registered her reservations. But he was too shrewd to challenge her.

Instead he said lightly, 'Why don't you go and have one of your scented baths? I'll make a few phone calls, then I'll give you the guided tour. And later I'll take you out for a meal. That will put everything into perspective.'

Nicky very much doubted it. On the other hand, a bath would be very welcome. She agreed.

Later she came downstairs in her last remaining change of clothes: sapphire velvet trousers and a softly alluring sweater the colour of cornflowers. It made her skin look porcelain and turned her eyes sea blue. Esteban, coming out of the study, stopped dead.

'You beautiful thing,' he said after a stunned pause. He sounded almost angry.

Nicky's chin lifted to a challenging angle. 'So?'

He stared at her for a moment, his eyes hot.

'What is it you're not telling me?'

Nicky jumped, disconcerted. 'You're imagining it.'

'Am I?' He was grim. 'You know we want each other. You feel it, just like I do. But then you remember something and you turn on me as if I'm your enemy. Last night—' He broke off with a frustrated, furious gesture. *'Why?'*

Nicky should have told him then. She knew she should have told him. She could not bear it.

She said in a high, tense voice, 'I thought you were going to show me round the house.'

He gave an exasperated exclamation. But Nicky was already turning away. Esteban shrugged and followed.

He took her from room to room like a professional guide. Except that no professional would have loved the place as he clearly did, treated it so carelessly and yet with such affection. He seemed to know the history of every stick of furniture, every tapestry, every fireplace. But it was on the paintings that he really came into his own.

'School of Botticelli,' he would say. Or, 'Tintoretto. The insurance is ruinous.' Or again, 'Van Dyck. A rather badly behaved ancestor, I'm afraid, but a nice picture.' Eventually he stopped in front of three garlanded girls in a midsummer copse. 'Raphael, according to my stepfather. Fortunately the experts don't agree with him or we wouldn't be able to afford the security.'

Nicky looked at the laughing girls. She felt hot and cold. Hot with embarrassment to be standing beside Esteban looking at all that luxuriant abandon. Cold with dread that she would never be able to throw off her inhibitions and dance in the sun.

Esteban frowned. 'One of them will have to be sold, though. I don't know how my stepfather will bear it.'

Nicky was struck. 'How odd. My parents regard all possessions as goods for barter.'

He looked down at her. 'Don't they have things they treasure? Think of as part of the family?'

Nicky laughed aloud at the thought. 'My parents? You're joking.'

'I don't mean a painting, necessarily. Something they inherited from their parents that stands for continuity.'

'Let me tell you about my parents,' Nicky said, glad of the diversion. 'They're the original flower children. Flowers don't make good heirlooms.'

He was taken aback. 'Flower children? And *you*?'

Nicky grinned suddenly. 'Peace and love, man. My upbringing in a nutshell. My parents are the last hippies. They made the Summer of Love last thirty years. So far.'

'So you're a rebel against parental conditioning?'

'I think I must be,' Nicky said reflectively.

She looked at all the voluptuous flesh on the canvas over her head. Constraint returned, sharp as a wind off the sea. She looked at her watch.

'When are we eating?'

Esteban looked from Nicky to the painting; and back.

'Ah,' he said, as if he understood everything suddenly.

He lent her the oversized waxed jacket again and put her into the low, gleaming Jaguar. The wind howled but the car seemed impervious to its buffeting. Esteban set it silently down the darkened lanes to a sprawling inn at a crossroads.

The restaurant was a tiny room, with just five tables. Every one of them was full in spite of it being midweek and long past the tourist season. And from the moment they stepped inside Nicky felt as if they were alone.

Alone and—she drew a wondering breath—in love. All her prickly anger had gone. Their discreet corner table was like a charmed place, where nothing existed but the candlelight and each other. Even the waiter hardly impinged on Nicky's consciousness. She was quite calm and she had total confidence that Esteban would bring the evening to the resolution that had been waiting for them since they were born.

He looked steadily at her across the flame as if he could see right down into her soul.

'Tell me about these flower-children parents.'

She did. For the first time she found herself laughing about the trials of life on a boat, instead of denying them.

'It sounds a tough childhood.'

'Well, my brother had the time of his life,' Nicky said fairly. 'For myself, I could probably have done with a bit more structure.'

'I sail a lot,' observed Esteban, 'and I love it. But I can't imagine living on a boat permanently. What did you do for privacy?'

He leaned forward, as if he really needed to know. Under his intense regard, Nicky began to feel slightly light-headed.

'Lived without it,' she said breathlessly.

She felt oddly detached, almost as if she were in a trance. That it did not matter what they said—it was their eyes that were talking.

'That can't have been easy when you were growing up.'

She watched his mouth. It was a beautiful mouth, sculpted and strong. Here, you would say, was a deeply sensual man with his desires under rigid control. She wanted to touch his mouth. She wanted to see what would breach that iron control.

She tried to concentrate on the conversation. 'Living on a boat, you tend to make your mistakes in public. Growing up was not easy. But it was fast.'

He reached round the candle and took her hand. Nicky gave a sweet, deep shiver. Esteban saw it. His eyes darkened.

And then the waiter came, bringing food. Unhurried, Esteban let her hand go and sat back, allowing the man to serve. But his eyes never left her face.

Nicky knew it. If Andrew Bolton or any other man had looked at her with such unrelenting scrutiny she would have run for cover. But in her trance-like state she gloried in it. She thought, I want him to look at me like that for ever.

They ate. They talked, though Nicky could hardly have said what it was about. And all the time he looked at her as if they were alone.

Esteban seemed as if he wanted to tell her everything about himself. He talked about his work, his travels, his sailing; about his stepfather—with affection—and, with a brevity that revealed how painful it was, his real father. 'Do you see him?'

'Not much,' he said curtly.

Nicky was so sensitised to Esteban this evening that she knew the matter could not be allowed to rest there.

'Why not?' she asked gently.

He looked into the candle flame. 'The truth, if you must

have it, is that Felipe has been trying to mend bridges ever since I was eighteen. I'm his only son and he takes that seriously. For a long time I would not see him at all. But then my mother died and the loyalties became less clear. So—we meet occasionally.'

'And why does that hurt?'

But he made a sharp, dismissive gesture and the subject was closed.

It was a shock, after their mutual openness. Nicky's calm confidence dimmed a little. She retreated, grew more polite, less spontaneous.

Esteban noted it ruefully. He called for the bill.

But in the car intimacy reasserted itself, silently. The stars were needle-bright behind the surging clouds. It made Nicky giddy to look at the sky. When the car came to that rise in the road, it looked as if they were going to drive off the cliff into the stars. She gasped and held on to her seat in pure instinct.

Esteban sent her a quick look.

He said abruptly, 'Look, I'll tell you why I avoid Felipe.'

Nicky waited. Esteban brought the car to a halt. She could sense him marshalling his words. Fluent and sophisticated though he was, he found this hard to say, she realised. They sat in silence for a moment under the wheeling stars.

Eventually he went on in a low voice, as if it was being torn out of him, 'My mother was terrified of Felipe in the end. He was passionate about her but he did not trust her. He did not trust her *because* he was passionate about her.'

The intensity of it shook her. She did not know what to say.

'Everything she did made him jealous. The whole thing was insane.'

Nicky swallowed. 'So she ran away with your stepfather and everything ended happily. Why should you blame yourself?'

Esteban gave a short laugh. 'You're missing the point. I'm my father's son.'

Nicky was bewildered. 'So?'

'They even call me the Latin Lover in chambers. They think it's a joke, of course.'

She winced, remembering. 'Señoritas fall over themselves for that Latin charm,' Piers had said. And she had fallen all right, hadn't she? She shut her eyes.

Esteban did not notice her withdrawal. He was deep in a blackness of his own. 'Given the right circumstances, I could do what he did.' His voice was raw with self-loathing.

Nicky's eyes flew open. She could not have been more shocked if he had got out of the car and tipped her over the cliff into the sea.

'*What?*'

He was looking directly ahead but she had an uncomfortable feeling that it was not the landscape he was looking at. For a long moment he did not speak. Then he gave a deep sigh and put the car in gear again. It slipped along the narrow lane in near silence.

'I've always known what I was capable of,' he said at last sombrely.

She forgot her own bad memories in the need to defuse the nightmare for him. But how? In the end she chose scorn.

'You mean you think you are some sort of clone of your father? P-lease.'

He smiled perfunctorily. 'No, not that. But that if I let myself care deeply for someone—if I stopped watching myself—I could go wild. Lose all control.'

In spite of her determined common sense, Nicky shivered at his words. It was quite clear that Esteban Tremain believed them.

'And have you ever? Lost it, I mean.'

He hesitated. She had a feeling there was something burning inside him that, even now, he could not bear to expose.

In the end it was almost inaudible. 'Only once.'

CHAPTER EIGHT

HALLAM HALL was black and massive as the Jaguar's powerful headlights raked the sky. Esteban brought the car to a halt outside the studded door and sat for a moment. Nicky looked at him uneasily.

'What is it?'

'Maybe nothing.'

But when he opened the Gothic door and reached for the light switch nothing happened. Nicky gave a small gasp. It felt like a scream. At once his arm came round her, steadying her.

'It's all right. I told you the power goes off sometimes.'

But they had been too close tonight and he could no longer deceive Nicky with a reassuring tone. She knew it was not all right.

Keeping his arm round her, Esteban felt along a shelf. There was a click. A powerful beam scanned the hallway. It was empty.

It seemed to her that some tension in Esteban relaxed. But all he said was, 'I'll give you a candle.'

He found one, already set up in an incongruous old tin holder. He lit it and gave it to her. The flame shook as Nicky took hold of it. She tried to control her shaking.

'There you are. You can go to bed without breaking your neck now,' he said lightly. 'I'll just take a look round.'

She lifted the candle to search his expression. 'What is going on, Esteban?'

The candle had set all the shadows alive. They made Esteban's face unreadable.

'Don't tell me it's nothing,' said Nicky strongly. 'I mended those plugs, remember.'

140

'And you should remember that I said I'd take care of you,' he told her.

He looked down at her. In the crazy light, his face was a dramatic mask of planes and hollows. Nicky held her candle higher. Suddenly, his mouth was brilliantly illuminated. It was a long, curling mouth, devastating in its sensuality.

Nicky's stomach turned over. At once he pointed the candle away from his face and picked her up. Nicky gave a small scream and clutched at him to save herself from falling. The candle flame flared wildly.

'What are you *doing*?'

'Taking care of you,' he said.

He shouldered his way past various tables and chests to the foot of the tapestry-hung staircase. Nicky held the candle straight out ahead of them, in case one of the thousand draughts blew the wavering flame on to his skin or hers. It made the shadows dance.

'You're crazy,' she said with conviction. 'Put me down.'

'Are you or are you not scared?'

At once Nicky fired up. 'Don't you start cross-examining me. Of course I'm scared. That doesn't me I want you to carry mean to bed...'

The moment the words were out of her mouth she wished she had said anything else. Esteban stopped at the foot of the staircase. He did not say anything. In the darkness Nicky felt her face heat. She could have screamed.

'*Damn.* I didn't mean...'

Esteban put her down. He did not let her go, though. She stood in the iron circle of his arms, effectively his prisoner.

'You mean you *do* want me to carry you to bed?'

Nicky jumped. It sent the reflection of the candle flame leaping all round the walls. Esteban removed one arm from her waist and steadied the taper.

'Nicky, are you scared of me?' he said softly.

Nicky felt suddenly breathless.

'Don't be ridiculous.'

'Then scared of me forgetting myself and doing all the things you don't want?'

Nicky did not know what she wanted. She stood very still, her thoughts whirling. In the restaurant she had wanted quite passionately to touch and be touched. She had even revelled in the way he looked at her; wanted more. Now—

Now constraint froze her muscles, as deadly as snake venom. She could not answer.

'I know.' Esteban touched her hair briefly, as if he could not help himself. Then he stood back, letting her go. 'Go to bed,' he said quietly. 'You'll be quite safe. I promise.'

He was not talking about people who sabotaged kitchens and they both knew it.

Nicky hugged her candle and ran up the stairs to her room. The pictured nymphs flared briefly into life as the candle raced past them. They seemed to mock her.

Nicky undressed but she did not go to bed. She blew out the candle and prowled her room in the moonlight. Her thoughts were in turmoil.

Even though she could not see it in the dark, she was conscious of the photograph on the chest. It seemed to glare at her accusingly. She ought to tell Esteban that they had met before. Even if he did not remember that night, he had the right to know that she did. She must be giving him so many conflicting messages. He had asked her *why*. He had the right to an answer.

Face it, she thought. You keep saying that you want to get away as fast as you can. But you grab every excuse you can find to stay right here. There is something between you and Esteban Tremain. Maybe it's unfinished business. Maybe it isn't. Either way, you aren't going to find out until you tell him.

Outside in the corridor there was a series of creaks, then a thud. Nicky stood still, ears straining. Without the central heating, the natural chill of the castle reasserted itself. She shivered, pulling her dressing gown tight round her. There was a loud crash, a series of thumps, angry voices...

She gasped, *'Esteban,'* and rushed out into the corridor.

From the end of the passage came the sound of steady cursing. A strong torch beam flooded the carved ceiling. The torch itself had ended up against a Chinese urn. On the other side of the corridor a crouched figure held his elbow against his chest and swore fluently. Nicky ran forward.

'What is it? What happened?'

Esteban picked himself up from the ruptured rug.

'He got away,' he said bitterly.

Nicky picked up the torch and gave it to him.

'Who was it?'

'I don't know.' He sounded grim. 'Not the person I expected, certainly.'

From outside they heard the sound of an engine firing like a rocket.

'Motorbike,' diagnosed Esteban. 'He must have left it out of sight.'

Nicky shivered. 'He must have been in the house when we got back. Are you going to call the police *now*?

'I suppose I'll have to.' He did not sound very enthusiastic about it.

She clutched his arm. 'Don't go after him yourself.'

He looked surprised. 'It's all right. I'll just—'

Nicky was shaking. 'Don't.'

Esteban put a strong hand over hers. 'Darling, it's all right,' he said soothingly. 'He's gone. I couldn't catch him even if I tried. I was just going to check the door is bolted and then reset the alarm.'

But Nicky would not let him go alone. She despised timid women and she did not exactly cling to his arm while he checked the doors. But she did not move far from his side, either. And when he went into the library to put in the call to a bored police constable she hovered so close that she bumped into his injured arm.

He gave a sharp exclamation and rubbed his elbow.

'What? Oh, no, sorry, Greg. My house guest just reminded me I've got a few bruises.'

The police constable became a lot less bored. Nicky approved but Esteban laughed at him.

'No, the man didn't hit me. We fell over each other, that's all. He's probably got as many bruises as I have. I'm more worried about what might be missing. I haven't found anything yet but we've got no power at the moment so I can't be sure.'

The loss of power interested the constable even more. Sighing, Esteban agreed that the police could come over the following morning.

He put the phone down and stirred the blackened log that was all that remained of the earlier fire. The embers glowed red and he flung on another log. A small flame caught. He turned briefly to Nicky.

'They want to see you too, I'm afraid. It looks like you'll have to spend another day here.' He kicked the log and added another two or three, not looking at her. 'You must think you're never going to get away from me.'

The fire was catching fast now. The flames crackled, leaping high in the old fireplace. Esteban stared at the flames broodingly.

'No,' she said in a strange voice.

Esteban looked at her quickly. 'Are you all right?'

Nicky hesitated. No, of course she wasn't all right. She had been terrified for him. Even now that he was safe her heart was beating so hard that it hurt.

She said harshly, 'I don't want to spend the night alone.'

For a moment there was a blank silence. The burning wood fizzed and chattered but the man hardly seemed to be breathing. Nicky cleared her throat loudly.

'I said—'

'I heard what you said.' His voice was rough. 'Is it post-intruder panic or do you mean it?'

Her heart galloped. Did she? She found she was holding her breath.

Esteban said softly, 'Nicky?'

She let out her breath with a great whoosh. It sounded like a sob.

He took her hands swiftly into his. She was shivering, not just with cold or reaction. When he touched her, she shivered harder.

'I mean it,' she whispered.

In the fight his shirt had ripped at the shoulder seam, so it fell from his waistband like a rag. Nicky saw his ribs rising and falling. The beam of the torch illuminated it like a spotlight. He was breathing hard. His chest was warm. Nicky twisted one of her hands gently out of his grasp and brushed her fingertips against the naked skin. His breathing stopped.

'Nicky,' he said in a strangled voice.

And then, quite suddenly, she stopped shaking. She felt like his powerful car, suddenly finding the right gear after labouring horribly uphill. She felt calm and clear-headed. The only thing she needed to make her fly was Esteban.

She thought, in faint surprise, I want him. Only him. He is the only one I have ever wanted. Why didn't I realise that?

She leaned forward and pressed her lips against the base of his throat.

Esteban was breathing again, carefully. 'Is this sensible?' he said, shaken.

His skin tasted of wine and wood smoke. Irresistible, thought Nicky, all her senses heightened. It made her light-headed. She felt suddenly, gloriously irresponsible.

'Who wants sensible?' she murmured.

'I thought you did,' he said on a flicker of amusement, though his mouth twisted as if he was in pain. He did not touch her. 'Didn't we agree that we both needed to stay in control?'

'So?'

He held her away from him. 'God knows I want you. But, Nicky, what good can come from two control freaks making love?' It sounded as if it hurt him to say it.

If you're going to break the habit of a lifetime, go for gold,

Nicky thought. There's no point in going slightly out of character. Turn Miss Prim on her head.

Quite deliberately she moved her mouth down his ribcage, savouring each sensuous touch, each spasm of reaction which he could not disguise.

'Broaden our horizons,' she said brazenly.

She loosened the sash of her old dressing gown. The shirt that she wore under it gaped. Deliberately she undid the last couple of buttons and pushed it aside.

Esteban's eyes flared. But he stood like a rock, his response under iron control.

Nicky took his hands and pulled gently. He resisted. She sank down on to the rug, urging him to join her. Esteban let her go but he did not follow her. He looked down at her broodingly.

'Last night you couldn't say you wanted me.' His voice was almost unrecognisable.

'I want you.'

Nicky lay back on the rug and stretched her arms behind her head. She did not care about her fire-lit nakedness. She lay there, eyes steady on his, offering herself without disguise.

Esteban knelt on one knee beside her. He caressed one lifting nipple as if he could not help himself. But he was watching her face.

'I'm possessive,' he said in a warning tone.

Nicky gave a little anticipatory shiver.

'So go ahead and possess me.'

It was said teasingly. But they both knew it was deadly serious. His eyes darkened.

'You don't have to pretend.'

'I want to make love with you,' Nicky said quietly. 'No pretending.' She was saying it to more than this man tonight. She was saying it to all the arid years when she had ached for Steve and not acknowledged it.

He gave a great sigh and came down on to the rug beside her.

'You'll get cold.'

'So warm me up.' Her own voice was unrecognisable too. Like the laughing provocation of the remark. Like the *confidence* of it.

He will think I do this sort of thing all the time, Nicky thought with just a flicker of concern.

But it was too late. Esteban flung himself out of the torn shirt. His other clothes followed, tossed away across the library like so many rags.

Esteban did not notice. His concentration was wholly on Nicky. He had said he was possessive; and he was. His hands swept down her body, claiming her, branding her. And his mouth was hungry.

Nicky was almost frightened for a second. She thought, *I didn't know*. And then her body took over.

She had never experienced such total absorption. Esteban explored without restraint and expected her to do the same. The only thing he seemed unaware of was how totally new this was to her.

Nicky's unpractised reflexes went into rapidly escalating response. A long way away, her mind watched and was amazed. But Nicky, shocked, scared and trusting, abandoned herself to Esteban.

It was like a tidal wave: not gradual but sudden, huge and terrifying. Nicky gasped and hung on to his shoulders. Esteban steadied her, murmuring. She was not sure what. Her ears were ringing as she was thrown up, up, up…

The momentum increased: his body's, hers. She felt tears and hardly noticed them as she strove fiercely.

Esteban flung back his head and shouted aloud. Suddenly Nicky convulsed. There was an explosion of light behind her eyes. She was *there*.

Afterwards they fell asleep from sheer exhaustion. But the cold meant their sleep was brief.

'I need to get you to bed,' said Esteban.

She hardly recognised him, his eyes were so warm. He

looked down at her with such rueful complicity and kissed one cold breast possessively.

'Or my next reason to keep you here will be hypothermia.'

He gathered her up, finding the old dressing gown and tucking it round her. This time she did not demand that he put her down. He carried her through the house to her room.

'What about you?' murmured Nicky, her head on his shoulder. She ran her hand down his naked spine, loving the feel of it. 'You must be freezing.'

'The exercise is keeping me warm,' he said drily as he mounted the stairs.

In her room he dropped her on to the bed and turned away.

'Don't go,' said Nicky, suddenly alarmed.

He grinned at her. 'No chance. But I've got something to wear in here somewhere. You don't want me freezing you to death.'

He pulled a towelling robe out of the wardrobe and slid his arms into it. Nicky watched for a moment. Her eyes assessed him with that new-found confidence.

She made up her mind. She snaked her way across the coverlet and began to pluck at the robe, teasing. Laughing, he pretended to fend her off. But she had learned her lesson well and the laughter did not last long for either of them. She stripped the robe away.

'We don't need that,' she said huskily.

They didn't.

It was not until early morning, when she lay wakeful with Esteban asleep beside her, that other thoughts returned to chill her blood. *What has happened to me?* Nicky thought.

She had gone wild. Felt wild. And now the wildness had burned itself out and left her on the other side of a great ravine, not quite sure how she had got there.

All her adult life men had accused her of coldness. Andrew Bolton had gone further when he'd called her a fraud. Nicky had accepted it. She had not even felt indignant. It was true. Now—

Suddenly she could not bear to lie there a moment longer.

She slid out of bed. And gasped. She had forgotten she was naked.

Behind her Esteban turned over, murmuring in protest. Nicky froze. But then he pulled the pillow under his chin and subsided again with a sigh.

The cold air struck at her shrinking skin. Nicky looked round for something to cover her. Then her feet tangled in his discarded robe. She remembered all too clearly how she had slid it off his shoulders. How she had twined round him, laughing, teasing, luring him… She shut her eyes at the memory.

Tell the truth, she told herself harshly. You were seducing him. Deliberately. You made all the running. Not once but twice. *You.* How could you?

Shivering, she bent and picked up the robe from where she had thrown it last night and huddled it round her. It smelled of his skin. Nicky held the lapel against her face and breathed Esteban in.

She sank on to the window seat. Outside the pre-dawn sky shimmered. Clouds rushed dizzyingly between the sea and the stars. Nicky felt as if she was falling. She braced herself against the cold stone of the window embrasure. It seemed as if her whole life was racing away out to sea with the clouds.

I'll never be the same, she thought.

Behind her, the man on the bed stirred. She sat very still. In vain. He moved again, more strongly. The bed creaked several times. Then stopped altogether.

Nicky did not turn her head but she heard him prop himself up on one elbow. She could feel him looking at her out of the darkness.

'What is it?' he said quietly.

Nicky did not know how to answer him. She knew she could not lie any longer. Some time during the night she has lost her ability to tell those light, necessary half truths with which she was used to defending herself from Andrew and men like him. Men who, ultimately, she had not cared about.

She shuddered at the implications of that. Did she care so much for Esteban Tremain, then?

But the truth—the whole truth—was so big and so complicated that she did not know where to start. Or whether Esteban would understand, even if she could find the words. She stared out at the turbulent sky, silenced by her own confusion.

Esteban slid out of bed and padded across to her.

'Nicky?'

He sounded almost tentative. Surely not. Not Esteban, the master of his life, his instincts and Hallam. And, now, of her body and her heart.

'Nicky, what is it?'

He cupped her shoulder. His palm was so warm that she felt the heat even through the material of his robe. Nicky shut her eyes.

She said, 'I'm not used—' And could not go on.

He waited. Her voice was clogged. She gave her head a little shake.

Esteban pulled at her shoulder gently, urging her to turn to him. Nicky resisted. She opened her eyes and stared out at the pre-dawn sky as if her life depended on it.

Eventually the pressure stopped. Esteban said gently, 'Used to what?'

It was a good question. Nicky could not answer it. She shook her head dumbly.

His hand began to move, almost absently, caressing her shoulder.

'Then let me guess.' His voice was warm. Amused, even. 'You're not used to four-poster beds? Medieval draughts? Making passionate love on top of a four-course meal?'

Nicky could not bear the tender, teasing note in his voice. She said harshly, 'I'm not used to sleeping with a man.'

The caressing hand stilled on her shoulder. There was a pause. It felt like the end of the world.

'Ah,' Esteban said at last.

She thought he would try to make her turn round again

but he did not. Staring out of the window, Nicky pulled his robe tighter round her. She was shivering. How could he stand there naked and not feel the cold? she thought with a flicker of temper.

He said as if he were no more than mildly interested, 'Is that supposed to mean that you usually sleep with a woman?'

Nicky gasped and swung round. '*No.* Of course not.'

In the dawn light she could see he was staring down at her gravely. His voice had misled her. He was not teasing at all. And he was a lot more than mildly interested. His eyes were passionately intent.

'How *can* you?' she choked.

There was a tiny pause.

'Well, at least it got you to look at me,' he pointed out drily.

'Oh, very clever.' Nicky was bitter. 'Are those the tactics you use in court?'

Esteban waved that aside as if it was not worth answering.

'The alternative is that you don't sleep with anyone,' he observed in a neutral voice. 'Are you trying to tell me you are a virgin?'

'After last night, don't you mean *were* a virgin?' Nicky flung back, suddenly and inexplicably furious.

This time the pause was charged. *Why did I say that?* Nicky thought. She held her breath. A part of her was utterly bewildered by what she was doing. Another part—the new, wild part—wanted to go on and on until she goaded him into... What?

'Yes,' said Esteban at last evenly. Too evenly. 'I'm glad you reminded me.'

He took hold of her, not gently at all, and hauled her to her feet. Nicky's head went back.

'Let me go,' she yelled. She was shaking with anger.

By contrast, Esteban was so quiet she could hardly hear him. 'Well?'

His naked body glimmered palely in the dark. Like some marble statue of a god, Nicky thought, crazily. You would smash yourself to pieces if you fell against stone like that. She rammed her forearm against his chest and levered herself away. She was panting.

'What do you mean, "Well?"' she snarled.

'If you've got something to tell me, tell me.'

'Tell you? What would I have to tell you?'

His jaw was like stone, too.

He said with precision and absolutely no sign of emotion at all, 'Is it true?' And when she did not answer he shook her a little. 'Was I the first?'

He was not rough. He certainly did not hurt her. But Nicky flinched as if from a blow. She was speechless.

Esteban said, 'That's it, isn't it? I was the first.' For a moment Nicky stared at him as if he were speaking a foreign language. Then, horribly, she began to laugh. He had been the first to break down all her barriers. She laughed until she was choking. Her breaths came in great gulps, straining her ribs.

Esteban took his hands away. Nicky was laughing so hard, she barely noticed. Esteban stepped away. She was alone.

Nicky put out a hand to the wall to steady herself. She tried to control the crazy laughter but it spiralled up and up, making her ears ring. She was light-headed with it.

And suddenly she was drenched in ice.

Nicky's eyes flew open in shock. Esteban was there again, holding a nearly empty glass, and her face was wet. The terrible laughter stopped dead. She put up a hand and rubbed her eyes.

'Here. You'd better drink the rest.'

He handed her the glass. Nicky hesitated.

'It's only water,' he said briefly.

He must have brought the water from his own room. While he was there he had taken the opportunity to pull on a shirt. Clothed, he did not look like a marble god any more. He looked a hundred times sexier.

Nicky took the tumbler from him and poured the water

down her throat as if it were medicine. She gave the mug back.

'Thank you,' she said in a small voice.

'You're welcome.'

It was bottled mineral water and he had brought it from his room. He poured some more and gave the glass back to her. This time she just sipped.

Esteban did not try to touch her. Instead he retreated to the end of the bed. He propped himself against one of the wooden barley sugar posts and crossed one tanned foot over the other.

'OK,' he said, as if they were working on some abstruse theorem to which there was a logical answer. 'What is it about sleeping with someone that you're not used to?'

Nicky folded her lips together.

'Is it because we don't know each other very well?'

'We don't know each other at all,' Nicky muttered.

'I wouldn't say that.' Suddenly, shockingly, there was a note of total intimacy in his voice. 'I know you cook like an angel. You don't like Renaissance painting. And you pack a mean screwdriver. It's a start.'

A start to what? Her own pulses told her.

'No,' said Nicky hoarsely. More to herself than to him.

Esteban folded his arms across his chest. He looked like a man who had suddenly scented an interesting debate and was willing to stick with it as long as it took.

'Are you going to tell me you're already in a steady relationship?' He sounded disbelieving.

Nicky winced. She had never managed a steady relationship. Never committed herself totally to anyone. How could he tell? Was it written all over her?

'You think what we've done involves some sort of betrayal?' he persisted.

The puzzled impatience was all too reminiscent of Steve on that moonlit beach.

'Only of myself,' Nicky said desolately.

Esteban snorted. 'You've taken a vow of celibacy?'

'You don't understand…'

'I understand all right.' Suddenly he was grim. 'We've got something between us. For a moment back there you woke up to it. Now the reaction has stopped fizzing and you're remembering that you don't like me. Well, tough. I don't like you all that much either. It doesn't make any difference.'

'Difference to what?' demanded Nicky. Though she knew.

Esteban looked at her across the shadowed room.

'The fact that we want each other,' he said quietly.

The room was cold. Outside the wind was rising. But Nicky's skin remembered the warmth of a Caribbean night and a scented breeze. She ought to tell him; she ought to tell him *now*. But something kept her tongue locked in a vice.

'Don't we?' said Esteban.

He held out a hand. Like a sleepwalker, Nicky went to him. The great bed towered over them like a ship. Nicky found she was shaking as if the world were breaking apart under her feet.

Esteban put his arms round her. The world steadied. But her heart didn't. Just like ten years ago.

She said, 'I have to tell you—'

'You're not used to it.' His voice was warm with amusement. 'I know.'

'Not that—before…'

But her words dwindled into suffocating silence. Esteban was too close, too intent. Her heart slammed as if it would drive itself out of her body and into his. She clung to him, shaking.

'Do you think I'm used to this?' Suddenly his voice was ragged. 'Do you think anyone could be?'

Nicky thought, He's shaking as much as I am.

She said harshly, 'Touch me.'

He got rid of the robe with agonising slowness. Bending, he moved his face across her throat, her shoulders, her breasts. He did not touch. He inhaled like a jungle animal scenting water—millimetres from her skin, but it burned like fire. He fell to one knee. Nicky grabbed his shirt to steady herself. She sobbed aloud.

It was exquisite. It was torture. It was the road to paradise she had glimpsed all those years ago under the Caribbean stars. It was *now*.

Esteban looked up. In the shadows she could not make out his expression. She did not need to. His ragged breathing, his low laugh said it all.

Pure triumph.

CHAPTER NINE

FOR the remainder of that night she did not dream. She awoke slowly. She was smiling and deliciously comfortable.

'Good morning,' said a voice. It sounded as if it was smiling too.

Nicky's eyes drifted open.

Four-poster. Open curtains to reveal a wide sky. The sea sparkling beyond a dark cliff. And dark eyes, warm with the knowledge of last night's lovemaking, so close they made her head swim.

Esteban!

She gave a little wriggle of pure pleasure. This morning he was wearing old jeans and an open-necked shirt. He had not shaved. His hair was still damp from the shower. Sheer lust took a firm grip of her abdomen. Nicky's smile widened. She held out her arms.

He kissed her but shook his head as she tried to pull him down to her.

'Time to get up. We have the fuzz calling on us this morning.'

Nicky laughed and let him go reluctantly. 'What time is it?'

'Nine.'

She yawned, stretching. The lifting breasts escaped the covers proudly. Esteban watched with amused appreciation.

'No use. It's time to get up. You can seduce me all you want when Mr Plod has gone.'

Nicky sent him a naughty look from under her lashes.

'Promise?'

He laughed. 'Behave yourself. How can I keep my mind on last night's intruder if you flourish those at me?'

156

He drew the covers firmly up to her chin. Nicky pulled a face.

'Spoilsport.'

He kissed her lingeringly. 'Temptress. There's coffee downstairs when you're ready.'

He went clattering down the hallway, whistling. Nicky sat up and considered what to wear. Last night's clothes were hopelessly creased. She compromised on her working trousers and a clean shirt of Esteban's which she filched from his drawer. It was not, after all, the first time she had worn a shirt of his.

The thought stopped her dead in her tracks. Her radiance dimmed. *I've got to tell him,* she thought. Now more than ever he had the right to know. She did not look forward to it.

So it was a constrained Nicky who went into the kitchen ten minutes later. Esteban was not constrained at all. He was slicing bread for a toaster which now worked. He was not actually singing, Nicky allowed, but he looked as if he might break into song at any moment.

She set her teeth.

'Esteban—there's something—'

He waved the bread knife in greeting.

'Feeling ready to face the law now you've got your clothes on?'

I will not blush, Nicky thought, indignant at this lack of sensitivity. I will not.

'I'm fine,' she said repressively.

Esteban looked her up and down appreciatively. 'You are indeed.'

For the first time that she could remember under a look like that, Nicky found she had no desire to clamp her arms across her breasts. No urge to hide. She liked Esteban looking at her. She was glad that he seemed to like what he saw. She forgot about telling him anything that he did not already know and gave a low, delighted laugh. She was not going to feel outclassed by his stepfather's Renaissance nymphs ever again.

He held out an arm. She went and leaned against him. He kissed her hair absently and carried on cooking one-handed.

'Toast? Cereal? The full English breakfast?'

Nicky rubbed her face against his shoulder. 'Who needs food?'

'That's what I like to hear. An appreciative woman.'

He slipped bread into the toaster and poured her coffee. Nicky took it and added milk.

'I took one of your shirts.'

Esteban's eyes laughed down at her. 'I noticed. I look forward to taking it back.'

Nicky purred. His arm tightened. But there was a sharp ring from the front-door bell.

'Just as well,' said Esteban ruefully. 'Or Mr Plod could have been seriously embarrassed.'

He went to let in the policeman.

There was only one and he had clearly known Esteban for years. He accepted coffee and toast and sat down at the kitchen table.

'Well, what can you tell me about your intruder?' he said, pulling out a grubby notebook.

Esteban gave him a concise account. The policeman wrote it down painstakingly. He looked at Nicky for corroboration.

'I didn't see anyone,' Nicky said apologetically.

'That's a pity. Still, at least he didn't come back after you'd called us. They do sometimes, you know. The cheek of these villains.'

Nicky thought of what the intruder would have found if he had returned to the library. She looked towards Esteban, her expression stunned. He kept a poker face but his eyes were dancing.

'Just as well he didn't,' he agreed gravely.

'Better show me where he got in, then,' said the policeman, getting up.

Esteban came back ten minutes later.

'They're bringing up a team to dust for fingerprints. I said we'd get out and leave them to it.'

'Very wise,' said Nicky drily.

He rubbed the back of her neck as if he had been doing it all his life.

'That's what I thought. God knows how long I'd be able to keep my hands off you. The wind has dropped. Come on.'

He insisted on lending her heavy boots as well as the waxed jacket. Nicky let him lace the boots up for her. She felt more cared for than she ever had in her life. She almost said so. But their unconfessed history kept her silent.

The path he chose wound downhill away from the sea. The pale sun, only just above the horizon, illuminated a sky like a powdered rainbow—the colours of amethyst, black cherry, toast. Sharp black shadows of trees lay across a lawn frosted to white. The air had the sharp tang of cold champagne.

Nicky drew a long breath.

'It is beautiful.'

Esteban looked down at her. 'I think so,' he said quietly. 'That's partly why I have tried to keep it going. Not just for my stepfather, though of course he loves it. If he thought he could never come back here, he would give up, I think.'

Nicky was startled. 'And is that a possibility?'

'Not as long as I can earn enough to pay the next bill,' Esteban said grimly.

'And can you?'

'Over time, yes. But we have our hairy moments.'

There was something in his voice which made Nicky scan his expression alertly.

'And is now one of those?'

Esteban was silent for a moment. Then he said slowly, 'Do you know me so well? Already?'

For some reason it made Nicky uncomfortable.

'I just thought—'

'Rightly.'

He strode on for a while in silence.

Then he said in a level tone, 'Now is indeed one of those moments. My stepfather's convalescent home has cost a fortune; between that and a poor summer, the deficit has got out of hand. The farm is up to the limit on its overdraft. I've got a big job in New Zealand next week which will pay the bills eventually. But clients can take their time to pay up.'

'Don't I know it,' said Nicky with feeling.

Esteban nodded. 'So meanwhile I'm scrabbling round to keep us afloat. Yesterday I talked Patrick into selling one of the paintings at last. But that could take almost as long to bring money in as my New Zealand clients.' He laughed, half angry half resigned. 'Impasse. I can't think of a solution.'

But Nicky was sensitised to his moods now. 'What's the solution you don't want to think about?'

Esteban jumped. 'Are you reading my mind?' He looked down at her searchingly.

There was a pause. He had not been able to find gloves for her to borrow. Now he took her naked hand and held it as they walked. Nicky's cold fingers twitched, then twined with his. Oh, *last night*. He had not answered her question but suddenly she did not care.

His hand tightened, hard. She knew he was thinking of last night too. It was sobering, this silent communication.

Esteban said slowly, 'It feels like we've always been lovers. You seem to know me so well. But—'

Nicky's hand tensed in his.

'Why do I think there's something you're not telling me?'

It was the perfect opportunity. She knew she had to do it. But somehow, when it came to it, she could not. *Later,* she promised herself.

She removed her hand from his and started to ask about the countryside. Esteban let her. But his expression promised that the subject was not closed.

From the smooth sweep of sward they plunged into an overgrown path. Puffball heads of dead flowers drifted against their clothes like frosted feathers.

'What are these?'

'Old man's beard,' Esteban told her. He removed one from her shoulder and held it out for her to see. 'A wild clematis. A weed.'

'It's beautiful,' said Nicky, watching it blow away down the path ahead of them.

'You will get on with Patrick. He likes weeds too.' He paused, then added deliberately, 'To say nothing of girls who look like his favourite nymphs.'

Nicky blushed but said honestly, 'Now you're reading *my* mind. Oh, not that I look like them. But I thought this morning that I sort of understood how they felt.' She looked up at him. 'I've never felt that before. Can you understand?'

Esteban's face was serious. He took her hand again. 'I think you and I have a lot of talking to do.'

They walked on, silent in their total intimacy.

The path dipped steeply into a wood. Nicky heard a rush of water. Then she saw the stream. It was below them, splashing busily as it eddied round smooth rocks and swirled about the struts of a rickety wooden bridge. She stopped and drew a long, delighted breath.

Across the stream the steep bank was vivid green all the way from the top to a line roughly opposite to where they were standing. Then it turned abruptly silver where the sun had not yet reached the frozen dew. It was very cold.

Nicky stood utterly still. She was conscious of Esteban behind her, the warmth of his body, his breath in her hair. His arms went round her waist. She tipped her head back, feeling his strength as she leaned against him, looking.

She said softly, 'It's magic.'

His arms tightened. But his voice was teasing when he answered, 'And you said you didn't do magic.'

For a moment she was bewildered. Then she remembered shouting at him in the showroom just a few days ago. It felt like another dimension of time.

'The magic seems to be mutual.'

'Yes.' But he was no longer teasing. 'Nicky—'

'Yes?'

He looked down at their locked hands. 'This is—unexpected. I can't help thinking I've bounced you into something you weren't prepared for.'

Nicky was shaken to the heart. After a moment she said evasively, 'Not that unexpected. You said you wanted more than a truce, after all.'

'Yes, I did, didn't I?' He looked up. 'I didn't realise how much more. So—it matters that you're holding out on me.'

Nicky looked away. He turned her cold face back towards him.

'How about telling me the truth now?' he said gently.

She thought, *Tell him now*. She even opened her mouth to frame the words.

'Whatever it is, I can deal with it,' he promised. 'Just tell me.'

Nicky looked in his eyes and read all the possessive intensity he had warned her about. Oh, yes, he could deal with anything, she thought. The problem was, could she? If she told him and Esteban saw her once again as the sexy, callow schoolgirl he had fought off, she thought she would die of shame.

She could not do it. He gave a small sigh.

'OK. Leave it for the moment.' He looked down at their hands again. 'You're frozen. Let's get you warmed up. Then we'll talk.'

He set a brisk pace until they came to the outskirts of a village. In the distance she recognised the inn where they had eaten last night.

'We must have walked miles,' Nicky said, glad of a neutral subject.

'A few. But we've walked straight down the hillside. The road winds. Tired?'

'Just beginning to flag.'

'Step out, then. Ian will have a fire in the snug and I have no doubt he will rustle us up a ploughman's lunch if we ask for it.'

Nicky's stomach rumbled. She clutched it, laughing.

'After last night's meal I thought I'd never want to eat again. But I was wrong.'

'You've had a lot of exercise since then.' Esteban's tone was bland.

Nicky looked at him sharply. His face was perfectly serious. So why did she think he was laughing? No, *know* he was laughing. She thought, Because I'm in love with him.

She stopped dead. Esteban looked down at her, startled.

'Stitch?'

Nicky felt as if she had walked into a brick wall. She shook her head to clear it. 'Yes. No. Not really.'

I'm in love with him. *I'm in love with him.* I've always been in love with him. Why didn't I realise it?

That was why she had thought about him, dreamed about him. That was why his image had haunted her all her adult life, interposing itself between her and any other man. It was not that his rejection had hurt so much that she did not dare to trust anyone ever again. It was that she was still in love with the man on the moonlit beach.

Only now he was called Esteban Tremain. And when he looked at her he did not despise her any more. He liked her; he laughed at her; he certainly wanted her.

But did he love her? Nicky's heart fluttered uneasily. She could read his moods but she could not read that. She realised she had not the slightest idea.

He touches me as if he loves me, thought Nicky, walking on in silence. Surely he loves me. It feels as if he does, said her hopeful heart.

Well, it would, wouldn't it? said her brain. After all, what do you know about love? You've been in the deep freeze for ten years. It hasn't exactly given you a wealth of experience to draw on. Whereas if there's one thing Esteban Tremain has by the bucketful it's experience. And he didn't say a word about love.

And you haven't said a word about your moonlit beach, her heart reminded her. Trust is a two-way thing, you know.

Nicky bit her lip.

'Esteban—' she began.

But they had reached the pub. He held the door for her.

'Go and get warm by the fire,' he urged gently. 'The snug is through there. I'll bring the drinks. What do you want?'

'Oh, anything,' said Nicky distractedly.

She went where he pointed. Her brain was in a whirl.

Which must have been why she hardly noticed the man standing in the lee of the staircase in the small telephone booth. Deep in thought, she walked past him, oblivious.

It was he who, looking up, nearly dropped the phone. He flung it back on its cradle and dashed out of the booth.

'Nick? It *is* you. Nicky.'

She turned then.

'Ben.' She stared, not believing it. 'What on earth are you doing here?'

Her brother was looking shocked. 'I was going to ask the same thing. Oh, Lord.'

He sounded guilty, Nicky realised. He looked quickly over his shoulder. Then he took her by the shoulder and almost pushed her out of the hallway into the empty snug.

'Have you come looking for me?' he demanded in a low, urgent voice.

Nicky thought she had never seen her laid-back brother so agitated.

'I'm working,' she said in bewilderment. 'I told you when we had lunch. The kitchen where everything had gone wrong. The house is up the cliff. We've just walked in.'

Ben looked at her with horror. 'You mean Hallam Hall?'

'Yes,' said Nicky, puzzled.

'For Tremain?' He sounded appalled.

'Yes. What's wrong?'

'I told you the man was bad news,' said Ben intensely. 'I *told* you not to have anything to do with him.'

Nicky began to feel alarmed.

'What do you mean? How do you know Esteban?'

Ben brushed that aside. 'You've got to get out. Go back to London now.'

An unwelcome suspicion crept over Nicky. She drew a steadying breath and said again, 'What are you doing here, Ben?'

'It's a job,' he muttered. 'Just a job.'

Nicky knew her freewheeling brother. 'What sort of job?' she said with foreboding.

'A girl I know,' he said in a rapid undertone. 'Tremain dropped her flat when he'd had what he wanted. She'd give up everything for him. She put me on a retainer to watch him and—well, she just wanted him to hurt a bit.'

'Hurt...?' Nicky was speechless.

'Nothing dangerous,' Ben said hastily. 'I told her I didn't do things like that. Just a bit of damage. Preferably with high repair bills,' he added in a practical tone.

She thought, This is my brother and I don't know him at all. Ben saw her expression. He shifted uncomfortably.

'It was cash in hand,' he muttered. 'I couldn't keep coming to you. Anyway—' his confidence reasserted itself '—he deserved it.'

'Deserved what?' said Nicky. Though she was almost sure she knew.

That was clearly what Ben thought. He said impatiently, 'I—er—adjusted the kitchen appliances. And his car.'

Ben had to be the intruder. The irony of it hit her. Nicky gave a harsh laugh.

Ben took an urgent step forward. 'Nick—'

'*My* car,' she told him.

'What?'

'You're not very good at this, are you, Ben? Did you really think Esteban would drive an urban runabout? That's mine.'

Ben whitened. 'I don't believe it.'

'He has a Jaguar XJ8. I imagine it was garaged in the old stables when you were snooping around.'

'I can't have been that stupid. I *can't*.'

Nicky shrugged. 'So the one with the massive repair bill is me.'

Ben looked round wildly as if he was trying to find another explanation.

'And I've been making a statement to the police this morning,' she said, her voice shaking. 'About the intruder last night.'

Ben winced.

'What am I going to do?' she said, more to herself than to him. 'How am I going to tell Esteban?'

'Tell me what?' said Esteban, coming into the snug with a couple of tankards.

Nicky looked round. She did not say anything. Her face said it for her.

Esteban's eyebrows flew up. 'What—?'

And then he saw Ben. He stopped dead. Ben took hold of her elbow. Nicky was wretched. 'This is—'

Esteban was not listening to her. She saw that he recognised Ben. The hostility was instant and unequivocal.

'We haven't been introduced,' he said with barbed courtesy. 'But didn't we nearly meet a few days ago?'

Ben said, 'You're Esteban Tremain.'

Esteban was being civilised. He put the drinks down and gave Ben a wide, polite smile. 'And you're Nicola's private life.'

'*No,*' said Nicky instinctively.

Ben's grip on her elbow tightened painfully and held her silent.

'You could say that,' he drawled.

Esteban was not that civilised. For a brief second his eyes flashed molten with rage. 'And I think,' he said with dangerous quietness, 'that you're my intruder of last night.'

Ben gave a mocking laugh. Nicky wrenched her elbow out of his grip.

'That's enough,' she said harshly. 'There have been enough lies. No more.'

'Lies?' said Esteban very quietly.

Ben said, 'Nicky—'

They both ignored him.

'So this was what you weren't telling me.'

Nicky met Esteban's eyes. She thought she had never seen such passion; such pain; such distaste. A cold hand clutched at her heart.

'I can explain…'

'I'm sure you can.'

He was very gentle and remote as the moon. If it had not been for those bitter eyes, she would have thought he did not care a snap of his fingers, one way or the other.

'As a liar, you're inspired,' he told her in congratulatory tones.

'Take that back,' said Ben fiercely.

Nicky turned on him. 'Go away. You've done enough harm.'

Ben paled. 'I never meant—'

'Just go.'

He did. The door of the snug banged behind him.

In the sudden silence, Esteban said, 'Were the lies really necessary?'

Nicky tried to marshal her thoughts. It was not easy with him standing there looking as if he hated her. She swallowed.

'I should have told you,' she said, not very coherently.

His face was a mask. 'I asked you if there was anyone else. I asked you.'

She sensed a slow fury building behind the mask. She refused to let herself be intimidated but it was an effort. She shook her head and said quietly, 'Not that. It's me.'

Esteban said nothing. His concentration was total.

Nicky moistened her lips. 'You and I— You've forgotten— We met before,' she finished baldly.

Esteban looked arrested. His brows twitched together in a black frown. But he still said nothing.

'I know you don't remember. Well, it wasn't very important. Except it was to me,' Nicky said, stumbling over the words as if she were a teenager again.

'What are you talking about?' It ripped out, savage.

Nicky quailed. But she had to tell him the whole truth now. Even if he looked at her with contempt or loathing after-wards, she could not let him go on thinking she had conspired with Ben against him.

'Ten years ago,' she said rapidly. 'Cotton Island. I worked on your boat one night—'

An oath, shocking in its ferocity, cut her short. Nicky flinched as if from a blow. Esteban's face was not a mask any more. He looked as if he was going to burst into flames of rage.

'*Pompilia.*' He spat it out like a snake striking.

Nicky stood fast but it was an effort. 'Th—that was my father's boat.'

A muscle worked in his cheek. 'Which he sold on May 4th that year.'

Nicky stared. 'What?'

'All I knew about you was that you were nearly sixteen and lived on *Pompilia*,' he said evenly. 'I traced that bloody boat all round the world. Do you know how many times she has been sold?'

'N-no.'

'I do. And I know the name of everyone who ever owned her or chartered her. There's no Piper on the list.'

Nicky could not believe Esteban had done that. She said blankly, 'Leon always sets up a company to own his boats. He says it's better for the insurance or something.'

'So why didn't he record himself as a shareholder of the company? He wasn't on *any* of the lists, believe me.'

'Trying to keep one step ahead of the creditors, I should think,' Nicky was shaken into admitting.

Esteban swore again.

'I suppose that's why he never seems to have moored at any decent harbour? Never shown his papers anywhere in the Caribbean? Never listed crew and passengers when he put to sea?'

Nicky stared. 'Are you supposed to?'

'It's a good idea,' said Esteban with restraint, 'if the boat gets into trouble, that the rescue services know how many people they're looking for.'

'Oh.'

'He was completely irresponsible, wasn't he?' Esteban was icy with fury. 'My investigators could not find any trace of *Pompilia* until, I suppose, he sold her.'

'Investigators!' Nicky was alarmed. 'Why did you try to find him?'

'I didn't. I tried to find you.'

She stared, astonished into blank silence.

He said more calmly, 'I wasn't proud of myself. You were so young. I should have kept a lid on the situation. When I had time to think about it, I realised—' He broke off. 'But you'd gone. That damned boat had disappeared. None of the port authorities seemed to know anything about it. Even the good old boys in the yacht clubs hadn't got any worthwhile gossip. I didn't know where to start looking.' He gave a sharp sigh. 'I didn't even know whether I ought to.'

Nicky swallowed. 'Why?' she said in a small voice.

'My motives are best described as mixed.' He looked at her broodingly.

She said, 'I thought you despised me. My whole life I've thought you despised me.'

His mouth twisted. 'Was that what this was all about?'

Nicky did not know what he was talking about. 'All what?'

He gestured at the door through which Ben had departed.

'The elaborate set-up.'

'The *what*?'

'Ben,' he said with distaste. 'Isn't that his name? It was a plot, wasn't it?'

Nicky winced. She hated having to admit what Ben had done.

'Yes,' she said in a low, shamed voice.

Esteban looked like stone.

'I should have guessed it,' he said harshly. 'If something is too good to be true, it means it isn't true.'

Nicky did not understand. So she said nothing. He gave a hard laugh.

'You even warned me, didn't you? I should have listened to you more carefully.'

He sounded so angry. This was a nightmare.

'Warned you?'

'''I don't like being messed about,''' he quoted savagely. 'Is that what you think I did, all those years ago? Messed you about?'

Something inside Nicky wanted to reach out to him; almost, if it had not been ridiculous, to comfort him. He stared at her as if he had never seen a specimen like her. As if she filled him with loathing. Nicky flinched.

'I thought I knew you. I didn't, did I? Not for a second. Every word, every gesture—it was all planned. And all false.'

'No,' said Nicky, understanding at last.

It was too late.

Esteban took a hasty step towards her. Nicky stared as if she had never seen him before. His mouth was compressed into a line of rigid control but the dark eyes were molten.

'You wanted your revenge, didn't you? Well, you had it.'

He seized her shoulders. Nicky was too dazed even to resist.

'And now I'll take mine.'

She read violent pain in his eyes. She put up a wavering hand, half protest, half caress. He caught it and held her immobile. His mouth came down on hers.

It was an assault on her deepest feelings. It felt as if he wanted to drain all the passion from her to the dregs. As if when he had finished with her, she would be a bloodless ghost. He did not use his physical strength against her; he used furious desire. Mutual desire.

When he let her go, Nicky felt naked and broken. Her legs buckled. She had to grab hold of a chair-back to keep her upright.

Esteban looked at her as if he hated her. As if she had made him hate himself.

'You win.' It was so low she could hardly hear him.

He turned his back with an awful finality. And walked out.

CHAPTER TEN

BEN offered to take her back to London. He was very chastened. Nicky refused.

'If you want to do anything for me, you can get my bag back from Hallam Hall,' she said.

Ben looked appalled. 'Tremain will kill me.'

Nicky was too weary to care. She shrugged.

'What has the guy done to you?' said Ben, torn between alarm and affront. He was not used to such treatment from his sister.

'Not him. Me. I did it all,' said Nicky.

'You're not yourself.'

Her laugh broke in the middle.

Ben doesn't know me, she thought. Esteban doesn't know me. I don't even know myself any more.

She turned away. She had never felt so lonely in her life.

She travelled back to London on the train, thanking heaven for credit cards and the forethought which had made her tuck her wallet into the back pocket of her jeans. She did not have her clothes, her make-up or her toothbrush but she had her keys and the means to get some money. The rest, if Ben did not retrieve her bag, was expendable.

She collected bread and milk and a couple of escapist videos and spent the weekend trying to put Esteban Tremain out of her mind. It was not a success.

What has happened to me? Nicky thought.

For years she had hated the man she knew as Steve. In London, before she'd known who he was, she had recognised Esteban as a male predator instinctively. It had sent her into

172

full retreat from him. And then at Hallam Hall everything had changed. Why?

Was it that first evening? She had not been very happy about spending the night alone in the castle. No, she thought in disgust, you can't get out of it that way. If that was the reason you would have fallen into bed with him the first night. You didn't.

The television screen flickered unnoticed. Nicky pressed the back of her fist to her mouth to stop herself crying out. Her lips was still tender from that final, forceful kiss. It was a potent reminder of the passion that had shaken her to the core. Not just Esteban's passion, either. Even as she realised that he would never forgive her, she recognised the depth of her need of him.

It was not just desire, thought Nicky. Heaven knew, her physical response to Esteban had left her with a hollow craving she did not think would ever be assuaged. But what haunted her was the hurt she had seen in his eyes behind the anger and betrayal.

If only she had never got involved with him again. Why on earth had she done it? Nicky demanded of herself. Because she had, hadn't she? Esteban might have been furious because of a misunderstanding. But he would not have had the chance to misunderstand, if she had not allowed him to make love to her.

Allowed him! Nicky stared sightless at the television screen. Who was she kidding? She had responded to him right from the start. But when she had failed to tell him she wanted him he had stopped and gone away at once. In the end, it was she who had initiated making love. It was all her own doing. Her responsibility. She could hardly say he'd seduced her, could she?

Not that it would be any better if you could, Nicky told herself in disgust. Which would you rather be—a weak-minded wimp who can't say no to an attractive man? Or a vamp who made all the running?

Neither, Nicky thought passionately. I want to be myself

again. No weaknesses, no commitments and nothing to be ashamed of either. In full control of my life at all times. I want that night when we drove each other wild never to have happened.

She curled up into a tight ball of misery on the sofa. She sat through three videos, none of which she could remember a word of. In the end sheer physical exhaustion released her. She slept.

On Monday she went to work as usual, except that she carried with her a large package. The first thing she had done when she'd got back to her flat was parcel up the boots and jacket he had lent her together with the shirt she had purloined. Her eyes filled, looking at the shirt, remembering how he had said he looked forward to taking it off. How it had made her shiver with anticipation.

She gave the package to Sally.

'Ship it to Hallam Hall,' she said crisply.

Sally took one look at her face and decided to ask no questions.

The others tiptoed respectfully round Nicky for the rest of the week. And Nicky, working like an automaton, got through a phenomenal amount of work, looked as if she was made of wood and never mentioned Esteban Tremain at all. Not even when a courier brought her suitcase and the showroom resonated with tactful silence.

Once Caroline wondered aloud whether he would be coming in to pay his bill.

'He's in New Zealand,' said Nicky, not looking up from her work. 'He won't pay the bill for weeks.'

The cheque came the next day. There was no letter with it. Martin thanked heaven. Nicky's expression became more wooden than ever.

Esteban was working all hours in final preparation for his trip. He was not best pleased when a tall, handsome man presented himself in the doorway of his room. He did not, however, as a hovering clerk half expected, throw him out.

'Felipe,' he said coldly.

He stood up, pulling on his jacket, and went forward to shake hands formally. The man who came in was sublimely confident, from his expensive tailoring to the grey wings of discreetly styled hair. He looked distinguished, like an ambassador, Esteban thought dispassionately. Or a film star who played a lot of ambassadors.

'You're busy,' the man said with easy charm. 'Forgive me. But I'm not in London for long this time.'

Esteban shrugged and closed the door behind him.

Felipe's smile was a brilliant flash of white in a tanned face. The likeness was unmistakable. They had the same high-bridged nose, the same deep eyes. Esteban knew it. It gave him no pleasure.

'I won't keep you from your work long. I wanted to see you.'

Esteban received the information without enthusiasm. 'Evidently. Why?'

The tall man sighed. 'Don't you think this feud has gone on long enough?'

Esteban did not answer that. 'What do you want?'

'I heard you were having some problems,' the other man said carefully. 'I wanted you to know that I am here.'

Esteban looked at him for a long moment, his eyes hard. 'I don't think Patrick would be happy to take your money,' he said at last, evenly.

'And you? What do you feel?'

Esteban just looked at him.

There was a sharp silence. Then the man nodded, as if that was what he expected.

'I see. I'm sorry. I hoped that after all this time you could understand, even if you could not forgive.'

Esteban made an abrupt movement, dismissing it.

'I'm not your judge, Felipe. It's not up to me.'

'In your place, I don't suppose I would forgive either,' the man said ruefully. 'In some ways we are so alike.'

Esteban did not answer that but he stiffened noticeably.

The man hesitated, inspecting a portrait of a grim-faced judge in full robes. Then, as if he was making a last gamble, he swung round to face Esteban.

'Esteban—your mother and I were too young. She hated being so far from her family and I resented not being enough for her. I never meant to hurt her,' he said with desperate earnestness. 'Surely you can understand now, even if you couldn't when you were ten. I just didn't seem to be able to control myself. And she—'

'Oh, yes,' said Esteban, as if he could not bear to hear any more. 'I can understand that. More than I ever wanted to.'

Felipe stopped dead. 'What?'

'The genes run true,' Esteban said curtly.

'What?'

'That's why I'm the last person to sit in judgement on you.'

He started to gather up the papers on his desk. Felipe watched him.

'What is this?'

Esteban's jaw set. He was clearly regretting his outburst. He did not look up.

Felipe said slowly, 'It's not just me you have to forgive, is it?'

Esteban's hands stilled. He looked up at last. His eyes were agonised.

He burst out as if he could no longer contain himself, 'Oh, God, Father. I hurt her. I must have been mad. I don't know what to *do*.'

Nicky's bruises faded but her inhuman efficiency did not. Her colleagues watched with increasing concern. When Ben rang to speak to her on Friday morning, Martin de Vries intercepted the call and closed the door to his office firmly.

'What's wrong with her?' he demanded. 'I've never seen her like this.'

'Neither have I,' said Ben miserably. 'She won't speak to

me when I call her at work. And at home she keeps the answering machine on and won't answer the door.'

'Bad,' said Martin. 'Do you know why?'

Ben admitted it.

'Then you'd better come round here and talk to her. I'll make sure she stays late tonight.'

He did. When she saw Ben, Nicky gave the first sign of life he had seen in a week.

'Get out of here,' she cried.

But Ben had toughened up during a wretched week. He seized her by the arms and held her still.

'Listen to me, Nick,' he said urgently. 'I've talked to the police. They say Tremain may withdraw the complaint.'

Nicky's face lost all colour. She stopped struggling in his grasp. Her eyes fixed on him painfully.

Ben drew a long breath. 'He won't talk to me. Can you try? Please?'

Nicky flinched. 'He's out of the country.'

'No, he isn't,' Ben said eagerly. 'He's at his chambers. I've just come from there.'

She hesitated. 'He hasn't tried to get in touch with me. How can I—?'

But Ben was a much loved brother, she reasoned. They had always got each other out of scrapes. And she had spent some considerable time alone with Esteban Tremain, after all. Another twenty minutes wouldn't hurt. Or wouldn't hurt any more than she hurt already.

'Oh, all right,' she said.

People worked late in chambers every night but Friday. That was the day of the week that they cleared their desks at four, or earlier, packed children or the tools of seduction into their cars, and piled off for the weekend in the country. Esteban had heard them clattering downstairs into the dark evening as the building emptied.

Anne appeared in the doorway.

'The courier has collected the papers for Auckland. I've

typed the Vereker Opinion but I'm only halfway through Raleigh Processors.'

Esteban blinked. His eyes were gritty with tiredness.

'That's OK. As long as I can have it by Monday afternoon. Anything else?'

Anne hesitated. 'Well—there's a woman. She didn't say what she wanted but she kept talking about the police. She's in the clerks' room.'

Esteban was puzzled. 'Police?'

'Could be blackmail,' said Anne, who had seen a lot of life since she'd started working for a barrister. 'Won't give her name. Blonde and gorgeous.'

'Blonde?'

Esteban was on his feet and out of the door before Anne could answer. No waistcoat, no jacket, and his shirt-sleeves rolled up to reveal muscular forearms. He did not seem to notice, much less care. He positively ran down the corridor. The clerks, thought Anne, would have the shock of their lives if they saw him now.

But the clerks' room was empty except for a slim blonde figure huddled in a damp coat.

Nicky had paced up and down in the courtyard for a long time before she'd plucked up the courage to go in. As she looked up at Esteban's tempestuous entrance, her heart nearly failed her. He looked so wild. So—her mouth dried—utterly sexy.

'It is you,' he said in an odd tone.

She could not think of a thing to say.

He pushed a hand through his hair. She had never seen him so dishevelled. She wanted to smooth it so badly it was like a physical need. She thrust her hands up her sleeves and folded her lips together, speechless.

'What are you doing here?'

'I—' Her heart was beating so hard she thought he must be able to hear it.

'Come to my room,' he said harshly.

Her pulses leaped. She followed him without a word.

'Now,' he said, closing the door firmly and putting his back to it as if he would never let her out again, 'you're here. Why?'

Nicky tried to remember. The look in his eyes did not make it easy. 'M-my brother.'

'Who?' He looked impatient.

'He said you would withdraw the charges if I came to see you,' she said rapidly.

He looked stunned. 'That man was your *brother*?'

Nicky nodded. 'He was stupid,' she said rapidly. 'But if you hadn't treated that woman Francesca so badly, she would never have convinced him to help in the first place. He's never done anything like that before. And he really—'

Esteban breathed hard. 'Nicky—'

'—doesn't know how he could be so stupid. What?'

'Shut up,' said Esteban, coming firmly towards her and taking her in his arms. 'Shut up. Shut up. *Shut up.*'

He threw a key on to the desk and kissed her comprehensively. Nicky gave a small sob.

'You can't want me. Not after the way I lied.'

'You didn't lie,' said Esteban, kissing her throat, her chin, her eyelids. He sounded breathless. 'You just forgot to tell me all the truth. And you would be surprised what I can want.'

Not lifting his mouth from her skin, he pushed the coat off her shoulders. Her business suit followed. His hands were practised but not quite steady.

'Oh, God, Nicky, I thought I'd lost you. I've got to have you *now*.'

They sank on to the floor.

It was a long time later when Nicky stirred in his arms and said dreamily, 'I think we both just behaved appallingly.' She sounded rather proud of herself.

Esteban was shaken by a soundless laugh. He hugged her close. 'Somebody ought to paint it,' he agreed lazily.

'Completely out of control.' Nicky was warming to her theme.

He kissed her. 'Don't wind me up, you baggage. I've never had any control where you're concerned.' He paused, then said painfully, 'That was what scared me so much in the Caribbean.'

Nicky struggled up on one elbow and stared down at him, astonished.

'Scared? You?'

He reached up a wondering hand and traced her mouth.

'I'd seen my father go crazy. I thought I was different. It took just one car ride and being hit on the foot with a jar of coffee to show me I was exactly the same. And you were fifteen, for God's sake.'

Nicky said incredulously, 'You *do* remember.'

He sat up. 'I remember all right.'

She gave a shiver, half voluptuous, half sad.

He said with difficulty, 'I don't know how I didn't recognise you.'

Nicky said wisely, 'You probably didn't want to. I didn't. I'm pretty certain I knew before I knew I knew, if you follow me.'

Esteban looked sober. 'When did you know for sure?'

'When I saw a photograph in your room. You were wearing sunglasses. It just—clicked into place. I didn't know what to do.'

'Why on earth didn't you tell me?' He sounded as if he was suffering.

Nicky shook her head. 'At first I just wanted to run. Later—' She bent her head, blushing. 'I meant to. But things kept interrupting. And then I lost my nerve.'

Esteban's arm clamped her to him. 'Were you so scared of me?'

Nicky looked at him in surprise. He looked sick.

It gave her courage to say, 'Not scared exactly. But I've always been sort of ashamed.'

'*Ashamed?* Of what, for heaven's sake?'

Nicky looked down at her rosy nakedness. She was reclining against Esteban's shoulder for all the world like one of Hallam's more disreputable nymphs. She smiled.

'It may be difficult to believe just at this moment, but I used to hate men looking at me.'

He did not smile back. His arm tightened painfully and she felt his lips move in her hair.

'Piers and his friends did quite a number on you, didn't they?'

'Not the number that you did. You were the one who called me a voluptuous Cleopatra.' Her smile died. 'You were the one who didn't want me.'

'I wanted you.'

She looked up. 'But—'

'You say you were ashamed. What do you think I was?' His voice was harsh. 'You were so young and scared and I—lost control. I was worse than Felipe.'

'*No,*' said Nicky, dazed.

'And then it happened all over again last week. Like a recurring nightmare. When I thought you'd set me up I went mad for a moment. I almost hated you. I wanted to hurt you.'

Nicky flinched. But she said steadily, 'But you didn't.'

He drew away a little and lifted her chin so she had to look up at him. He touched her mouth gently. His face twisted. 'You're very generous. I know I wasn't—kind.'

Nicky's eyes were steady. 'No. But I probably deserved it.'

'Don't say that,' he said sharply. 'It makes me feel like Felipe.' He shut his eyes for a moment. 'I always dreaded—' Nicky hugged him. 'You were shocked and you nearly lost it for a moment. That's all. You didn't *hurt* me. Not the way you hurt yourself.'

He said on a little shaken breath, 'Oh, Nicky, I love you. I'll never hurt you again. I swear it.'

He held her very tightly.

Nicky said, 'So why have you let this whole week pass without a word? Why did you just send that beastly suitcase back to the showroom? It seemed like you didn't want me again.'

He lifted his head and looked down at her eloquently.

'Is that what it seems like?' he asked drily.

Nicky gave a little wriggle of pleasure.

'Well, maybe not just at this moment,' she allowed. 'But it was pretty horrible marching about outside trying to get up my courage. It was raining too.' She shivered.

'You're cold,' said Esteban remorsefully.

He looked round for her clothes. They were strewn widely and he could not find her tights. But he collected the rest and helped her to dress, kissing her as he helped her pull on the garments.

'Well, you don't look very respectable, my darling,' he said, sweeping her hair clear of her collar and kissing her ear, 'but at least you won't die of cold before I get you home.'

Nicky was suddenly shy.

'Home?'

'My home,' Esteban said firmly. 'I'm not letting you out of my sight again until you marry me. I have an apartment below Tower Bridge.'

Nicky raised her eyebrows. 'And what about my apartment?'

Esteban was not thrown. 'Fine. I'll pack a suitcase and we'll go to your home. Or you pack a suitcase and come to mine. I am infinitely flexible. I'm just not letting you go.'

'Control freak,' said Nicky blissfully.

Esteban was hurrying into his own clothes. He looked up at that, his expression unexpectedly sober. 'Not any more. This last week has taught me that. I can't afford control if I want to hang on to you.'

Nicky was moved. She went up to him, buttoning his shirt like a long-married wife.

'How did you work that out?'

He grimaced. 'With the help of my father, in the end.'

'I thought you didn't talk to him.'

'I didn't. But he came here and saw the state I was in. He gave me some excellent advice—along the lines of not doing everything that he did, admittedly—and persuaded me that I had to stay here and sort things out with you, not go off to New Zealand. So I sent off the work I'd done on the case to the local man and bowed out.'

Nicky was conscience-stricken. 'But the money you were going to earn—you said Hallam needed it.'

Esteban put his arms round her and held her against his chest.

'Felipe again. He has always offered to help but I was too proud. He convinced me that there were things more important than pride.'

Nicky rubbed her face against his shirt-front. 'So why didn't you come to me?'

'I was going to. I was planning it very carefully.'

Nicky was bewildered. 'Planning?'

'There were,' Esteban pointed out drily, 'one or two impediments. Francesca needed a smart reminder of what would happen if she tried any more of her tricks. I couldn't expose you to her malice before I'd got that sorted out.'

'Oh,' said Nicky. She had wondered about Francesca Moran.

'And then there was the glamorous intruder. You said you were not involved with anyone. But you were clearly intimate.' The dark eyes looked fierce for a moment. 'I could have killed him when he said he was your private life.'

Nicky shivered, remembering. 'You said that.'

'He didn't have to agree.'

'He was trying to protect me.'

Esteban said something rude under his breath. 'I knew I was going to have to clear him out of the path one way or another. So I rang the police a couple of days ago and said that I knew him and he'd done it for a bet.'

Nicky was impressed. 'Didn't they charge you with wasting police time?'

'I'm a local employer,' Esteban said cynically. 'All it cost me was a lecture on my irresponsible friends and several tickets to the Police Ball.' He chuckled suddenly. 'In fact that was going to be my excuse to ring you up. I thought I would point out that you got me into it, so it was your moral duty to come with me to the blasted ball.'

'When?' demanded Nicky.

Esteban was startled. 'I don't know. Before Christmas some time. That's when it usually is.'

'I mean when were you going to phone me up?' said Nicky impatiently.

'Not phone. Stand on your doorstep. Tonight. With my heart on my sleeve and a mega helping of humble pie in the shape of two dozen roses,' Esteban said drily.

Nicky choked. 'What?'

'I told you, I've been taking advice from my father,' he said. The amusement was back in his voice. 'He has a rather Latin attitude to these things.'

'Why not until tonight?'

'Because I didn't manage to persuade de Vries to give me your address until today. Apparently your colleagues finally convinced him that you were eating your heart out for me,' he added complacently.

'Eating my—' Nicky was indignant. She strode about the room, mock affronted. 'It's a foul lie. How can you—?'

Her attention was caught by the judge's portrait. She blinked. So that was where the missing tights went. Nicky began to laugh.

Esteban had been settling down for an enjoyable battle. Now he raised one eyebrow. 'What?'

She grinned, pointing. 'For a couple of control freaks, we lost it pretty comprehensively this evening, don't you think?'

Esteban turned, following her finger. He took in the judge's new adornment. His shoulders shook.

'Would you say lost it?' he drawled. 'I'd say we reached new heights.'

He extended a long arm and tugged at the tights. There was a moment of resistance. Then they fell, clearly laddered beyond repair, and the portrait lurched sideways. It was too much. Nicky let out a delighted peal of laughter and clung to Esteban.

He looked down at her, his mouth curling wickedly.

'I can see you're going to be a terrible influence,' he murmured.

Nicky looked up at him. There was so much love in his eyes, he was almost unrecognisable. Her laughter quietened.

'I hope so,' she whispered. 'I do hope so.'

The wicked mouth was fierce on hers.

'Count on it,' said Esteban.

LIVE THE EMOTION

Modern Romance™
...seduction and
passion guaranteed

Tender Romance™
...love affairs that
last a lifetime

Medical Romance™
...medical drama
on the pulse

Historical Romance™
...rich, vivid and
passionate

Sensual Romance™
...sassy, sexy and
seductive

Blaze Romance™
...the temperature's
rising

27 new titles every month.

Live the emotion

Next month don't miss –

MARRIAGE AT HIS CONVENIENCE

*Passionate, successful and devastatingly
handsome, these tycoons are definite husband
material. They certainly want to marry – but
for convenience alone. Only blistering
attraction with their contract brides –
wasn't part of the deal!*

On sale 7th November 2003

*Available at most branches of WHSmith, Tesco, Martins,
Borders, Eason, Sainsbury's and all good paperback bookshops.*

Coming Home for
Christmas

Three brand-new seasonal romances

HELEN BIANCHIN   LUCY GORDON   REBECCA WINTERS

On sale 7th November 2003

*Available at most branches of WHSmith, Tesco, Martins, Borders,
Eason, Sainsbury's and all good paperback bookshops.*

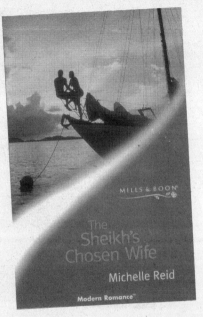

MILLS & BOON®

Live the emotion

PENNINGTON

BOOK FIVE

Available from 7th November 2003

Available at most branches of WHSmith, Tesco, Martins, Borders,
Eason, Sainsbury's and most good paperback bookshops.

PENN/RTL/5

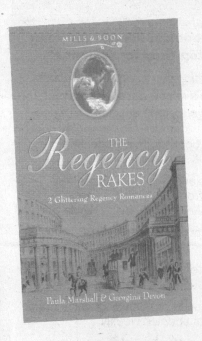